T0367334

THE BIRTHDAY BASH

Elizabeth Sorrells

iUniverse, Inc.
Bloomington

The Birthday Bash

Copyright © 2011 by Elizabeth Sorrells

All rights reserved. No part of this book may be used or reproduced by any means, graphic, electronic, or mechanical, including photocopying, recording, taping or by any information storage retrieval system without the written permission of the publisher except in the case of brief quotations embodied in critical articles and reviews.

This fiction work is based on a story of complete fact. Names, characters, place and resemblance to actual events or locales or persons, living or dead, have been changed to protect those involved, and still alive.

iUniverse books may be ordered through booksellers or by contacting:

iUniverse
1663 Liberty Drive
Bloomington, IN 47403
www.iuniverse.com
1-800-Authors (1-800-288-4677)

Because of the dynamic nature of the Internet, any Web addresses or links contained in this book may have changed since publication and may no longer be valid. The views expressed in this work are solely those of the author and do not necessarily reflect the views of the publisher, and the publisher hereby disclaims any responsibility for them.

Any people depicted in stock imagery provided by Thinkstock are models, and such images are being used for illustrative purposes only.

Certain stock imagery © Thinkstock.

ISBN: 978-1-4502-8049-5 (sc)
ISBN: 978-1-4502-8051-8 (dj)
ISBN: 978-1-4502-8050-1 (ebook)

Printed in the United States of America

iUniverse rev. date: 01/03/2011

For Scotty

Acknowledgements

This journey seemed far too terrifying to travel but I could never imagine the knowledge, insight and wisdom of where I'd go and who I would meet. Without the distress and horror, I'd never have met some amazing humans out there, who have patiently endured the drama of my world.

Mary Belk, Faye McFarland, Deborah Williams, and Effie Albrecht Piliouni are friends that I now know: my life wouldn't have been complete if I'd never have crossed paths with. They all have amazing stories of their own that have helped me where no one else could have reached. Their encouragement and belief in the effects of the written word to heal the soul literally carried me through the work. You've helped me achieve my dream, and for that I thank you so much.

Diane Walden has been just like a laser beam of light, pointing me in the directions I must go. Her tender support and hard work in protecting victims has touched my soul and helped me continue to realize, that the only way to endure permanent pain, is to help others going through it. Mrs. Diane, I love you too.

George Zubowitz, I can never say this enough, you helped me save myself. To the "group" of friends I repeat, we're the sane one's living in an insane world.

Momma, you've sacrificed the ultimate and been robbed of so much. This is your story too. I pray its words bring the healing your scars deserve. I'm proud to be your daughter and friend. I love you.

Siblings are both blessings and lessons from God, the very ones who share our spirits and souls. I thank God for mine and love them.

Maw Maw and family, without you there would be no me.

My children and grandchildren, beautiful stories in themselves, I adore you all.

Jerry, I will always love you.

June, Tina, Lisa, Diane & Candy, I thank you for your calm patience and forced humor.

For each and every one of those who asked if my book was finished yet, thank you for your persistence. Without it there would be no book.

WHY I WRITE
By: Seven's "Big Sis" Mae

Nothing about life prepares you for murder. Though you are completely saturated with its presence, nobody really thinks it could get that close, until POW! Hitting you from behind, it's ignited into your mind and heart. It just happens, some will say. Every hour of everyday, it's "happening" to someone new. Our time of tragedy had come, ready or not. After a year, it stings just as bad, as the moment his heart stopped. My mind still won't accept that the brother I loved so much endured so much brutality, so much hate. Sure it was no secret that he had grief the entire previous year, with his wife. As a result of that, Seven's troubles intercepted with the local police and even the same District Attorney's Office that would be trying his case against his murderer. Yet, they had been the ones wrong about him, and now he would never have a chance to defend his life.

Remains after autopsies are far from pleasant and not something most humans look forward to observing. I'd hoped to catch a glimpse of the boy I'd once known. What my eyes beheld would only add to the many distressing images, in my mind's eye.

Every one of us, hoping that maybe, just maybe, we would catch just one last glimpse of the beautiful human he once had been. After all his body had been put through, the autopsy wouldn't help restore him in any way. With objects like 'bone cutters, hand saws, brain knifes and cranium chisels', no restoration would be done. A corpse may hide many valuable clues, both inside and out. With a victim of crime, the ultimate autopsy is required, with every major organ removed, weighed and examined. In Seven's case, all the damage had been to his head, so that's where the forensic pathologist would have started the examination.

Huddled together for support, we made our way into the back of Thompson Brown Funeral Home, a local place of familiarity, yet not back in the prep area. As if in a grisly time warp, a door was opened by the tall funeral director, and we filed into an empty room, with only Seven's remains lying on a metal table. A thin paper sheet covered him to his chin, and though with some morbid curiosity, I refrained from examining him any further than his head and face. Seven no longer had the color of life as I searched in vain for the brother, I'd once known, while a loud ringing pierced my ears. Sickness crept up my throat, and the air seemed to leave the room. His face returned no expression of peace.

I left the room first, with the rest of them holding back with the cadaver.

Running outside, needing fresh air, and without any thought, I sat down right in the front of the Funeral Home, on the ground. How could this be happening? Just where and when did this all begin? Why? Why? Why?

Putting my face into my hands, I now had this new image for my memory banks, of his grey, swollen, drilled, broken, beaten and autopsied head and face.

Determined is what I've become, and holding absolutely no fear of retaliation from those who killed him, I will tell his side of the story, and set the record straight on exactly who Seven Scott Levine truly was underneath all the lies. Writing is all I really can do, not for any other reason but to clear my own mind. It's my communication from my heart, mind and soul. I'm unable to do anything else with this pain. Promising Seven that somehow, I would get his story out there, giving him the justice, and the final say. Maybe those who wished him dead, believed in their ability to shut him up forever, yet they certainly didn't account for his oldest sister, setting the record straight.

Making no claims at being a great author, I have got the guts to claim I loved Seven so much more than those who wanted to control him. Physically he is gone, but on paper I will see that he lives beyond that tragic night. I will erase the lies told about him and replace his dignity and respect, with the truth. One thing that offends me so is the way people want to put the blame of his murder, on himself.

"Well if he hadn't been out at that time of night", and "If only he had left her."

Look, if it makes you feel better to think that way, fine, but you're wrong. No one deserves to be murdered. Seven wasn't a homicide victim who programmed himself for a violent death. It's just more comfortable for some to suggest that a victim is partially responsible for their own fate. For the family left behind, it's a painful concept to accede.

At this point, the one that brutally beat Seven from behind sits in jail waiting for his opportunity to defend himself and be the star of a murder trial. He wants his justice, even though he gave Seven none.

My heart goes out to every person that has lost a loved one to homicide. In my process of healing, I've tried to find things to be grateful for. Though Seven was fatally injured, I did get to tell him I loved him, and held his hand when he died. There is a place where his remains lay, that we can sit and talk to him. We do have a suspect in jail, and a few answers for questions after the fact. Yet, Seven's absence far outweighs any benefits. So, I must write, or lose my mind to grief.

PART ONE

WHERE, WHEN, WHY and HOW IT STARTS

Chapter One

"Please, please, please, send me a sister or brother." Little Mae sat on her knees beside her bed, holding both hands together before her face, with her eyes squeezed shut. The lights were out, and she wasn't supposed to be out of her bed. Most nights she'd just stay under her covers, but every so often she felt it important to pray harder. Despite the fear of what might try to grab her from underneath the bedstead, nothing dissuaded her from the belief God would provide what she needed.

"Someone that I can talk to and I could share my room with." Praying wasn't something she did at meal and bedtime exclusively. Having no one else but her beloved German shepherd and God to talk too, she chattered all day with a constant flow of ideas, questions, needs and fears.

"Help my daddy and mommy to be happy. Thank you. Amen." Without a second in between, she'd slid silently back in her bed. Closing her eyes, she knew her prayers would be answered.

Some of Mae's earliest memories were situated in the middle Seventies with the Vietnam War coming to an end. The little blond girl, filled her days exploring the thick woods of her parent's land, situated in the center of twenty acres of uncut and overgrown woods in western Alabama. The house and acreage was private and secluded, which only added to Mae's solitude.

She was a fearless youngster while exploring the dense acreage with her dog King. Ever mindful of the dangers lurking around, she was careful of rattle snakes, spiders, scorpions, poison oak and ivy, as well as the threat of long abandoned deep wells. Playing in her own carefully controlled fantasy world, she had no fears in her dark and enchanting forest. It was in the walls of her house, she would have every reason to fear for her life.

The "Police Uniform" was created for someone like Mae's father, Joel Lee Tripp and he took tremendous pride in wearing it. With or without the "magic badge" on his chest, he lived and breathed discipline and control. Mae could never be sure what any twenty four hour period might bring in the form of lessons she needed to learn.

"Like this!" Joel stormed in after a difficult day on the job, grabbing his four-year-old daughter by the arm. "When you try to kill yourself, you need to cut this way, not this way!" His gun swinging in her face, as his finger traced lines across her wrist.

"Yes sir!" Mae never questioned her father's orders. Love came in the form of control, discipline and appeasement, using his favorite Vietnam War military belt. Holding his small and helpless daughter by one arm, allowing both of her legs to dangle, while her feet were kicking, he'd whip her as many times it took in any given day, to teach her right from wrong. Growing up, Mae wasn't aware of what a child abuser looked like, nor did she understand why her daddy felt the need to teach her such violent lessons. She didn't realize her life to be unusual.

Mae's mother, Mary Baker Tripp, was as befuddled as her daughter was, as to why Joel turned out to be so brutal to his daughter and discontented with his marriage. Fresh out of high school, Mary had fell head over heels in love for the tall, popular and good looking Joel Tripp. Even though Joel joined the military, with the draft forcing many young men to fight in a war, far from home, she married him, and moved to where he was stationed. Mary was a catch herself. Full formed, blond and petite, she had been a majorette for years, as well as shared the same circle of friends as Joel. The couple seemed destined to live happily ever after.

"I'd never been so lonesome in all my life." Mary described her early marriage, the days before Mae's memories. "Joel worked out in the world as a military police, while hiding me from the dangers he claimed to be lurking in the streets. I wasn't allowed any military wife acquaintances, and was required to make quick and brief trips out in the public for basic necessities only." Being young and naive, she believed making her husband happy was all she had to do, and trusting him was part of the process.

In the early years of the marriage and being stationed in Michigan, it was a distance from the southern climate, family, and friends, and the culture shock kept Mary obediently behind closed doors. Quickly under Joel's command and control, Mary determined to make her marriage work. Once they finally moved back to Alabama years later, Mary hoped her obsessive husbands gripping hold would loosen up. Instead, being near their families and hometown support, made Joel Tripp worse than ever.

Visiting Joel's parents, Clay and Marion, down in Florida at least every year or so, kept little Mae in touch with her beloved grandparents. They never denied their youngest son's family love, actually doting on and spoiling Mae as much as time allowed. They wouldn't involve themselves in the affairs of his marriage, no matter what he did. It was during one of their eight hour trips down for a visit, that Joel would pull one of his famous stunts of abandoning his family, to demonstrate his moral.

Mae loved visiting the sunny state of Florida with the salty taste in the air and the golden sand holding back that massive water called ocean. They had only been their long enough to unpack the car before she was eagerly asking to go for a walk to the little tourist shop, up the sandy road. Paw Paw and Maw Maw Tripp gave her a few dollars in case she found something she liked, and Mary gave her permission to leave the yard all by herself. Sea shells lay all around, causing Mae to pause often to pick some up to examine closer. The shop was only a few blocks away, and just as she walked up to the front display table holding Sunshine State souvenirs, she noticed her daddy pulling the car into the small parking area. Mae briskly made her way to him, noticing their suitcases sitting in the back seat, the same ones she'd just witnessed being unloaded from the vehicles trunk. Looking around the little shop, a few tourists walked about, and she hoped it would deter a beating. He was rolling down his window, which she took as a positive sign she wasn't getting the belt.

"Tell your mother, I've gone home." He was unusually calm, nearly cheery.

"Yes sir!" Nearly saluting as she backed up and watched with confusion as he pulled the car onto the road, back towards Alabama. Suddenly scared, she ran back without haste to inform her mother as she was instructed. Once back, no one seemed to notice Joel and the luggage were gone. It took Mae a few minutes to really get Mary's attention, because she was in the middle of talking to Marion. Being brought up not to interrupt adult conversations, Mae patiently waited until they had a quiet moment, and then she announced the news.

"Daddy said to tell you he has gone back home." Mae's words were followed by a long silence from all the adults looking down at her.

"What?" Both Clay and Mary quizzed together. Mary jumped up and started for the bedroom, while Mae began to cry as she repeated slowly.

"He went home." Shrugging her shoulders, Mae didn't really know how else to put it.

All three adults were shocked and upset. This was exactly what Mae didn't want, but somehow she felt she was always the bearer of bad news or the cause of most commotion.

There was no way to call Joel and ask him why he left, and no one would have persisted for an answer from him to start with. Paw Paw Tripp brought his son's family back home, and Joel never gave a reason for abandoning them.

Joel's behavior, though disturbing, was tame in front of observers and family. In the privacy and seclusion of his house, Mae's father made it very clear; he could simply kill them all. Sometimes his rage and anger, slipped out of the confines of his house. One day it caused a car "accident".

Two days after the car wreck, Mae returned to her first grade classroom. The teacher encouraged Mae to describe what happened to her, to the entire class. Terribly shy, at first Mae couldn't bear the thought of everyone's attention on her, but the class full of curious youngsters, implored her to explain. Still nervous, the teacher sat Mae on her lap, and allowed the children to sit around them on the floor. Carefully, Mae began to recount what she'd been through, fearful she might reveal what really happened.

"Daddy was driving, and I was sitting in the front seat with Momma. The car started slipping and sliding, and Daddy couldn't keep it on the road. I hit my head, and blood was covering my eyes and it was going in my mouth."

"What did it taste like?" Red headed Warren questioned out loud, while politely raising his hand for permission to speak.

"Ewe..." Most of the girls wrinkled their noses in displeasure.

The teacher quietly reminded them that questions and comments come after the story. She then looked down and smiled, heartening Mae on.

"An ambulance picked Momma and me up. I had to stay in the hospital all day and sleep there all night." Mae sat quietly for a second, to let that sink in, because staying in the hospital had been no fun at all.

The same boy was bouncing around with his hand up again, dying to ask the question everyone else was whispering, if the ambulance had its lights on, but the teacher motioned for him to put his hand down.

"Mae, what was it like, in the hospital?" The teacher wanted Mae to finish.

"They stuck me with lots of needles, and I had to have these put in my head." Mae pulled the bandage off her new scar going across her forehead. All the children were impressed to see the tiny stiches.

The actual true version of the accident would never be known, and for Mae became part of her haunted collection of locked up memoirs. Only after her brothers murder years later would she be able to recollect the factual events of that day.

Joel Tripp, dressed in his Valley Point Police uniform, was running late. Everything was to blame for the tardiness, except for Joel himself. Unpunctuality drove him nearly insane and he still had to drive Mary to work and drop Mae off at her great grandmother's house. As they left the driveway, Joel was yelling at his wife.

Mae sat squashed in between her mother and the door. She was accustomed to hearing her two parents fuss, and she drifted in and out of sleep to the roaring sound of his voice, bouncing within the confines of the tiny Toyota. It was the tone of her mother's terrified vocals that made Mae's eye's open wide.

"I tell you what!" Joel screamed in a military tone. "I will kill us all Mary, I'll kill us all right now!"

"NO JOEL! NOOO..."

It was too late; Joel had already floored the gas pedal, steering straight for an old Oak Tree. Luckily, he lost complete control, and only managed to throw his wife and daughter into the windshield. Joel suffered no injuries, and even though Mae was admitted into the hospital for observation, her daddy never stepped foot in the hospital to check on her, until his police caption made him. It was reported as a simple accident.

Joel was the law, inside and out of his home. Mary had felt trapped for years, while Mae grew up believing such things were normal and part of daily life. Feeling so alone, Mae had believed that having a sibling could help solve so many painful problems, if not for her parents, at least to ease some of her own solitude.

"Please, please, please, Dear God, send me a sibling."

Chapter Two

Little Mae could have simply slipped from this world with her terror and turmoil. Fortunately she did have her mother's family to provide her with the tender love a young girl needs. Mae's grandfather, Owen Baker was a spirited fellow, well known and respected in Chambly County, Alabama.

"I love you little one." Owen wasn't shy with his affection for Mae and he never let her leave his presence without hugging her and telling her. Thulah Jean, her grandmother, was Mae's biggest fan. After Mary had given birth to Mae, she came home for a bit, while Joel served in Tuy Hoa, Vietnam

Infant Mae would start her days in that little brown brick home situated on Highway 51. Back then it was known as Route 1, and was a well, traveled road that Owen had watched as it was first paved many years before. The old brick house was built by his father "Edward R. Baker", with the money his two sons sent home while they were serving in World War II. It sat on five acres of pasture land, which back in the day, was considered a rural farm. Mae would run and play all day long out there, alone for many years, being the oldest grandchild of Owen and Thulah. They both called her affectionately, "Doll Baby" and Mae always knew, they kept her close to their hearts. Mary's two younger siblings, Mae's Uncle Frank and Aunt Denise both joined in on the spoiling of their niece, so while Joel didn't seem to like her, the family took up the slack in loving her.

Another crusader in Mae's life was Anne Grey, her great grandmother. Anne was the mother of Thulah Jean, and she lived in what Mae considered the big city limits of Lanyard. During the weekends Mae would usually be at the country home of the Bakers, but during the week days, she walked to and from school, from Granny Anne's house. In Mae's eyes, Granny Anne was amazing, and Mae was taught so much about being a "Southern Lady" with her charm, quiet nature and honest opinions. Anne demonstrated to her great granddaughter how to quietly endure life and to see people in a particular way.

In the early mornings when Mae was dropped off by her parents, Anne would have a cup of hot Tasters Choice instant coffee and a warm bowl of grits with bacon chunks, waiting for her. Sitting on her wooden floor, Mae would watch "The Little Rascals" and "Tom and Jerry" before walking the four blocks to school. It was the seventies, so it was safe for a six year old to walk the streets. After school, Mae walked by the local bakery and drug store, and would spend the nickel or dime; Grannie Anne would have given to her. Drivers Bakery had chocolate shaped gingerbread man cookies and the corner drug store, "Red's", had penny candy. Mae considered her blessings every time she had those two little brown bags of goodies to take back to her Granny's, but it was rare for the gingerbread man to ever remain fully intact.

The afternoons were always the same when she'd get back to Granny Anne's after school, they would sit on her front porch swing. That's where Anne would listen as Mae told her about the day, as they sat watching the neighborhood activities. Anne had retired from the Lanyard Textile Mill which sat within view of her front yard. It continued to be the main employment of the area. She lived alone in her small mill house, her husband Ransom Grey, called Rance, had died years before Mae was born, in a car crash

During those early years of her life, Mae wasn't sure what other's thought of her father's behavior. No one offered to defend or step in to stop him, so she assumed it had to be normal, regardless of how unpleasant it felt.

All that speculation was put into clear perspective one Saturday morning, inside the Baker house. It was before the days that her parents owned the land and home in the woods, and they were temporarily staying with Owen and Thulah. It was tough times and two families living under the same roof, didn't make anything easier. To make matter's worse; Owen was recuperating from a broken hip and had to use a walker to get around. It made him more ornery than normal.

Mae had gotten up early for the Saturday morning cartoons, she herself just getting over a bad case of pneumonia. Wanting a bowl of cereal, she asked her daddy to pour the milk for her.

"Pour it yourself."

Mae, in her long flannel gown, opened the refrigerator and took hold of the glass container, full of milk. Before she could get the container across the room, it slipped right out of her hands, crashing to the cement floor.

"Now look what you did!" Grabbing Mae off the floor by one arm; he spanked her with his bare hand, twisting her around with every smack.

Dropping her, he thrust a dish towel into her hand. "You clean up every drop!" He walked back into the living room, leaving her to get the glass and milk off the floor.

Once she was finished, she'd lost her chance to eat cereal, spilling all the milk. She hoped to at least get to see her favorite show, Land of the Lost. Joel was sitting in her favorite chair in front of the television, so Mae crawled up on the couch. Not wanting to bring any more attention to herself, she silently sat looking at the program playing, wondering if her daddy was really watching it, or just making sure she couldn't watch her favorite show. There was no way she was going to ask him to change the channel.

Owen Baker was not one to hide his feelings, and when he witnessed his "Doll Baby" being smacked around in his kitchen, it had made him mad enough to want to kill Joel Tripp. Unable to hardly walk, the anger he was feeling had him determined to do something about 'that boy, beating on that baby'. Forcing himself out of bed, he'd started cleaning the house, sweeping the living room, while using the walker to move about. To see Owen doing house chores was a sign to those who knew him, he was highly agitated. Mae was watching her grandfather, who looked furious to her, but she didn't know why. As he circled around, he got to Joel's two feet.

"Move your feet." Owen stood over Joel, who had also been watching his father-in-law.

Slowly, Joel retorted, without budging his feet an inch. "You can ask me nicely."

Mae could feel the air in the room; it began to tingle like an electrical current flowed through, as Owen stiffened up.

"I said to move your feet."

Joel smiled a wide grin. "Well I said, not until you ask me nicely."

Now the entire room became static, with the hair's on her arm starting to stand on end, Mae pushed herself back against the couch, and pulled her two legs close to her body, wrapping her arms around them She watched as her grandfather brought the broom handle up in the air, above his head.

"I said to move your GD feet now!" He began to threaten to smack the hell out of Joel, who only continued to beam from ear to ear.

"And I said..." Before Joel could finish, the broom was whizzing through the air, and smacked him really hard across the head.

Owen didn't stop with one hit, and as the broom handle went up and down, he got madder and madder with each contact mark his weapon made. Mae's mouth was wide open, with a blood curdling scream flowing full force like a siren. Never had she witnessed anything so graphic and violent as the two powerful males came to blows right before her eyes. She believed one was going to kill the other; she just wasn't sure who was going to do what. With it happening right in front of her, she couldn't escape off the couch, and couldn't stand to watch either man hurt the other. She tried to squeeze her eyes shut, but they kept popping open upon hearing the thick wood, crack her daddy's head again and again.

Both Mary and Thulah came rushing into the room, with looks of alarm on their faces. Thulah rushed for Mae, while Mary lunged in the path of her father's now broken broom handle.

"DADDY STOP...! What are you doing? Stop...!" Having placed herself in front of her husband to protect him, Mary was now facing her father, who had completely deflated in spirit. Owen realized what he had just done. He stepped back, and looked over at his wife.

Thulah sat holding tightly to Mae, humming into her ear, as she continued to shiver with shock. Ashamed of his behavior, Owen took a seat, and listened while Mary fussed at the display of violence she'd just witnessed from him.

They moved out that day, and it would be years before either Owen or Thulah would be allowed to see Mae again, even though they would live within a mile or two of the Baker house at all times. Mae hugged her Paw Paw before she left, and he apologized for scaring her.

"It's okay Paw Paw." She patted his cheeks, and could easily see the tears in his eyes.

"I'll see you later Doll Baby." He choked out, as she skipped across the room to her mother, unaware it would take so long to feel his warm hug again. The only indication had been the loud wailing of Thulah, who fully believed Joel's promise to keep Mae from them.

The relationship between Joel and Owen never repaired, though Mary soon realized her husband had instigated the entire scene. The situation taught Mae that though obviously other people didn't like her father's behavior, no one had the power to stop him.

Chapter Three

A decade of life brought many things Mae's way, but she wouldn't have a sibling to share it with. She'd never stopped praying, hoping, dreaming and believing, but as the years went by the knowledge a sibling wouldn't solve all her problems became apparent. The idea was still a silent wish.

"Mae come in here, I've got some important news." Mary came home that afternoon, walking in the door excited. Mae noticed the blushing tone on her mother's cheeks. She smiled as she rubbed at her daughter's hair. "What have you always wanted more than anything?"

The question coming out of left field, made Mae's mind go suddenly blank. She wasn't sure what she had last asked for. Looking at her momma, she smiled with curiousness.

"A baby Mae, I'm going to have a baby. You're going to be a big sister."

"What is it going to be, a girl or boy?" Mae waited, holding her breath.

"Oh, well, we won't know until the baby gets here." Mary chuckled. "Which do you want?"

Mae had given it thought. "A baby sister..." She felt such happiness inside her heart. Mae wrapped her arms around her momma. "I'll have a baby sister." She looked up at Mary, who appeared blissful too. "But if you have a boy momma, I'll love him too!"

Mae's life would never be the same again. Another human would be coming that she could share everything with. As easily as it would be to stay happy with the pregnancy, Mae suddenly began to have a brand new fear with the new life on its way. What if her Daddy treated the baby like he treated her?

Joel was not pleased at all, and his behavior toward his wife became so menacing, she did something that her husband never believed she'd ever do, she filed for divorce. After all the years, and all the close calls with death, something inside her snapped, and she'd had enough. Before she was even due, she moved Mae and her into the Baker house.

With her parents separating, Mae found life to be taking a sudden turn for the better. It was one of the happiest times of her life up until then. She'd always felt with those years without a sibling, God wasn't listening to her. Mae even believed God was punishing her through her father. Now she began to believe God hadn't abandoned her, and did care for her to be safe and happy.

Mary on the other hand, was feeling brand new insecurities for the first time in her life. Being pregnant added to her stress, while the end of her marriage made her view herself as a failure. Though she was determined to make it work out for the best, she'd never really planned beyond, being with Joel. She couldn't take the idea of being under his domination, or watching him over discipline his daughter one day more. Looking out for her children, she started looking for a home to raise them up, free of fear.

Within that year of the birth announcement, Mae's life changed in more ways than she'd ever imagined. Just leaving her daddy was something she never dreamed would happen. Mae had no clue what divorce really meant, other than she wouldn't be living with Joel Tripp anymore. She still visited him some, but he wasn't ever in a good mood, spending his visitation, belittling Mary to her daughter. Mae didn't think her daddy wanted the new baby, but on the morning Mary gave birth, Joel was there to see the little one.

Mae had spent the night with Granny Anne, but neither of them got much sleep as they lay there all night long, waiting for the phone call. Right as the sun came up, the loud ring made them both jump. Anne reached over, picking up the receiver, as Mae listened to any indication of what was going on.

"Well I'll be..." Anne smiled, looking over at Mae, whose eyes were squeezed shut. She hung up the phone. "You're a big sister."

Nearly exploding, Mae opened her eyes. "Is it a girl or a boy?"

With her full attention, Anne teased her great granddaughter. "Well that doesn't matter."

Mae sat up, considering it shouldn't matter, but she'd still like to know.

"It's a boy." Anne laughed, proud for her.

They both got up, dressing quickly and gobbled down a bite of toast and scrambled eggs. Granny Anne and Mae got into the large white Cadillac and heading down to the hospital. Anne drove her car with extreme care and caution, but in Mae's opinion, it was just too slow.

Thulah met them both at the front door, and led the way through the many doors and hallways. As they turned the last corner, Mae noticed her daddy standing still and looking into the maternity ward window. Thulah stopped abruptly, wondering how Joel found out about the birth so fast. She didn't want a confrontation with him.

Mae looked at her daddy, standing there with his arms crossed, and for the first time ever, she felt sorry for him. Walking over to him, he looked down at her in such a sad way.

"Well, you have a baby brother." He smiled, and Mae thought she saw tears in his eyes. Standing on her tip toes, she looked into the glass, at the tiny baby boy.

"Oh...he is perfect." She carefully examined him, taking in the sight of his tiny toes and grasping fingers. "Erik Mark Tripp." She whispered into the glass making it fog up. Mae was mesmerized upon seeing the gift from God. Joel put his hand on her shoulder, it was an unusual gesture, and Mae looked closely at his hand, before she looked up at him again. He was looking at his son, something he had never beheld before and it broke his heart to know that the family he once had, was now forever gone.

Chapter Four

"May I have the bedroom with the bathroom?" Mae requested while running around in what was to be their new safe house.

"You sure can." Mary followed Mae as they took their first tour. She'd found a nice home for her two children, and in the months after Erik's birth, Mae began to adjust to life without Joel under the same roof. No more objects being tossed around. No more yelling, screaming, or hate spewing. No more death threats. Mae believed that without her daddy having to look at her every day, maybe he would actually enjoy her occasional company.

Mae would visit him regularly once the divorce was finalized. Depression had attached itself to Joel's heart though and losing control of his wife filled him with fire red rage. Mae easily became his puppet and spy, unaware of the things he requested like pictures and paper's, were wrong to retrieve for him. He would get his new girlfriends to babysit Mae or leave her with complete strangers. She would always be made to do cleaning chores. During the Alabama Football season, she'd dust during the entire game. Joel was obsessive compulsive and her cleaning would have to pass his meticulous military inspections.

Her parent's divorce hadn't stopped the arguing between them, it made it far worse. The fights commonly circled around Mae, and now Mary fussed because she didn't like her ex-husband getting his daughter to steal, spy and clean for him. It angered her to find out Mae had been left in the care of odd girlfriends and strangers. So though the divorce happened, Mae would never be able to escape her parents nor seem to be able to enjoy one without infuriating the other. Their hate for each other would dominate her entire childhood.

Things settled down though, and they got into a weekly routine. Mary surprised her daughter with a piano for her tenth birthday, something Mae had always longed to have. Weekly lessons were added to the already demanding schedule of Mary's. She'd always tried to counter balance the damage she feared Joel was causing Mae. Extracurricular activities could very well have been created by Mary. Throughout Mae's childhood, Mary had put Mae into anything positive she could find. Tap, ballet and jazz dance classes. Gymnastics, cheerleading and swimming kept Mae fit and pushed her out, somewhat, from her shell of shyness. Mary was a Girl Scout Pack Leader, which gave Mae invaluable instruction on basic survival, and priceless time with her mother.

With little Erik though, Mary's time was spread thin, and caring for a newborn kept her exhausted. She continued with her full time job at the hospital's emergency room, and with less time, Mae dropped all of the extra stuff. She didn't mind giving up anything, with her new brother, piano and own bathroom, she liked being at home more than she had ever before. She also spent more time at the Baker's and Granny Anne's, which she credits with keeping her grounded while the divorce was happening between her parents.

Church began to fill in every single Sunday, no matter whose house she was spending the night at on Saturday night, except while with Joel, whom was a professed atheist. After Mae's prayer was answered concerning a sibling, she floated around in a faith like never before. Climbing tree's all the way to the top if possible, Mae craved to get as close to God as she could. She'd pray while hanging onto the swaying trunk, and sang thanks as loud as her voice could go. One of the worst lessons about life was just around the corner though, something even as damaging as Joel Tripp had been.

Ricky Levine met Mae's mother, and like a spider with caught prey, he spun his web around Mary with pure precision. Mae had envisioned her new 'step father', a tall and handsome doctor from the hospital where her mother worked. Instead, Mary had met her new boyfriend in a bar; on the one and only night she'd occasioned the place since her divorce. Mary hadn't had the energy or time, so it took her friend Peggy month's to get her out on the town. Peggy's husband accompanied the two women, and it didn't take long for a willing suitor to approach Mary. At first glance she wasn't so impressed with the man, but having another man's attention made her feel good about herself again. She hadn't felt good about herself in a long, long time.

The night passed, and Mary soon forgot the man, who had requested her name and number. She figured him to be too intoxicated to remember, and hoped he wouldn't call. A few weeks later, he did call, and it impressed her to think, he hadn't so easily forgotten about her. They started talking, and she gave him a chance once she found out he was a single father, raising two little girls. Soon, she invited him over to the Bakers, to meet Mae and Thulah.

Hardly as tall as Mary, skinny and dark haired, Mr. Levine, didn't fit any dreams of Mae's. Thulah's expression mirrored Mae's own confusion. This couldn't be the man her oldest daughter was now seeing. When Mae locked eyes with Ricky, something within her twisted and an acid taste seemed to seep up her throat. As he smiled at her, she didn't return any emotion; instead she gave her momma a bewildered look. Mae tried to set herself at ease; there was no way that her momma would end up with such a man. She was far better than the likes of him.

Mae allowed the prospect of receiving more siblings into her life, two beautiful young girls, Terri Lynn, seven and Angel, five. Having always wanted a sister too, God was flooding her with answered prayer. The first night the three came over to eat supper with Mary, Mae and Erik, the two little girls ran around like they lived there. Instead of being excited over what could be new sisters, it bugged Mae as Terri Lynn eagerly tapped at little Erik lying in his crib.

"No, don't do that, don't touch him, you might scare him. He doesn't know you." Mae oozed protection.

"Well, I've always wanted my own baby brother." Terri Lynn wasn't one to back down to anyone or anything. The two girls eyed each other.

"Well, I've prayed for this baby, so..." Mae could comprehend the little girl's dilemma; still she wasn't coming down from her stance.

Terri Lynn, had always longed for a brother, and instantly took to Erik. Both Mae and Terri Lynn had been the 'oldest', but now Terri Lynn was losing that position to Mae. So from the start the two of them were at odds and almost hourly, locked horns with each other. Terri Lynn staked claims to most of Mae's property, which Mae had never had to share one second in her entire life.

Angel on the other hand felt she was losing her 'baby' position to Erik, yet she was still the baby girl and proud of it. She kept both Terri Lynn and Mae on their toes, taking on the task of tattle telling on them even before they knew what they had done

Before any of them realized it, a wedding was being planned and Ricky was moving his girls into the brick home. After the December 1979 wedding, they would all be called family. Transitions for the three girls were in order, and all that goes with joining two separate families to form one.

It had all happened so fast, the birth of Erik, the divorce of her parents, a new house and then an entire new family line. Within one year, Mae went from zero siblings to a house full. She tried to be happy, she wanted to be content, but something felt like it was moving beneath the surface, something sinister.

Ricky Levine was not a well man, but his illness wasn't displayed for all to see. Mae's daddy noticed it right away, being a law officer, but his concerns were of no issue to the new family. What Joel Tripp had picked up on was the subtle clues put off by a child predator.

Mae wouldn't figure it out until after her momma's wedding to Ricky, a month after to be precise. He'd come into her world and managed to take over her mother's life. She now had to share everything she owned, with a smile on her face. Something about the way he looked at her made her feel uneasy, but she couldn't comprehend what it was.

The magnetism that had drawn Ricky to Mary was the fact he had the appearance of being a good single father. Joel Tripp had literally attempted to kill his own daughter, and here was this man, raising two young girls all alone. Their mother had abandoned her family, years before, leaving Ricky alone to take care of them, which he seemed to do with joy. There were things about Alicia, the girl's mother that Mary had just taken Ricky's word for. Unlike Joel, Alicia wasn't a pressing issue, at least not at that time, but the truth behind Ricky's first marriage would be making its way to the surface, in due time.

Sitting around eating dinner at a tableful of people, was something Mae had a hard time getting used to. Terri Lynn was a smacker, and little things like that started to irk Mae, while Angel cried if something she didn't like was placed on her plate. Nothing irritated Mae more than the way Ricky stared at her. It was after one of these meals, that Mae finally lost her composure, and allowed her true feelings to show.

The meal was finished, but they all continued to linger around the table, because the conversation was on what everyone wanted for Christmas. The lists from Terri Lynn and Angel were exact and long, while Mae hadn't really given it much thought. She knew what she wanted though.

"I want a puppy." Mae had to leave King behind with the divorce, and it had been the most painful part of the end of her parent's marriage.

"Me too, me too, I want a puppy too!" Terri Lynn stood up jumping.

"I want a puppy too!" Angel chimed in with her big sister.

"NO!" Mae's voice broke its quiet tone. "No, I asked first." It had started to get on Mae's nerves how Terri Lynn seemed to want everything she had.

"Well if you get a puppy, you will have to share it." Ricky spoke to his new stepdaughter with parental authority, something which Mae didn't believe he deserved to have.

"No, I won't share my Christmas present." Mae crossed her arms and stared back with defiance at him.

Her daughter's reaction had turned the fun conversation into a first time family fuss, and it shocked Mary to observe Mae's attitude. "Mae, that's not nice."

Having upset her mother bothered Mae even more than the idea of having to share her Christmas morning puppy, but she didn't care. She was in a stare off with Ricky Levine, the very first stare down of thousands more to come.

"I think you need to just go on to bed for the night." Mary continued to get onto Mae, who happily got up and walked out of the room, continuing to stare at Ricky; her new perceived rival.

A few weeks later, Ricky would finally make his first criminal move on Mae. It happened on a Friday after Mae brought home a bad project score from her Science class. Mary had tried to help Mae, but her daughter's lack of school performance, had been a result of what was happening at home. Ricky had reasoned with Mary, to let him try to talk to Mae, to take the kids and go over to the Bakers house, and leave him alone to work with Mae. Mary had no reason to fear her new husband, and she figured he might be able to break through the thick protective shell; Mae had started building around herself since the new marriage. After they left the yard, Ricky found Mae sitting in the back yard.

"Mae, could you come here for a minute."

Mae still spent a lot of time outside. Looking up from a book, she jumped up, laying the book down in her seat. Ricky waited at the back door as Mae pushed past him. The house was unusually quiet. "Where is Momma?"

"She's gone to your grandma's."

Mae didn't believe him, and checked to see if the car was actually gone. "Why didn't she take me?" She turned questioning him, finding him standing right behind her. He was smiling and had a strange look about him.

"I told her I wanted to try to reason with you." He reached out his hand for her to take. "Come on."

Mae walked past him, without taking his hand. She still had a hard time believing her mother left her.

Ricky pressed on. "Come with me, I want to show you something." He was smiling as he started for her bedroom, walking in and sticking his head back out to see if she was following. "Please Mae."

She walked slowly toward her door, even though something was telling her to run. Looking into her room, he stood in front of her mirror. "Why didn't Momma tell me she was going to Maw Maw's?"

"Because I asked her to let me have some time with you alone…" He walked to her, and took Mae's hand. "Come here, I want to show you something." He pulled her in front of her mirror, and made her look at herself. "Look, at how you're growing." His comment made her uncomfortable as he stood behind her, holding her in place. Without warning he grabbed her with a force she'd never felt before, throwing her backwards onto her bed. In an instant he was pushing her legs apart, and laying down on top of her.

"Stop…" Mae couldn't register what was being done in time to stop him.

"Oh come on, you'll like it." Ricky pushed her hands up above her head, and tried to smell her neck.

"No, I won't! Get off of me!" Mae's automatic response system kicked in, and for the first time in her life, she fought back. "Get off me now!" Out of Mae's mouth, a strong and demanding growl made Ricky stop. He got off Mae and walked to the door.

"Don't tell your mother…" He grinned before leaving her. "She won't believe you."

The deed had been done, and Mae was left to figure out why it happened to her. It felt like she was falling into a bottomless pit. Above her the light was growing fainter and dimmer, while the darkness loomed beneath her, pulled her to perpetual fear. She wanted to tell her mother, she wanted to run out and tell the neighbor, but at the same time, the embarrassment and humiliation that filled her heart, shoved her into a deep and dark hole of secret shame.

Ricky loved wrestling, and would spend hours on the floor, using the moves he saw on television, on Terri Lynn, who actually loved to fight. It was kind of like watching a pit bull, maul a rabbit, so Mae wouldn't hang out to see Terri Lynn get twisted up, punched and in the end, be forced to beg for mercy. The simple wrestling games became a normal past time event. Ricky hid a staggering fact that he was a raging alcoholic, who effectively hid the amount he consumed per day. In all appearance sake, Ricky worked hard and dedicated himself to doing a good job. Being such an unassuming man with a small frame, he didn't fit the image of predator. With a lifetime of working in slaughter houses and meat departments, lifting heavy cow and pig carcasses to slice apart, Ricky was no wimp or weakling. Despite his small stature, he was extraordinarily strong.

Mary was completely unwitting to what was being down to Mae and Terri Lynn. She continued to hold her full time job, while juggling her new household. Neither girl shared their pain with anyone, especially Mary.

Being beat was nothing new for Mae, and though Ricky did give it plenty of effort, he quickly found out, his stepdaughter had a thick, tough, and stubborn exterior. He found ways of getting around all that, by beating his own daughters, and making her watch. Mae found it more horrific, than receiving the brutal blows herself, and she'd submit to whatever he wanted her to do or say, just to make him stop torturing his own daughters.

Ricky and Mae developed a mostly silent and covert war between each other that only Mae's daddy seemed to recognize. Unfortunately before Seven was born, Joel had transferred from Valley Point Police Department in Georgia, to Cocoa Beach Police in Florida. Mae was on her own, and though she had her momma and her grandparents, Ricky had them all convinced at that time; he was only a loving father.

Chapter Five

"Go, go, go…!" Mae pushed her bike behind Terri Lynn's and tried to get around to the front. She was whispering, as loudly as she could. "Move, come on, follow me."

Terri Lynn looked like she was having a sudden change of heart.

Mae couldn't let her renege now, it could blow her cover. She took hold of Terri Lynn's arm. "What are you doing, chickening out?"

"I ain't no chicken." Terri Lynn jumped onto her two wheels, and started peddling.

Suddenly she was leaving Mae behind, who had to shut up and start her own two legs going up and down. The coldness in the night air surprised them both, as their teeth started chattering, long before they reached Highway 51, a block from their home. They had a long way to go, planning on going down to Florida, three hundred miles away. Both had a change of clothes, and between them three dollars.

Terri Lynn and Mae had become close allies. Both wanted to escape the confines of a troubled home. They shared a bedroom and would sometimes lie at night and talk before going to sleep. They had decided to run away from home, and without much thought or plan, they made their first attempt on a Sunday night. They snuck out of the bedroom window, and got on their bicycles, and started riding for their freedom. Within a few blocks they were stopped cold in their tracks when some large barking dogs ran out to greet them.

Mae kept Terri Lynn calm, warning her not to give the dogs something to chase. Narrowly they escaped being attacked, and effectively curing them of the desire to run away on their bikes every again. Quickly they turned back, giving up on the crazy idea. Before they went home though, they stopped together at a tiny church named Three Pines Baptist, got on their knees and prayed.

"Dear God, thank you for not letting those dogs eat us. Help us get back home." Terri Lynn's was quick, while Mae tried to take advantage of the moment.

"Dear God, please protect our family from evil."

The two rushed back home, and snuck back in, never to be discovered they ever left.

It was the summer of 1981, and Mae was now twelve-years-old. In the fall she would be attending Lanyard Jr. High, as a seventh grader. Mary was in her late months of pregnancy and was home all the time having quit her job at the hospital. For Mae it was a strange welcome to have her home full time, and she'd hoped with the birth of another sibling, things might change.

Ricky, was a master manipulator, and managed quite well to continue his criminal behavior. The pregnancy made his unprovoked attacks worse. The last thing Mae wanted to do was to hurt her momma, and somehow she got it into her head, if Mary knew what was going on, she would blame her.

Erik turned two-years-old on June 19th and Mary would give birth to Seven Scott Levine, one hour past midnight, June 20th. The two brothers would be eternally linked sharing their birthdays.

Mae had been as tickled about her mother's third pregnancy as she had when Mary was expectant with Erik. She'd hoped for a girl, while Terri Lynn had prayed hard for a boy. From the beginning of Seven's life, Mae and Terri Lynn fought over the blond baby and both claimed the title older sister.

"You have Erik, Seven is mine!" Terri Lynn wanted him all to herself.

Soon enough though, no one wanted to change the diapers.

After Seven's birth, Ricky became more antagonistic towards Terri Lynn and Mae. Things for him started to unravel when his first wife wandered back into the picture. Alicia's presence troubled Mary, because though Alicia appeared older, her actual age at the time of giving birth to Terri Lynn had been 13. This new fact unnerved Mary even more, when Alicia's younger sisters, made legal accusations against Ricky for molesting them. Alicia wanted to see her daughters, and her girls were desperate to see her. So now, not only did Ricky and Mary have to battle Joel Tripp, they had Alicia fighting them too. It was rather difficult for Mary to believe her present husband to be a child molester, how could she have made such a terrible mistake? The worries took seed, but doubt followed soon behind with Ricky denying the accusations.

Ricky could have been on "The Days of our Lives" with his superb acting skills. Somehow he managed to turn every disagreement with Mae, into a battle over 'the other parent'. Mental and emotional abuse was being tossed at Terri Lynn and Mae every day.

Fearfully, Mae had started trying to tell her daddy what Ricky was making her do, as well as the physical assaults she endured. Never had she ever imagined living with her daddy, now she began thinking about it. Raised in Chambly County, Alabama, Mae relished the rustic south. She had never thought about living anywhere else. If she moved to her daddy's in Florida, she'd be away from her momma and brothers, a painful thought for her. Maw Maw, Paw Paw, Granny Anne and all her friends, would be left behind. Everyone and everything she'd ever known or loved.

Mae wrote her daddy letters, long ones, where she attempted to provide him with enough reason to come rescue her from her tormentor. Hiding these letters, until she could find a way to get them mailed, she'd often worried they could be intercepted by Ricky. Worse than that, read by her mother, so she sent encrypted messages. Many letters were found and read by Ricky and instead of getting help; Mae would get in trouble for making up "lies", and would be accused of trying to get her parents back together. Ricky twisted everything around this issue. Mae never wanted her parents anywhere near each other, but Mary could easily see how Joel was twisting his daughter against her new marriage.

Ricky was a smart man, and he watched Mae closely for signs that she might spill the beans on his sexual advances on her. Mae wondered herself if anyone noticed what was going on. She started school, and felt like it was printed across her forehead, but no one seemed to recognize her distress. The letters she wrote to her daddy would be hidden under her mattress, until she could find the money for a stamp, but just writing it out on paper, made her feel somewhat better to get it off her chest. It worked out until Ricky found her letters.

Walking into her room after school one evening, Mae's bedroom had been ransacked. It appeared as if a police search had occurred with everything opened up and emptied onto the floor. Her bed had been stripped, and the mattress flipped up. She knew in an instant that the letters she'd written to her daddy had been found. Ricky appeared in her door way, with his sinister grin, and alcohol breath.

"So I'm abusing you?" The words slurred from his lips.

Attempting to ignore him and fight back the tears, Mae turned her back on the inebriated idiot. Reaching down, she started picking her things up off the floor. When her bedroom door shut, she swung back around to find him pulling an object out of his pocket.

"I found this." He tossed the object over to her. "It was under your mattress."

Quickly, Mae handed it back to him, embarrassed for touching it.

"A vibrator…" His teeth were showing as he chortled. "Do you know how to use it?"

Mae feared her lunch was going to come back up her throat. "NO!" She answered while backing away, trying to get as far from him as possible.

"Oh sure Mae, it's yours, I found it under your side of the bed." Chuckling to himself he took a step closer.

Mae started shaking her head back and forth. "It's not mine!" She announced with honesty, because it wasn't. They both stared at each other for a minute. He then took the object and licked it up and down.

"If I'd known you had this, I could have helped you with it, and taught you how to use it." Licking his lips, and sticking his tongue way out to do it. "Mm… you taste good." The object slid into his mouth.

Mae's blood began boiling, while his disgusting actions started making her nauseous.

"Leave me ALONE!" The shrillness in her voice made him nearly trip trying to get back out of the room. He was fearful Mary would come in. Tossing the massager back at her, it fell to the floor. He opened the door and proceeded to the kitchen where Mary was reading Mae's letters, written out of desperation to her father.

"So, what punishment does she need?" The sound of his voice continued to heat her blood.

Mae's shy character was replaced by a hostile warrior, and for the first time in her life, she completely lost her cool. Despite all the years of abuse, she'd provided few fights. As if she had nothing to fear, she confronted Ricky in the kitchen.

"You're nothing but a lying drunk!" Mae pointed her finger at him. They both glanced over at Mary sitting at the kitchen table, who was still trying to take in the contents of her daughter's written word.

Mae looked back at Ricky, and stood her ground. She seethed her hatred for him, and wanted to scratch his eyes out of his head. She wasn't prepared for the full frontal attack; as Ricky ran towards her with both hands reaching to grab her. Shoving Mae backwards into the hallway wall; hard enough to force the air from both of her lungs, he then lifted her easily off her feet by holding onto her thin hair. He began tossing her back and forth down the hallway, banging her head into the wall with each step.

Fearing he was going to pull her head bald, Mae started kicking and scratching, attempting to free herself from his grip. She was no match for the drunken adult male, dripping with hate.

"Stop it!" Mary appeared behind Ricky, yelling at both of them, which only angered Mae more.

She felt she'd done nothing wrong to start with. A voice she'd never heard before started coming from her mouth, saying words, she'd never spoken before. A searing heat began to make its way through her veins, as she found herself fighting for her life. Breaking free from his potent grip, and somewhat stunned by his viciousness towards her, Mae ignored Mary's pleas, and bolted out of the house.

She didn't want to listen, she just wanted to escape. Her ears were ringing and tears soaked her face as she continued to wildly run down the road. She didn't know where to go or what to do, as she pulled handful after handful of blond hair, leaving a trail behind her. Sure she'd been disciplined to the extreme by her own daddy with his military belt. Never had a grown man attacked her with such animosity, in all her twelve years.

From a neighbor's phone, Mae called her Maw Maw, who showed up and sat out in the car, listening to Ricky explain Mae's troubling behavior. He claimed Mae had attacked him, unprovoked, and he'd had no choice but to defend himself. It shock Mae how easily he could convince others of his authenticity, while promoting her as a crazed, lunatic who was desperate to get her parents back together.

Mary continued to be a stay at home mom after giving birth to her third baby. She found it easier to handle five children by taking care of them all first hand. She could sense something going on under the surface, but was completely blind to the truth. The two baby boys, kept Mary on her toes, and with the three older girls, she had plenty of house hold chores to do and pass around.

The first two years of Seven's life, Mae resigned herself to endure Ricky's perverse behavior. Her father offered for her to come live with him in Florida, but she didn't want to move and hated the idea of going to a new school. Clandestinely she just wished Ricky would either die or go away.

Despite her refusal to move away, her worst fears would still come true, when Ricky decided they needed to move to middle Georgia. He'd obtained a job managing a grocery store named, Rubo's.

Deathly shy, Mae crumpled in spirit and depression began to eat away at her like cancer. She would pray every night.

"Please God, make Ricky go away."

The stress made her face break out with acne, which made her feel like she had the plague on her face. She began to self-mutilate, taking her pencil's eraser, and rubbing the skin off her hands. The strange act, as painful as it was, felt good. She couldn't help but to start considering suicide or murder. Feeling trapped in an endless nightmare, she could find no to wake up or escape from.

Alcohol continued to play a major role in Ricky's obscene behavior; he loved to drink Canadian Mist. Mary never realized how much her husband drank. He kept a bottle in the refrigerator that she assumed he took a couple of sips out of each day. She would be the one to buy his alcohol every month, so she never knew the trick he was playing on her, which was that the bottle in refrigerator was full of water, and he kept a separate bottle, which he emptied daily.

When Ricky moved the family, there was only three weeks left in school, so when they started their new schools, they only had two weeks to attend. This didn't leave Mae much time to acquire any friendship, except with one girl, named Sharon.

Her new friend had invited her to come over, which Mae decided to take her up on. Sharon had a boyfriend, and his name was Marty. After an hour at Sharon's, Mae was getting tired of hearing the girl go on and on about how wonderful Marty was. It surprised them both when Marty showed up with one of his friends. Mae wasn't impressed, and pardoned herself with the excuse that she had left chores undone at home, and needed to go. She started on the ten block walk home, bouncing a tennis ball with the rhythm of her step. Unbeknownst to her, Marty had started following her, and out of nowhere he ran up, grabbing her ball.

"Give me back my ball." She warned him while squinting her eyes and putting her hands on her hips.

Believing himself to be funny, he pushed her ball down his pants. "If you want it, go get it." He grinned at her, daring her to take it from him.

Without further thought, she marched right up to him, pulled his pants out with one hand and got her ball with the second.

"Like this?" Mae scorned at him, as she yanked the ball out.

Resuming her walk he continued to follow, having never met anyone like her before. Most teenage girls would have giggled and begged for the ball back. Penis's really had no effect on Mae, nor was she afraid of them. This fascinated Marty, and he walked her all the way home, trying to figure out what it was that had him so intrigued with the Alabama girl. He like her, and told her he wanted to see her again.

Mae laughed at the prospect, but then she felt suspicious. "Why?"

He quickened his pace so that he could walk backwards in front of her, eager to both slow her down and look her in the eyes. "Because… I like you." He nearly tripped over a rock, but regained himself fast enough to prevent falling on his butt.

"You don't know me." She had no time for his advances, and he'd started bugging her like a fly buzzing around her head.

"Well, I want to know you." He held his two arms out, which made her stop for a moment to give him a long glare.

"Sharon is my friend and I'm not interested in hurting her feelings or making her mad." Mae stepped around him, wishing he'd just go away.

"She's just my friend." He reasoned while crossing his arms back and forth. They were now standing in Mae's front yard, and she wasn't about to invite him in.

"Oh, I think she intends on marrying you one day." Mae teased, putting her two hands on her hips.

Marty began backing back out her yard, knowing he'd left his friend back at Sharon's house with no explanation of disappearing. He couldn't help himself, and now that he knew where Mae lived, he would be able to find out more about her. He laughed at Mae and shouted back to her while backing out of her yard.

"That's never going to happen!"

Mae spent the rest of the evening, thinking about the irksome young boy, and how much her new friend, her only friend, was in love with him. The house was quieter with Terri Lynn and Angel gone to their mothers for summer visitation. But with Erik and Seven running around with energy unknown, it was far from silent. Other than meeting the new young boy, Mae resigned her weekend to lazily lingering around the house.

For Ricky Levine though, he had other plans for Mae, and would pick this weekend to succeed his worst attack ever on his step-daughter.

Chapter Six

"Mae, I'm going to get some fried chicken, do you want to come with us?"

Mary was standing at Mae's bedroom door, looking in at her daughter who continued to linger in her room, even though it was almost one o'clock in the afternoon, on Saturday. With Ricky home it was the safest place to be. Mae looked up from her magazine article and could see both boys excited about the prospect of both riding in the car and getting some chicken. Seven was pushing his blond head through Mary's legs, while Erik tugged at her purse, which hung loosely from her arm.

Giving it some thought, Mae declined the offer. "Nah, I'm just going to stay in my room, or watch Poltergeist." The horror movie was scheduled to come on that day, and it was one of Mae's favorites.

Mary stood in the door way lingering for a moment; she had a funny feeling in the pit of her stomach, but couldn't quite place it. "Are you feeling okay?"

"Yep feel fine." Mae got up to show her mother that nothing was wrong. Mary went on out the front door while Mae started for the back den. The room was empty, and she would have the television all to herself. She turned on the set and took a comfortable place on the couch. The movie was already on, and Mae realized she'd looked at the program schedule wrong, it had been on for over an hour. Debating whether to go back to her room or watch the rest of the flick, she had just started to lie down; when Ricky walked into the room, and took a seat in the recliner across from her. Immediately feeling uneasy, she glanced his way and found him looking right at her. She tried to return her focus to the movie, but she could sense something sinister flowing through the room. In the next second he was on top of her.

He said nothing as his hands went straight to work, one grabbing at her hands, while the other attempted to unbutton her shorts.

"What are you doing? Stop it! NO! NO! NO… stop…STOP IT!"

Panic nearly choked her, as she began to struggle with the demented man. He began to use his upper body to push down on her face, while his right hand began to try to make its way into her pants. Mae determined herself to fight, she had to stop him, but he was strong, much too strong. He had one hand on her throat now, as she started slapping at his head and face. Ricky was unable to maneuver his way in her pants, so he just grabbed her crotch and squeezed it really hard. Pained, she began to really freak out, kicking both legs, while unnatural sounding screams began coming from deep within her soul.

"This is it!" Her voice was screaming inside her head. "He is going to rape me! He is going to choke me to death!"

His weight pushed down harder, as his grip felt like he was trying to rip her vagina off. As fast as he started the attack, he stopped, and returned to his recliner as if nothing had even occurred.

Mae couldn't believe what had just happened, as the air sucked back into her lungs. Her bruised breasts and crotch confirmed it. The shock was pulsating through her veins, but she couldn't make herself move.

The front door opened up, and both boys could be heard doing the happy chicken dance through the house. Nothing made them happier, than chicken legs and biscuits, and as they buzzed past Mae their exuberance cut through the thick air.

Mae hadn't moved. Devastating terror still held her partially paralyzed as Mary walked by.

Mary had no reason not to be in a good mood, as she smiled down at her daughter. "Well are you hungry?"

"No thanks." The words found their way out of her mouth. She tried not to look at her mother, terrified she'd see straight through her. Mae continued to look at the TV, as if she were really enthralled in the 'scary' movie. She pulled her spirit inward, fighting hard to keep the salty water from escaping her eyes. Two thick tears broke through and slid down her face as she quickly scratched at them.

Mary could feel the atmosphere's heaviness and she tried to read her daughter, but Mae had become a difficult person to comprehend. As she was preparing the boys plates, Mary continued to look at her from the kitchen.

Mae got up, without looking at Ricky, and started for her bedroom.

"Are you ok?" Mary pressed Mae before she managed to get away.

Stopping, Mae knew her mother was trying her best to figure out what was going on.

"Sure." Glancing over at Ricky, he sat with his back to Mary, and was smiling at her distress. Mae could feel something on the inside of her go sour, as a dark hatred mounted inside her heart. She forced her face muscles to relax, realizing they were still frozen in shock. She looked beyond Ricky to her mother and wanted to scream what a monster her husband was, it was like holding back a tsunami.

"I'll eat in a little while. My stomach feels funny." Mae fought hard not to show her mother an ounce of alarm, while a battle churned in every molecule of her body, to prevent herself from attacking the evil man.

She needed to throw up, feeling Ricky's hands still on her. Closing her bedroom door, she made her way to her half bath, where she proceeded to vomit. Collapsing on the floor, she cried and cried. Who could she call? Where could she go for help? She had no other choice but to run away, kill Ricky or commit suicide. There was no other way around it, Mae picked herself up off the floor, and started pacing back and forth. The boiling blood making its way through her frozen body, giving her the sensation of being stung by dozens of bee's.

"Enough!" Her angry voice in her head was screaming obscenities and threats. Mae laid down, pulling her pillow over her head, trying to block out the noise. "I'm not killing anyone!" She cried while arguing with herself. None of it was fair. She'd just have to run, and get as far away from Ricky as she could. She spent most of the day in the seclusion of her bedroom, until late that evening.

Deep in thought about how she would plan her escape, Mae was sitting outside on the front porch steps when Marty surprised her by showing up unannounced.

"Hey!" He was grinning and appeared to have put on some of his nicest clothes. "So what are you up too?"

"Oh, my step dad just tried to rape me earlier, and I'm contemplating killing him." The incensed voice in Mae's head screamed, but out of her mouth came a quiet. "Nothing..." She looked down at her feet suddenly, the tears returning without her control to stop them.

"What's wrong, what's happened to you?" Marty sat down next to Mae, immediately concerned.

Looking over at him momentarily, Mae debated telling him the truth, the whole truth.

"I am running away." The words spilled out.

"Where are you going? What's happened?" Moving closer to her, he leaned down to whisper. "Let me go with you." His excitement annoyed her.

"Shh..!" Mae put her finger to her lips. "I don't want anyone to hear!"

He glanced behind his back and started speaking softly. "Where are you going?"

"I can't tell you." She looked him in the eyes. "That way, you won't know if they ask you." She didn't want him to go, but at the same time she feared to run all alone.

"I can go if I want; I have problems too!" His face displayed both pain and irritation.

"What problems do you have?" Mae wanted to swat at him like a fly.

"Look, I want to go, and if you don't let me, I'll tell you Mom right now." He stood up, as if he planned on marching right into her house.

"Go ahead!" She irritably called his bluff.

Marty sat right back down, nervous that he couldn't push her buttons. "Mae, I wouldn't do that, I'm sorry. I just don't want to lose you now that I've found you."

"No, you'll get in trouble."

"Please, Mae, Let me go with you." He reached out and took her hand.

"Okay, you can come with me." The words slid between her teeth as she pulled her hand back. "You'd better not tell anyone!" She was angry with herself for so freely spilling the beans to what was really a complete stranger. It just felt good to have another human to talk to.

Chapter Seven

The plans had been ironed out the evening before, and Mae woke up the next morning with a heavier heart than she had ever had. Running away made her very sad. She loved her mother and brothers, and had concern for Terri Lynn and Angel. How could she leave them all with such a horrible monster? It tore at her heart to even look at Erik and Seven that morning, they were especially watchful of Mae, both boys sensing she was up to something.

Mae had tried to go about her day like normal, but had her things packed and sitting outside her bedroom window. Marty was supposed to meet her by the rail road tracks after ten, and it was nearing that hour. She patrolled her bedroom, trying to get the nerve up to make her move. First she would have to get past Mary, without giving away anything. It wasn't like she was just leaving to go to the store; she would be leaving for good.

"Momma…" Mae had to go, it was time. She made her way into the kitchen. "May I go to Sharon's house for a little while?"

Mary was cleaning the dishes from the morning breakfast. "Well, have you folded the laundry?"

Mae had forgotten her basic chores. "No, but…" Mae could hardly speak the words. "I'll do them when I get back."

Mary frowned at Mae.

"I won't be gone long." Mae looked her mother in the eyes, and lied.

"Well, be back after lunch, do your chores, and you can stay gone all day if you want." Mary continued cleaning, while Mae slowly agreed.

"Okay, I will."

Once out of the house, she grabbed her bag and ran as fast as she could to Marty, who was waiting by the rail road just like she'd told him. Immediately they began walking on the tracks, their plans were to follow the rails all the way down to Florida. The idea sounded simple enough, but neither teen accounted for the 98 + degree temperatures. Every step farther away, Mae felt both elation and fear. Marty quickly became a pest.

"I'm taking my shirt off. Why don't you just take your shirt off too?" He grinned at her.

"I certainly hope you don't think I'm going to have sex with you." Mae couldn't help but to put it bluntly.

The words made Marty tense up a bit, and walk with a slower pace. "Why? What's wrong with me?"

"I'm on my period."

The answer hadn't been expected, but it was a good one for Marty. "Oh…"He picked his pace back up, but neither spoke for a long time.

Mae thought about sex and how she despised it. It had been nothing but a weapon used against her, something she was ashamed of, and full of guilt over. Marty would soon figure out that running away hadn't been some elaborate plan to get him laid.

Later that evening they made a camp next to a creek. At first it was fun for Marty, playing a game of house but as the sun started disappearing and a black unlike any either had ever experienced took over, the surroundings took on a scary and ominous feel. Without any source of light, the blackened woods became threatening, with every noise amplified. Having a small flash light, and nothing else, Marty's playfulness soon vanished.

As Mae made her way back to their sleeping bags, from taking a nature break, she teased Marty.

"I just saw something with red eyes!"

Without further prompting, he was up and packing his things together.

Snickering to herself, she innocently quizzed. "What are you doing?"

"I'm out of here, I ain't staying!" Marty fussed while taking quick glances all around into the dark circling in on him.

"I was just playing, I didn't see anything." She eased herself down, hoping to calm him some. It didn't work.

"Well I don't care, and I don't like this place." Looking at each other, she figured with one flash light, they would have to come to an agreement of some kind.

Neither of them expected the commotion of noise just beyond the veil of black. It must have been a nice meal for either a wild cat or dog, but from the ears of two young teenagers, it sounded like the "Texas Chain Saw Guy" had a young victim. Without further discussion, they found themselves walking along the tracks, quite slowly, but none the less with intense focus of getting to light and life.

Wood, gravel, wood, gravel, went the blinded pace of their feet. Marty held to the flash light, so Mae couldn't see too much of anything. All day long, they had only seen two trains, and they had hid as they went by. Mae kept looking back, sometimes thinking she could see something keeping up with them just beyond the darkness. Long ago their eager conversations had ended as hunger and tiredness took over the mood. Wood, gravel, wood, gravel, and every so often they'd stub a toe. Wood...gravel...wood...hole.

"Wait!" Mae reasoned quickly. "We're on a bridge Marty, shine the light." Sure enough, the failing light showed the tracks were going across a bridge.

Mae stopped. "We can't go across this!"

Marty turned, shining the light into her eyes. "Why not…?"

"Because…" She reasoned, while blocking the light with her hand. "A train might come."

"Well we can't stay here; we just have to take our chances." Marty concluded, turning his back and continuing his pace.

Swallowing hard, Mae took her own blind steps, finding it more difficult if she looked down.

"We don't know how long this bridge is, nor what it's going over. It could be a thousand foot drop!" She fussed as one step at a time, she progressed. He had begun to get a bit ahead of her, leaving her alone with her fear of a train, a steep drop or the chain saw man.

"Some experience this has been." Mae mumbled to herself, as again she turned to see if her phantom was still behind her. It wasn't, but a bright light was.

"Marty, it's a damn train!" She screamed as she forgot her patterned steps and took to an all-out race, passing him right away. As if he didn't believe her, thinking she was trying to trick him again, he shined his light back to the brighter light.

"It's a train!" He announced, and started running behind her, when suddenly, his right leg fell straight through two wooden cross tracks. His screams of pain pierced into the blackness all around, turning Mae around completely.

"What?" Running back to him, she took the flash light to see what damage had been done. With a train coming toward them without mercy, Mae had no time to examine him. "GET UP!" Pulling him to his feet, she started to run while holding and pulling him, as fast as she could. As soon as her feet hit gravel, they jumped from the tracks, within seconds of being hit.

They both lay face up, catching their breath, while the assailing horn from the conductor's car went past. Before the entire train went by, with the brisk breeze blowing, Mae knocked on the flashlight, as it threatened to go out for good. With what little light it offered, she gazed at Marty's injured leg.

"Well, it certainly looks broke." He didn't deny her prognosis, feeling every bit of agony associated with broken bones. They would have to find help.

Chapter Eight

Marty was having a grueling time trying to walk, and his excruciatingly protracted steps had started to get on Mae's nerves. She was angry at him for not listening to her concerning the bridge, and though she felt somewhat sorry for his injury, she also felt he deserved it.

It was only two am, and they had made their way to a sleepy town, having abandoned the idea of walking to Florida on the rail road tracks. Hobbling along, with Mae now carrying his bag, Marty was beginning to show signs of an early retreat.

"If someone stops us, you let me do the talking." Mae exercised her control. As if she was seeing into the future, a sheriff's car pulled along beside them. Mae knew the law enforcer would know something was off with two teenagers walking the streets at such an hour. Marty looked drunk, staggering around, hardly able to stand, while Mae held his pillow case of stuff and her step-father's bowling bag. (The only thing she could find to put her belongings in.)

The old sheriff rolled down his window. "I'm going to ask you, what are you two doing out at this time?"

Mae had over a decade of experience with a police officer, and she knew exactly how to act in their presence. She knew how closely they watched every move and action, not to mention demeanor.

"We're walking to my Aunt's house." She casually answered, while Marty began to turn really white.

"You're Aunt's house? Who is your Aunt?" The sheriff prodded.

Mae knew this man would probably know the majority of people in his own town. "Sadie Williamson…" She offered and added. "She lives just two blocks down." She pointed toward a group of houses.

This answer only made him smile slightly. "Really, well I don't know anyone by that name. Is she expecting you at this hour?"

Scratching her head, and looking down, she answered. "Well, no, she doesn't know we are coming over, but that's because of the argument, and we just decided to walk over." The sheriff was eyeing Marty, who continued to waver back and forth. "His leg is hurt, that's why we are going to Aunt Sadie's." Mae offered, while helping to support Marty.

The sheriff didn't look convinced. "Well, my advice is to get to where you're going, and get off these streets. If I catch you two out again, I'll arrest you."

Just like that he pulled off, leaving the both of them out of breath. Without further word, they took off running, as best as they could. Making their way behind a residence, they sat against the house in the dark shadows, trying to regain their composure.

"I really thought we were going to jail." Marty laughed. "Why didn't you tell me you had an Aunt?"

Mae eyed him with a sideways glance. "I don't have an Aunt, and if he catches us out again, we will be going to jail. I know he didn't believe me." Her head rested back onto a complete stranger's home. Exhausted and feeling sick at her stomach she added. "We have to get out of this town, before the sun comes up." Her words made Marty start to turn pale again. He had already imagined "Aunt Sadie" fixing him up a nice warm bed.

"I don't think I can keep walking." Marty whispered mostly to himself.

"Well you stay here then."

Mae had no intentions of going back home, none what-so-ever. Nestled inside the bowling bag, she had brought with her a bottle filled with Old English Lemon Oil furniture polish. Having studied lethal ways to kill herself, she'd ended with the precautionary remarks on the back of the household chemical.

"DANGER HARMFUL OR FATAL IF SWALLOWED. KEEP OUT OF REACH OF CHILDREN. CONTAINS-PETROLEUM-DISTILLATES." On the very top in even bigger writing, "CAUTION: COMBUSTIBLE MIXTURE." Other than Drain-O and Bleach, the ingredients in the furniture oil would offer her freedom from a life plagued with a child molester. Standing up, she started to walk away.

"Wait!" Marty slowly got to his feet. "I'm coming too."

Mae did feel bad about his leg, but she'd also warned they shouldn't go across that bridge. Carefully they walked the dark back roads of the sleepy town. Only a few vehicles were riding about, and they kept a close eye out for that sheriff's car. Not really certain where they even were, it wasn't hard to figure out they were lost. A large pickup truck with monster tires drove past them, and then stopped, backed up and stopped beside them. Two young guys were inside, and asked where they were headed.

"We're trying to get out of town." Mae answered, letting her guard down instantly. They didn't strike her as law enforcement, and who knows, they could have a way to help them. She was becoming desperate to get away.

"Really…" The driver looked them both over really good. "Where are y'all headed?"

"Florida…." Marty blurted out, with Mae giving him a dirty look.

"Wow, you two are in luck, Dan here is fixing to go to Florida." The driver pointed to his passenger who smiled and waved.

"Yes, that is lucky." Mae squinted; feeling like a trap was being laid out.

"My name is Stanley, by the way." He offered her his hand to shake.

Letting her hand go into his, she certainly didn't have much more to work with. "So, Dan can give us a ride?" She looked across at the passenger.

Dan shook his head up and down, while looking at the driver. "Yep, but he has to pack his truck first, do you two mind waiting?" Stanley looked from his passenger back to Mae.

Mae looked at Marty. He seemed tickled to death over having a ride, versus walking.

Dan's house was only a block over, and they met up at the back of his truck, backed into the driveway. Mae couldn't shake her uneasiness over the fortunate luck.

"Something just doesn't feel right about this." While whispering to Marty, she started debating in her mind to just walk away. Headlights could be seen coming down the road, giving Mae the sudden urge to run. Dan stepped up next to her. That's when she knew the jig was up, that the two guys were young deputies and had been told to be on the lookout for them.

"It's a set up!" Mae warned Marty, but it was too late. Two sheriff cars pulled up out of nowhere.

"Easy now..." Dan put his two hands up like he was trying to catch a stray animal. Marty looked around but gave no indications that he would try to get away. "Everything is going to be alright." Dan eased his way to Mae.

The old sheriff walked up smiling like he had caught himself some big time criminals. "I told you two not to let me catch you out on my streets."

His expression made Mae want to puke. None of these idiots had a clue what they were actually accomplishing, putting her back in with a child predator.

Instead of running, she gave in, considering she had a second plan in place. She let the sheriff lead her to the back seat of his cruiser. Holding onto her bowling ball bag, as soon as he shut the door, she began digging in the bottom, feeling around for the bottle of furniture oil. As Marty was being questioned, she found her bottle, and took it out, examining it for leakage. She then noticed Marty was being lead to the car, so she hid the bottle. As he assisted Marty into the back seat, he noticed the blue bag and took it. He gave them another grin and shut the car door.

"I'm so sorry Mae." Marty began, as she turned her head from looking at him. "I had to tell them where we came from, they made me." He was crying. "Please don't hate me!" He begged, as she slowly twisted off the bottle cap.

In her mind she was thinking how they wouldn't be able to figure out what she had taken, and by the time they did, she would already be dead. As she raised the bottle to her lips, Marty panicked and grabbed it. Somehow he seemed to know her intentions immediately.

"No way are you going to kill yourself with me, I can't let you do it." He struggled with her for the bottle.

"Stop it!" Mae hadn't anticipated his prompt reaction. "You don't know what you are doing, let me have it!" She seethed at him, as the contents of the bottle splashed all over both of them.

The sheriff noticed the two of them fighting and opened the door. "Give me that!" He took the bottle.

"NO!" Mae screamed at both Marty and the sheriff, who also took the top of the container.

The door slammed shut and the sheriff walked off examining the contraband he'd taken. Looking over at Marty, her expression made him extremely uneasy, being locked up with her in the sheriff's car.

"I don't care Mae; I couldn't just watch you kill yourself. I don't care, be mad at me." He boldly announced, while holding to the doors arm-rest.

"You don't have a clue." She whispered, not sure what to do anymore.

They arrived at the two room sheriff department in what they'd come to find out was Reynolds, Georgia. Marty and Mae had managed to walk about twenty miles from Fort Valley. Sitting in front of the sheriff's desk, Mae had decided after the bottle incident, to stay silent. She listened as the sheriff tried to get their story from Marty, who couldn't talk without looking at Mae. This made the sheriff intrigued all the more in her story, which she refused to answer as he questioned her. Marty watched her, and had been worried ever since Mae stopped talking to him.

The sheriff held up her bottle of poison. "What's this?"

Marty shook his head back and forth. "It ain't mine!"

Mae's eyes met the sheriff's. "So you're just gonna plead the fifth huh?" He grinned briefly, but it soon disappeared when he saw her return expression.

Holding the bottle up in the air; he started shaking the liquid. "Is this some kind of new drug? Where did you get it? Did you make it, or did someone give it to you?" He sat it down before them on his desk, and then folded his arms to wait for answers.

"Why don't you just have it analyzed in your lab?" Mae finally spoke, mostly out of irritation of his assuming she had nothing better to do than drugs.

"Oh, you can count on that little lady; we will know what it is come tomorrow." He grinned at another deputy sitting across the room.

"Well good, so now what?" She asked while folding her arms up tighter.

"Well your parents will be picking you up shortly, so just sit tight."

The words turned Mae's world inside out. "My parents, how do you know my parents?" She looked over at Marty realizing he had told them everything.

"Oh, we know who you are and where you are from; you were reported runaways out of Fort Valley." The sheriff's answer made her dizzy, as she lowered her head down to her knees. Marty shifted around in his seat, having become slightly terrified of her reactions. Unable to even stop herself, she'd started crying, really hard.

"Don't send me home, put me in jail, but please don't make me go home." Mae begged, while hiding her face in her hands. The quick change in her demeanor had taken the sheriff off guard. He sat up in his wooden chair.

"Why don't you want to go home?"

His question seemed easy enough, but he just had no clue what he was asking her. The truth, a secret she had kept for years, was screaming at her inside her head.

"BECAUSE MY STEP DAD WANTS TO SCREW ME!" She wanted to scream out loud, but sobbed even more. She wanted to tell her desperate secret, it was just too terrible to reveal; too embarrassing to speak of.

"Honey, I can't help you, unless you tell me what's going on." The sheriff had turned from iron clad, to fluffy soft, in an instant.

Slowly Mae looked around at the two sheriffs and Marty looking back at her with what happened to be sincere concern. She wanted to tell someone so bad, and she could feel the words coming up her throat. "Well..." She looked down at the floor, suddenly embarrassed. "My step father has been molesting me." There, the words had come out; finally after four years of torment, she had actually spoken the truth. Everything went silent, as the two sheriffs' gazed back and forth at each other.

Marty reached his hand over and put it on hers. "Mae, I didn't know, why didn't you just tell me?"

"Well Mae, I can assure you, I will have it investigated." The sheriff tried to comfort her.

"Oh thank you, so much." She cried, relieved that she wouldn't have to go back home and face her momma. Running from Ricky, was easy, but running from her momma had been much more difficult. Mae knew Mary would be scared, hurt and angry over her daughter's actions. She didn't feel up to facing her mother.

The sheriff still looked concerned at the young girl whose disposition went from low too high in only split seconds. "How long have you, well, has your step dad been molesting you?"

Now that he was helping her, Mae freely gave him information, almost happy to finally have someone to tell about the torment she'd been experiencing.

"For four years, since he married my momma."

"Really…" The sheriff took off his hat finally, laying it down on his desk.

"Well, where am I going to stay?" Mae asked him smiling; it felt good to have such a painful thing off her chest.

"Oh, you have to go home, we can't keep you, and we have to release you to your parents."

His words felt like bullets hitting her in her heart. What had she done? She started looking around for an escape. "Oh no, I can't go home!" Mae glanced at the front door.

The sheriff stood up suddenly, anticipating her ability to bolt. "Sweetie, we just can't put you into our jail cells, you're a minor and there is no way you can stay here, not even for one night."

Pesky tears continued to trail down her checks, while the sheriff slowly sat back down.

"It will be okay, I will help you," He promised her.

"Help me now!" She cried out loud, but knew it was a waste of time. Any minute her momma would be walking in the door to pick her up. Marty's parents arrived first, and his mother gave Mae an ugly glare, which she couldn't blame her. The entire ordeal had turned into a waste of time and only made things worse, worse than ever.

It would be the very last time Mae ever tried to escape by running away for the rest of her life.

Chapter Nine

"YOU LIED TO ME!" Mary was beside herself with fearful fury. "You stood right there and told me you'd be back home after lunch to do your chores!" She paced back and forth in the den, while Mae sat slumped on the couch. They had picked her up, Ricky and Mary, neither saying a word to the sheriff except thank you, but the second they were in the car, Mary lit into her daughter. She hadn't stopped fussing the entire time it took to get back home. Now she continued while Ricky sat watching Mae in the recliner.

"Damn you Mae, I'm tired of this crap! I'm sick and tired of being lied to!" Mary was so upset she smacked Mae across the face. "You get off your ass and get those clothes folded like you promised!" Mary was crying with rage. She had been terrified when she realized her daughter was gone without a trace. "I hate liars, and you're a damn liar!"

Mae was exhausted; it was close to six in the morning. Obeying her mother, she looked over at Ricky as she walked over to the basket of clothes waiting for her. He sat smiling, enjoying her torment. While Mae folded the laundry, Mary continued to fuss. Mae could feel her spirit dying, while her heart felt like it was bleeding. She felt guilty for hurting her mother.

By eight in the morning, Mae had become numb from the pain and a zombie from exhaustion. Mary had calmed down, but wouldn't let her daughter go to sleep, for the lack of sleep Mae had caused her. Mae wasn't mad at her mother's anger, but was worn down from the entire experience. She was happy when the sheriff didn't mention the secret to her mother, but she worried what the revelation of that secret was going to do.

A knock at the front door made Mae jump in her skin. She watched as her mother walked past her bedroom to go answer it. Both boys stopped to stare at their oldest sibling, whom had made their momma both cry and scream. They had been unusually quiet and nervous. They knew Mae was to blame, and intended on keeping their eyes on her.

"Mae, you have a visitor." Mary announced dryly.

As Mae entered, an official looking man with a suit and tie stood smiling at her. He put his hand out for Mae to shake, which she did so quickly.

"NO, NO, NO!" Mae's mind was screaming. Being in the room with her momma wasn't how she'd envisioned the secret coming out. "Please, don't tell her." Mae's eyes pleaded with the stranger.

"Well, I'll leave the two of you to talk." Mary took immediate leave, to Mae's slight relief.

"My name is Don Daniels and I work with the Family and Children Services." His demeanor did nothing to put her at ease. "Do you want to sit down and let me ask you a few questions?" He pointed to the living room couch. Mary had retreated to the den in the back of the house, so Mae obliged him and took a seat. "Now…" He sat down and began pulling folders from his briefcase. "We received a call concerning you." Mae watched him prepare for what she would be saying to him, but in no way did she feel comfortable in telling him anything. Looking over at her only after he had everything in order, and making eye contact, he finally requested to hear what Mae had to tell him.

"My step father has done things to me." Her mouth was moving, but she could hardly believe how easily the words were coming out. Mae felt like she was having an out of body experience.

"What kind of things?" Don began to write.

It was harder than it had been in the Sheriff Department. "He has tried to make me have sex many times." Mae looked down, sad and ashamed.

"Exactly how many times has this happened?" Don asked as he looked down at his pad of paper.

"A lot..." She hadn't counted the amount of times through the years, but in her head she tried. "I guess six to seven times." Somehow she figured he didn't believe her, and wondered if the sheriff had.

"Have you told your mother?" He pushed his glasses up on his nose as he looked over at her.

"NO!" Mae looked at him as if he'd lost his mind.

"Well you're going to have to tell her." His demand didn't surprise her, it was something that she'd known since the first time Ricky forced himself on her all those years back. What did surprise her was the fact he meant right that moment.

"I can't tell her." The uncontrollable tears began flowing down her face and she pushed herself back further on the couch.

"Mae, I can't help you, unless you tell her." Don carefully explained, with a sudden look of sympathy.

He had said the magic word, help, and as if given a shot of endurance, Mae felt her head nod up and down. "Okay."

"Mrs. Levine…" Don quickly called for Mary, and her slow footsteps, along with both boys running could be heard making their way toward the news.

Mae's heart felt like it had traveled up to her throat, as Mary stepped into the room and sat across from her daughter. Erik bounced over to sit next to Mae, while Seven decided he wanted to get up close and personal with Don. The toddler was trying to get into the service workers bag. The moment would have been cute, except Mae knew what was fixing to be thrown at her mother.

Don easily enough deterred Seven with his keys, giving him the chance to promote the needed conversation. "Mrs. Levine, your daughter has something to tell you."

Mary looked directly at Mae, her eyes wide with obvious irritation. She didn't know what stunt her daughter was trying to pull. She wasn't prepared for the terminologies that were fixing to come her way.

"Ricky has been…" Mae faltered, now finding it impossible to make her vocal cords work properly. "Ricky has been molesting me."

The silence in the room was a testament to Mary's extreme shock. Mae began to shiver and tears poured out of her eyes as she watched her mother's hands come up and cover her face. She began sobbing really loud, while both boys took to tending to their wounded momma. After a few moments, Mary got up and disappeared into the back of the house, with both boys on her heels.

Don had put everything back into his briefcase and stood leaving at the door. Everything started feeling like a nightmarish dream as she watched him walk right out the front door, shutting it behind him. She got up to look out the window, but the man's Volkswagen Rabbit was driving off. Within her mind she could hear herself saying. "I have no other choice."

Programmed; Mae made her way to the kitchen and opened the cabinet under the sink where the chemicals were kept. Taking the Old English Lemon Oil polish, she walked over to the cupboard and took out a coffee cup. Pulling the covering off the polish top, she easily poured the oil, filling it to the brim. With her cup in hand, she started walking through the empty house, not even looking to say goodbye, she walked out the front door.

Having only lived in Fort Valley for a couple of months, she didn't have any idea where she was or where she intended on going. She couldn't see anyway; crying uncontrollably, she blindly made her way a block or two from the house, before she stopped abruptly. This was it, the time had come, and without another thought, Mae drank the entire cup of lemon oil.

Chapter Ten

Mae had stopped and drank the furniture polish, while on a Church lawn. The lemon tasting, oily substance, continued to slowly slide down her throat, as the large cross on the top of the churches steeple caught her eyes. Feelings of dark and trembling shame began to emerge within her heart. What had she just done? How could she take it back? Trying to take a deep breathe quickly revealed the inability to do so with her lungs filling with fumes from the polish. She felt like she was going underwater and every gulp for air resulted in piercing pains flowing through her chest. A dark shadow loomed and sent out a cold lonely feeling. Deplorable and depressing thoughts attacked her. "You're dying!" "Your life is over!" "Death is going to hurt!" "You've murdered yourself!" "You are a failure!"

In utter despair she cried out. "I'm sorry God…" But it was all she could speak with so little air left. The world began to turn around her, like she was sitting on a merry go round; she struggled to stay on her feet.

"I'm sorry, I don't want to die." A weak whisper uttered. Somehow she forced the uncontrollable fear from subduing and enveloping her life's light. "Please, forgive me." She continued to silently pray as she stumbled and fell forward. She quickly got back onto her feet; the dizziness making it difficult to stand. An invisible, titanic wave pushed her forward, while every muscle in her body began to seize with panic, but she kept walking.

The persistent black shadow started to follow her, throwing questions into her mind. "How could you be so stupid? Dead is dead, gone, finished, over and kaput!"

Mae urgently decided she didn't want to be dead. Not aware of any direction that she was going, perhaps walking in a suffocation shock circle, she looked up to see a large black woman standing before her, pointing in a direction. They were both standing in the middle of a street and without a word; she went where the woman wanted to send her. Actual visions of her past began playing in her mind, while the world around her turned black and white, like Dorothy's life before landing in Oz. This was it, this was what death coming felt like, and it came from all directions. Looking back from where she'd just walked, the lady was gone. Now she stood in a small parking lot, the parking lot of the Fort Valley Police Department.

She opened the thick wooden door with glass panes that rattled and two officers abruptly looked her way. Pulling all the air she could into her lungs, the intense pains in her chest squeezed more tears from her already wet and swollen eyes. One officer began to walk with confusion written all over his face toward her.

Mae gasped with all the effort she could put forth. "I've drank furniture polish." She tried to take in more are, as her lungs felt as if they would blow up any second. "I can't breathe." The effort made her fall forward and the officer carefully, helped her to a chair. The officers looked at each other, wondering if what they heard was correct. It wasn't something either had ever heard before.

"Did you just say you drank furniture polish?" The officer sat down pulling a chair right in front of the distressed girl.

"Old English, Lemon Oil." Mae's head lifted up and down.

The seconds seemed like hours as both officers looked back and forth confused, but then both sprang into action. One dispatched an ambulance, while the other officer tended to the suicidal girl. He wasn't quite sure what to ask her. Struggling to deal with the situation he asked basic questions.

"Sweetie, what is your name?"

Looking at him, Mae struggled to get more air in, but with each breathe her lungs felt like they would burst.

The officer began to turn white as he looked over to his fellow officer. "She isn't going to make it." Unable to wait another second he jumped up. "I can't sit here and watch her die right before my eyes!" The officer broke procedural rules and scooped the suffocating girl up into his arms.

"What are you doing? The ambulance is on its way." The second officer reasoned.

"She don't have time, she won't make it if we wait!" The officer waited as the second officer opened the station door, and then let him open the patrol car door too. She could hear them briefly talking, as she felt her body curl up in a fetal position. It helped her to close her eyes, but she'd open them ever so often, catching the terrified officer looking back at her. His mouth was moving, but the sounds coming out were severely distorted, similar to Charlie Browns school teachers' voice.

The officer was panicking, frightened that this young girl, who could very well be the age of his daughter at home, would die in his care. In less than five minutes the cruiser slid into the hospital parking lot. Outside a small group stood ready with a stretcher. The officer promptly removed her from his back seat and laid her onto the already rolling bed. Oxygen went onto her nose, which immediately made her just want to sleep. Now the voices all around began to come in loud and clear.

"Furniture Polish…" One nurse asked another as Mae was being pulled into a seated position.

A cup was offered to her. "Honey, either you drink it or we will have to tube you."

Nothing about being "tubed" sounded good to Mae, not good at all. Grudgingly she swallowed the cup of liquid chalk. Another cup was offered which she drank slower. Still having trouble breathing, she just wanted air. By the third cup, she didn't want any more of the substance.

"I know this isn't pleasant, but you've got to drink this." Her nurse persisted. Everyone moved about but she felt like all the eyes were looking at her. Taking the cup, and putting it to her mouth was all it took, and she began to regurgitate into a pan they had ready. Somehow this process made everyone happy, as the lemon oil smell floated all around.

"Yep, it's Old English Oil alright!" The nurse laughed. Be it behind their humor Mae saw fear and concern in their eyes. Their humor still puzzled her, but maybe it was their way of avoiding the awfulness of what was happening.

They saved her life, and she felt gratitude towards them immediately. Laying back down, with the oxygen mask back on, she floated in and out of a sleepy dream. Exhaustion consumed every cell in her body. They put her into a private room by herself, with the officer who brought her to the hospital, watching over her. Outside the door her momma wanted to see her, at least Mae thought so. Maybe her mother couldn't see her, but she knew her mother was out there. She opened her eyes to see the officer looking down at her crying.

"Why would you do something like that?" His hand slid across his face in an attempt to stop the wet drops.

"I'm sorry." Mae mouthed under the mask.

"Don't be sorry; just never do anything like that again."

Mae realized her problems hadn't gone away with her attempt. She had made things even worse. If revealing the secret hadn't made her momma want to disown her, then her present condition wouldn't make it any better.

Don Daniels walked in briskly, both eyes as big as half dollars. Looking at the Police Officer he nodded, but then walked right up next to Mae's bed.

"Why did you do that? I was there to help you."

"You left." Her voice muffled under the plastic.

Don's head nodded slightly as he looked down to the floor. "I know, but I was coming back, but you're right, I shouldn't have left you."

His words offered her little consolation now. He too had started crying and turned to talk to the Officer. Between them they discussed the issues at hand.

Ricky Levine was inside the hospital's chapel, where the sheriffs' department was questioning him. This news made her feel sick, when she'd always dreamed it would elate her. It hurt so bad to think what her momma had to now be going through. Would she believe the accusations made against her husband? Or would she doubt her oldest child? What could she be feeling to know, her husband tried to rape her daughter?

Mae wanted to just disappear, closing her eyes; she fell into a deep sleep. It wouldn't be until noon the next day that she completely woke up. Opening her eyes, she couldn't remember where she was, or what had happened. Tubes were blowing oxygen into her nostrils, as she looked around the room, pulling from her memory banks.

"Well good morning..." Mae's eyes focused on a woman sitting in a bed beside hers. "I was just praying for you." The woman announced, as she took her hands down from a praying position. "My name is Sarah." Mae continued to look blankly at the stranger, without saying one word, she turned over, putting her back to the woman.

"Praying for me?" Mae thought to herself silently. "She doesn't even know me!" Tears immediately formed in her eyes, as she remembered exactly what had happened.

"They just brought our lunch in; I know you must be hungry." Sarah spoke while lifting the tray off her own food. Laughing out loud, Sarah joked. "If you don't want yours, I might. Mine just doesn't look that good."

Mae turned her head to look at the woman again, and for some reason, just looking at Sarah's bowl of clear broth, made Mae's stomach growl really loud. Just as the woman said, her food was resting at her feet, on a large rolling tray, Sarah helped by pushing it closer.

Mae eyed the strange, but nice woman. "Thanks." Mae hoarsely spoke. Lifting the lid it revealed she had the same meal as Sarah, a steaming hot bowl of brown water. Under another lid, she found red Jell-O, which seemed more appealing. As she tried to get the wiggly food into her mouth, a large nurse walked in.

"We're going to need to take some blood." She smiled while showing off her needles. Mae hoped she was talking to Sarah, but the nurse pushed her food tray back, and laid her supplies down on top of Mae's legs. "Now this isn't going to be fun, no fun at all." The nurse began explaining the necessary procedure. "I will be taking blood from your arteries, to check your white cell count, and see if you're getting enough oxygen in your blood."

The words were foreign to Mae, and she couldn't get past the "no fun, no fun at all." Why did nurses have to announce such facts?

"Now I'll need for you to lie completely still, you can't move one bit, or I'll have to start all over again." The large nurse had Mae's left arm, because the IV had been put into her right arm. "Now, this isn't like taking blood from your veins, which you can easily see through the skin. We have to get down to the tiny arteries and hopefully find one." Suddenly she stabbed the needle straight down into Mae's wrist.

With force she began twisting it all around. Without meaning to, Mae's arm twitched with painful reflex and the nurse yanked the needle back out. "Great, because you moved I have to do it again!" She sounded disgusted.

After her fourth attempt Mae decided she didn't want to be stabbed by the woman anymore. "That's it, no more!" Mae pulled her arm away, willing to fight with this nurse who obviously didn't know what she was doing. "I don't have any arteries!" Mae reasoned bravely and seriously, rubbing her wrists which were now terribly swollen and bruised. "Come back on another day!" Mae looked at the round nurse whose hands rested on her hips.

Slowly the nurse backed out of the room. "I'll be back in thirty minutes." She warned as she walked out the door.

After she left, Sarah began talking. "Wow, I know that had to hurt, I am so sorry she did that to you."

It felt good to have someone witness the abuse for a change. "I think she was trying to cut my arm off with that needle." She examined the damage.

Sarah laughed at Mae's sarcasm.

Eventually another nurse showed up to finish what the first one couldn't. With the second nurse, it only took her one stick and she poked into an artery, to Mae's relief. After the blood work showed she was receiving enough oxygen, it was announced she could be released to go home. Mae wanted to go home, even if Ricky was there, she didn't want to leave her mother and brothers. Don Daniels showed up with a shock for Mae though, she wouldn't be going home; she would be going to a place called a foster home.

Chapter Eleven

Being placed into a foster home hadn't been something Mae ever considered happening. The concept itself was outlandish to her. Instead she'd thought Ricky would be forced to move. The images Mae had of a foster home, was of a large room with beds and hundreds of orphan children running around. So as they drove up to E.T. and Mandy Griskeys yellow brick home, in a nice upper-middleclass section of Fort Valley, she was relieved to say the least.

E.T. and Mandy hadn't long been accepted as foster parents. Marion Mae Tripp would be their very first foster child. They had a nice home that had been big enough for their four kids. Three had already finished college, while the fourth was still at home. As it turned out, her foster sister, Gennifer, was Mae's age and would be starting high school like her in the fall. Mae had her own bedroom with Gennifer's room right next door.

Mae and Gennifer became fast friends from the start. That fall they started high school together, which for Mae was something she'd feared having to do all alone, but now she had a comrade. She became a member of the Peach County Trojan Marching Band, playing a flute. Mixing in with the hundreds of other kids, Mae could pretend everything was conventional in her life. She started attending weekly therapy sessions, which would consistently remind her of how messed up she felt, and how no matter where she was, she couldn't escape her life.

After she revealed her secret to her mother, it felt as if her life were shot out and over. All the good things were gone. She'd lost her mother and siblings. Everything felt screwed up. No matter what she did, she would be hurt, and end up hurting others.

Mae visited with her daddy at one point during the year in foster care. Joel had found a new woman named Tessa and announced their marriage plans. The visit would leave Mae perplexed, because Joel didn't act the same as he had in the past. She didn't know if he was sincere, or trying to convince somebody of something.

Every month Mae visited Mary and the boys. They had moved into a much smaller house, which sat a block away from Rubo's Grocery, where Ricky was still the manager. He wasn't allowed to be at the home while Mae was visiting. These visits were awkward, between her and her mother, neither knew what to say to the other. Mae knew she had put doubts in her momma's head, but she didn't know who her mother doubted more, Ricky or her. The visits home would leave Mae feeling depressed. Neither of her baby brothers seemed to notice she was even gone, living innocently in a world of calamity.

The next year of her life went by, and in many ways she'd forever be changed from the encounter of living with the Griskey's. Her experience of living with a completely differently family, gave Mae plenty of insights she would never have known existed. Two unified parents, working together, for her, not against her. It was both touching and terrifying to Mae. In the back of her mind she knew it was only temporary, and eventually she'd have to tell E.T., Mandy and Gennifer, goodbye.

Nightmares would wake her in a wet sweat. She couldn't shake the feeling something bad was going to happen. She continued to feel depraved and guilty for causing her momma undeserved pain. Telling the truth hurt when no one believed her. What hurt worse the truth or the disbelief, Mae didn't know, but she worried relentlessly if she'd made the right decision to tell her momma the secrets about Ricky.

Mae continued to feel the need to cause harm to herself, it was a strain to fight off the impulses. She'd swallow entire bottles of prescription pills she found in E.T.'s medicine cabinet. No one even noticed her sicknesses as self-induced. What exactly she hoped to accomplish by doing such things she didn't know. She just knew she hated herself. She didn't want to die, but life hurt too much to live.

Her freshman year at Peach County would bring her memories that lasted a life time. She met a boy named Jacob Jones, who would one day be her future husband and father of her three kids. In typical high school fashion, Mae saw him the first time during a pep rally. Giving him a note soon after, the two of them, though strangers, called themselves, 'going with each other'. When he asked her on her first date to see the country group 'Alabama', it took a month before Mae could give him an answer. Being a ward of the state of Georgia, she had to have special permission to go, with precise times and places filled out on an official form.

Once the year of the foster home was over, Mae would be moving to one of three places. Down to Florida with her daddy, over to Alabama to live with the Bakers, or back home with her momma and Ricky. Because Ricky never admitted hurting Mae, and it was her word against his, no charges had ever been filed. As Mae's time drew near to leave, Gennifer and she began to realize their epoch together was about complete. The two would always remember that year together as sisters, and stay in touch on and off, throughout life.

Ultimately, the decision to go to Florida to live with her daddy had been a hard one to make and one Mae wasn't sure she wanted to go through with. Standing in the parking lot of the Department of Human Resources that early morning, hugging her new family goodbye, Gennifer and Mae cried like twins being separated.

Joel beamed with pride and pleasure, being elated that after working so hard to get custody of his daughter, the time had come to take her home. As he pulled the car out of the parking lot, Mae noticed Jacob leaning against a parked car across the street. He waved bye to her, and she had the urge to ask her daddy to stop the car, but knew better than to make the request.

Florida wasn't a bad place to live, and Joel had a job with NASA as a security guard, which paid him much more than the Cocoa Beach Police Department had. He had a nice modest brick home, in a safe and friendly neighborhood.

Tessa, Mae's new step mother, didn't really seem to like sharing attention with her teenage stepdaughter. Joel had a way with women, and his uniform hadn't ever hurt his prospects either. He could make any female feel like they were the only woman in the world, spoiling them with shopping trips and surprise presents. Mae had never felt jealous of any of her daddy's girl's, always knowing they couldn't take her place as his only daughter. Tessa tried really hard to relate with her, but being in the state of depression Mae was in, she wasn't letting anyone else new into her world.

Mae still didn't know if she'd made the right choice coming to live with her daddy. It had only been a couple of weeks, when one afternoon Mae mentioned she might want to go back and live with her momma.

"What the hell did you just say?" Joel's eyes widened and his face started turning redder than his hair.

They had been sitting in the living room laughing and talking one minute, and in the next moment, the room was ten degrees hotter. Tessa was terrified, having never seen him so enraged.

"You just want to go back to that damn Jacob boy! I won't allow it, and there is no way you're going near Ricky Levine again!" He stomped back and forth across the living room.

Tessa was petrified, having never experience the wrath of Joel, she sat wide eyed listening to her new husband as he ranted.

"I won't allow it! I'll go right now to the store, buy some chains and chain your ass in your bedroom before I let you go back." With that said, he headed out the door, slamming it behind him.

"Oh Lord, we've got to get you out of here." Tessa jumped up, looking out the blinds. "I've never seen him so mad before."

Mae calmly smiled at her step-mother; having survived Joel's attempts to kill her, being chained up would be a cake walk. Still it hurt really bad to hurt her daddy's feelings. She knew he'd worked really hard to gain custody and control of her, not just in the previous year, but since he suspected Ricky Levine was putting his hands on his daughter.

Her bond with her daddy had never felt that loving or intimate. Apprehension and limitations had dominated most of her life with him.

She did love him, and she knew without doubt he loved her. The biggest thing about being near him was she believed she could never live up to his expectations. Then there was the unconscious fear he might try to kill her. She felt he tried to show her love, in his own way.

After that day, they were both strained to be near each other. He didn't buy any chains, but after Mae mentioned moving back, he would hardly look at her. Controlled fear had always been Joel's key feature with Mae, and that was something he no longer had over her.

Ever since she'd revealed her secret, it was like a new persona would come over her at times. Gone was the victimized girl, and in her place appeared a fire filled bitch. Sure she still feared her daddy could kill her easier than deal with her, yet she believed that once he dropped her back off at Mary's he would soon forget she existed anyway.

Chapter Twelve

Mary and her ability to put her life back together had been difficult. The past year had been a nightmare for her. She'd fought the fear off that Mae was telling the truth. Why would she come back home, if Ricky had hurt her? It didn't make sense. Neither did the very prospect that Ricky would do something so horrible, without her noticing something. How could such a thing happen right under her nose? Mary resigned herself to believe Mae was crazy like her father. Regardless, she wanted her daughter back, and felt her heart coming back together having her home.

Mae had thought about the fact she would look like a liar, if she moved back in with the very man she accused. She didn't care what people thought about her, not as much as she cared about her momma and siblings.

Terri Lynn and Angel were living with their mother during the summers, and they both hardly noticed Mae's absence. Both of the boys would hold no memory of it what-so-ever. No one talked about her accusation, and eventually Mary and Mae began to look at each other eye to eye again. Mae wanted her mother to know the truth, and she felt just like glass embedded in the skin, it would eventually work its way out.

Ricky moved them into another home, big enough that Mae had her own room. It wasn't a pretty house, and Mae was glad it couldn't be seen from the passing traffic, being down a hilly dirt road. A man named, Driver, rented it out, even though he had been living in it. It looked like a work in progress to Mae, and the dirty landlord left a red circle of clay where he slept on the floor in the living room. The funky smelling man lived across the dirt road in a tiny camper shell, with his dozen or so, wild pit bulls.

Jacob was happy to have Mae back, and with her living at home and not in the state's custody, their relationship grew more intense with the freedom. Jacob's friend provided both of them a ride to school and back, which gave the love birds daily contact. They planned class's together and spent time at the mall or movies on occasional weekends.

Mae continued with the Marching Band, but wanted to drop the flute. She had sat outside during band camp watching the rifle team twirling those heavy wooden guns in such choreographed crisp and precise motions. It was amazing when they threw them up in the air, and so gracefully reached out and caught them, while never skipping a beat to the rhythm. Making her way to the band director's office, she felt he could help her with information on how to get on the elite team. The office was tiny, and had a few students lingering and joking around with Mr. Lindsey. Mae stood in the door way, politely waiting for the opportunity to ask him her questions. After a few minutes of listening to the jargon going back and forth she interposed herself.

"Excuse me Mr. Lindsey, I'd like to join the rifle team, how do I do that?"

The room went very quiet, with everyone now looking at her. She tried to not feel as stupid as they were making her feel. Then they all started laughing, with Mr. Lindsey laughing the hardest.

"You can't twirl a rifle!" Mr. Lindsey laughed while slapping his leg. It made the other's start laughing all over again.

Mae turned around, walked back outside, and straight over to the girls flinging the guns all around. It hadn't occurred to her, until she started getting closer to the spinning pieces of wood, the entire team was black. They noticed her walking over, and continued practicing, ignoring her, and it took about ten minutes before the teams captain noticed the quiet and shy acting blond girl standing to the side.

"What's up? You want to twirl the rifle?" She flipped her gun around and around like it was nothing at all.

"Yes, I think so."

"Well do you or don't you?" The girl stopped the gun in a snapping motion, and handed it to Mae. The other girls started making their way to them.

"Well, I do, but I don't know how…" Mae started to hand the heavy wood back.

"Well you can learn." She pushed the gun back at Mae.

Mae was now ready to just run away, but her two feet stayed put like cement post. The other's snickered and giggled, but the captain turned on them quickly.

"She wants to twirl, give her a chance. Could you twirl the gun the first time you put it in your hand?" She questioned the girls, who suddenly took on respectful attitudes. She instructed them to go practice. "And Stacy, if you can't twirl it three, you are in trouble."

Turning her attention to Mae again, she smiled and offered her hand. "I'm Cheri, and you can do whatever you believe you can do, and that's about all you'll do."

The pretty captain could have been an angel for all Mae knew. Cheri's strength and drive invigorated Mae to try her very best. Focusing on twirling kept Mae's mind occupied from her tormenting fears, and when somebody told her she couldn't do something, it lit a fire within her, to do nothing else, but prove them wrong. Mae won her spot on the rifle squad, respect and all.

After a few months back home, Ricky tried to befriend Mae again. He and Mary remained married, but a wedge had developed between them. She no longer fully trusted him and watched his every move, very closely, especially concerning Mae. Ricky now was trying to reason with Mae, that Mary's new relationship with The Jehovah Witnesses was causing problems. It was the first time, Ricky tried to converse with his step daughter since she moved back. He'd approached her as she stood in the front yard practicing.

"It wouldn't hurt you to go with momma." If he was looking for her help in manipulating Mary, he'd come to the wrong one. She kept him at bay as she swung the wooden gun all around.

Ricky didn't want to go to church with Mary, but he didn't say that out loud. "Well, I'm not sure if I'm comfortable with the requirements."

Flinging the gun up to spin it in the air, Ricky took a few steps further back from her. She didn't want to talk to him, but he continued to stand there, more amazed than fearful. She had no intentions of belittling her mother's choice of faith. The Witnesses had given Mary needed friendship, good advice, comfort, peace and hope; things that had eluded her for years. Who was Ricky or anyone else for that matter, to question Mary's faith in God? Mae concluded Ricky didn't like the way Mary trusted the witnesses, compared to how much she trusted him.

Ricky wouldn't give up that easily, always desiring drama and aggression. Within the first year that Mae moved back, family arguments and discussions started again. Slowly Ricky began to conjure up how much Mary mistreated his children, while Mary defended her mothering, and accused him of being the child abuser.

Mae escaped the family situation with her social life that circled around Jacob. Throughout that first year back, Mae's self- mutilation continued. She'd tried to give herself food poisoning, and rubbed Vick's vapor rub on her chest and ran in the icy morning weather; trying to catch pneumonia. She tried to break her arm by letting the car run over it, ate glass and poured Pine Sol in her eyes. It was an obsession; she didn't even realize she had. Painful confusion continued to shadow her life, no matter how many times she tried to convince herself she was happy and safe. Her past wouldn't let her go.

Where Mae turned her pain inward, Terri Lynn threw hers out. Terri Lynn had started drinking her daddy's Canadian Mist, and Ricky knew it, but let her do it without informing Mary. It had become a sick way for him to control his oldest child.

Before the first year back was finished, Ricky found another house to live in, just around the block; a nicer home with five bedrooms. Mae was happy to get out of Driver's house; the place gave her the creeps. She tried to blame the new darkness she was feeling on the location she was living, but it really had absolutely nothing to do with what was brewing under the surface. Mae had a fire in the pit of her stomach that at times, she feared, could burn out of control. She wanted to find a way to dissolve the intensity of the heat within her, before anyone discovered it blazing.

Chapter Thirteen

"Poor little thing." Ricky's pitiless and unpleasant side began to show more and more with each passing day. His voice whispered from behind.

Mae turned to glare at him for an explanation as to why her pet hamster lay on top of its cage, massacred. She'd only opened her bedroom door, and stood outside, horrified with what she'd come home to.

"The boys wanted to see if it could outrun the cat." He grinned at her. "Obviously it couldn't."

Jacob had bought the critter for her, and teased that it was their baby. The two of them continued with their relationship. He'd just dropped her off after taking her out to eat at Waffle House. Mae knew her brothers would have no concept of such and that Ricky himself wanted to kill her pet. It was an indication that his sinister behavior was starting back up.

They had moved into the Five Bedroom Home, which would become the last place Mae would share the same roof under with Ricky. Each girl had a bedroom to themselves, while the boys shared theirs. Life was as normal as it could get in the home of a child molester.

Curly red headed Erik and golden locked Seven were inseparable from each other. Mae always wondered how it must have felt to have someone to talk to from the beginning of your life. Neither boy had any memory of life without the other in it. They took care of each other and took up for each other. They were best friends and shared mischievous memories. With three older sisters, it was them against the girls most of the time.

Terri Lynn and Mae continued to be the big sisters in the house. While Mae had stopped Ricky from molesting her, Ricky continued to manipulate his oldest daughter. It didn't go unnoticed by Mae, and she spent lots of time watching the interactions between father and daughter. In the meantime, she dreamed of finishing school, and marrying Jacob Jones.

There was a nice swimming hole back behind their house, beyond a long wooded trail. Terri Lynn was the one to find it and show it to Mae. They would sneak away during the hot summer days and cool off. The creek was an oasis in the Southern heat, and once Terri Lynn showed it to Mae one day, it wouldn't take her much to talk Mae into going for occasional dips to cool off and escape the scorching sun. It was on one of these hot days that the two girls had snuck away from Angel and the boys unnoticed. Mae had on a two piece with cut off blue jeans and a t-shirt. She was subconscious about being in the slinky suit but her one piece was white, and the creek would turn it into a light brown. Terri Lynn had absolutely no shame in her body, or cared what color her suit might turn, she proudly wore her bikini, showing off her young woman curves.

As soon as they arrived, Terri Lynn jumped right on in, while Mae dipped her toe in cautiously. She walked around the edges, as Terri Lynn attempted to float. Eventually, Mae eased herself into the water, after taking her shorts and t-shirt off. The creek had a deep pool, with water falls cascading swiftly over smooth rocks. The two girls splashed and laughed at each other. They had survived many things together over the years, and gotten close, even though they still went round and round at times. Terri Lynn had a healthy sense of humor, which was something that kept Mae laughing despite the pain. Other people always had a hard time understanding Terri Lynn, but Mae knew exactly why she was a bit on the wild side.

Neither girl noticed the man standing to the side watching them play. Whenever they did notice him, Mae grew fearful, while Terri Lynn started flirting. Mae made her way to her clothes, as Terri Lynn struck up a conversation with the intruder. He'd started answering her questions.

"Yes I work at the auto body shop. I was just checking on you two; it's a dangerous place out here."

Motioning for Terri Lynn to get out of the creek, Mae apologized, while she quickly got her clothes back on. "Sorry, we didn't know this was private property."

"Oh it is, but it's ok if y'all want to swim, just be careful." He smiled while backing away.

After he left, Terri Lynn went on and on about the handsome fellow. His dad owned the auto shop next door to their home, and he seemed harmless enough, except Terri Lynn was in love with him. Mae never suspected her step-sister would land such a catch, since she was only fourteen.

A few weeks later local high school gossip had some girl trying to steal Lisa Crews boyfriend. Not that Mae paid attention to gossip, but is did stick out to her because the boyfriend happened to be none other than Marc Maynard, the same auto body shop worker they met at the creek.

Mae confronted Terri Lynn, asking her if she was the other girl, to which she laughed at Mae, refusing to give her an answer. The worry over whether Terri Lynn was the other girl was confirmed when Mae caught her sneaking out her window one night.

"Just what do you think you're doing?" Mae had walked in, and completely forgot what she'd come in for in the first place. Shutting the door, she placed her hands on her hips.

"What does it look like I'm doing?" Terri Lynn didn't look like she'd been caught; she did appear irritated at the interruption. She continued to sit in the windowsill, with one leg in and one leg out.

"I know what it looks like, but why don't you explain it anyway."

Terri Lynn put her eyes on Mae. "I'm seeing Marc, and he's waiting on me."

"No, don't go, just don't go." Mae hoped to deter her.

She ignored her, and brought her other leg out. "Oh I'll be right back."

Terri Lynn never listened to reason, so Mae felt she had no choice but to inform Mary. Mae wanted it to stop before something bad happened; something like Terri Lynn being lynched by Lisa Crews and her friends.

The wedge between Mary and Ricky had grown significantly since Mae had returned home. It had become a 'your kids, my kids' situation. So when Mae told her momma about Terri Lynn's affair with the older neighbor, Mary tried to evade trouble by telling Ricky about the relationship Terri Lynn was in. When he asked her how she found out, Mary told Ricky that Angel told her. Mary was afraid if Ricky knew Mae had been the one to tell, an argument would result.

The affair was immediately stopped. Weeks passed and Terri Lynn got over her fling, while Marc was proud to dodge a bullet or jail time. Then it happened. The truth came out.

It was a weekend that Terri Lynn and Angel were gone, on a late Friday night. Erik and Seven had fallen asleep earlier than usual, playing in Angel's bedroom. Because Ricky was working late, it had been a nice quiet evening.

Turning off her lights around ten thirty, the headlights shining across Mae's room signaled Ricky was home. Mae had a five inch, black and white television which picked up about three channels. Usually she'd have on the tiny earphones, but she didn't really care to listen to her limited variety of shows.

At first nothing unusual happened once Ricky made his way into the house. Mary sat at the kitchen table when her husband sat down across from her.

"You are nothing but a liar." Ricky pointed across the table, slurring his words.

Mary looked over at him with a questioning look on her face. "What are you talking about?"

"You told me, that Angel was the one who told you Terri Lynn was seeing that Marc guy, and that's a lie." His voice grew louder.

Mae got up and tip toed to her door, pulling it open slightly, allowing the kitchens light to brighten her room.

"Mae is the one who told you, not Angel. Why did you lie?"

"Well, because I knew it would cause an argument if you knew Mae told me."

"You are nothing but a sorry liar!" Ricky seethed.

Mae couldn't hear the conversation, but she could easily hear Ricky's voice booming through the house. Suddenly she heard the kitchen table and chairs sliding around, it was a scuffle, and she jumped out of bed, running to the kitchen door. Ricky had Mary pushed up against the cabinets, with his hands around her throat. Once he noticed Mae, he took his hands off Mary, and he and Mae shared a moment of a stare down. Mae hated this man, had from the first day she met him, and he had hurt her in so many ways. Putting his hands on her momma awakened her sleeping bear. The one that had been born that day Ricky attacked her in the hallway so many years before. The part of Mae, that fought him off before he could rape her.

"Mae, go back to bed." Mary's voice was strained, as she tried to make everything appear okay.

Mae's eyes were squinted at Ricky, who smiled back hatefully. She backed out of the room watching him and warning him with her glare. Mae didn't lie back down; instead she picked up one of her twirling guns and sat on the edge of her bed ready to do whatever it was she might have to do. The guns used were pieces of heavy, thick, wood, shaped like rifles, being decorated with metallic tape to match the school colors of black and gold. They were old fashioned ones that the school had replaced with heavy duty fiberglass versions. Mae had obtained three of the old replaced wooden ones, one for

Terri Lynn, Angel and herself. Mary and Ricky continued while Mae was listening.

"I'll take my kids and leave!" Mary was screaming.

"Good, get out of my house and take your two brats with you!"

Ricky had miscounted, and Mae knew her momma wasn't about to let that go. "You mean my three beautiful children!"

With that they began pushing each other around.

"Oh no, Seven ain't going nowhere, he is my son!" Ricky's words seemed to growl as they came out.

Mae had made her way back into the kitchen, holding her weapon in front. Wrestling around in the kitchen the two didn't notice she was standing there.

"You've got to be insane, if you think I'd ever leave my son with you!" Mary pushed back and Ricky slid backwards a foot. For a second the two locked eyes, then Ricky took off for the boy's bedroom. Mary looked over at Mae, as her daughter tried to hand her the wooden gun. Mary took it into her hands, as Mae turned to go get another wooden gun in Terri Lynn's room. The two parents were both headed toward the boys. As Mae made her way to the living room, she noted Mary had put her weapon down. Erik and Seven's bedroom as well as Angel's were on that this side of the house, while the other three bedrooms were on the other end. The boy's room was closer, and that was where Ricky had gone, while Mary went past to Angel's room where she knew the two boys had fallen asleep playing.

All this was happening really fast, as Mary made her way back with four year old Seven, sleeping in her arms. Mae was watching this scene unfold, feeling elated as Mary made her way nearly to the front door, before Ricky exited the boy's bedroom. Red faced mad he looked over at Mary holding Seven, and for a split second he started toward them, when WHAM! He punched Mae in her stomach so hard; it lifted her off her feet. Like a rag doll, she flew back and landed in a recliner. All at once, Ricky had Mary and Seven both in his hands, trying to rip the two apart. Unable to catch her breath and feeling paralyzed; Mae struggled to get back up.

"Leave them alone! Stop it you're hurting them!" Her screams were muted beneath Mary's and Seven's. The commotion had awoken Erik, who now stood watching with confusion, holding his little hands up over his ears.

Taking two steps toward them, Ricky abruptly went from attacking Mary and knocked Mae off her feet entirely. They had an old fashioned woven rug that she landed on and before she could regain any type of composure, she felt the steal toed end of his boot making contact with her back. Like a jack hammer, he kicked and kicked at her. Mae rolled up into a ball with both arms trying to cover and protect her head and face. Still he continued his assault, making contact with the back of her head many times. Trying to look up, she saw the faces of Mary and both boys, looking down at her with shock. Ricky continued kicking, while throwing profanity from his mouth. The feeling of nausea was all that kept Mae from passing out, as she oddly began to focus on not throwing up on herself. Once his foot struck her forehead, something in her exploded, and she lost it. Though everything was occurring so fast, she felt the feeling of a slow heartbeat pumping inside her skull.

"Kill him. You have to KILL him. Kill him now. Kill him before he kills you." The bear was wide awake and madder than hell's fire. Mae tried to describe it as her "bear" or "dark shadow", the one who steps in. Years later in therapy, Mae would name her LIZ.

While the boot continued to make its marks on her, she found herself face to face with her wooden gun on the floor. In Mae's mind, she could see herself hitting Ricky in the head, hard enough to knock his skull off his shoulders. Pushing herself up, now on her knees, her hands reached for the heavy wood. Picking it up by the smaller barrel end she took the weapon as far back as she could. Turning to eye Ricky, he realized Mae had a fix on him, as the weapon whizzed through the air. Her gun made contact, POW! Striking his leg and breaking his Femur bone, cracking it nearly in two.

Ricky's leg wasn't her intended target, but it stopped him instantly.

"STOP…! No, No!" He began to motion with both hands, while staggering towards the couch away from Mae and her weapon.

Tossing the gun onto the floor LIZ started screaming expletives at him. "YOU STOP, You sorry piece of shit, F U, I'm calling the f *#!ing police, I hate you!" Mae's finger was pointing at Ricky, her eyes were bulging, her skin was red hot and she couldn't shake the need to rip his head off. Never in her entire life, had such vulgarities passed from her lips.

Both boys continued to watch the disturbing scene, petrified with fear, while Mary stood uncertain what to do or who to protect.

Mae took off out the front door. She ran as if a wild animal was giving chase. She made her way to the auto body shop owner's house. Marc answered the door, and tried to make sense of her hysterical babble. Leading her to the telephone on the wall in their hallway, Mae fumbled with the numbers, unable to push the buttons without touching two or even three of them at a time. Marc took the phone away and successfully made the call to 911. While trying to calm Mae, he explained to the dispatch that a domestic fight was going on next door.

Taking her back outside to his front porch, to wait for the police, Mae stood on tip toes trying to see what could be going on at her house. Marc was shivering and asking her if she wanted a blanket, noticing the fact she only had on a long night shirt and panties.

"No." Mae answered him, still crying uncontrollably and trying to watch her house. Where were those police? Without warning, as if she was under mortar attack Mae hit the concrete of his porch.

"Here he comes!" She screamed, seeing the station wagon pull out of their yard. "He's looking for me!"

Marc hit the porch, crouched down on all fours. "Where…where is he?"

As the vehicle drove past, Mae pointed while hiding behind the bushes. "Right there, there he goes, oh my God!" None of this was helping Marc stay calm; Mae knew he just wanted her off his porch.

The sirens were coming, and one by one, sheriff's cars began pulling into their front yard. Still lying flat, she could see the lights flashing all over the now waking neighborhood. The station wagon, which had turned around, pulled back into their yard. Jumping up, Mae looked down at Marc who continued to lie low.

"Thank you." She offered and walked away. Making her way back home, Ricky stood out front, completely surrounded by a circle of law enforcement. High beam lights hit Mae as she made her way across the front yard, and she could hear Ricky yelling and see him pointing right at her.

"That's the one, that's the one who started it, look what she did to me, she broke my leg!"

Mae could hear some snickers because she was merely a young girl, and this grown man was accusing her of breaking his leg nearly in two.

Mary was relieved to see her daughter, but was also crying and terribly injured. She had been the one driving the station wagon around, desperately trying to find Mae.

"We're leaving, get your things."

"Momma, I don't want to leave." Mae had plans with Jacob the next day. "Make Ricky leave!" Mae pleaded with Mary to not take them to Alabama. Mary began sobbing, putting both her hands over her face.

"What else can I do Mae?" It was noticeable her mother was in pain with both sides of her face swollen and red. Mae gave her momma no further fight, and they packed up and left, with Ricky still running his mouth to the sheriff.

Mary would describe what had happened once Mae had left the house to call the police. It made her blood boil.

"I'd decided to pack, and had taken Seven into the bedroom with me, putting him on my bed as I got the suitcase out. Ricky came into the room, holding your wooden gun over his shoulder."

"I've done told you, you ain't taking my son."

"I turned to face him and told him that I wouldn't leave Seven there with him."

"I'll kill you before I let you take him." Ricky threatened.

"That's the only way, you will get him Ricky; you'll have to kill me."

So that's what he tried to do.

"At first when I saw the gun suddenly swinging at me, I had no time to think before it slammed into the left side of my face. Stars appeared and the room tilted, as a dark silence enveloped my ears, except for a loud ringing sound. Everything began to move in slow motion. I believed I was fixing to die, and then he hit me again on the other side, Wham! That hit knocked me back into full consciousness, and Seven's piercing screams made their way back into my perception. A voice in my head said, fight back or your children will watch him kill you."

Listening to Mary tell her what Ricky did, only made Mae feel a hundred times worse that she didn't kill him when she had the chance.

Mary continued. "When the gun swung at me a third time; I grabbed it in mid-air, and pushed him backwards onto the bed. Calmly I told Erik to take Seven outside, get into the car and lock the doors. Miraculously Erik obeyed, walking over to his terrified baby brother. As soon as Seven's hand went into Erik's he stopped crying, got off the bed, and followed his big brother out to the car."

After a minute or so, Ricky quit attacking, allowing Mary time to get out and try to find Mae. Her mother's story gave Mae the chills to imagine the two boys witnessing the attack. She cringed to think of her gun smacking against Mary's skull. Ricky could have murdered his wife, right in front of her boys.

They left town that night, headed for the Bakers house in Alabama. After a few days, they went back, and things were just left unsaid for the time being.

Mae wanted to go back, where she could be with Jacob, no longer wanting to move back to Alabama where her past was. Jacob had become very important to her, and if she had to put up with Ricky to be near him, she would.

Chapter Fourteen

Jacob had become the man in Mae's life. Starting their junior year, the high school sweethearts were entering the third year of their relationship. All their peers recognized them as one of those "long term couple's"; as well as many teachers who had put up with the pair in their rooms.

Mae's siblings loved Jacob, especially the boys, who considered him a big brother. Sometimes Mae would actually get a little jealous of the time Erik and Seven could monopolize with Jacob, but that was the case with anyone who got his attention and time from her.

At the beginning of their relationship there had been no sexual contact, to the consternation of Jacob. After Mae moved back in with her mother, they became more intimate. By the third year, Mae became pregnant.

For the first few months' they kept it a secret, but as time went by, her belly began to grow. Other girls in school noticed the small bulge and rumors began to fly. It was the day of their Junior/Senior Prom that all hell broke loose on Jacob.

Thulah had purchased Mae a beautiful pink Prom dress, and it had taken her nearly all evening, to get herself dolled up. Mary had her camera ready to take pictures of the two teens; she couldn't help but to be proud of her beautiful daughter. Mae's shoes clicked on their wooden floor, as she paced back and forth waiting for Jacob to arrive. After he was an hour late, she started to worry. What if he had another date? Why else wasn't he here? They had been planning this night for months. What if he had been hurt or something?

Mae had made her way to the back porch, where a nice breeze blew across their laundry hanging up. Wanting to just sit down and cry, she had her back turned, when Ricky walked up on her.

"This doesn't surprise me one bit, I could have told you he had someone better than you."

Turning around to face him, his words somehow managed to hurt Mae.

"He's not like that!" Her words were choked up as they came out, but she held back her tears. There was no way she was going to let him ruin her planned happy day!

Pushing past him, she started for her bedroom, where she planned to strip off her fancy dress. Instead, she could hear the sounds of Jacob's car pulling into their driveway. Meeting him at the door of his car he looked sick.

"Where have you been? I've been waiting for hours. We were supposed to be there early for pictures." Mae cried to him.

Mary had made her way outside with her Polaroid, smiling at how nice the two of them looked with their outfits. Jacob had on a white tuxedo with a pink cummerbund that matched the pink of Mae's dress.

"Oh you two look adorable." Mary beamed, having one of those precious memories playing out before her.

Mary and Ricky had plans for the weekend themselves. Once Mae left for the prom, they planned on leaving for the weekend to go to Alabama to stay with the Bakers. Mae had never been left at home alone; both Terri Lynn and Angel were with their mother. So Mae was looking forward to not only going out for a night on the town all dressed up, but getting to enjoy the house all to herself for a couple of days. Jacob and Mae began to pose for pictures, while Mary snapped one after the other, Jacob whispered why he had been late.

"Tammy Messer told her mother you are pregnant, and her mother… called mine." He explained while they put frozen smiles on their faces.

"So your family knows?'

"Yes, they do."

They whispered, hiding their dilemma from Mary, who picked up on nothing. She started telling Mae rules to follow while they were out of town through the weekend. The prom couple got into the car, and started down the road.

"What did your parents say?" Mae probed before they pulled out of the driveway.

"Well, they fussed and cussed at me, I didn't think I was even going to get to go tonight. We have to go there…" He began but Mae cut him off.

"Where do we have to go? Not to your house? NO! No way! No! No! NO! There's just no way Jacob!"

"Yes, yes, yes, way Mae!" Jacob continued to be pale from the previous encounter with his parents.

Mae began to contemplate the idea of jumping out of the vehicle; she didn't want to ever see his parents again. Suddenly she was sweating, and just wanted out of the fluffy material. "I think I'm going to be sick." She bent over, putting her head down between her legs.

"It will be okay; I mean we couldn't keep it a secret forever." Jacob was speeding, like his parents had given him just so much time to bring Mae back.

At his house, Mae could feel all the eyes on her. Jacob's parents, Lee and Shannon Jones, didn't mention anything about Mae's condition; however the air was thick enough to cut with a knife. No one spoke, but energy could still be felt tingling about from the previous argument between parents and son. His older sister Amy and younger sister Sue both eyed Mae's belly. Shannon took some quick pictures, and the two made their way to the prom. Once they got there though, with the current situation, neither felt much like having any fun. Jacob would have to go home to his distraught parents, while Mae had to start figuring out how to tell Mary her condition. They ended the night early; and he dropped her off at the empty house.

Chapter Fifteen

Ricky Levine had told Mae not to let his brother, Randolph, in the house. Now Mary had many other rules for Mae to follow while they were out of town for the two nights. No cooking, lock the doors, etc. Ricky's only request sounded odd to Mae, but then she thought everything about him to be abnormal.

The family history on the Levine side wasn't as sound, stable, loving or secure. Ricky had two brothers, Randolph the older and William the younger. All three had been given up by their parents to the state's system. Not one of the boys would ever know who their parents were, or how to find them. They knew however, that they had at least two older siblings that stayed with their mother. Ricky's only memory of his biological mother was sad.

"I only remember they were taking us away, and Momma tried to explain she had no choice. I hid under my bed and they yanked me out by my feet."

They grew up wondering why their momma and daddy; didn't want them. After floating around in foster homes, Ricky and baby William ended up living with Alfred and Mattie Pearl Penny in Penton, Alabama.

Mae didn't like staying out on the Penny's run down and creepy farm. The only bright spot about staying out there some weekends would be Ricky's adoptive mother, Mattie Pearl. She was such a sweet and docile woman, as well as one of the best cook's Mae ever knew. Waking up to her breakfast feasts was amazingly delicious. You'd leave the table thanking God for both the food and Mattie Pearl.

Ricky's two brothers, never saw the side of Ricky that Mae saw. They both looked to him as the clever one, and trusted him with their own lives at times. Randolph had it the roughest, never really finding a permanent place to call home. The Penny's didn't want him. Neither of his brothers had Ricky's tendencies, or posed any threat to Mae. Randolph had one daughter, and when she was only three, she was taken away from him, and he never saw her again. William had a large family, and though they were a bit rough around the edges, or as some say, a bit red neck, they seemed healthy and happy enough.

Why Ricky's parents gave up the three youngest, no one alive knows. Two older children, Louise and Cleve, stayed with their mother after the parents divorced. Years later, Louise searched for her three younger brothers, and found them. She explained that she also found their long lost father, sitting in a chair in a nursing home all alone. Walking up to him, she explained that he was her father, and she was his oldest child and only daughter.

The man looked at her and bluntly stated. "I have no children."

Over all the years of being around Randolph Levine, Mae never felt any fear of him. Unlike Ricky and William, Randolph was a large man, standing several feet higher than his younger brothers. An alcoholic, who seemed to have nothing to live for, Randolph kind of floated around following his younger brother Ricky. Despite herself, Mae liked him and his humorous ways. He lived in a trailer park, just across a cotton field from their five bed room home.

"Don't let my brother in this house!" The two brothers had normal arguments every now and then, and because Ricky had helped Randolph's ex-wife, take his daughter away from him; they were not presently getting along.

Mae had gotten up on Saturday after prom night, cleaned her messy bedroom, folded her expensive pink prom dress and put it back into its box. Taking a bath, she put on her McDonald's uniform, and started putting on the finishing touches of her hair and make-up. Jacob would be arriving shortly to take her to work, and after she got off, they planned on going out to eat. Mae still worried about the fact, his family was aware of her pregnancy, but had started thinking about what Jacob said.

"We can't keep it a secret forever."

A knock at the front door, brought her out of her room, expecting Jacob had come over early. Standing outside the screen when she answered the door, was Randolph.

Pulling on the latched screen, he smiled at her. "Hey let me in."

"I can't..." Mae began but stopped, not wanting to just come right out and tell him Ricky didn't want him in the house. "I'm getting ready for work."

"Well, I need my mail." He pulled hard on the screen door. "And it's right there..." He pointed at a pile of mail sitting on the coffee table.

"No, you don't have any mail here." She tried to explain.

"Why won't you let me in, so I can look for myself?" Again, he yanked hard on the rickety screen, and Mae got the feeling he knew he could easily rip through it.

"Jacob is picking me up, I have to be at work in a few minutes, I am not finished getting ready." She tried to ease the situation.

"Well, I need my mail." He wasn't going to go away. Instinct told her to slam the door, but respect kept it open. Mae walked over to the mail and thumbed through it.

"No, nothing for you, but..." She walked back to the door quickly. "Ricky had some mail in the car."

"When will he be back?" Randolph took his hand off the door finally.

"Tomorrow afternoon." Mae knew the second she said it, she'd made a mistake.

"Oh, so you're here all alone?"

"Well, unless they come back early." She tried to make it sound less dangerous for herself.

Randolph left, and Jacob soon arrived, taking Mae to work her six hour shift. After work he picked her up and they spent some time together, mostly going over their situation, and plans. Around eleven pm, Jacob walked her into her dark and empty home. Immediately she noticed a small picture lying on the floor, and wondered what had made it fall. Normally, they would have taken advantage of having the house to themselves, but neither was in the mood for that with a real baby on the way. Turning on the TV, they both sat down, blankly staring at the program.

"Well, I guess I will go on home, got to be in by curfew." Jacob stood awkwardly leaving.

Maybe being pregnant made her more emotional, but she felt sad as he left. Life had been so complicated before, but now with another human's life at stake, things had gotten serious. In deep thought, Mae's mind was numb with decisive questions, when she abruptly caught a glimpse of something out of the corner of her eyes. Looking right, she noticed the curtains floating upward with a brisk breeze blowing them. She began glancing back at the TV and laughed at herself for being so easily scared. All of the sudden, this fear enveloped her, with her mind racing, that picture on the floor, when Jacob and she had first walked in. Very slowly she looked back toward the curtain, which continued to be blown about. That window contained an old piece of tin, not glass, and so the curtains blowing wasn't what brought her to her feet. It was the absence of that tin, which always made a high pitched whistling and squeaking sounds.

When the realization that someone had been in the house slammed into Mae, every hair on her body stood on end, as a tingly sensation went over her. The house seemed suddenly huge, with every noise amplified. The darkness started to close in around her, what should she do? Paralyzed, she began to feel the dread that someone could still be in the house. She couldn't just stand still and do nothing, so she slowly tiptoed to the kitchen. Flipping on the light, her eyes scanned the room. Nothing looked out of place at all, as her hand checked the knob of the back door. It was unlocked. Trying to ease her own mind she began to dismiss any harm, maybe the tin fell out finally, it could have happened. Grabbing a kitchen knife regardless, she could hear her daddy's police instructions playing like an old tape player.

"Don't use a knife, unless you are trained to fight with one, otherwise it will be used against you."

She put the knife down on the kitchen table. Digging under the kitchen sink in the cabinet she found some oven cleaner. Removing the top she tried to muster up the courage to go to her bedroom.

Looming before her was the darkened hall, with it's even darker four doorways. What if the intruder was just lying in wait for her? Taking steps, but not wanting to, she peered blindly into the rooms, as she slowing stopped at her own door. Using her hand to slightly push the door open, she slid the light switch on, and quickly swung the door open for surprise. Complete silence hit her, but the scene before her struck terror in Mae's heart.

Completely torn apart, ran-shacked and left in shambles was her room. Mae's eyes attempted to take it all in, while her cowardice made her take off running back to the kitchen. She had to call for help, she thought to herself as she started for the front door. She'd have to go outside to get to a phone, and before she got near the door, Mae stopped, afraid that whoever tore her room apart, could be waiting outside. Turning back to the kitchen, she tried to calm herself down, again, checking the back door.

Who would do such a thing? Looking the kitchen over, she picked the knife up again and fearfully headed back to her room. As she passed Mary and Ricky's room, she peered inside, and could see the Polaroid camera still sitting on the corner of the bed where Mary had left it. Nothing looked touched in their room, and as she looked in hers, nothing made sense to why her room was ripped apart.

Shutting her bedroom door behind her, Mae slid her old sewing cabinet in front of it. Still standing in front of her door, she slowly examined the mess without moving. Every drawer was open, with contents tossed; clothes covered the floor with knick knacks broken about. Her alarm clock was missing along with several tapes and albums. Lying across the bed was Mae's beloved prom dress, covered in the pink nail polish she had bought especially to match. The nail polish covered most of her clothes and bedding. Tears began to roll down her cheeks as she tried to imagine who would do such a mean thing to her. What enemies did she have? This was extremely personal, directed at her it would appear, but why?

She got no sleep that night, keeping the light on, holding tightly to the knife and watching the door knob. Jacob arrived the next morning to pick her up for church. They called the police, and looked around for evidence. The back window had been the entrance, as Mae suspected, with the tin laying on the ground as proof it had been removed. Cigarette butts and beer cans lay all around, and Mae's first suspect became Randolph. Later that afternoon, when Mary and Ricky got home with everyone, Mae told them what happened. Though Mary looked concerned, Ricky accused her of trying to start trouble for Randolph.

"You made the whole thing up."

"What?" Mae couldn't believe what she was hearing. "Why would I do such a thing?" Mae tried to argue. "That makes no sense! Why would I destroy my own dress, tear up my room and get rid of my alarm clock, tapes and albums?"

"No one ever understands why you act the way you act, why you like to kick up trouble the way you do." Ricky reasoned back.

Chapter Sixteen

"Momma, I'm going to have a baby." There she said it.

Mae and Mary had just got back from the laundry mat, and they sat in the car in the front yard. Mae had tried all day while with her momma, running errands, grocery shopping and even the hour laundering the clothes. It had taken her weeks to get the courage up, to let her mother down. She was holding her breath, looking over at Mary who now seemed frozen, with one hand on the door and one on the steering wheel. She didn't look at Mae right away, but sat looking out the front windshield.

"Momma, I'm sorry." Mae didn't know what else to say. She had to tell her mother, before she heard it from someone else or spotted her growing belly.

"I've known…" Mary began and turned her view to her first born. "Well, I've been suspicious."

They sat looking at each other, and then they quickly looked away. Mae couldn't take it back, and she really did need to have her mother's help. Still, she knew Mary had to be upset.

"What should I do?" Mae questioned, wanting her advice.

"Mae, you've got a baby inside you, so now, you will have to make adult decisions on your own."

Mae looked at her like she was crazy, but considered what she said. "Okay."

"I mean, I don't know what you're going to do. I seriously can't believe this is happening. Let me know what you decide." Mary wasn't registering it properly, and was actually feeling shock waves rushing through her soul. She knew what Mae had in store for herself, and it was terrifying to think about.

Mae needed her mother like never before, but she knew she might have dripped one too many drops into Mary's cup of sanity. She looked at her mother hard as Mary opened her door to get out of the suddenly sizzling hot car. Mary stopped getting out, turning back around to look at her daughter again.

"I love you Mae, and will support any decision you make." With that she got out, leaving Mae alone with her mind full of daunting thoughts.

As Mae's belly grew, so did her many options. Her daddy said he would provide for an abortion, while Uncle Frank, Mary's brother, offered to house her until the baby was born, and then she could give it up for adoption. Jacob's mother also offered to take the baby, to which Mae politely refused. She already loved her baby. She named her Melina, and had no intentions of giving her away.

Jacob and Mae decided to get married the summer before their senior year of high school, the baby being due late autumn. Mae moved into Jacob's parent's house, even though his parents weren't thrilled. Lee Jones didn't like Mae one bit, but Shannon knew she'd better learn to tolerate the mother of her soon to be oldest grandchild.

Despite being married so young, the soon to be parents were determined to finish school. They both were in attendance at the start of the year. It was hard for Mae to not feel subconscious with her almost nine month pregnant belly hanging out. Regardless, she wanted a diploma, and luckily the school offered a hospital homebound program. Being so far along, she was offered the service, to which a teacher came to tutor her weekly. Once she was able to return, she'd be able to complete school with her Senior Class.

During this time Ricky took a job in another city, Americus, Georgia; promptly moving the family away. It hadn't been something Mae had anticipated. Immediately their absence made her heart grow weak, and she sank into unhappiness unlike any she'd ever known. Mae couldn't understand her sadness, she should be happy, being away from Ricky, and having Jacob as her husband, and the baby in her belly. Twisted up on the inside over emotions, Mae felt guilty for feeling so sad, and annoyed with her mindset of fault.

Melina was born in the first week of October 1986 and by Thanksgiving; Jacob was taking Melina and Mae to visit Mary and the boys, making an attempt to lighten his wife's depression. They surprised Mary with their visit, since she had no phone to call and tell that they were coming.

Erik and Seven would for the first time set their eyes on Melina, and both fell in love with her. The boys pretended Melina belonged to them, like Mae had given them a gift of a little sister. Seven would have subtle memories of the day he first saw Melina, but he had other memories about living in Americus, that he wasn't so fond of.

Christmas that year wouldn't be merry for Ricky Levine and most certainly horrible for those living under his roof. Within weeks of Thanksgiving holidays, Ricky would land himself in a lot of trouble.

Mae happened to answer the phone in the house, while Jacob answered the line out in his father's garage, the day the news came in.

Jacob beat Mae to the greeting as they both picked up. "Hello?"

"Jacob? Thank God you answered the phone." It was Thulah, and she sounded upset. Mae sat down and quietly listened to them talk.

"Yes mam?" Jacob wondered why Thulah would be calling him and not Mae.

"Lord, I don't want Mae to know, but she needs to get down there to Americus." Mae didn't have any idea what had her grandmother so upset, but it already had her tearing up. Something horrible had happened to her family; she tensed up to hear it.

"They've arrested Ricky, I don't know exactly why, but I know Mary has got to be upset." Thulah continued talking, but the words didn't sound that horrible to Mae.

"Maw Maw…" Mae cut in.

"Mae? Well, I just told…"

"I heard you Maw Maw, what was he arrested for?"

"Well…" Thulah faltered like she didn't want to say. "Something about molesting the sheriff's daughter, I don't really know the details, I just know your momma has got to be torn up, and all alone down there."

The words did all kinds of things to Mae, from happiness to horror. Ecstatic he was locked up; but confounded for Mary, the boys, the girls and most certainly the victim. Mae wanted to throw up and cheer at the same time. She hung up the phone, really unable to think clearly. She'd not stopped him, and now someone else had to live with the memories of Ricky Levine's hands on them.

Jacob knew he had to get Mae to her mother, and Shannon offered to keep her little granddaughter, so they could get down there fast. Pulling up in front of the apartment building where they lived, Mae could see the two boys sitting outside on the curb.

"Hey, you guys!" Mae jumped out trying to surprise them, but both simply looked up and calmly asked where Melina was. Once Mae explained that she'd left her, Seven started expounding their dilemma.

"The police got daddy, and we can't get him out of the jail."

Erik nodded his head up and down in agreement. "Momma's crying."

Mae's heart was breaking to see the fear in their tender and young eyes; it wasn't fair that they had to be put through such bull crap. She looked over at Jacob and motioned for him to talk with the two young ones, while she went inside to find Mary. She was sitting on her couch, all balled up and crying.

When she saw Mae walk in, she was surprised at first, but within seconds, she crumpled into Mae's waiting arms.

"Ricky's a child molester." Mary could hardly speak; her soul felt like it had been hit by a Mack truck. She was facing, her deepest and darkest demon. She cried and cried for a long time before she was able to explain what she'd heard about her husband.

"Well, I was gone this weekend, to get baptized in Macon, and Ricky didn't show up. Terri Lynn was supposed to have a party, that we weren't supposed to know about, but we did; a going away party. Ricky stayed behind to keep her from having a party, but was supposed to come to Macon to be with me at my baptism, but he didn't show up. Angel, Erik, Seven and me had to ride a bus back from Macon."

Mary wasn't making much sense to Mae, but she didn't intrude, allowing her mother to get it all out.

"Well, he said he didn't pick us up because of Terri Lynn, but Angel went to school today, and everyone was talking about Terri Lynn's party. Angel came home and told me, so I went down to the grocery store to confront him, but they told me he was taken by the sheriff's department." Mary started crying again, but kept telling her daughter the rest.

"I rode around all over town trying to find the sheriff's department, and they told me Ricky wouldn't be coming home for a long time. They explained that he had molested a bunch of girls at Terri Lynn's party; one of them was the sheriff's own daughter. Ricky provided all of the girls at the party with a keg of beer." Mary got up and began walking around the living room. "I got home, and some angry parent met me at the door, cussing me out for being such a horrible person. I tried to apologize and tell her I wasn't home at the time, but still she looked at me so ugly. I come in the house, and hidden under the couch is beer cans, and in my bed, under the mattress, girl's underwear. I don't know where Terri Lynn is, she's run away."

Mae didn't know what to say, nor did she know how to comfort her mother.

Mary wanted to get as far away from Americus that she could. The Jehovah Witnesses provided her and the boys a house back in Fort Valley, free of rent. Terri Lynn was found in Alabama with Alicia, and soon after Ricky's arrest; Angel moved to live with her mother too. For Erik and Seven, various and profound changes occurred when Ricky went to jail.

Saturating Mary's soul was an overwhelming depression, worse than she'd ever had. She felt the sting of guilt for the humiliating crimes Ricky sought to commit on every single victim he snagged. How could she endure the knowledge of two daughters being so terribly hurt right under her nose? Having spent her entire life trying to trust men, but for whatever reasons unknown to her, men had always seemed to prey on her. What was it that brought such people into her life?

Regardless of the pain of a cheating first husband who tried to kill her, and the major crimes committed by her second, who also had a crack at killing her, she somehow managed to put within all five of her kids, a sense of protective love. Mary was an outstanding mother, but she completely felt like she'd failed her kids.

Her pain and anguish would consume her for years to come, as would her desperate desire to protect her two boys and keep anyone who could possibly hurt them far away. This was the second time in her life that she was on her own, but the first time as a single mother, with no income. With the assistance of her church, she managed to get through that first winter with her boys. They both were confused as to why Ricky was in prison, but neither wanted to discuss it with their momma. Anyone could see she was depressed and sad, no matter how hard she tried to hide it. One day, she sat crying; wondering what she was going to find to feed her boys that night for supper. Seven came inside, excited to have found an old grown up garden. He handed her his prize, a turnip. His sunny smile could light up a room, and he grinned from ear to ear.

"Look what I found." He proudly announced then finished with. "What is it?"

"Son, you've found our supper." She smiled back at her baby, taking him into her arms. "Do you think you could find more?" Eagerly Seven jumped down from her arms, happily bounding off to find more turnips to feed his family.

Both boys developed a protective bond with their mother that started with their early childhood, but grew stronger after Ricky was locked up. Like two little men, they took on the challenge of being in charge of the house, and kept Mary laughing. No matter what happened, they all had each other, and that was all they needed.

Chapter Seventeen

Mae and Jacob were lucky to have so many people backing them, and supporting their goals. Living with Jacob's parents and sisters, they both persisted with their education, determined to graduate with a diploma in hand. Many teachers, family and friends, encouraged and assisted them in trying their best. During their senior year, being married, young parents, and working full time jobs to pay for Melina's extensive list of necessities, kept them extremely busy. Unlike all the other seniors in school, they were taking an advance course of what 'adult' life had in store for them.

It was the end of January, and the winter that year was frigid in the southern states. Infant Melina would sometimes sleep with Jacob's older sister Amy, which suited the young parents just fine, lacking enough time in the day to get any sleep with a newborn.

Amy had a job and would be the first in the house to get up. She would bring Melina to Mae or Jacob, so she could get ready for work. This had become a routine, and on this morning, it started out normal enough. Not long after she handed the infant back to her parents and went back to her room, Amy began screaming at the top of her lungs, throughout the entire house. Mae could have sworn that she had hollered rat, but Jacob had heard something entirely different.

"No! She said fire!" Jumping straight out of bed and right into his pants, Jacob was already heading out the bedroom, down the hall toward his sister.

Mae took Melina closer into her arms, and listened carefully to what was being said in the other room.

"I came back and the entire bathroom was on fire!" Amy was still shrieking hysterically.

"Call 911!" Jacob was on emergency autopilot.

Mae decided she'd better check out the damage herself, and slowly got out of bed, holding tightly to the baby. Something was holding her back, and she noticed Melina had a tight grip on the comforter. Mae wrapped the bedspread around the both of them, grabbed the baby's bottle and headed to the kitchen. At first nothing looked out of place, no smoke no flames. Amy hung up the phone, white as a ghost, and took off running toward the living room. Following suit, Mae looked into the living room, seeing a little bit of black smoke floating across the top of the room, she took another step and stopped. The entire laundry room was aflame.

"Well, Melina, it's time for us to leave the building." Running across the living room, holding the baby tightly against her body, they got out the front door. The front window glass was shattering, but Mae kept running, jumping into the open door of Shannon's mini-van. Jacob's baby sister, Sue, sat inside the vehicle, having obeyed the pre-arranged fire drill instructions. She was crying, silently watching with her two eyes wide, at the out of control flames, licking at her home. Sue was only a year older than Erik, and like the boys were to Mae, she was very special to her big brother Jacob. Mae looked in the direction that the young girl was staring. That's when she realized what horror she was really looking at.

Lee and Shannon's bedroom was beyond the bath and laundry rooms.

They had no exit out of the house, with tiny windows that had screwed in bars. There was a door, but when they had done some reconstruction on the home years before, they welded it shut. A fast and steady beating noise could be heard, as Lee's fist's pounded to break the door open.

Little Sue was praying for the door to open, while Jacob ran around cutting gas lines off, and Amy began moving everyone's cars away from the growing inferno. Mae sat watching the metal of the door giving way to the pressure of Lee's pummeling. Miraculously, the door flew open, and tiny Shannon was tossed out by her struggling to breathe husband.

Everything was lost, everything except what was most important, their lives.

Jacob, Mae and Melina stayed with Mary and the boys for a few months until the Jones got a new double wide trailer placed in front of where the burned house had stood.

The experience was fun for Erik and Seven. They were thrilled to have both Jacob and Melina; living with them. Mae was loved, but not as much fun since she had become a momma. The boys, including her husband's rough housing with each other made her a nervous wreck around little Melina.

Both boys quickly got use to Melina waiting for them when they got home from school. When it came time for them to move back into the Jones's, both boys were upset to see them go.

Mae and Jacob continued to be seniors in high school, despite all the obstacles. The week after the fire, they had returned to their classes. It had taken a while to gather up a small wardrobe of clothes, and needed school supplies, but they bravely walked the halls with their second hand clothes on. The last hour of the first day back, both Jacob and Mae were called to room 222. They arrived outside the door at the same time, looking at each other confused. Mae let Jacob open the door, and they both were surprised to see the room full of their senior class members. A collection had been taken, and they wanted to give it to the determined young parents. With the fire, came so many opportunities to see the good in so many people, and experience love from authentic and sincere human souls. Mae learned what could be replaced, and what couldn't.

Chapter Eighteen

Graduation came, and with it great pride for the seniors, from their families and friends. Not sure what to do with the diploma's, but gratified none the less, they promptly moved out of the Jones's and into their own trailer. They had made it, and now as they sat in their empty place, the accomplishment was followed with uncertainty, especially since they were expecting their second child.

Mae gave birth to her second daughter, Cameron, in early February 1988. It had been a difficult birth, one which Mary had hung by her daughter's side the entire time. A few months later, Mary would baby sit while Mae worked a part time cleaning job in the afternoons. Mary would come over after school with the boys, who now had another little sister to watch over.

Mary had starting making plans though, and when she announced to Mae one afternoon what she was going to be doing, it took Mae by surprise.

"I'm moving back to Alabama."

It wasn't bad news, but it dismayed Mae none the less. She tried to appear happy.

"Oh really...when?"

"Well, this weekend more than likely, I've saved for a moving truck and just about have things packed up."

Swallowing hard, Mae encouraged her mother. "That's good."

It was good, very good for Mary and the boys to go back home where they belonged. Mae was learning a fast lesson about life, that nothing is permanent; everything was temporary.

The boys would be raised by the same people who had instilled love and security into Mae. As Mary left the state of Georgia, she closed that chapter of her life for good.

They moved in with the Baker's and the two boys were by far ecstatic with the attention they received from their grandparents. Childhood for them became carefree and happy, with all the room they needed to run, explore and play. Paw Paw stood in where their paternal parent was absent, to the joy of both boys. Having each other, Erik and Seven continued to be best friends, and for those first few years back in Alabama, it seemed their childhood had more chance for survival than Mae's ever had.

Seven desired being outside far more than Erik though. To locate him you'd have to walk down through the overgrown pasture which had become his playground. He loved the solitude of being enclosed by trees, and being able to sit and think in the tranquility of nature. The school classrooms nearly drove him crazy; he despised being shut inside for any length of time. Playing, running, swimming, laughing, dreaming and living were things better done outside than in. He wasn't hard to please; his only desires were to be happy and make everyone he loved, happy too.

Toward the end of 1988, Jacob enlisted into the Navy, and Mae moved back to Alabama, with both of her baby girls. With Jacob going away to boot camp, Mae tried to encourage Mary in sharing a house and the responsibilities associated with it. While Mary worked, Mae could watch the boys and girls, and Mary could do the same for Mae while she worked. Cautiously, Mary agreed, desiring to move out of her parent's house anyway.

Once again, Mae was living with her brothers, who were excited having their big sister around and even more pleased to have Melina and Cameron to watch over. Every afternoon, they rushed home from school, to check on their niece's. They bragged about being such young uncles. Mae's first credit debt was at a furniture store, where she purchased needed beds for Erik and Seven to sleep on.

This arrangement Mae had made with Mary would have worked out fine, except within a couple of month's Mae left her all alone, taking the girls with her and moved to Waukegan, Illinois to be near Jacob while he finished school, at the Great Lakes Naval Base. Her daughters move hurt Mary in so many ways, mentally, emotionally and financially. Without Mae's help, she couldn't afford the rent, utilities or food. She had no one to watch the boys at night while she worked. Yet, Mae didn't care. All her concern was with Jacob. Though strapped, Mary didn't move back into her parent's home, she managed to find a cheaper house that sat across from Southside School in Lanyard. Granny Anne lived within several blocks, and she helped with the boys.

Mary and Mae didn't speak for the next three years, until the end of 1991.

The split between mother and daughter didn't directly affect the two boys, they were finally home. Just as Mae had done a decade before, the two boys would spend their school days, walking to and from Granny Anne's house.

Through the years many things had changed about downtown Lanyard, and many things hadn't. Driver's bakery still sat next to the Old Lanyard Post Office, and across the street "Red's" corner drug store still ran its business. As she had done for Mae, Granny Anne provided the boys with breakfast and change for after school snacks at the bakery. The walk to Lanyard Elementary was the same as her, except the old Elementary school building had been torn down, and the new building sat across from where the other had been. A large playground replaced the old building and a tunnel under the street had been installed so that students could get across the road without interference of traffic.

Erik and Seven walked together the four blocks home, which took them through the tiny downtown section. Granny Anne would wait as she had for Mae, on her front porch swing in the warmer weather. With harsher conditions outside, her gas space heaters blazed in every room while she sat in her favorite Duncan Fife chair, keeping up with the, "Guiding Light." A

Matriarch to generations, yet nothing significant or tragic ever happened at her address, except eating pound cake and climbing apple trees.

Mary held a full time job at a local discount retailer. Though she could have gone back to her hospital emergency room position, the hours and benefits suited her needs better at the department store. She mothered the boys with a loving passion, and believed her protective barriers would prevent any harm from ever reaching them. Both boys were being guarded by a circle of family who had only their best interest and needs at heart. Other than their father's, Ricky's being locked up and Joel Tripp's troubling Mary for visitation and refusing to pay child support, nothing was wrong with either son. There were no obstacles in their way, no monsters to have to fight off. Seven and Erik were just fine, until one day.

Playing at the park was one of many things they found to do after school. They had recently acquired bicycles, and were riding around enjoying their new freedom of transportation. Other people were at the city park, and a group of boys were playing ball. They offered for Erik and Seven to join them in the game. Everything went as it would normally look at a playground, until it was time to go.

"Hey, let me ride your bike." The largest boy got in front of Erik's bike, blocking his path.

Erik considered it a moment, but knew they had stayed longer than they should have, and Granny Anne might be worried about them.

"I can't today, maybe tomorrow." He was hoping they could play ball again.

The boys balled up fist smacking him right off his bike certainly wasn't something he'd considered though. Without warning, Erik was being beaten and kicked.

Seven panicked, having never imagined witnessing his big brother being attacked. He was just a little fellow, the smallest one left in the large group of boys now mobbing Erik. Running home in fear they would kill Erik, he flew into Granny Anne's house.

"They are beating Erik up!" Seven ran to grab her car keys and purse. Anne didn't move so fast, suffering from a bad hip, but without any more prompting; she'd started for the back door toward her old Cadillac. Little Seven was anxious to get back to his brother. As Anne slid into the driver's seat he gave her further instructions.

"His at the park… they are at the park."

Within a minute they were pulling up to find Erik laying on the ground all alone, he was crying and in shock. They were all in shock. Granny Anne called Mary at work.

"Mary, some man has beaten Erik up, and stolen his bicycle." Anne could hardly talk; she was so shaken up by the scene. She'd never in all her life, witnessed something so senseless.

Mary couldn't believe what was happening either. Her two boys were good boys, and they didn't bother anybody. How could someone beat on either of them? Asking her son what had happened to him, she assured him it would never happen again. Erik was bruised up on the outside, while Seven wore his experience on the inside. Trusting others was becoming harder for them both.

Erik described the assailant as a man. They drove around looking for a man on a boy's bike, and eventually found it parked in a yard. Mary spoke to the man's mother, and it turned out the boy was an overgrown bully, who was three years older than Erik. Mary hoped the conversation with his mother would deter any more attacks.

It didn't. The attacks grew worse, and even sinister and criminal. They would continue for months before Seven, finally told his mother. He had to go against Erik's wishes to do so, because Erik was hiding the abuse. The more his mother got involved, the worse and more perverse the attacks got. Not to mention being ashamed of what the bully was doing to him, in front of his gang of followers, every day after school. The first few weeks were horrifying to both boys, Erik always trying to protect Seven, who would run away as fast as he could for fear of the pain they could cause him. He would hear Erik scream out in pain, begging for mercy and other times Seven would see Erik give the bully a good fight. But not one fight was ever fair, and Erik got good at hiding the bruises and scars. Seven told his mother mostly out of pure fear for Erik's life.

The subsequent years in the legal system did not offer much in the way of justice, nor did it stop the bully, who made Erik's torment his life's mission. It created something within each boy that they would carry around with them at all times, for the rest of their lives.

Chapter Nineteen

Being far away from Alabama, Mae lived on the Norfolk Naval Base with her family of three children and a military husband. While Erik was being tormented, she had no idea with her life running full steam ahead, parallel to their tragedy down south. She had given birth to her third and final baby, a son named James Robert in the snowy December of 1989. With her husband going out to sea, no family or friends around to help, Mae had her hands full with motherhood. Mary and she still hadn't spoken since Mae left her the year before. When Ricky got out of prison in 1990, it made their rift with each other worse than it had ever been, when Mary took him back.

Mae wrote Mary a letter, soliciting and petitioning her mother to keep Ricky away from her brothers. Mae reminded Mary to consider not only what he had done to her, but to dozens of other innocent girls. Her request made to Mary in her written communication didn't produce the results she expected.

Mary's response was the most painful thing she had ever wrote to her daughter, which was that Ricky, unlike Mae, had never abandoned her, and he, unlike Mae, was helping her with the boys, not hurting them.

Unable to understand how Mary could possible write or believe such, Mae felt like her heart was broken in two. She tried to comprehend but she just couldn't understand Mary's decision.

Unknown to Mae was how both boy's had worked for weeks trying to persuade their mother to take their daddy back. They had begged and pleaded with her, not knowing what he did to get sent away in the first place. Neither boy had memory of watching him beat Mary with a wooden gun years earlier. They had never seen him hurt anyone, or do anything wrong. Ricky had always been good to them both, and they wanted him back. Mary let him move back in, though she continued to keep him at arms-length, she made her boys very happy by allowing Ricky in their lives.

It wasn't until November 1991, that Mary spoke to Mae. Month's before, Paw Paw Baker had been diagnosed with terminal lung cancer, and on a Thursday afternoon, Mae received a phone call from her Maw Maw. Thulah was crying so hard on the other end of the line when Mae answered, it was difficult to understand what was happening. Mary took the phone from Thulah.

"Mae, if you want to see your Paw Paw before he dies, you better come home."

Just like that, their conversation wasn't long, but it was intense. Driving thirteen hours, with all three babies in her conversion van, Mae made it by Saturday morning, and she got to spend the last day of Owen Baker's life with him.

Late that evening, with a room full of family and friends, they watched him take his last breath. Mae's only living protector was dead, and she sat alone with him for a long time, while waiting on Thompson Brown Funeral Home to come pick him up.

In the middle of all this was Ricky Levine. He had managed quite well to blend himself back up into the family. Catering to Mary, and going out of his way to do anything for anybody, Ricky wanted to be accepted, yet

Mae couldn't shake her heavy feeling's concerning him. After burying Owen Baker, a new immediate depression found its way into Mae's life.

Losing her beloved Paw Paw was difficult, but watching Ricky try to fool the same people all over again, boggled her mind. Mae's marriage was also in shambles, but she had told no one about it. Riding back to Virginia, she had the urge to run away again, just hit the road with her three children and disappear. Crying the entire way back, she couldn't pinpoint all the reasons for her tears. Being around her family again had made her heart start to ache. She longed to be closer to them, not thirteen hours away. With her marriage failing, she considered moving back home to Alabama.

Mae hadn't told her family about her crumbling marriage, the death of Owen was sad enough. She held another secret, more disturbing than the pending divorce; something that she spoke to nobody about. Something that had disturbingly changed who she would be forever and something she shamefully tried to bury from her own recall. The funeral had been plagued with Ricky's presence and Mae wasn't sure if that could be what was making her so forlorn. She'd begun to feel like a dirty, no good, waste of human skin.

Since Jacob had joined the military, many things had changed with the southern sweethearts. Mae continued to be plagued with unwanted abuses in her life. It wasn't so much Jacob, but nothing felt right about living life since giving birth to her third baby. He was perfect, sweet and almost born on a schedule, but after he suffered a virus and a trying hospital stay, darkness covered over Mae's life. Unhappiness was going to come with her previous tragedies, but no one warned her about postpartum depression. It had gotten so bad; Mae was forced to take anti-depressants. Jacob didn't know what to do about her invisible pain, and couldn't comprehend her sadness. They had started arguing after James Robert's birth, and by the time he was six month's old, the two were only playing happy home for the children's sake.

They had an arrangement where they took turns each weekend going out, while the other parent stayed home with the kids. Somehow their weekends got mixed up, and he had planned on hanging around the house with the kids, and he didn't want Mae around.

"Why don't you go out with Kitty?" He tried to encourage her to go out and have a good time. He had been working on her for hours.

"I don't really know her Jacob, and besides I don't have anything ready to wear. Why don't you just take this weekend too, I don't care. You go have a good time." Mae had tried the bar scene, but it mostly gave her a headache. Jacob was determined, and went upstairs, picking out an outfit that he figured she'd score in.

"Who knows you might find someone that can put up with you." Jacob teased, but Mae knew it was really sarcastic truth. They had tried to stay friends; he only had a year and a half left before he could leave the military with honorable discharge. The plan was to get through the rest of his time, without killing each other.

Mae got dressed and went out with their neighbor Kitty and one of her friends named Kathy. During the evening, Kitty took them to a military sports bar, where for the next four hours; Mae sat and talked to a nice Officer. The bar closed at two a.m., and Mae found Kitty and Kathy outside, talking to a young group of military men.

"We're going to follow these guys to a party." Kitty giggled while tugging on one man's shirt.

Without any cash on hand, Mae couldn't call a cab. She certainly wasn't in the mood to party with anyone. She got in thinking the worst case scenario; she could wait in the car while the two older ladies painted the town red.

They drove down to Virginia Beach to a nice motel along the coast. She followed the women, who were following the marines. Once inside the room, it was empty, no party going on at all, and Mae figured it wouldn't take long at all for the ladies to fizzle on down.

One marine took his chance with asking Mae if she wanted to go for a walk or something. Mae looked him up and down, immediately on guard. She turned him down politely.

"We could ride over to the 7-11 and get something to eat." He persisted.

Mae thought about all the fast food joints, and wondered why he'd want to eat out of a convenience store. "No thank you, I'm just going to sit here and wait for my friends…to get done, with whatever they are doing." Looking down the hall, she hoped it wouldn't be long.

"Well suit yourself." Dejected he left her alone.

Watching the door shut, Mae reached over and grabbed a folded blanket off the couch, wrapping it around her entire body. It was freezing, and she just wanted to curl up and go to sleep. Taking hold of the TV remote she snapped on the box, and yawned really big. Her head was starting to pound with what felt like a migraine. Within minutes, she'd fell asleep sitting straight up.

The sensation of falling startled her eyes open, while something pulled at the blanket she was twirled up in. At first she couldn't remember where she was. Many voices could be heard, as she tried to adjust her eyes to the bright lights and get her senses about her. Attempting to get up, she was pushed back down with unexpected force.

"Get off me." Pushing at the one attempting to climb under her skirt, both of her arms were grabbed and pinned to the floor. Looking up she couldn't count the number of faces, while more hands were touching, rubbing and groping her from head to toe. Mae started screaming, but a foot was put over her throat and a pillow quickly covered her face.

Panic seized her as she struggled to get air. It felt like a pride of lions pulling and ripping at her. An old familiar voice started screaming obscenities, but her viciousness was no match with the determined group. She continued to try to scream, though the sounds were muffled under the pillow and roar of the crowd. Her panties were being ripped off, while the room grew even louder. Blacking out wasn't an option, she feared they would kill her for sure, with every second, the assault got worse.

"This can't be happening to me! How is this happening?" Mae tried to stop struggling, hoping to at least be granted some air. She heard laughing, and with an intensity she'd not ever felt, she determined to fight back. Her spunk was met with cheers, as the many hands flipped her over to her stomach, giving her a chance to see the large number of people watching her rape. A humiliating darkness inched its way across her soul, and the pain being caused was met with numbness. She squeezed her eyes shut as someone began to sodomize her.

"No, no..." Tears streamed down her face, as bones in her arms and ribs felt like they were breaking under the pressure and weight of so many attempting to attack her at once. Spit, sweat and semen were dripping all over her. Some were cheering on the brutality, while others were making fun.

At some point the gripping hold was lightened enough; she broke free, pulling at what clothes she had left, she ran out of the room, down the stairs, running until she fell in some sand, where she proceeded to violently vomit; over and over. Mae cried, not sure what to do, or where to go, suffering from shock.

Kitty and Kathy found her outside, waiting by the vehicle; neither woman said on word about what had happened in the room, leading Mae to wonder if it had really happened to her at all. By the time she got home, the sun was already coming up.

Walking inside, Jacob looked like he was happy that she had stayed out all night. He figured, she must have gotten lucky, but she looked awfully pale walking past him without saying a word.

Mae went into the bathroom, turned on the shower and got straight in, with her clothes still on. Jacob found her sitting in the tub, letting the scalding hot water burn her skin. She couldn't talk, or explain what had happened, as her husband realized something was seriously inappropriate.

"What's wrong with you?" Flinging open the shower curtain he looked down at the crumpled mess she was in.

"They...raped...me. You wanted me to go out!" Sobbing without control, Mae just wanted him to let her be.

"What? When? Where...who are they?" Anger pushed through what his eyes and ears were experiencing, but it didn't make any sense. "I'm calling the police!"

"NO! No you're not calling anyone!" Mae pulled the shower curtain closed, while he pulled it back open.

"What? You were raped...I'm calling the damn police."

"No, there was too many, no, just leave me alone!" She tried to cover her face with her hands. "Please, just let me deal with it. I don't matter to you anymore, so don't bother yourself with it." Mae stood up with difficulty. Pulling the shower curtain closed and holding it, she just wouldn't talk to anyone about what happened. She scrubbed herself clean of all the evidence and stayed in the water until it ran cold.

Jacob helped her get dressed. Everything was sore from the neck down. Deep purple and black bruises were showing up all over her arms, legs, neck, and torso. Unable to lift her legs to go upstairs to her bedroom, she eased herself down onto the couch in the living room. A deep, yet restless sleep drowned out all the noise of kids and electronic gadgets playing around the house, while she lay motionless, with her back to the room. At some point she turned over with great pain, looking out the front screen door. She could see her husband, talking to Kitty outside. The next time she opened her eyes, her husband stood above her looking down upon her.

"I just talked to Kitty, and she has a different version than you." He had started explaining. "Seems that you were the life of the party, and you WANTED them to do that to you."

Mae looked up, but made no comment.

"Kitty says, you were asking for it." He finished with a matter of fact tone. Waiting for an explanation he sat down on the coffee table, sitting face to face with her.

Mae was hurt, stunned and humiliated by his accusation, as the violent rape itself. Why would she ask to be attacked in such a manner? Silently she looked him in the eyes, if he, her husband and father of her three kids didn't believe her, how would anyone else? Without saying one word, she stiffly turned her back to him. She had made the right decision to keep her attack silent; there was no way she ever wanted to confront anybody in that room, ever again.

Chapter Twenty

Seven is gone. He is forever departed and his murder has awakened the parts of me I'd believed to be locked up and forever hidden. I had assumed I'd always have the time to share life with him, but now it seems to have disappeared so fast, when back then, I felt a paralyzing fear; it would never change.

Since his birth, I was there, holding, feeding, changing, playing, singing, laughing, fussing and sometimes crying with him. I'm eat up now with guilt over not spending near enough time and energy, admiring him. I've never felt this feeling, like something so precious and priceless, has been so brutally taken right from me.

Our entire family has been robbed of so much with his murder, the effects ripple outward in an eternal pattern of pain.

Returning to my yesterday's hasn't been easy, but with a fine tooth comb, I searched for every fragment of remembrance that I could find of Seven. What I've uncovered is how I dripped with pain and a desperate need to survive. I begged for understanding from God, as to why this sorrow was allowed. The past caught up to haunt me, and remind me of my experiences.

I unconsciously needed to relate to my brothers pain. I had to know what he went through. The last few seconds, of the last moments in time when another human hates you to the point they want to kill you. Unlike Seven though, I'd survived.

I wanted to know why he hadn't. It's just wasn't fair.

Seven's slaughter has opened up every wound I'd ever suffered. Nothing I thought I'd learned or credited myself for understanding made any sense anymore. This had me cut in half and everything felt ripped out. No matter what, it could never be fixed. No matter how angry or sad, it can't ever be changed. I'm forced to face it every day, for the rest of my life. HOW?

My life has invoked the character I have become, and in going over my story, I'm trying to understand my own capabilities.

I have my theories on his murder, and how I suspect it involved a large group of people attacking him. I can feel it in my bones, he was mobbed and robbed. The ruptured and silent spirit of Seven's, lying in the ICU, testified to me and questioned me.

"Why Mae...? Why would they do this to me? I've done nothing to them! I don't understand! My family needs me, I need them, and they cared so little for my human life, to beat me to death?"

Seven lay suffering, second by second, a torture for him and us, for absolutely no excusable reason. The memories will now shade every single second of my existence, for the rest of my life. It has shattered any and everything I ever comprehended, into little pieces of naught.

My heart and mind knew intimately what the touch of evil felt like. I'd stood in it, tasted, smelt, heard and handled it. My experience was rich, but the effects left me numb and frozen on the inside.

Now I struggle with rage and anger. His murder has forced me to dig inward to my past struggles, and take an inventory of pain. I have nowhere else to go until the throbbing ache that his homicide has caused, is lightened up in its intensity. I can't move forward through this, pretending nothing has happened, because this has definitely changed me like nothing ever before. I feel if I am silent through this travesty that it affirms he deserved his fate, and there is no way Seven deserved his early and untimely demise.

I can't escape my history, and this time I choose not to be silent. I will not be encouraged by those who choose for me to be hushed, in order to survive an impossible situation of corrupt or unjust power in the family, community, or world. One day I will release a rage that shakes the skies, once I can comprehend how to handle it.

How do you come to terms with the unthinkable?

I want answers, and those around me want me to move on. Seven is dead and gone, no matter what. So why must I continue to drag myself through this grief? What if I actually find the answers I am desperately searching for? That and only that, answers, will give me the necessary peace my soul needs to survive this event, pass through it and come out on the other side. I really wish I could move on or as some say, get over it. That's a nice thing to wish, but unless I obtain full amnesia, I will never be free of the memories.

Chapter Twenty One

Mae's marriage was finished, the sweethearts were through, and the two were moving back home. Jacob went back to his parents in Georgia, while Mae was finally making her way back to her sweet home Alabama. Shannon had offered to help with the three small children, and because Mae had no income, she believed for temporary purposes, the kids staying with their daddy wouldn't hurt. The drive between parents was less than two hours, so Mae could see them whenever she wanted.

Ricky Levine was still in the picture, and Mae wasn't sure how she was going to deal with the dark presence in her life.

It was a difficult decision to separate from her babies, but it was for the best. Mae needed a car, home and income to afford them. Every other weekend, she'd drive over and get them, bringing them back to Alabama for the weekend. Mae had moved in with Thulah, and it was pure joy to watch her children run around where once, her small feet had roamed. It was hard to take them back, and the pending divorce wasn't turning out as nice as they had originally premeditated.

Words can hardly describe how good Mae felt to be back near her family after so many years apart. Despite Ricky's existence, Mae wasn't a stranger in her mother's house. Keeping her eyes and instinctual senses on him, she doubted prison had done anything to help the sexual predator she knew him to be. His health was failing him, to the point he'd had open heart surgery. It gave him access to some potent prescription medications, so though the Canadian Mist was gone, it had been successfully replaced. He'd become an active Jehovah Witness, almost too lively a member, Mae perceived. He'd act sick, but then play a rough game of basketball with the boys, to which Mae kept mental notes on. Something inside her heart, said he wasn't finished with his crimes. Regardless if at times it felt like a tug of war with him over her mother and brothers, he wasn't going to keep Mae from her family.

Angel continued to live with her mother, but wanted to move back in with Mary and Ricky. She couldn't for the fact Ricky, couldn't live with any minor girls. She was finishing high school, and for Erik and Seven, a good sister to have around to provide rides for them. The three of them had been close in age, and strong in sibling bonds. They shared in the fact that Ricky hadn't ever sought to cause them pain and they had no memory of Terri Lynn's or Mae's.

Terri Lynn was now married and a mother of a son named Stan. Busy as ever, she wouldn't stay still long enough to ever address her issues. They were far too painful and Terri Lynn suffered in silence and gave herself over to living life on the edge.

Alabama was a beautiful place to belong to, and Mae had missed it more than she realized. So much discomfort and despicable injustice hadn't been isolated to her home state, it was everywhere. As much as she noticed the evil around her, she'd force herself to find the good. That was part of her survival, too live one day at a time, and not let anything worthy go without notice.

Jacob wanted to keep custody of the children, to which Mae would start the battle of her life. It hurt so bad at the prospect of losing her children, but she could comprehend Jacob's worry, maybe she wasn't mentally capable of taking care of her kids. If she couldn't mother them though, she didn't think she could breath.

Painfully she continued to hurt herself, she needed to do it. Glass had become her preferential object to cut herself with. The need would come without warning, but it was something she'd done so long, it had become as normal as blinking an eye.

Oddly, one day, after cutting herself strategically in places no one could see, the thought hit her, that what she was doing was insane.

"Why do I need to feel pain?"

Before she could ever find the answer, she'd have to learn how to ask the proper questions.

"Why do I need to cause myself pain?"

The question went round and round in her head, there was no logic to anything she thought about. She had too much to think about. So much pain, it was far too scary to dwell on anything, and something's she wouldn't allow herself to recount. Mae needed help, she picked up her phone book, calling number after number, until she found a place she could go to for assistance.

No one knew about her need to hurt herself, only a very few noticed the marks left. Afraid of anyone knowing, yet terrified no one cared. She decided to face off with herself in a room with a professional holding a pad and pen. She began talking, and talking, and talking. At first she would have to chip away at the years and years of issues, one at a time. Some issues would take years to come to terms with, while others less than an hour. Why it was embarrassing to have to ask for help, she didn't know, but she knew enough about what her heart, spirit and soul would do without assistance; die. She refused to abandon her life, no matter how insignificant it felt.

Every so often, Mae would take her three over to Mary's. Ricky was given the impression from Mae that he shouldn't even look; much less ever touch her children. With Mary, Erik and Seven watching over them also, Mae tried to believe nothing like what Ricky did to her, could possibly happen to her three babies.

The boys adored their nieces and nephew, spending every minute with them laughing and playing.

Mary kept her eyes on her husband, an eagle eye on his every move. Ricky knew he was being observed, and continued to be on his very best behavior. As always though, what's seen on the outside, if scratched away at, could reveal something else entirely just below the surface.

The black of Ricky's soul was the color of tar, and his view would never be understood. Causing others agony was his life's mission, it was what made him feel good about himself, to feel in control of others destiny. He had been devalued from the start of his life. Thrown away like garbage. His only male descendant would not be done that way, and ultimately Ricky began to see Erik as a threat, not as a boy he helped raise, definitely not his son.

In the months before Owen's diagnosis of terminal cancer, he was the first to take notice of Ricky's actions. Owen had noticed his grandson's swollen red welts, and he questioned Erik.

"What happened to your legs?"

"I got in trouble." Erik tried to hide the marks to no avail.

"Ricky did that?" Owen didn't like either man his oldest daughter had married, and he didn't mind setting them straight. When Ricky showed up to get the boys, Owen was waiting for him. Age and hard living had worn down the once six foot tall Baker. It didn't matter; he was still full of fire.

"I saw those marks on my grandson's legs, and I'm going to tell you one time and one time only." Owen had his rifle lying across his lap, looking up from his couch at Ricky who just walked through the living room door. "If you ever put your hands on Erik again, I'll kill you just as soon as look at you." Owen stood up, still much taller than Ricky. "Do you understand me?

Ricky tried not to pass out. His heart was beating against his ribs. "Well, I've..."

"That's right, you've been warned." Owen looked Ricky through his eyes, and into his soul. When Owen died months after, Ricky figured no one would ever know about the stern warning from his father-in-law.

The unnerving encounter had made Ricky's blood boil, and he took matters into his own hands. Under the surface he'd work hard to destroy Erik's happiness. It would take years to find out exactly what he did, but its effects could be felt immediately after that day.

It had always been a fun activity for Erik and Seven to compete with each other in most things. Who could run the fastest, jump the longest, climb the highest and ride their bike the furthest. Lately though, Seven had started taking everything very personal, and where he use to take losing in stride, now-a-days, he got really mad.

"Boy you better watch out!" Erik turned to face his little brother, sweat dripping from his forehead.

"You cheated, you stopped bouncing the ball, and then you moved. That's traveling!" Seven grabbed the ball off the ground as it rolled back to his feet after rebounding off Erik's back.

"It's a game dude..." Erik turned his back again, and again the ball hit him, this time, painfully in the back of the head.

They were at each other instantly, rolling around in the dirt, fist making contact. Ricky came out as if on cue, to separate the two.

"That's enough." He strongly man handled them both, but push Erik backwards, knocking him off his feet. "If you ever put your f*#!ing hands on my son again, I'll kill you."

At first both boys were shocked, but then Seven got to his feet and started walking inside the house, leaving Erik on the ground, beneath Ricky's pointing finger. Erik stood up, confronting the little man would be easy, but he couldn't bring himself to hit Ricky back. From that day forward, Ricky began attacking Erik nearly every day, finding arguments in everyday function. Though Ricky found pleasure in causing Erik pain, what was really excruciating for Erik was Seven's anger toward him. Erik decided to keep the trouble from Mary, who continued to work her full time job.

Seven grew distant from not only Erik, but also his mother and sister Mae. His temperament turned distressing, but everyone just gave Seven his space. No one knew what had turned the young boy's world upside down. It was oblivious to those that loved him; he'd suffered a tremendous blow to his spirit. That his own father had planted a seed of doubt into his very heart, and robbed him of the security he'd always had.

Chapter Twenty Two

As if overnight, Seven developed an obscurity around him. Erik was the first to notice it, being witness to his brother's daily grumbling and altered perceptions. Their once tight friendship was now nothing more than slim threads threatening to snap apart. Whenever Ricky physically attacked Erik, Seven would walk away, never coming to his brother's aid. It hurt Erik, when he tried to talk to Seven, and his brother slammed the door in his face. All of this would go on while Mary was at work, but when she came home, Ricky and Erik would act like nothing unusual was happening, while Seven kept to himself more than ever.

Seven's studies started to be affected too. He'd always had a hard time with school, even though he was highly intelligent. The restrictive confines of the classroom nearly drove him insane, he preferred the beauty and awe of nature to the stark greyness of the school's interior. Around the time he moved to F.W. Burns Jr. High in Westwood, Alabama, the typical teenage hormones kicked in. Many things became serious for Seven, and he lost his once smiling and enlightened mood, exchanging it with an argumentatively angry persona. He associated with a tight circle of friends, and his daddy. He was cross with Mary, and most of her family

Erik and Seven's lives would be led completely separate, though they had always been tied at the hip before. Ricky seemed pleased with the split between brothers. He worked hard every day to find something to crawl all over Erik about. Unlike the abuse on Mae, which was more sexual in nature, Ricky hated Erik, and wanted him to go away.

Watching his daddy abuse and belittle his brother began to unnerve Seven though. It began to tear at his heart. He couldn't help but love Erik; his brother had always been his best friend. Even with Ricky's encouragement to set his big brother straight, Seven began to take up for Erik, which only made Ricky the madder and more determined to separate the boys.

Ricky had explained to Seven, that he was his only son and that Erik was not. It wasn't a secret that the boys didn't know, but Ricky wanted to clear up the fact with his only son, that he noticed Mary's family treating them differently. He pointed out the differences to Seven, whom hadn't noticed anything; until his father trained Seven's attention to it. There was no difference, at least no one thought of the boys as different, but after Ricky pushed these thoughts into the preteen's head, Seven couldn't help but consider his father's advice. He had no reason to believe his father would lie to him.

"Mae is the reason I had to go away to prison; she accused me of molesting her. That's why your Momma's family doesn't like me and that's why they don't like you."

Though initially Seven had believed his daddy's lie's that Erik was loved more, Seven loved Erik too and it pained him to lose his close bond with his older brother. These words had torn everything Seven had loved away from him. All the people Seven had ever loved and trusted Ricky had cleaved him away from them. Seven didn't know what to believe, and turned to his new friends at school to fill in the void of losing his family bonds.

Mae had easily noticed Seven's awkwardness around her, but she figured it to be normal teen-age behavior. She drove up one day to pick up a suitcase, she'd asked Mary to borrow. She pulled her car up behind the house, and entered through the back door. As she walked in Mae felt as if she were walking into "something going on". Both Erik and Seven were sitting down on the couch, looking down at the floor, while Ricky sat in a recliner across from them, with an "I didn't do anything" look on his face.

"What's going on?" She questioned while making her way to the closet where the suitcase was kept. As she walked back through, Erik had gone outside, while Seven and Ricky continued to sit in the living room. "Well, I'll see you later." Neither said one word, as Mae made her way out. Closing the back door, Erik was sitting all by himself, still looking down toward his feet.

"Erik, is everything okay?" She stopped, holding the suitcase up, and gave her brother an intense stare.

He said nothing, as his head shook back and forth.

"Okay then." Mae didn't believe him, but couldn't make him tell her anything either.

Getting into her car and turning on the ignition, she had just started backing out when Seven ran out the back door. Mae stopped to watch him, as he made his way to her car and stuck his head into the driver's window.

"Get Erik out of here, daddy's going to beat him if you don't." He began to back himself away from her car.

"What?" Mae put the car back into park.

"He has already beaten him once; get him out of here because he isn't done with him." The look in Seven's eyes made it apparent to her, that Ricky was dropping his false persona and the abuse had started up again.

"Erik, get in this car now! And you too!" Mae motioned to Seven, who shook his head no, and backed away from her further. Erik obediently came down off the porch and made his way to her car, walking with his head down.

Ricky came out the back door with his arms folded, and it was at that moment Mae felt such hatred, more than she'd ever felt for him before.

"It's over, you've done messed up now!" Mae pointed her finger as she warned him. Their eyes locked and that same old sadistic grin he used to give her came across his face. The damage was already done; nothing could erase all the pain and misery he determined himself to cause.

Erik began explaining that Ricky had been attacking him nearly every day, for one reason or another.

"The man will never put his hands on you again." Mae attempted to be calm, while a hurricane of emotions flowed through her veins.

Mae drove straight over to the department store where Mary was busy working in her blue customer care vest. At that time she worked in the fabric department and that's where Mae found her.

"He's up to it again Momma, Ricky's been beating on Erik." Mae let that sink in a second. "Momma, the man hasn't changed one bit."

Something inside Mary finally cracked, concerning her husband, and it was that very day, she finally drew a line down in between her and Ricky Levine. His good times of abusing her kids were over.

But Ricky wasn't going to give up that easily, especially on his only son.

Chapter Twenty Three

The divorce of Seven's parents sent him on a troubled journey of despair. Ricky had come full circle; better than he had ever been before. Having his son convinced that he wasn't adored and loved like Erik, made Seven desire to please his father all the stronger.

With Seven's gang connections, Ricky used it to help teach his son how to make a fast profit. Ricky's diagnosed heart condition, gave him plenty of prescription medications to sale. One particular pill that brought lots of money on the streets was his Oxycodone.

Seven had plenty of buyers and his ranking in his gang went up as his notoriety exploded on the drug scene. His tough exterior was backed with violent outburst; he became someone you didn't want to cross. Ricky knew his son had started drinking and taking some of the pills he trafficked, but Ricky thought he had Seven under control. The only thing Ricky had control over was ruining people's lives. He began playing 'divorce' games with Mary, using Seven as the weapon. With his parents separating, Seven's demeanor turned gloomy and depressed. Gone was the sweet little boy. In his place was a hollow hearted and confused young teen, being drugged up and destroyed by his own father.

Granny Anne unexpectedly died of heart failure in December of 1993, and away went the family's moral compass and guide.

Mary moved into Granny Anne's mill home with the two boys to get away from her husband, but Ricky began stalking her every move. Ricky didn't have a clue how to move on, and began using Seven in all kinds of disturbing ways, to keep an eye on his soon to be ex-wife.

Seven at first didn't want his momma leaving his "sick and dying" father. When that didn't work, Ricky tried to convince Seven that Mary had a new lover.

Ricky would park outside and sit, watching Granny Anne's house, for hours at a time. Mary didn't know he was stalking her to start with. One day he called her and informed her that he knew what time she went to bed, because he saw the lights go out. Attempting to ignore his continued criminal antics, Mary kept all her blinds and curtains closed.

This behavior wasn't invisible to Seven, who couldn't figure out which parent to trust. While his father fed him lies about his mother, and his mother grew more distant from his father, Seven became more and more confused. This went on for nearly two years, before the divorce case ever saw a court room. In that time, Seven's behavior was out of control, with Ricky assisting on getting him addicted to numbers of prescription medications and allowing him to drink alcohol.

With Seven's abnormal mood swings, Mary assumed it was the divorce proceedings that had Seven all messed up. She hoped that with time, her son would understand.

As Mae had grown into a young mother herself, she'd long ago gotten over the injustice of losing her childhood. Well, she was actually working on it in therapy, but she held no notions that Ricky would ever admit, all the things he had ever done to her. Mae didn't have any expectations of anything the day Mary and Ricky met at the Chambly County Courthouse for their divorce proceedings.

Mary's attorney, Barker Reynolds, was what Mae described as a "rogue Rottweiler" loose in the courtroom. Ricky had a new and inexperienced attorney named, Steve Parker. The case started with Ricky Levine being called to the stand.

Sitting in the very back of the courtroom, Mae had worn a black dress, and sat with Mary, Thulah and Mary's friend, Peggy. What happened next, no one could have foretold, but for Mae, it was one of those moments in time she'd never forget.

As Barker stood up, to take his turn questioning Mr. Levine, the words that came out of his mouth, made Ricky turn a greenish-grey color.

"Mr. Levine..." Barker's voice carried throughout the big room. "Who is that girl, right there?" His finger pointed toward Mae, at the back of the courtroom. "The one dressed in black?"

Ricky's eyes followed Barker's finger to her, and with the rest of the spectators, everyone looked. Nothing came out of Ricky's mouth; he looked scared, as if he was seeing a ghost from Christmas past or something worse.

"You know who she is don't you Mr. Levine, you know her very well?" Barker continued while walking around, with his back to Ricky. "Because, Mr. Levine, she happens to be one of your many victims! Isn't that right?!" He swung around and walked right up to the witness box. "Isn't she one of your pedophile victims?"

Mae was in shock, not expecting Ricky Levine to be put on the spot. It was giving her a warm and tingling pleasure to see him squirm.

Ricky looked up at Judge Bryant listening to the case, and then his eyes met Mae's from the back of the room. "Yes, she is."

"What's that Mr. Levine; speak up because I didn't hear you." Barker had his prey in a gripping hold. "Didn't you spend time in prison, for molesting many others also?"

"Yes." The defeat could already be seen on his face.

Ricky managed to receive visitation, but would never obtain custody of his son.

After the divorce, Seven went numb, and decided neither of his parents could be trusted with his well-being. He had a problem's at school too. Just like Erik, Seven had a bully that decided to target him. Unlike Erik, who wouldn't run, Seven found running to be an easier way to handle the situation. It would have worked out fine, if the school hadn't called Mary to inform her, he'd been absent for over a week.

Mary couldn't understand how her son wasn't in school, when she personally dropped him off every morning. Going home she found him hiding in the shed in the back yard. It turned out, as soon as she dropped him off, he'd walk back home and stay until after school.

Scolding him, Mary could understand why Seven didn't want to deal with some boy beating him up. "But you will have to find some way to handle him. It's the law son; you have to go to school." Mary had put one bully away, but she knew it took years in the legal system. She hoped the two boys could somehow come to terms with each other. She talked to the school staff about the problem her son was having, but it did little to halt the tormenter.

Seven found the answer to his problem, by befriending his assailant. It was easier to follow him, than to go up against him. J.B. as the bully was called, taught Seven many dangerous tricks of the trade for dealing with life. Coupled with Ricky's continued determination to destroy his ex-wife's family, poor Seven couldn't figure out which way was up or down.

Chapter Twenty Four

Mae was attempting to come to terms with her distressing past in therapy. She'd learned how repression was a natural mechanism by which her brain was attempting to protect itself from threatening thoughts by blocking them out. Where Mae thought she couldn't stop thinking about past pain; it turned out, she'd block most of it out entirely. Pretending she had it all together, Mae had never stopped self-mutilating throughout her life since her early teens. For years she had harmed her own body and kept it concealed from everybody, because she was embarrassed she did it. With therapy she would try to figure out why she had the need to start with. The need wasn't an everyday event, but whenever bad things happened, or people she loved, hurt her feelings, Mae would quickly and mechanically hurt herself in private, taking a broken piece of glass, and slice her forearms, to watch them bleed. Initially, just glancing back in time at her past, she had to learn to be patient with herself. She didn't want to hurt herself anymore, and she was determined to find her cure.

The custody battle with Jacob was taking its toll on her emotions, and her moods were on edge. She had hired Barker Reynolds as her attorney, but he never assured her she would win. They both had mud to sling at each other, but inevitably like with all divorces, the children got caught up in the middle.

Holding a job wasn't hard, but presenting herself to the public was exhausting. Inside she felt as scared as a three year old in a haunted house. It was difficult to trust anybody. She worried constantly that others would look into her eyes, and she the petrified little girl, screaming to get out. She wanted to present a tough exterior, to ward off anyone, looking to attack. She never wanted to be a victim of anybody's again. Sometimes she worried what it would take to send her over the edge entirely; she tried to keep her spirits calm and her soul at ease.

"Okay, you lose your kids. So now, what are you going to do?" Her therapist was teaching her to allow the worst case scenario to come to mind, so she could learn to deal with it squarely.

Mae looked at him hard, and allowing the thought in her head felt like swallowing nails. Big tears escaped her normally controlled emotions. "Well, I'd get on a visitation schedule and start paying child support."

He smiled at her. "That's right Mae; you will survive this no matter which way the judge decides."

The pending custody case would take almost a year to see the inside of a court. She was allowed to see the three children whenever she wanted. After realizing she would survive losing custody, and never be removed entirely from her children's lives, she began analyzing some of her past, starting with the damage done by Ricky. As she began her descent into her trauma, she was met with opposition from another male, as Joel Tripp moved back to Alabama and right into Mae's life and home.

Loving her daddy had never been a question for her; it had been a major part of the problem. Despite all the pain he'd caused, Mae had always needed him and his approval of her. On the surface Mae appeared excited and happy to have her daddy back in Alabama, but within her heart and soul, a terrified little Mae screamed to get away from Joel Tripp. Desperately she had always longed to have a "father/daughter" relationship with him, but that had always been hampered by the fact Mae couldn't live up to his expectations.

Immediately after his return, Mae's life erupted out of control. Innocently at first, her daddy stepped back into her life, but quickly it became apparent that Joel wanted full regulation of not only her existence, but Erik and Mary's as well. Mae's breakdown took a few weeks in the making, before her second suicide attempt. Having already sought help for her mutilation problem, the return thoughts of suicide wasn't anything she ever thought she would suffer from again.

Joel Tripp had many changes in his life, after being committed to the state mental hospital in Florida. His parents were both dead, and he lost his sanity along with his job at NASA. After moving back to Alabama, he stayed with Mae, while looking for a house to buy. During the day he also looked for employment.

On the particular day that Mae insists caused her nervous breakdown, Joel had gone over to Mary's house, unbeknownst to Mae. While Mary was at work, he let himself into her home, which she had managed to keep in the divorce settlement with Ricky. He sat and talked to Erik and Seven for a while, then brought Erik over to Mae's house.

Mae wasn't aware of any of her dad's antics, so when Mary called to find Erik, she laid into her daughter first. Mary voiced her displeasure in Mae for allowing Joel to come into her house and take her son, without her permission. She was on her way over, so Joel Tripp better be ready, because he had crossed the line!

Mae questioned her daddy and told him of how mad he had made Mary. His response wasn't anything she had expected or wanted to hear.

"He is my son too, and I've had enough of her damn shit!" He suddenly lost that docile demeanor that had plastered his face for days. "I tell you what..." He roared as he began pacing back and forth in the living room. "I know how to fix this!" He smiled at Mae and pointed his finger into the air.

Looking over at Erik, who had never experienced this behavior from his father; Mae got a mirror view of what her own face must have always looked like when Joel blew his top.

"Daddy, you shouldn't have just gone up into her house." Mae's words did nothing more but pour gasoline on the fire.

"That's my damn son too Mae!" He growled while pointing at Erik. "I don't have to deal with her shit anymore, and do you know what I'm going to do?" His tall, six foot frame grew inches whenever he lost his mind, and the heat of his rage would cause the temperature in the room to go up. "I tell you, I have the solution to this problem right out there in my car, under my seat, and I am going to empty it into her head!"

Mary's car pulled up into the yard, making Erik and Mae stand up and look.

"No! You sit down and don't move!" Joel ordered Erik, who was now showing signs of distress himself. He sat down, as did Mae. Pushing the screen door open, Joel marched straight out to his car, while Mae jumped up and grabbed the cordless phone.

"It's going to be just fine, you are not in any trouble, and this isn't about you." Standing in the door way, watching the scene unfold, Mae added. "Just stay there Erik; no matter what, don't look."

She couldn't allow Erik to see his father killing his mother. Debating what to do, should she call the police on her own father, or just wait and call after he killed her mother? What the hell was she supposed to do? Mae held the phone, looking at the numbers, and then looking at her parents. The questions were flying through her mind, while the seconds were ticking away on the clock.

Mary went right for Joel; verbally she attacked him, red faced yelling, pointing and threatening, while Joel slowly opened his car door.

"You will not come up into my house, you have no right! Nor do you take my son without permission." She wasn't going to back down to him like he remembered; Mae could tell her mother was angry enough to physically rip Joel's head off.

He kept reaching down toward his floorboard, which Mae began to fear, he would produce his shiny 38 special. Squeezing her eyes shut, Mae couldn't believe what she was witnessing again, after so many years; it was like she'd gone back to the 70's. Should she wait for the gun to come out? Or should she call and have her daddy arrested? What if both parents were arrested? All of this had made the beautiful sunny day, surreal with prospects of double homicide occurring by nightfall.

Like a light switch being turned off, Mae could feel a dark stranger looming from her past. She'd never imagined having to deal with it again, believing she'd been cured of ever wanting to just be dead. It wasn't worth it though; life was far too confusing and painful. Nothing really ever changed; it just kept coming back around. At that moment, Mae began to wonder if she wanted to live another second longer.

The shadow followed her everywhere she went, all day and all night. She loved her children with every molecule of her being, but the hateful thoughts would question if they would be better off without her? How could she even think such things? Her common sense would argue the children didn't deserve to live their lives with a reality of a mother who had abandoned them to suicide. She fought it off like she'd never had to fight before.

She was spiraling out of control, and couldn't do anything to stop it. The dark assaulted her with more and more absurd questions and facts. What good was she? If she had been worthy, then why had God allowed her so much pain? It was punishment, for sins! Church became a constant, as she attempted to fight back, to refuse to give up on her life.

A trigger of Mae's mutilation that had taken a while to figure out was that when someone she loved, hurt her, it caused her so much intense internal pain, she'd physically attempt to take control by attacking herself. An unconscious way to counter balance the pain she couldn't control, with pain she could.

The results of that day Joel came so close to shooting Mary, would leave both parents angry at their daughter. Mary had assumed Mae was in on what Joel had been doing. She didn't like Mae letting her daddy stay in her house; it bugged her how easily Mae opened her world up to him. Joel was irate as he accused Mae of always taking her mother's side. No matter which way Mae turned, she was hurting the two people she had nothing to do with choosing as parents. The two people she couldn't help but want to love and be loved by. Both parents continued to put her in the middle of their disputes and hatred.

Once Mary found out how close she came to being shot by Joel Tripp, she was angry that Mae hadn't called the police. They confronted each other one evening in Mary's house. Mae had hoped she could reason with her mother, but Mary wouldn't budge an inch over her feelings concerning Joel.

"You have no right letting that man in my house!" Mary was still seeing red, weeks after the incident.

"I didn't let him in your house!"

"You knew what he was going to do! I'm sure you knew something was up when he showed up at your house with my son!"

Mae tried but couldn't articulate her words, and they began to come out at such a pace and in such profanity and seething anger. These feelings she tried to keep under control, and only allowed them out in the safety of the therapist office. She'd never spoke such words to her mother, but she couldn't help it.

Mary was as lethal with her tongue as Mae, and the two went to battle with words. The onslaught had both boys shut up in their room, neither one enjoying listening to the two degrade and put each other down.

"What did you want him to do, shoot and kill me? Get out of my house!" Mary threw out the fatal stabs. She had no idea what was on her daughter's mind, and at that moment, she didn't care. She hated Joel Tripp, and anyone who was on his side.

The words Mary spoke to her daughter were on target. Mae took off out the back door. Her mother had every right to be hurt and angry. Since the day it had happened in her front yard, Mae had felt such guilt over how close to death Mary had been. Having both parents angry at her for loving the other, was more than she could take. Getting into her car, she drove back home at break neck speed, with tears blinding her eyes. Nothing would ever be right, no matter which way she went. She couldn't hold onto anything she loved. She feared she was going to lose her kids, her attorney showed no signs of the case being an easy one. Her mother was right; she was not a good person.

Death was the only way to find any peace, and as her car sped home, she considered crashing into a tree, just like her daddy tried to do years before. If only death was certain, and just crashing into something held no guarantee of demise. No, she wouldn't try to injure herself; she'd be more successful than that. She cried from that day on, irritating trails of wetness flowing non-stop out of her eyes.

She had a life, three beautiful children, a loving family, a good job, and every reason to live, but it was too late, the plan was put into motion. Her brain circled around and around the injustice of life, and how even if she had a happy moment, it was far more temporary than the painful ones. Mae gave no clues to what she was thinking; she went to work on that Monday as she normally would, smiling at her customers at the convenience store. Her fellow employees would be in shock to hear what she'd end up doing later that night in the quiet of her home. No one near her would have ever guessed.

That evening she had visited Joel, and he noticed something about her that disturbed him, but he couldn't put his finger on it. "You look…tired."

"I'm having trouble sleeping at night." She wasn't lying to her dad, she couldn't sleep.

He gave her a bottle of sleeping pills that he'd had prescribed to him for the same problem. "Here, try these, they help me."

At home later, she sat on her couch, crying and holding that bottle of pills. She'd already bought a box of sleeping pills, and was thinking how horrible her daddy would feel, if she used his pills to end her life. She knew what that would do to any parent, and instead of taking his pills, she swallowed the entire box she bought herself.

Walking around in a daze of emotions, Mae waited patiently for the pills to start taking effect. After twenty minutes, she began to feel sluggish, and her body began to struggle to stay alive, while her spirit refused to give into the sinister darkness. She picked up the telephone, and called her therapist, deciding to talk to him about the issue she now faced. They carried on a conversation for well over ten minutes, and just when he thought he'd adverted trouble with his patient, she gave him the bad news.

"Oh, well, I've already swallowed the pills."

"What? When? Oh Lord! No Mae! Oh no…"

An ambulance was called, and they got Mae to the hospital. Pumping her stomach helped some, but she'd given the pills long enough to dissolve into her system. For two days she slept, waking up occasionally to catch one or the other parent, looking down at her with worry. After that, she was placed into a mental hospital, where she'd spend the next week being observed and counseled. It was during this week of her life, she'd be transformed forever.

Spending those days in a mental hospital, opened her to the realities of her own life's story. True she'd been hurt, but sitting in group, surrounded by everyday people, who hurt too, opened a door inside her soul. Looking into their faces, Mae could picture them outside the hospital, holding normal jobs, with families and friends, why would they want to die too? Out of all the people she would have the experience of meeting; one lady would never leave her mind.

The lady didn't speak much, and at first Mae didn't notice anything unusual about her. The lady didn't resemble your average "crazy", more like your sweet grandmother or Sunday school teacher, except for the circle of staples, around her neck. The metal anchors also were needed to hold her hands and feet onto her body. That sweet woman had literally tried to cut her own feet, hands, and head off.

Now Mae might have thought she'd always felt pain, but after the experience of meeting another human, whose pain was far worse than she had ever imagined, it opened her every sense to human sorrow and how it affects one and all.

Change occurred within Mae to such a level, that she never looked back. Her new awareness, made her grateful to be alive again, no matter who or what might come along in any twenty four hour period of time to erase her sanity. Never again, has she felt an urge to take her own life, in that dark place where there is no hope. She challenged not only herself, but anyone who came to her with their shadow of sorrow, to hold on to hope at all cost.

Chapter Twenty Five

Ricky continued to envelope Seven's life with alcohol and prescription pills. The divorce from Mary hadn't stopped his need to be in her life. Within time, Seven began to recognize his father's behavior towards his mother as dangerous and criminal. In the back of Seven's mind, he started believing his father could possibly be wrong about his family. In his heart, he hoped so.

The only one who knew that Seven had become hooked on pills was his father, who'd provided them for him to sell to his school friends. Slowly the excessive liquor and medications began to create an ugly monster. Everyone noticed the change in Seven, yet it was blamed on his parents unpleasantly long divorce battle. No one could have known the extent of the damage Ricky was purposely causing. It gave him something to point his finger at Mary about, questioning her parental skills and accusing her of neglecting Seven, while spoiling Erik.

Seven had stopped blaming Erik, recognizing the relationship with his brother as authentic, no matter what his daddy said about it. It would be with Erik that he found his foundation of trust, and the two continued to be best friends. Erik had gotten his license and a nice little car, which gave the boys a new sense of freedom. It nearly cost both of them their lives.

Both of the boys had stopped over at Mae's house, visiting for just a minute, before they jumped back into Erik's car to ride back home. Watching the little silver Neon pull out of her driveway, she frowned as Erik gunned the engine and tore down the road. She had a new boyfriend, a local man named Rex Smithfield, who stood outside with her, observing the teenagers driving away.

"If he doesn't slow down, he's gonna wrap himself around a pine tree." Shaking his head back and forth, Rex spoke mostly under his breath, but Mae heard him and agreed.

Within fifteen minutes they got a phone call. The boys had wrecked the car, both were taken by ambulance. Erik had lost control going too fast around a sharp curve; ultimately they hit a pine tree, and literally wrapped the car around it. Erik was trapped inside the vehicle, while Seven was ricocheted out the back window, throwing him with such force; it bent the metal frame of the front seat he was in and left both of his shoes in the front floorboard. Landing fifteen feet out the back of the car, Seven jumped up, panicked over his brother being trapped. Seven was so upset; they had to tie him down to the gurney to keep him still.

Both boys were very lucky, Erik ended up having to go to Birmingham and stay for observation, while Seven was released with a badly bruised back and leg. Mae brought him home with her, where he paced the floor all night long, worried over his brother. He had been given pain pills. These unlike the ones his daddy gave him, actually had his own name on the prescription bottle.

Weeks later, Seven would end up being hospitalized, with his kidneys shutting down. Once he had his own pain pills, he swallowed them down, and went to his daddy for more. Suffering from actual pain, his tolerance levels went up, as did his need for more medications. Now, lying in the hospital with the threat of losing his kidneys, Mary confronted her son. Though he tried to make it seem insignificant, it was obvious he needed help with his problem.

Though Mary had uncovered the truth concerning her son's addiction to pills, it was a lot harder to stop him than she thought it would be. She took her son to the juvenile officer, Pete Grimsby, hoping the man could scare Seven straight. It would be harder than that to reach Seven, whose father had given him permission to destroy his own life.

Ricky had also taught his son that all law enforcement was bad, and because Seven was his son, the law would never give him a fair deal. Seven didn't trust anyone, much less some strange juvenile officer who threatened to lock him up.

He was growing up to be one of the most charming boys in the world. He developed his bad boy exterior, but upon spending more than thirty seconds with him, he would draw you right into his life forever. Despite his father's cold heart, Seven's heart was warm, loving, tender and true. Being an intent and intelligent listener, Seven held no punches and gave it to you like he saw it. His laugh was contagious and sincere, which he shared with anyone willing to chuckle with him. He was well aware of his problems created by his harsh mistakes. He shared his inadequacies' with anyone who cared to listen, and was also willing to seek help, but somewhat skittish over whom he could actually trust.

Mary took him to Gadsden, Alabama, to a rehab called, The Channel. After only one night, Seven ran away, and showed up at home the next day.

Promising his mother, he could get better all by himself, and would change his ways. Knowing he needed a change, Seven broke away from his crowd of friends. This was a big step on his part. He cleaned up his image, and started having relationship's with many sweet and beautiful girls. The mothers of Seven's girlfriends, loved him as much, and for a couple of month's Seven made many positive and rewarding changes, all on his own accord. He kept the truancy officer at bay by actually attending school and stopped doing drugs of any kind, completely.

Ricky still had influence with his son, but as Seven got older, the shingles fell from his eyes concerning his father. Ricky determined himself to control his son one way or the other. If he couldn't have Seven's devotion, then no one would. Escaping his father was nearly impossible, but with his new outlook on life, it became easier for him to disassociate himself from his paternal parent.

Seven would somehow attract the type of people that wanted him all to themselves; the sort of people that would prefer to destroy Seven, then to share him.

Fate would arrive for Seven one day in the form of a beautiful girl.

"She is the girl I'll end up marrying and spending my life with…" Seven came in one late afternoon and announced his true love to Mary. He held a large grin on his face, and his eyes were sparkling with joy. "If… I ask her out."

Having already met several "girlfriends", Mary didn't take notice of this certain girl being any different than the rest.

But Seven's premonition was on target, he had found the girl of his dreams. Sylvia Dean Myers was a knock out gorgeous teenager with thick dark brown hair that touched below her waist line. The brunette doll had dark penetrating eyes that seemed to look right into your soul, and from day one, Seven was madly, passionately and desperately in love with her. Initially no one noticed anything wrong with Seven falling for this particular girl. Within the next year though, his family would have a definite opinion of what was to become a lifetime of despair.

Ricky Levine was losing control over his maturing son. Without the toxic effects of prescription pills, Seven wouldn't listen to his father's schemes to make some fast money. Though as Ricky left Seven's life, Sylvia walked into his place. Soon she would seek to control every scant moment of Seven's world; worse than Ricky ever had.

Chapter Twenty Six

Sylvia Dean Myers was a complicated and complex individual. In the summer of 1996, Seven was fifteen and Sylvia thirteen, when the two first met. Once Seven asked her to be his girlfriend, he would never imagine the time clock started ticking toward the end. Instead, he felt it was only the beginning of his intended and dreamed about life.

Seven's new girlfriend was eaten up with issues though, too many to name. Her major tragedy was the loss of her beloved father that took place before she was a preteen. This event had not only traumatized her, but her entire family. Her mother, Lisa, had even shot herself, in an attempt to kill herself, in her grief. In reality, Sylvia had lost both parents. By the time Seven found her, she had developed an obsessive and deep desire to control everything and everyone around her. She was threatened by love and tenderness, assuming people just wanted to take advantage of her. Constant turmoil and crisis pushed her through most days, and though she couldn't commit to just one person, she enjoyed being able to control Seven with his love for her.

He loved how strong and powerful this young girl seemed. Sylvia immediately became dependent on his presence in her life, and that thrilled Seven even more. Those who knew him could tell he was happy with that constant grin crossing his face and the way he started carrying himself with his head held high. He had new directions and outlooks on life, which included taking care of Sylvia.

At Thanksgiving that year, Seven brought Sylvia to his family's dinner, introducing her for the first time. Nothing unusual was noticed about the young beauty. No red lights or sirens went off warning anyone what was to come with this new relationship. Everyone was more relieved to see Seven looking better than ever, with a positive stance for his future.

It would be easy to just blame Sylvia for what was to become of Seven, but in her defense, Seven made the choice to have her in his life. No one could have known how persuasive and manipulative she was, even at such a young age. She had found her perfect someone, and she didn't want to share him, not even with his own family. She knew there was something beautiful and special about Seven, and her only desire was for him to be utterly devoted to her and her long list of needs.

Having put his old gang behind him, he started hanging with Sylvia's circle of friends which included her older brother, James. Seven had cleaned up by removing the toxic prescription pills once provided by his dad, out of his daily diet. With his new circle of friends, a new form of getting high called huffing was introduced to him. Extremely cheap and dangerous, it's like playing a game of Russian roulette, because every time you get high, you could possible blow up your own heart. Using gold and silver spray paint, they'd spray it into a bag, and then huff the chemical back out of the bag. Soon, everything Seven owned had either gold or silver paint on it. It took Mary a while to figure out what was actually happening to her son with this new high. By the time she caught on to the dangerous new sensation, Seven was hooked not just to the high of huffing paint, but also the exhilaration of being in love with Sylvia Myers.

Of the entire emotions humans feel, love may be the most confusing and the easiest to misidentify. Infatuation, possessiveness, sexual attraction, jealousy and passion have often been mistaken for true love. What the two young teenagers had was in its worst form, obsession.

Behind the handsome young guy with the beaming smile, Seven was a very modest man. He was never happier then when he was surrounded by his family and friends, those he loved and needed in his life. His family meant more to him than any amount of money. Yet his life always seemed to be running faster and faster toward something…but what?

Seven's bliss had always been love of family. Loving them had been his greatest joy, and Sylvia had become very much like family to him. What she brought out of him was a loyalty to his true love of massive extremes. He was willing to sacrifice his own life for hers. The problem was she certainly didn't mind letting him.

In the summer of 1997, Seven had acquired a job working with a private electrician. He was due to be going out of town, and his girlfriend, simply didn't want him to go anywhere. Seven was scheduled to leave on an early Monday morning, but late into the night before, Sylvia showed up after midnight.

Mary was at work on the third shift when she looked up and spotted Seven and Sylvia walking around the store. She was surprised to see her son, considering he had to be up early for his ride to work. She chastised him, and told him to go home. She had no clue the two were out riding around in Sylvia's mother's van, until Lisa called Mary at work, soon after the two had left the store. Lisa informed Mary, that she hadn't noticed it at first, but that Sylvia had taken her keys out of her purse.

Whenever Mary got home early that morning, her phone was ringing as she walked in the front door. It was Seven, calling from a gas station.

"Hey Mom, can you come pick me up?"

"Where are you?" She began fussing at him. "You're supposed to be leaving for work here shortly! Are you in Sylvia's mothers van?"

"I know Mom; I'm in Fayette, near the library. Can you come and pick me up or not?" His tone was urgent.

"Well, it looks like I've got no other choice now do I?" Mary hung the phone up. "What was he doing in Fayette? He need's this job…" Grumbling to herself, she grabbed her keys and headed out the door.

Desperate is what she had started being, feeling an irrecoverable desire to put some distance between Seven and Sylvia. Since he fell in love, it was difficult to keep him away from her. They both had started slipping into each other's windows at night, and Lisa would call Mary to tell her she had put Seven out after finding him in her house.

Lisa liked Seven, but didn't condone his sleeping with her daughter. Mary would have to do the same, whenever she found Sylvia hiding in Seven's room. Sylvia's excuse to be there was always a good one, which Seven would defend.

"She can't go home Momma!"

He would have, what he believed to be a good enough reason, to just take her in and support her. Sylvia's two older siblings, James and Beverly had fights with her weekly. Beverly's boyfriend Ray would beat on Sylvia also, at least this is what Seven believed. With a passion, he desired to protect Sylvia from any and all pain.

The drive took about ten minutes and as she arrived in the tiny town's limits she saw her son standing on the side of Highway 51 next to a church. Pulling over to pick him up, she noticed Sylvia sitting down on the churches steps. Seven opened the door, and motioned for Sylvia to get in. Mary noticed that Sylvia appeared bruised and shaken up.

"What happened?" Mary stared at the ugly bruises on Sylvia's face.

"We wrecked the van." Seven slid into the front seat, after putting Sylvia in the back.

"SEVEN!" Mary nearly went off the road herself, looking back at Sylvia. "Are you okay?"

Sylvia only nodded her head up and down. Both of her eyes were blackened, bearing a resemblance to a raccoon.

"We lost control on a dirt road, we didn't know where we were, and we got lost, and wrecked." Seven tried to calm his mother down.

"Seven, you've got to go to work, remember? What were the two of you doing in Fayette on some dirt road? Lisa has called me, and told me her van was taken." Mary was now fuming, and couldn't help but feel like this was all a plan on Sylvia's part to keep Seven in town. "You just got this job! You need this job!" As they passed by the house, Mary dropped her son off, and took Sylvia home, so Seven wouldn't miss his ride for work.

On the way to Sylvia's home, Mary asked her. "Do you want me to go inside and talk to your mother with you?"

"No, it's okay." Still in the back seat, Sylvia looked into the rearview mirror at Mary's two eyes looking back at her with concern.

Mary drove herself back home, debating what the two kids had done. She didn't worry much about having sent Seven on to work. After all, it had been Sylvia who stole the keys and van. Sylvia had woken Seven up, and got him into the stolen van with her. Who was the one driving the stolen van? Sylvia was only 13 and Seven just turned 16, but neither had a license to drive. Who wrecked the van? Obviously it was Sylvia who had the suspicious air bag bruising all over her face, not Seven. No, sending Seven out of town for work was for the best.

Later that day, Lisa called Mary again, and got really irate once she found out Seven had left town.

"Your son not only stole my van, but he totaled it out!" Lisa nagged.

"You're full of crap Lisa; you called me and told me Sylvia took your keys and van!" Mary defended her son.

"You dropped your son off over here, I saw you!" Lisa threw back.

"No I did not; your daughter picked my son up!" Mary's voice was raising an octave.

"Sylvia told me exactly what happened, and it was your son who stole my keys and van." Lisa accused with vehemence. "Then he took my daughter, in my van and wrecks the vehicle with my daughter in it!" Lisa cried.

Mary could now understand why Sylvia didn't want her to go in and talk to her mother, when she drove her home. Sylvia had completely blamed Seven for the entire incident.

"No, Lisa, it was your daughter driving the van and your daughter who wrecked it." Mary tried to calmly explain. "I mean your daughter was hit by an airbag, which is located in the steering wheel. Look at her face!" There was nothing Mary could say to change Lisa's mind. Mary made her mind up at that second, she didn't like Sylvia and she certainly didn't like Lisa.

Lisa's brother was the registered owner of the wrecked van. He made a police report in order to get his vehicle's insurance to either fix it or total it out. The result was an investigation of the stolen and wreck vehicle by two minor and unlicensed drivers. A court date was set.

Month's had gone by, so all the evident bruises were long gone from Sylvia's face. Right before the judge, both Sylvia and Lisa accused Seven as being the thief of the van, as well as being the one who was driving it at the time of the wreck.

Pete Grimsby the juvenile officer looked over at Mary and Seven, giving them both a "shame on you" look.

Though all of this playing out before her in a court of law was surprising, what really shocked Mary the most was when Seven addressed the judge.

"It's true, I did whatever they say I did."

Mary bumped her son with her arm. "No you didn't Seven, why are you lying?"

But he ignored her.

Seven would spend the next year of his life locked up at the Juvenile Detention Center, located outside of Birmingham, Alabama city limits. Mount Harper is where they send the bad boys, and to where Seven would spend an entire year locked up for Sylvia.

This action of loyalty to Sylvia deeply disturbed Mary and Seven's siblings, but on the other hand, it prolonged his life. Huffing paint had become an obsessive habit of his, so his being locked up kept him from the dangerous practice. The bonus was it separated him from Sylvia.

After his first initial depression of being locked up in a place he couldn't escape from, Seven's head started to clear up of all his warped perceptions. With each visit and phone call from his family, he began to sound more like himself.

It was during one of the visits with Seven, that he educated Mae on the lies his dad Ricky had told him, about how his mother's family felt about him.

"I thought… well I believed you couldn't love me or even like me being around you. I figured, I reminded you of what my daddy did to you. That's what he told me." Seven revealed his secret with shame and guilt still dripping from his soul.

Mae was shocked, not just with the evil lie told by his father, but that her brother had spent even one second believing such nonsense, much less years of his life.

"Seven, I love you with all my heart, always have and always will. You're as much as my brother as Erik. How dare anyone say otherwise?"

He had also believed Owen and Thulah didn't love him or like him. It broke Mae's heart to think of his now shattered memories of childhood. She wanted to personally, put Ricky out of his misery.

Because of Mount Harper, the relationship between Seven and Mae grew deeper than it ever would have, if he had not been forced to stay put in one place long enough to find out the truth. After finding out what Ricky had told his son, Mae would spend the rest of her life worried at all times, that Seven doubted her love.

Seven's heart warmed to the knowledge he was loved dearly by every single member of his family. Mae's three children, Melina, Cameron and James Robert, worshipped their Uncle Seven and enjoyed visiting him, even though he was locked up. For the first time in his life Seven realized how important he was to his family, and it inspired him with new purpose to live. He felt good, and started planning his life apart from his previous relationships. If anyone had taken Sylvia's accusations against him wrong, he had. It made him realize, his life meant nothing to her.

While in Mount Harper, Seven would develop a new love for 'birthday's'. Turning seventeen that year, a visit with him fell around his birthday. Mae and her three, Mary and Erik, brought a picnic of food and drinks, along with a cake. They all sat outside and Seven shared with all his fellow inmates. He would become hooked on the sensation of sharing and fellowship on his day of birth - all the way to the last minutes of his life.

Chapter Twenty Seven

Dear Mae, What's up big sis!! Not much around here. Just sitting around, reading your letter. I'm glad I have changed. I feel a lot better than I did before I came here. I'm glad that you are explaining things to me. I have been through a lot of painful things, but you have been through more. All we can do is learn from these painful experiences. All my life, I did think that no one loved me, but now I know that my family loves me and I love my family very much!

I wish I would have listened to you and Mom, but I was hard headed and didn't want to listen. But now I see.

So what have my little angels been doing? I hope they put their clothes up, I'm pretty sure they have. I just got done with mind. What's Rex been up to? Probably working huh? Tell him not to work too hard and take care and I'll see him soon. Tell the angels that I said hey and to behave and I'll see them soon too. I'll see y'all later. Love ya, SEVEN

While Seven finished up his time at Mount Harper, Mary moved their home. She had her doublewide relocated onto her parent's property.

The Baker's had five acres total, including the wooded pasture land. Generations had walked the long ago farm, which provided all the early twentieth century necessities. Edward Baker and his tiny wife Jane Stone bought the property from Jane's mother. Together they raised their five children on the farm. So years before little Marion Mae frolicked the property, it was marched on by dozens of family members. By the time Mae and her siblings and cousins came along, it was a deeply rooted home for many.

Mary's younger brother Frank and sister Denise had families also. Uncle Frank married his sweetheart Kate Catherine, and they had two children, Marie and Mark. Aunt Denise married an extremely quiet fellow named Jack, and they had three boys, Cross, Bobby and Lewis.

Mary, Frank and Denise had their own childhood memories of the farm.

They remember their grandmother Jane, catching chickens in order to wring their necks for Sunday dinner. Jane was a wonderful story teller, sharing terrifying tales about the wild wood cats that roamed the woods behind the house. They would listen while bundled up on a large feather mattress. They loved spending the night, and waking to the sounds and smells of breakfast being cooked, in the little brown house. Their grand paw Edward use to walk to the back of the acreage and fish in the fresh water creek running across the back of the property line. Whenever it was time for supper, Granny Jane sent their dog Bo to fetch him, to which the dog faithfully retrieved his owner every time. After Edward died and Jane had to be put into a nursing home, Owen and Thulah moved into the house with their three kids, who were in their late teens.

Once Mae came along, she held the position as the only grandchild of Owen and Thulah for five years, and was the center of attention at the Baker house during that time. Aunt Denise would give birth to Cross once Mae was five and soon after Bobby. Mary then had Erik, while Uncle Frank and Aunt Kate had Marie. Aunt Denise had her final child, Lewis, followed by Mary giving birth to Seven the same year. The last grandchild of the Baker's would be Mark, Uncle Frank's son, and the only one to carry on the Baker name. Once Mary married Ricky Levine, Terri Lynn and Angel, rounded out all the grandchildren, all of which were raised to call the Baker's land their home.

Out of all the grandchildren, all of which held The Baker house and land close to their hearts, Seven was the only one who dreamed of living there. Something about the place soothed his troubled soul, and in his heart, he felt it was the safest place on earth to be.

Uncle Frank and Aunt Kate lived in Louisiana, and would only visit a few times per year. Aunt Denise lived in Southern Alabama, near Muscle Shoals, and could visit more often. Mary's boys, Erik and Seven, were not only cousins to Denise's two younger boys, Bobby and Lewis; they were like brothers, because they were so close in age.

Seven and Lewis would disappear usually for hours at a time, into the dense pasture land, and reemerged only to eat. So many family events and traditions tie the bonds that hold generations together. Birthday's, Easter hunts, cookouts, Thanksgiving and Christmas. The land meant family, and for Seven that's all he ever really cared about.

By the end of 1998, once free of Mount Harper, Seven's outlook had changed concerning his life and what he wanted to do with it. Finding out his father had lied to him; he realized how precious he really was to each and every one of his family members. He rededicated his life to his siblings, building unique bonds with each one. Having always taken pride in being an Uncle to

Mae's three, as well as Terri Lynn's son Stan and Angel's young son's Simon and baby Bruce, he spent time with each one.

Seeing his home sitting on the Baker land was like a dozen Christmas's and birthdays all in one. Mary had put their home on the only place Seven ever felt safe, the Baker land. Some folks like to travel the globe, but Seven's bliss could be found right there on that five acres. As if a child again he played, running, jumping, climbing and exploring every square inch of that property. Everyone felt warm and fuzzy feelings concerning the Baker land, but Seven, belonged there. It was almost like that land completed him in some way, and as he loved it and it seemed to love him back.

Chapter Twenty Eight

Sylvia had never left Seven's mind. He kept his feelings concerning her away from his family to start with. Actually he couldn't stop loving her, no matter what anyone said about her, she seemed to be a destined part of his life and soul.

Mae didn't concern herself over her little brother's girlfriends; she had her own family to contend with, as did Terri Lynn and Angel.

Mary didn't want Seven anywhere near the girl.

Sylvia's troubles were far from over, and it wasn't long before Seven was drawn right back into her life. Throughout the year of 1999 while the world worried over the Y2K computer disaster, Seven's family helplessly watched him fall deeper and deeper in love with Sylvia.

In April that year, Joel Lee Tripp died, and Seven would serve his siblings Mae and Erik, as the head pall bearer at their father's funeral. Seven had chosen to be an active part of his siblings lives, and he wanted to help anyway he could.

He helped his mother and grandmother, Thulah, by doing odds and ends around their homes. He visited all his sisters' families often. Realizing what his father had done to Mae and Terri Lynn, it touched his heart, and it seemed he felt he owed them for his fathers' crimes against them.

Not only did he want to take care of his entire family, he wanted to take care of Sylvia's too. Lisa, Sylvia's mother, had become very sick, and Seven would do anything she asked of him. Though Lisa really appreciated and like Seven, her brother Lonnie and daughter Beverly, despised him.

Beverly was much older than Sylvia; more like a second mother to her little sister. She blamed Sylvia's behavior on the stress their mother was in. Sealed minor records hold the secrets of a troubled girl. Sylvia had issues, and Seven wanted to do nothing more than to take care of her and make her demons go away. With Lisa being sick, Beverly was left with the control over Sylvia, and she absolutely didn't like Seven being anywhere near her family.

Sylvia would later tell Mae, that she and Seven led Beverly to believe that she had another boyfriend, who was not Seven. They continued to sneak around, while Beverly was convinced "Jay", was her boyfriend.

That summer, Seven and Sylvia went with Rex and Mae to Six Flags over Georgia. Seven nor Sylvia told Mae that they were not supposed to be seeing each other. Only Seven's family knew how much he loved her, more and more every day. No one could see anything dangerous or unusual with their relationship, it mimicked all the other young teenage love stories.

By the end of the year though, things would take a turn for the worse for Sylvia. She ended up incarcerated again into a girls' juvenile detention center. While she was locked up, at the beginning of 2000, her mother died. Beverly blamed her sisters issues for the strain that ultimately killed their mother, and she bitterly refused to let Seven anywhere near her Sylvia. Beverly would never accomplish keeping the two of them apart, nothing nor no-one, would or could ever come between Sylvia and Seven.

Their relationship only grew stronger despite how Beverly grew more determined. Once Sylvia became pregnant, she told Beverly it was "Jay's" baby, which seemed to make Beverly happy. Every time she saw Seven, she hated him more, and threatened to lock him up for statutory rape if he didn't stay away from her little sister. Beverly liked Jay; the one she believed was the baby's daddy.

Seven excitedly announced the pregnancy to his family, in the summer of 2000. He couldn't keep secrets from his mother or siblings, and besides, he wanted everyone to share in his happiness, especially his Momma.

Mary wasn't thrilled, but she knew by looking at Seven that her approval really mattered to him. She could only try to support her son, who wanted nothing more than to own up to his responsibilities concerning his child. While Seven began putting in more time at work, trying to start saving money, Mary invested a thousand dollars in fixing up a nursery, and preparing room for Sylvia to move in after having the baby.

Sylvia continued indicating to her family that Jay was the soon to be father.

As the middle of summer rolled around, Seven wanted to get married to Sylvia for his nineteenth birthday. All the preparations were made, blood work and license was obtained. Cake and punch for a small reception afterward. Seven floated around on cloud nine for weeks leading up to their big day. Unfortunately on the morning of the planned wedding day, his wallet went missing, with his identification. Searching all day, Seven looked so sad and let down, while trying to assure his bride to be, that everything would work out. Though they didn't get married on his birthday as planned, it didn't detour Seven one bit. Seven loved Sylvia and their baby, and nothing could keep him from taking care of them.

The next day his wallet reappeared in the laundry basket. He kept his spirits up despite the minor mishap, but something in the pit of his stomach began to sour. Something didn't feel right. He worried that Sylvia didn't want to marry him.

"I think Sylvia hid my wallet, to keep from getting married." Seven confessed to Mary one late night..

"Why would she do something like that?" Mary had a hard time believing Sylvia didn't want to tie Seven down.

"Because; her family doesn't accept me, or want me anywhere in her life…" Seven was confused, but he tried to keep things in perspective. Nothing mattered but making Sylvia happy, and whatever he had to do to accomplish that.

It didn't take long for Beverly to uncover the marriage plans or the fact Sylvia was seeing Seven, and telling him he was the father. In a rage, Beverly became determined to keep her sister from the devil, Seven Levine. Hell would freeze over before she ever let Sylvia be with Seven. With full control and custody of her minor sister, Beverly threatened to put her into a state home or juvenile detention.

"And if that baby in your stomach belongs to Seven, you'd be better off to abort it or miscarry." Beverly would never except any spawn of Seven's. She washed her hands of Sylvia, and made plans to lock her away until her twenty-first birthday.

In desperation to keep Sylvia out of juvenile jail, Seven made a phone call for help. He didn't know the man he was calling, but got the number from Sylvia. Seven appealed to the man and was relieved when the fellow decided to help Sylvia. Eagerly the man drove from Georgia to Alabama to pick up Sylvia, and take custody of her until she was of age. He agreed with Seven, who was only a stranger to him; they didn't want Sylvia giving birth behind locked doors.

Sylvia and her siblings had an older half-brother named Craig, from a marriage their father had previous to their mothers. Craig lived in Athens, Georgia, and Seven encouraged Sylvia to move to Craig's house until she turned 18. Her due date for delivery was only a few days before her birthday in January.

Sylvia didn't trust Beverly or want to go to jail, so she took off to her oldest brothers, who welcomed her in with open arms. Craig had no problem at all with Seven, he tried to talk him into finding work in Athens, but Seven had a home, and intended on bringing his future wife and child to it, once Beverly had no control over their lives.

Rumors continued to swirl around him that he wasn't the only prospective father of Sylvia's baby. Any chance Beverly got to talk to anyone that cared to listen; she would inform them Jay was the father. She would even go so far as to explain, she knew when the baby was conceived, because she caught them having sex not long before she got pregnant. Seven would hear all the stories, but stayed adamant over his belief, he was the dad.

While Sylvia was safe in Athens, Seven spent every moment preparing for the arrival of his child. With his mother's help, Seven got everything the baby would need, including bed, car seat, stroller, clothes, diapers, bottles and dozens of odds and ends. Mary would provide the transportation back and forth every week to Athens, so Seven could see Sylvia. He was working hard to provide her with everything he thought she might need. Happily he looked forward to the day he could bring his baby home to the Baker's land, where he now dreamed of raising a family with Sylvia.

Seven continued loving the land, and would still spend the night back in the woods. Of course, Sylvia had spent some nights back there with him, but he also shared his campground with Terri Lynn and a close friend named Jason. Out of all the grandchildren of Owen and Thulah Baker, Seven was the only one who literally slept out on the land. He dreamed of putting a home back in the woods, where the small creek cut through. All his simple dreams were coming true, and he wouldn't let anything or anyone crush his aspirations for happiness.

As January grew closer, Sylvia's belly grew bigger. After finding out she was pregnant, she and Seven had quit doing all drugs. Seven grew clear headed and determined to provide for his family, while Sylvia became increasingly depressed. She missed her mother, and having her own baby, made her think about Lisa all the time. She would fuss at Seven that he wasn't with her enough, though he tried to explain he was working for their future.

His focus was always on Sylvia, and her needs. What she needed, he needed. Sad to say though, Sylvia needed a lot of attention. Though the family had gotten a small taste of what she was capable of doing to Seven when he spent a year of his life locked up. Having counted that as a needed blessing, Seven had no intentions of ever being locked up again. Between work, visiting Sylvia, eating and sleeping, he was too busy to do anything else. Anytime, Seven was away from Sylvia, it literally drove her crazy. She allowed herself to believe Seven was seeing other girls, whenever he wasn't with her. No matter what legitimate alibi he had, she always felt he had others on the side, and she'd spend what little time he had with her, accusing him of cheating.

Chapter Twenty Nine

Bella Dawn Levine was born late one evening in the first week of January 2001. Mary and Thulah had traveled over to Athens, to be with Seven and Sylvia for the birth.

"Seven came running out of the delivery room, nearly skipping to us." Mary relayed the birth announcement to Mae soon after the new arrival, and explained how Seven reacted to the delivery.

"'It's a girl Momma! She's a perfect little girl! Oh Momma, she's so pretty! We have a little girl!'" Seven announced, crying and dancing about.

"He couldn't believe she was so tiny and she was part of him. He was beaming with pride." Mary too, was bursting with pride for her youngest son.

Pictures show him gazing in wonder, holding her close, as he rocked her gently.

A week later, after Sylvia turned eighteen, Seven brought his family home to the Baker land.

Mae would begin taking pictures right away of her new niece, and of the two proud parents. Seven appeared scared in many shots, while Sylvia looked uneasy.

No one knew what was going on in either parents mind. As all new parents go through that initial shock of bringing a tiny human home and learning to adapt to a completely new way of life. No one saw anything going on under the surface; everything appeared as it normally would, as stressful as being a new parent can be.

Before Bella was three weeks old, Seven and his family would get a first-hand, clear view, of what they would be dealing with for the remainder of Bella's infancy.

Along with a pressing need to provide everything Sylvia and baby Bella needed, Seven was emotionally overwhelmed. Though he knew a baby was on the way, until the moment of actually seeing her and listening to her tiny cries, did he realize how serious the situation was. She was beautiful, and he couldn't get enough of the fact she belonged to him and that he had made such a pretty baby with the girl he loved.

Reality slapped both young parents in the face. Before the baby, their only goal had been to be with each other. Now here they were, a small family, living together, and it apparently wasn't what Sylvia thought she wanted. Seven worked every day, leaving her at Mary's house, where he assumed she would be okay, but Sylvia didn't want Seven to leave her for one minute.

Another issue that became an object of wrath for Sylvia was because

Seven refused to change Bella's diapers or give her a bath. Instead of trying to understand why he wouldn't, she made it her jumping point for other inadequacies she found in him.

Seven had always wondered what had made his father a child predator, and sadly, he worried about what people thought of him, because of his father's behavior. He feared that because of Ricky's pedophilia, he might be thought of as a monster too. He couldn't imagine anyone hurting his daughter. He loved Sylvia so much for giving him little Bella. Blindly he was assured by his family, that Sylvia's dark and depressed mood was normal.

Around this time, Aunt Denise's youngest son, Lewis was staying on the Baker land also. He was living temporarily with Thulah, whose house sits about 75 feet in front of Mary's. Lewis and Seven had always been as close as brothers; with Lewis being only six month's older than Seven.

Innocently enough, after Seven would leave in the morning, Sylvia would call up to Thulah's, and ask Lewis to come help her with the baby. Not only did Sylvia start calling on Lewis, she began to take trips during the day time. Her friend Reese Parker would come pick her and Bella up.

To begin with Seven wasn't thrilled, but he tried to allow Sylvia freedom. Whenever he got home from work, she would complain about having to stay home all day, while he got to get out. She began to let it slip, that Lewis was taking better care of her. This started a small fire burning in Seven's mind, wondering what was going on while he was at work. Soon he would be informed by her that she was visiting, Uncle Mac Lorne, who Seven knew was an old drug dealer friend of hers. All hell broke loose as Seven vented he didn't want her nor his infant daughter around those people, no matter how innocent she was in visiting them.

"I forbid you from taking my baby over to that place!"

With time and experience the entire family of Seven's would learn the hard way, that to forbid Sylvia Myers from anything is like shaking a red cloth at a bull.

She then began to entice Seven into thinking she and his cousin Lewis, were seeing each other, to which a bitter battle between the once loving cousins began.

The Baker family had always been loving and respectful of each other, but Sylvia wasn't anything like them. If getting what she wanted, meant she had to destroy an entire family to get it; that was no problem for her at all. She even told Seven, his brother Erik was looking at her all the time, and making her feel nervous. By the time Bella was three weeks old, Sylvia dropped a bombshell onto Seven. After he got home from work, she announced she was leaving him, and taking Bella with her.

"You can leave, but you're not taking my daughter!" Seven drew a line, refusing to let Sylvia take his child to God knows where.

"She ain't your daughter!" Sylvia's words were like bullets hitting Seven right in his heart.

"What?" He had no air to breath in his lungs suddenly, and his world began to fall apart as her words made their deadly mark.

"You idiot, she belongs to Nathanial Walker; she ain't even your baby, so you can't tell me what to do with her!" Sylvia began putting Bella into the infant car-seat. "And I ain't staying here with your Momma, I don't like it here."

Helplessly, Seven watched as Sylvia tossed the baby into their newly acquired used car, and drove away in a rage. What had just happened? Her words had torn his heart out, and he didn't know what to do.

Finding out Lewis had gone behind his back had already weakened his heart. He had always known how some people rumored Bella was Jay's baby, but he was in on that ploy to trick Beverly. If at any time, he had thought Sylvia had been with another man, he never would have signed that birth certificate. Everything he had worked so hard, for so long to accomplish, had crumbled around him in one moment. Loosing Sylvia was painful enough, but whenever she took away his paternity and baby daughter; Seven's heart shattered into pieces.

Chapter Thirty

Nathaniel Walker wasn't a stranger to Seven, they had at one time been good friends, living in the same neighborhood, and sharing classes back in their earlier school days.

"Sylvia Myers is pregnant with my baby, and I'm going to support her and the child."

Nathan was so convinced that he was the daddy of Bella, he had already informed his wife, and mother of his two children. Taking care of Sylvia was his top priority. It was too bad that Seven Levine thought the baby was his, but Nathan figured his old friend would get over it.

If there was only one other man involved, it would have been bad enough, but Lewis had also been easily seduced. Unlike Nathan he found himself full of guilt over hurting his cousin. Similar to Nathan, he would continue to be willing to do anything for Sylvia. The relationship put a strain on Seven's entire family.

Mary blamed Lewis for causing problems between Seven and Sylvia.

Aunt Denise charged Sylvia for bewitching her son.

Thulah was mad at Sylvia, Seven and Lewis, all three for the mess.

Seven grew despondent, and couldn't figure out what he had done wrong. He'd lost Sylvia, his daughter, and two best friends. Overnight he changed dramatically. His pain tripled with the knowledge so many of those he thought he could trust had stabbed him right in the back. Everything he had so much hope for was now only a shattered dream. Loving Sylvia was one thing, but loving that baby girl was a love Seven had never experienced before, much less anticipated it being taken away. Sylvia not only had control over him with his emotions for her, but now she could easily manage him with the love he had for his daughter. Holding her close to his heart, examining her little toes and fingers, listening to her tiny cry, he never expected to fall in love so hard for someone he never met before, and now she was gone from his life. It tore his soul apart to hear that another man fathered his baby. He just wanted to make Sylvia happy. He had provided everything she asked for and more. He had loved her with every molecule of his being. How could she so easily, play games with his life? Why couldn't he make her happy?

Mary had never seen her son so sad and it made her worry. The day after Sylvia left and robbed Seven of his paternity, Mary watched her son carefully. Observations revealed he didn't care to live anymore, and then came his direct approach.

"I want to die." Was just about all he could articulate.

No one believed Seven would attempt to kill himself, having never threatened to do such a thing. This was different, his heart was bleeding, and he was experiencing grief like never before. He spent that day planning how to do it. Having put huffing paint behind him, it became part of his plan. The pain he was feeling was so intense, he couldn't comprehend living one more day under its pressure.

While Mary tried to secure the only weapon on the property, her daddy Owen's rifle, she talked to Mae on the phone.

"I'm worried about him, but I have hid the gun so he can't find it. Even if he does find it, I know he has no bullets for it."

Mae tried to assure her mother that Seven was very strong, and he would pull through this, but Mary wasn't so sure. As they talked, Seven had put his plans in action. Hiding something from Seven on the Baker land was futile, he knew every square inch. Easily finding the 'secured' rifle, he had gone across the street to the old gas station, where he got some bullets for his grandfather's twenty two rifle. Mary just happened to glance out her bedroom window, while still talking to Mae.

"OH MY GOD!" Mary screamed into the receiver. "He's got the gun!" The panic in her voice could be felt through the phone.

The hairs on the back of Mae's neck stood on end. "Momma call 911, I'm on my way!" Immediately, Mae got into her vehicle and made her way to the Baker land, only ten minutes away, but it felt like ten hours before she pulled onto the property. A few police had already arrived as Mae jumped out of her van. Without a word, she tried to run down toward the trail, where Seven had gone, but the police wouldn't allow anyone to go down into the woods. Erik and Mary both stood by, looking helpless.

"What are we supposed to do just stand here and wait until we hear a gunshot?" Mae's words brought urgency to the surreal moment.

Erik couldn't stand it, and ignoring the police, who were hiding behind their patrol cars, he ran down the trail, determined to stop his brother.

While Mary and Mae stood by waiting for a gunshot, Sylvia appeared, having got a ride with a friend. She too attempted to run down to Seven, with the cops stopping her in her tracks. She didn't choose to stand with Mary and Mae, but hung around watching.

The silence was unbearable, and the seconds felt like hours. Mae noticed a young police officer, with a giant grin going across his face. It struck her the wrong way. What could this police officer possibly find amusing about the horrifying situation? Before she could inquire, Mary spoke up.

"Just what is it that you find so amusing about this?" Mary folded her two arms and glared at the smirking officer.

Mae wondered the same, but was slightly surprised at Mary's bluntness.

At first he looked shocked that she would speak to him that way, considering he was the law.

"I don't appreciate your attitude one bit." Mary continued without giving him time to answer.

"Well mam, if you have a problem with me, you can file a report with my chief." The officer continued grinning.

"Oh, you can bet I will, Woody Muck!" Mary pointed her finger at the cop, who suddenly lost his grin.

"Now, Ms. Mary, you know me." The officer tried to reason with the upset mother, but it was too late.

"Yes I know you, and remember you well. That's why when I file my report I won't get your name wrong."

Woody had worked at the Department Store with Mary before he became a cop. Now he tried to smooth things over but the situation was grim. The last thing Mary needed was some smart ass cop making light of Seven's threats. Mary worried what could be going on between the brothers and the gun.

They continued to wait for what seemed an eternity before Erik suddenly appeared holding the gun above his head. All the police who were hiding came out, pointing their guns at Erik now, until he handed over the weapon.

Mae took off toward the woods, running as fast as she could, to get to her baby brother. As she approached him, he was standing, looking lost and defeated. Blankly he looked back to Mae. Wrapping her arms around Seven, she hugged him tightly.

"Why? Why Seven? Don't you know how much we need you? Don't you know how much we love you? How much I love you?" Shaking him, Mae looked into his eyes that were now brimming with tears. The smell of spray paint wisped past her nose, and she noticed the empty can sitting on the ground. Pulling him with her, Mae began walking back towards the house. Not knowing what to say, she continued trying to encourage him. "It's going to be okay, I promise…" She began.

"NO, it's not okay!" He began to speak with tears streaming down his face. "She ain't my baby."

Mae wouldn't accept that. "Yes she is, I know it, I can feel it in my bones Seven. Bella is yours."

She tried to help, but Seven was beyond her grasp. He couldn't believe it anymore, and it hurt no matter what anyone said.

"Listen to me…" Mae continued to try to make her brother understand. "I don't care what Sylvia says! Besides, she isn't worth you killing yourself over."

Later Erik would describe what Seven was doing when he showed up.

"Luckily I got to him when I did, because another minute and he would have shot his own head off. He was just standing there, with the barrel of the gun in his mouth, and his fingers were trying to push the trigger back. He didn't see me, and didn't stop me from taking the gun out of his hands. He continued to just stand there, looking past me."

Seven had huffed paint, so that he could pull the trigger. It was something he could never have done sober.

Having lost not only Sylvia, but his daughter, Seven was in constant, desperate pain. He wanted to be Bella's father so bad, it had become a mind numbing situation. Desperately he longed to have Sylvia back, but that was only a shattered dream now.

The only thing Bella was to him now, was another way for Sylvia to use him, control him and manipulate him. Her power and control was extended over Seven's entire family, who worried about Bella as well as Seven's mental state.

Chapter Thirty One

Seven's sobriety went down the tubes. He couldn't stand feeling the pain caused by Sylvia's lies. Was Bella his baby? He didn't know for sure anymore, realizing his true love had apparently been seeing other men. Now she had his cousin Lewis following after her, and since it was difficult for Seven to be angry at Sylvia, he turned his fury on his cousin.

"You stay the hell away from Sylvia! I mean it Lewis; I'll kill you if you don't!"

Sylvia learned quickly that Bella was a great tool in dominating Seven's family. They loved Bella so much, but Sylvia refused to let them see her, unless she got something out of the deal. She didn't need Seven's family; she had her own, as well as a growing list of prospective fathers and their families. She moved into a home with Charles Wheeler, a guy fresh out of jail, living with his parents. She continued to tell Nathan Walker, he was the father, and she was seeing Lewis also. She never stopped trying to get to Seven. Every single day, she would find him, and relate how well her life was without him..

Close family bonds would eventually pull Seven and Lewis back together. Mary and Denise had always loved each other's kids, just like their own. Seven couldn't help but to love Lewis, no matter what Sylvia did in attempts to fracture their relationship.

There were other key factors in the two cousin's rekindled ties that had absolutely nothing to do with the drama Sylvia created. The Baker family didn't have time to play games with Sylvia once it was discovered they were losing one of their own.

Aunt Denise had become a respected and loved RN, who had worked hard to get through school, while raising her three boys. Though her health had begun to deteriorate, it took years to diagnose the rare disease. The news took the entire family by surprise. She was suffering from Scleroderma, a rare condition, also known as Systemic Sclerosis. It can affect many organs and tissues in the body, particularly the skin, arteries, kidneys', lungs, heart, gastrointestinal tract, and joints. It is an autoimmune disorder, in which the body's immune system attacks its own tissues.

Mary was losing her baby sister, and Sylvia's playing around with Seven and Lewis didn't go over so easily now that Denise was dying. Mary felt Sylvia had absolutely no excuse for her seductress behavior, or the way she was treating her son and granddaughter.

The strain of losing Denise was enough for the family to endure, but Sylvia could care less. She enjoyed the unscrupulous power she had not only over Seven and his family, but all the families of the other men she was seeing.

It didn't take her long to figure out how much she could control Seven, and his entire family with their love for Bella. From the tender age of three weeks, Bella became a pawn. She enjoyed the unscrupulous power she had not only over Seven and his family, but all the families of the other men she was seeing. Charles Wheelers parents wanted nothing more than to protect the infant from Seven Levine and from what they heard, his mental family.

No matter how hard Seven wanted to be free of Sylvia, it was never going to happen. She never had any intentions of ever letting him go. Even though she was sleeping with so many men, Seven regrettably still loved her with all of his heart. The bond between the two would only grow stronger the more Sylvia hurt him.

"I've got Sylvia bringing the baby over her for a visit this afternoon!" Seven showed up at Mae's front door, excited over the news. He looked at Mae, hoping she'd be pleased with his impromptu arrangement, to which she welcomed him in. He had on nice clothes, and had strategically put on what he claimed was Sylvia's favorite cologne.

"What time is she coming over?" Mae worried that Sylvia wouldn't show up, and how it could crush Seven's weakened spirit. "Has she decided that you're the daddy?"

"I don't care if she is my baby or not, I love them both, and I just want to take care of them."

His sincerity touched Mae; it was something she knew her brother meant. He perceived Sylvia as his equal, a strong woman, whom he would give the stars and the moon to if he could. Seven had tried to come to terms with the fact that Bella wasn't his daughter.

"After all, she has green eyes." He enlightened Mae. "Which neither Sylvia nor I have. But, Nathan Walker..." He further explained. "Has blue-green eyes just like Bella's, and strawberry blond hair. That's who her daddy is."

Mae refused to believe that eye color had anything to do with what her heart and gut instinct told her, which was that Bella, belonged to her brother. She didn't argue with him though, refraining from ruining his good mood. She felt that he had lost the baby once, and just couldn't bear to lose her ever again. Mae was content to just see him happy again.

As he waited for Sylvia to show up, he played around with Melina, Cameron and James Robert. Growing up, they were like his little siblings and they all three adored having him at their house.

Arriving on time, Sylvia brought the baby inside. Seven was excited to see Bella, but the baby had been kept from him for so long, she didn't show any signs of recognizing him. Instead of allowing that to dampen his spirits, he moved his attention to Sylvia, as Mae took over showering her little niece with past due affection. Sylvia was riding with her friend Reese Parker, who had the car still running. Reese had a baby that belonged to Sylvia's brother James, but the two were not raising the baby together.

Seven was thrilled to see Sylvia but she didn't share in his exuberance. They stood outside talking on the front porch, Seven holding onto her hand, begging her to stay with him for just a little while. Seven could have many women, but he stood there, begging her like his life depended on it. At one point, she agreed and Seven came inside to get the baby to take outside. Before he got back to the porch he noticed Sylvia running toward the car, which was already backing away. Handing his daughter to Mae, he ran out the door, jumping from the porch with both arms wide opened.

"WAIT! Wait! Where are you going? Sylvia! Please wait!" Seven screamed as the car backed away. He ran toward the car and slammed his hands on the front hood. "Why are you doing this?" The car pulled forward threatening to run over him. Backing up with his hands in the air again he screamed. "Fine leave!" He pulled his Timex watch off and threw it at the car as it sped away.

Chapter Thirty Two

Without Sylvia, Seven had no direction in life, and no reason to do anything. He went through the emotions of wanting her back, and never wanting to see her again.

By March 2001, Sylvia had moved out of Charles Wheeler's parent's house, and moved into her Grandmother Sadie's apartment. Beverly had taken it upon herself to be "in control", of baby Bella. She continued to try her best to persuade Mae into realizing the truth about Bella's paternity.

"I know how much y'all want Bella to belong to Seven, but I saw Sylvia and Jay having sex, and nine months later, she gives birth to a baby that doesn't look anything like Seven."

Nothing would sway Mae's determined gut instinct, and Beverly's words floated in one ear and out the next.

Baby Bella would be without the needed stability and security necessary for a newborn baby. Before long she became sick with respiratory infections. One late evening in March, Mae received a phone call from the local hospital; it was Seven.

"Would you mind watching the baby tonight while Sylvia and I do some talking? Bella's sick, and she just doesn't need to be out on the streets."

Mae figured Seven knew she'd have no interest in assisting him with talking to Sylvia, but he had no doubts she'd want to get Bella off the streets.

Eager to always see the baby, Mae didn't ask Seven what he was doing with Sylvia; her primary concern at that moment was the sick baby. It angered Mae that both parent's needs and wants seemed to be of more importance than taking care of a helpless human.

Early the next morning, Seven and Sylvia showed up together to get their baby. Mae tried to talk them into letting her keep the baby until they figured out what they were going to do. They refused the offer, even though neither had anywhere to go.

After Sylvia's behavior, Mary didn't want her back in her home, and Sylvia's family never liked Seven, so if the two were together, they were on their own.

Late on March 5th, or early March 6th, while Mary was working on third shift, Seven and Sylvia broke into her home. The next morning whenever she got in, she wasn't happy to see them.

"Pack your things and get out of my house!"

"Mom, the baby is sick, and we needed to get her out of the cold." It always shocked and surprised Seven when his family members didn't forgive and forget Sylvia's behavior as easily as he seemed to.

"I don't appreciate you breaking into my house!"

"She is sick Mom, she needs her treatments, and I don't give a damn."

Both young parents demanded Mary let them stay there, and they used the baby's medical situation as an excuse to let them.

It didn't work with Mary. She hadn't been allowed to see her granddaughter in months, and she wouldn't permit them to use Bella as a tool or weapon against her.

Both Sylvia and Seven vehemently argued, and then they both began threatening her life.

"I'll burn this house down!" Sylvia continued to entice the growing out of control event.

"Get OUT! Neither of you should have rights to that baby!"

"What are you going to do call DHR?" Sylvia took a step toward Mary.

"Somebody should!" Mary wasn't aware Seven had a gun, and once the Department of Human Resources was mentioned, he began to rant and rave along with Sylvia.

"Anybody try's to take my baby, I'll kill them!" The gun went off and a bullet whizzed by Mary, narrowly missing her. Seven swore it happened by accident, but Sylvia said it was justified.

"If anyone ever tries to take my baby, I will kill them! I'll snap their neck!"

Both Seven and Sylvia had started doing drugs again, and Seven was not a nice person when he was under any kind of negative influences. He was extremely temperamental, easily agitated, and dangerously despicable. The mention of the DHR set Seven ablaze, with Sylvia urging him on.

Mary didn't want to, but she threatened to call the cops if they didn't leave.

The next day someone did call DHR, and for some reason, Seven and Sylvia assumed Mary or Mae did the calling.

They were both homeless with a sick infant, and had made both Seven and Sylvia's families mad. There were other families that Sylvia had allowed to bond with the baby, Charles Wheeler and his parents for one. Also, Nathan Walker believed Bella belonged to him. It didn't matter, Sylvia always convinced Seven, that Mary or Mae would be the guilty party for making the call.

Mae didn't call the DHR, but she did want to confront Seven over shooting at her mother. Whenever she received a phone call that day from her brother, she didn't expect him to be so hateful and angry at her.

"Why did you call DHR on us?" His accusation took Mae off guard.

"I didn't. Why did you shoot a gun at Momma?" She threw back at him.

"Cause she threatened us. Look, how about you just stay out of my life!?" His remark felt like little pins poking into her heart.

"How about you growing your dumb ass up and if you're not going to do nothing but try to kill our Mother, how about you stay the hell away from her!" She wouldn't be told what to do by her little brother.

"Just leave us alone, and don't you worry what I do or don't do." The phone went dead.

Later that day, Mae would also receive a phone call from Sylvia, who threatened to kill anyone that tried to take her baby. No doubt the two were desperate. Mae thought hard about it. She couldn't understand how Seven could actually believe his mother or her to be the ones who made the call. On the other hand, they had discussed it, over concern for the baby's well-being.

Within a couple of days, the two would be separated again, and Seven would be calling Mae, apologizing for what he accused her of, but mostly over the mishap with the gun.

"I'm sorry; I know you didn't call DHR."

Mae wasn't mad about that.

"And, I swear, I didn't mean for the gun to go off, I didn't know it would even shoot."

"Seven, it's not right…"

"I know…I can't think straight when I'm with her."

Sylvia had put him to the curb, and gone back to her grandmothers. He knew there was no excuse for his behavior, nor could he take it back.

He promised Mae that he would go talk to Mary, and apologize for what happened.

A wedding had been planned for the end of that month for Aunt Denise's middle son Bobby. Given Aunt Denise's grave condition, it gave the family time to celebrate with her. A trip to go up to North Alabama was made, with Thulah, Seven, Lewis and Mae going up together. The ride up was interesting, as Seven and Lewis sat together in the back of the van.

Sylvia had tried her very best to not only hurt Seven and his entire family, but to destroy a lifetime friendship between cousins, to which she failed.

Seven needed his family, always had, always would, and with God's grace, the cousin's battle over a loose woman, didn't completely destroy their bond. Seven warned his counterpart though.

"You'd better be careful and watch your back; she ain't nothing but a drama queen who likes to play games."

Throughout the time together, Mae tried to reason with her brother over the baby. She appealed to him that he needed to know whether the baby was his or not. He couldn't go on through life with Sylvia holding it over his head.

Seven agreed and before he went back home, he had determined to find out once and for all if Bella Dawn was his or not.

Their precious time with Aunt Denise was the sole purpose of the journey. It would be the last opportunity to enjoy the wonderful person she always had been. Though Scleroderma was robbing her life, she didn't allow it to stop her from living.

Seven found strength in seeing his beloved Aunts will to live life to the fullest. It encouraged him to hold on and fight for his own.

Chapter Thirty Three

Being able to attend the wedding and getting out of town for a few days helped Seven clear his head and think about what was important to him. He came back, wanting proof about Bella, and he wasn't willing to forsake a relationship with his daughter, or play diversions with the mother. Sylvia could do whatever she wanted, but if Bella was his, he would exercise his rights.

This newfound attitude didn't sit well with Sylvia. She wanted to be chased around and she enjoyed playing games with people's lives. She refused to let him see the baby anymore, as well as his entire family, throughout the rest of March. It seriously enraged her that Seven could move on past her, and appear to be happy without her. She couldn't afford for Seven to know whether or not he was the daddy. If he wasn't, she lost her control and power over holding the prospect above his head. If he was the parent, he gained rights, which enriched his dominance and influence in his daughter's life. Sylvia didn't want any man to have management over her, but she neither had intentions of ever letting Seven go.

Sylvia continued using Lewis, and tried to pit the two cousins against each other constantly.

Lewis didn't want to fight with Seven, but couldn't resist Sylvia. She called him every day, begging him to help her, in one way or the other.

Watching her with all the guys she had with her at all times, Seven wanted to be able to move past Sylvia as easily as she had him. He started seeing another girl named Mindy, which only caused a full blown war with Sylvia. He grew tired of fighting everyday with her, and just wanted his sanity back.

Mindy knew Seven loved Sylvia, and they shared a friendship, but once she became a target of Sylvia's hate, she was forced to cut ties with Seven completely, or wish she had.

Seven would be allowed few friends.

By the beginning of April, Bella's lung infection grew worse and she ended up being hospitalized. She would spend her days and nights in an oxygen tent.

Aunt Mae took the opportunity to see her niece, even though she had to endure Charles Wheelers' parents, who believed they had more right to the baby then she did. For Mae, having to put up with Sylvia's family had been enough, so these strange people had no idea who they were messing around with. She visited the baby every day, ignoring the indifferences with the strangers in Bella's life. It wasn't hard for Mae to understand why they loved the baby. She knew the infant was adorable.

Mae observed Sylvia during the visits, who seemed content with her new life, surrounded by Charles and Lewis at all times. Sylvia displayed her new tongue ring Charles got her, while she lay across his lap. Mae didn't pay much attention to the tongue ring, her eyes stayed fixed on Lewis, who could hardly look at her.

Aunt Denise meant the world to Mae, as did her three cousins. Lewis was like a younger brother, and had even lived with Mae one summer a few years back. It was easy to see Sylvia was using him, he even knew it, but seemed helpless to do anything about it.

Once Seven made himself less available to Sylvia, and began pursuing a DNA test, she took it as a personal threat. She told her sister about Seven's attempts to take her baby away. Beverly's husband, Ray, took it upon himself to call Seven and leave him a disturbing message.

"You'd better listen boy and listen up real good; I will personally kill you if you ever come near Bella or Sylvia again. I will beat you to death with my own two hands."

Ray's message sounded threatening enough that Seven decided, with the backing of his family, to take the message to the police and file a report. Seven wanted to go one step further; he wanted to talk with DHR personally, over his concerns with his baby. Thulah, Mary, and Mae went with him to try to get some help for Bella, but they would all find out the hard way, Seven had no rights as long as Sylvia denied his paternity. He was told to get an attorney.

Sylvia would still lead Seven on, using Bella. He was torn over loving his baby, and worrying she wasn't even his. Longing to just see her, it was easy for Sylvia to lure him right into a trap. Still living with her grandmother on and off, she invited Seven to come over and visit with Bella for a little while if he wanted.

"Oh yes, I'd love to!" He jumped at the opportunity, thrilled she finally offered.

"Well, I don't want to have to explain anything to my family, so you'd better just come through the window in my bedroom."

Her instructions sounded odd, but Seven figured she was right concerning her family. They absolutely forbid him from being anywhere near the baby. Arriving at the appointed time, just like Sylvia said, the window was open. Crawling in head first, something grabbed ahold of him, and yanked him down to the floor. The lights were out, so it was hard for him to see who or what had him. He felt a fist start beating on him, hitting him over and over. Seven was still unsure who had him, and though he struggled, he wasn't going to hit back.

Danny Morey, an old family friend of Sylvia's, had been told by her that Seven threatened to steal Bella, and really feared he would try that night. Danny sat in wait, just in case Seven tried to kidnap the baby or hurt the mother. With his bat in hand, he had full intentions of beating Seven to death. When he was finished with him, Seven was a bloody mess and ended up lying around for a week with a concussion and battered face.

His body and spirit was sore and fading. His mind was growing desperately sick of the on-going situation.

Witnessing her son's hammered face, Mary tried her best to set limits and boundaries on him. She wanted nothing more, then to protect him, and help him. Reaching him was impossible, every topic was too distressing for him to confront. The more she tried to help him, the furtherer he pushed her away. She could only be a witness to the destruction, while praying for a miracle.

Seven was an adult now, no longer a young boy and with his depression came more excuse for him to choose to numb himself to the pain.

For the remainder of 2001, the new eternal on and off relationship between Seven and Sylvia persisted. Turning twenty that summer, Seven continued to use drugs to numb his sorrow. He had some time sober while living with his sister Angel and her family. Everyone wanted to help him, and at times his depression would lessen. While with Angel, Seven managed to hold a job, and almost got his act back together, but not every member of his family had his best interest at heart.

Ricky Levine made himself, and his medicine cabinet full of prescriptions, fully available to his son. Soon, Seven was pulled right back into the life of selling pills for a fast profit. Once he was hanging around his father again, his depression took on a more dangerous pathway of self-destruction. Ricky was still a miserable man, and continued to seek out ways to spread his self-induced deprivation to anyone within arms-length.

"Let's go to the movies!"

Regardless of any pain he continued to dwell in, Seven never stopped pursuing bonds between all of his siblings. He was always insisting "they spend time with him." He showed up at Mae's on a Friday evening, determined to go out with his big sis.

"I mean, I thought to myself today, I've never been to the movies with you, and I thought it would be fun. Rex could even come."

There was something so sweet and sincere with him, that even though movies weren't her thing, she considered it. Both Mae and Rex had flaming germ phobias. Nothing about sitting in a room full of people, appealed to either of them. Yet they both decided it was a great idea, and with the three kids gone to their dad's for the weekend, a perfect opportunity. Seven insisted on paying their way, and seemed content with himself for taking the time to spend with his sister. Watching him though, Mae couldn't help but feel uneasy. Something sad lingered in his eyes, and even though he produced a laugh and kept a grin on his face, she felt the time she had with him to be precious and ticking.

Seven was the only sibling of the five that actively pursued all of his relations, and in the process, developed deep bonds with each and every one. Sure he was troubled with addictions, betrayals and outrageous lies told to him by people he should have been able to trust. But Seven was within himself, trustworthy, and loved sharing his life with those that loved him back.

Seven loved Bella so much with an affection that had snuck right up on him when he held her for the first time. For the first year of her life, he got to be her daddy as much as Sylvia allowed him to be. Being heartbroken, threatened and even beat couldn't make the devotion he had for his daughter just go away.

Was Sylvia jealous of that love? Could that be the reason she wouldn't allow it? Was she serious when she remarked. "I don't like sharing Seven with anybody; I want him all to myself."?

There was no doubt that Seven loved Bella, he tried his best throughout the first twelve month's to be not only a daddy but a worthy mate for Sylvia, but nothing was ever good enough for her. It wasn't fair for father or daughter to be robbed of their one and only chance to bond. The first year would leave Seven numb from the experience and leery of being Bella's father. He'd tried to get a DNA, but Sylvia didn't show up. He let her be with anyone she wanted, and took a beating just to see his baby. What more did she want from him?

Throughout the year, Seven's family had never denied or stopped supporting Sylvia, and she certainly didn't mind asking for their financial assistance. The baby always needed something, and though Bella had a long list of prospective daddy's none of them or their families seemed to care about Bella's basic necessities.

The yo-yo relationship took its toll on Seven mentally, physically and emotionally. He continued to pursue DNA, and in December 2001, he appeared in Chambly County for the second court ordered paternity test. He was eager to know once and for all whether or not he was Bella's father. Unfortunately, Sylvia wouldn't appear that day either, but it didn't seem to surprise Seven like it did his distraught family. He most certainly wanted to know if he was the father, but he grew increasingly tired of playing Sylvia's games. She knew how powerful she was holding the truth over so many people's heads. Seven had told many friends that Sylvia wouldn't show up for court because she couldn't afford for the truth to be known.

For Bella's first birthday, Sylvia went into hiding, so that none of Seven's family could see her. By this time though, her behavior was becoming a little more predictable. The second year would be worse in that no one knew where Bella was. Around March 2002, about the time another court date had been set for the DNA, Sylvia left town and disappeared for the next eight months. The rumor was she had gone to Ohio with Danny Morey. Running away and disappearing would become almost a hallmark of Sylvia's, who believed that by hiding, the problems couldn't find her.

One thing for certain, Seven had no intentions of chasing Sylvia or Bella around, as long as they were with Danny. It was impossible for him to forget the beating he had been tricked into. The black eyes and bruises didn't hurt half as bad as the knowledge Sylvia had set him up to get hurt.

During the second year, Seven tried his best to move on with his life. The pain could be seen on his face every time he talked about his daughter. What he wanted was to be free of Sylvia's control.

"Bella ain't my kid, and I don't want her to be."

Seven would say this, but his face would reveal otherwise. The eternal connection to Sylvia was what he wanted to be liberated from.

In November 2002, Sylvia finally turned over DNA to the courts, and by December the truth was finally known. It hadn't ever crossed Mae's mind as being any other way than the way it turned out. Bella was 99.99%, Seven's daughter.

The happiness was only dimmed in the light of Denise's death. Knowing for a while she wasn't doing well, everyone hoped her disease would taper off. Instead, her immune system started strategically attacking its own organs, and one by one, everything started shutting down. Thulah had moved to North Alabama to help take care of her dying daughter.

Mary had started the process of transferring stores, so she too, could move to Muscle Shoals and help take care of her little sister. It had become painfully obvious, her sister would not live. Denise had made one last trip home, and her condition was grim then. She could hardly hold her head up, and she wanted to plan her own funeral.

At the time of death, Mae was working at a local funeral home, as the Administrator, as well as apprenticing to be a Funeral Director. She tried to help her Aunt with the preparations, but it was far too difficult for either of them to conceive of the thought of life without the other.

The death rocked the entire family to its foundation. Thulah would never be the same after burying her 50 year old baby. Mary and Frank lost their little sister. Cross, Bobby and Lewis lost not only their Momma, but their best friend. Mae as well as the rest of the cousins lost one of their greatest fans. Putting her into the cold December ground was one of the most difficult days of their lives, and like all deaths do, it changed them all in an instant.

Chapter Thirty Four

Seven finally knew he was a father, and though he had this knowledge, it brought no rewards or blessings. He'd believed that once the truth was known, Sylvia would finally allow him to see Bella, without having to have his teeth knocked down his throat by her boyfriend's or hateful words from her family.

With her new proof of paternity, Sylvia's main goals were to pursue child support and continue to control and manipulate Seven. For the next three years, between 2002 and 2005, the relationship between the two mainly consisted of both running away and to each other. The few times Seven did see Bella; she was only confused, which would leave him wounded.

"I just want her to know who I am, and how much I love her."

Danny controlled when and where Seven could see Bella. Usually it would be at Mae's. She was allowed to see Bella monthly and never had a bit of trouble out of Danny. He was always on his best behavior around Seven's family.

"I seriously respect Danny, because he is taking good care of my daughter."

Despite the beating, Seven admired the stability that Danny provided Bella, and though he couldn't do the same for her, Seven was proud someone else would.

What Seven did obtain was a large past due child support amount, being totaled from the day of Bella's birth. Judge Spruce had no tolerance for dead beat dads, and refused to listen to any excuse for back child support. Whenever Seven tried to explain the situation the judge quickly shot him and his plea down.

"Boy, you signed the birth certificate so you knew you were responsible for the baby."

First Seven was robbed of being a parent, and then he was jailed for it. No matter what happened to Seven, it seems he always got the cruel side of justice tossed at him.

Like the time before with Mount Harper, the family tried to believe that Seven's being locked away was a good thing. He had been a drug addict since his early teens when his father introduced it to him. His life was confusing and painful, and anything he could find to numb himself, he'd go to excessive lengths to get. Loving Sylvia and Bella brought him torrents of agony. Drug use, was about the only thing Sylvia wanted to share with Seven. He felt lost, no matter where he was. Being locked up prevented Sylvia or his influences from getting to him, and he felt a strange freedom; only while he was secured behind bars.

With Seven locked up, Sylvia continued playing games with other's lives. Danny didn't see what was coming his way, the "what goes around comes around" part. Every man she ever had would become part of her life that she refused to let go of. One way or the other, like a pit bull with a rabbit, she just wouldn't let go. While she was living with Danny a guy named Peter Roder had moved in also. Pete was hiding from the law at the time Danny took him in. While staying under Danny's roof, Sylvia became pregnant again, in July 2003.

This second pregnancy of hers upset Seven, who had hoped the two of them would eventually work it out. It also amused him to know, he wasn't the only man she sought to destroy the soul of.

"I wonder which guy this baby belongs too?" Seven laughed while talking to Mae from a collect call from jail. "Poor Danny will find out how it feels!"

Sylvia was also seeing another man named Fabio Ranchez, The list was extensive but Seven was completely exempt due to the fact he was in Chambly County Facility for five months, and couldn't possibly be the daddy.

Jail didn't do the trick for Seven this time. Instead it put him in direct contact with some old friends. Getting out didn't really appeal to him. What reason did he have to be free? Bella didn't know him, or show any interest in wanting to. When he got out in March of 2004, Sylvia was ready to pop with her second child. As soon as he was free though, she began making her phone calls to his family and friends trying to regain her control over him. She tried her best to convince him he should put his name on the second birth certificate too. Both amazed and amused that she had the audacity to even suggest such a thing, Seven declined to make the same mistake twice, still hurting over what was pulled on him with Bella. No one except Sylvia forgot what the past few years had been like.

When Seven got out, he wasn't a happy person. Unable to shake his depression, he would end up making a very bad decision. It would haunt him for years, and take complete control of his life.

He'd been staying with Mary, and had started receiving phone calls from Sylvia before he got home the first day out. Wanting to see Bella, but not wanting to see her mother, he attempted to keep the conversation simple to no avail. He'd served time now for his daughter, but Sylvia still controlled the relationship he could have with her.

It took two weeks before Sylvia finally agreed. Seven had worked, and had a paycheck to put toward child support. With his promise of payment he was given an afternoon to spend with his child.

It had been stressful for Seven's family to sit by and watch as he grieved for Sylvia and longed for his daughter, but nothing disturbed them more than his next choice of action.

Mary had been hurt over the loss her son suffered over with Bella, and she'd wanted nothing more than to see him spending time with the little one. She'd missed her granddaughter herself, and was excited that they would be bringing the toddler to her house, without the mother in tow. She believed Seven deserved time with his child. Excitedly she had put the car seat in, and was waiting patiently for Seven to announce he was ready to go.

"Seven, we're going to be late." Mary could hardly wait any longer. Her son came out of his room, all cleaned up unlike she'd seen him in the past year. They headed outside and towards the car, when someone drove up that Seven knew. He started to walk to the car…

"Tell them they'll have to just come back another time, we've got to go." Irritated, Mary headed to her car, got in and started the motor for emphasis that they were leaving.

Seven bent down to talk to the guy, who Mary recognized as Tracey Miller. The last time she had seen the boy was years back whenever she came home from work one morning, and had to call the police to toss him out of her house. She wasn't thrilled to see him now.

"Seven!" Mary got out her car, leaving it running. "Let's go!"

Seven had started to walk around to the other side of Tracey's vehicle. "It's okay mom, we'll go pick her up."

Mary knew very well that if she and Sylvia shared anything more than loving Seven, it was hating Tracey Miller.

"That's crazy; you know she won't let you take Bella if you're with him." She began walking toward them, pointing at Tracey.

"Yes she will." Seven quickly jumped into the car as Tracey started putting it into drive.

"Wait!" Mary was fired up now, and rushed back over to her car, ripping the carefully place car seat out. She hastily made her way to the two young men, opened the back door up, and tossed the seat in.

"You'll need this!" She slammed the door and gave Tracey the ugliest face she could make. She hoped he knew how much she despised him.

"Mom, I'll be right back!" Seven yelled out the window.

She watched as they pulled away, turning into the wrong direction from Bella. In her heart, she could feel Seven had just made a horrible mistake.

The two didn't go pick Bella up; instead they headed out of town to where Tracey lived in Anniston. Sadly, Seven had no clue what was going on behind the scenes, but would quickly find out. Before they went to Tracey's house, two girls had been picked up along the way. They all four were in the car, as Tracey pulled into his driveway. Unexpectedly a hoard of police vehicles swarmed in around them. Tracey immediately jumped from his car and took off running, leaving Seven and the two girls behind, completely stunned. Apparently the local drug task force had been watching Tracey for some time, and it just so happened, the bust on him was going down that day. The items inside the trunk of Tracey's car were enough to charge them all for manufacturing methamphetamine.

Seven was placed into the Calhoun County Jail, and faced major felony charges, that would put him away for well over twenty years of his life. Finding himself locked up again, this time far from home, and facing serious time, Seven grew indignant with the man he saw in the mirror. He had no one else but himself to blame for his critical mistake and foolish decisions.

Dear Mae: Hello, how are you doing sis? Me, I'm doing pretty good, just wish I was at home. Thanks for all that you have been doing for me lately. I know that I have let you down again. I won't ask for y'all to believe in me again. Won't sugar coat it at all, I've gone and f*#!ed up pretty good. I got myself a Class A and Class B felony. The good news is that a lady has come down to talk to me about rehabs. All of them are a year and a half or longer, if not more. I only have a choice of three out of ten because the rest cost money. But I have written to them, and I am waiting for replies. Maybe I can get my bond lowered and get Carl and them to get me out, but I don't feel like asking so I probably won't. Thanks for the pictures. She is so pretty and getting so big. Shame I missed so much of her life. Tell her I love her and I will see her soon hopefully. Tell Sylvia to write me, I have something to tell her, I'm sorry and I'll make it up in time. You know I wasn't using drugs, was drinking, guess that's a drug. How is Maw Maw doing? Tell Mom, I love her. How's your youngen's doing? Well better go, don't feel well. See you sis and thanks. Love you, Lil Bro S.S.L

Soon Mae would be excepting his collect phone calls, and he tried to explain what had happened.

"I swear I had absolutely no idea that Tracey had a lab in the truck of his car. Hell, all he mentioned was he was having a party. I know, I know, I shouldn't have just left, and I know Momma is mad."

"You have no idea." Mae had been listening to her mother's voiced complaints over Seven's choice that day.

"I know, I should have just gone over and picked up Bella. But I just didn't trust Sylvia..."

"Seven..." Mae agreed with Mary, and was irritated with her brother's thoughtlessness. "Your daughter was what should have been your top priority."

"I know...it's my own fault. I shouldn't have ever gotten into the car with Tracey."

Mae didn't want to fuss at Seven; she knew he was already having to face a severe punishment, being locked away from the ones he loved. She'd only wanted him to have a relationship with Bella, and was frustrated his time with his daughter was slipping through his fingers.

"How could I have been so stupid?"

Hearing him choke up, brought Mae to tears with him.

"I've really messed up my life this time."

Chapter Thirty Five

Those that loved Seven were furious and hurt with him.

Mary wouldn't accept his collect calls. She refused to visit. He would receive no aid or support from her in anyway. She watched him walk to Tracey and away from his only child. There was no way she'd ever be able to forgive him for being so senseless.

"If he's doing that kind of crap, then his butt needs to be locked up!"

It would take Mary month's to calm down. She wanted nothing more than for her son to buck up, mature, and do what was best for his daughter. To do what was best for him.

"He promised me he would be right back!"

Mae would be the one to accept his collect calls, and write him letters. For her it was upsetting to know what both Bella and Seven were missing out knowing each other.

Little Bella was growing up fast, turning three in January 2004, while her daddy was locked up. She'd become a permanent fixture around Aunt Mae's and Uncle Rex's house, spending more and more time there.

Seven's time locked up in Calhoun County was incredibly terrifying to him. The facility was nothing like the small Chambly County jail, and he was a stranger in a sinister place. Effectively isolated and alone, he fought to stay sane. Never before had he realized how easy it could have been for him, to just get his life straight. Now, it would appear that all his chances were gone.

Losing more than just his freedom was the loss of his job with Carl Pacer. Owning his own business, Carl had taken a young strong Seven under his wing after he got out of Mount Harper years before. Installing, repairing and replacing windows had been a job well suited for Seven. Carl liked him a lot too, and they worked out of town mostly. Carl had been a good father figure to Seven, and helped get Seven through those years while Sylvia was keeping his daughter from him, by working hard and keeping busy. While Seven had been in the Chambly County jail for past due child support, Carl had promised to hold his job for him. Now though, Seven couldn't see Carl holding that position open for twenty years.

Giving birth to her second child, Liam Scott Roder, in March 2004, Sylvia had gone on with her life. No one, not even Sylvia, was sure who the daddy of Liam was, though Danny's pal, Pete gave the boy his last name. Danny wasn't an individual you'd want to double cross, so soon after Liam's birth, Sylvia left town again, this time with Pete, taking off for Pensacola, Florida, where some of his family lived. Seven's family had no idea where Bella had been taken during this time. But Sylvia didn't stay down in Florida for too many months, before she moved back.

Eagerly Mae got in touch with Sylvia and arranged for Bella to spend the night over. The toddler was growing up quickly, and had begun to talk, a lot. Most of her conversation was innocent and sweet, but then something's that she shared were shocking.

"I have a new step daddy named Timothy!"

It was a name that Mae hadn't heard before, and she wondered if the fellow was real or not. The baby had so many men pretending to be her daddy that she couldn't keep up with all of them.

"Don't you mean Pete?"

"No, Momma married Timothy. I don't like Pete, he hurts me. I like Timothy." She swirled around while talking. "Timothy is nice because he buys us lots of food."

"What about Danny?" The baby was talking, and Mae wanted to know.

"I like Danny. Danny is really nice." She ran off, leaving Mae's head full of questions that she knew the baby could never answer. The words, "Pete and hurts me…" also circled around in Mae's mind.

Mae doubted Sylvia would actually get married. It had been something Seven had begged her for. But when Sylvia showed up to pick Bella up, she confirmed her daughter's announcement.

"Yep, I'm married." She would elaborate no further.

Mae wanted to question Sylvia about Pete hurting Bella, but she figured that might be why she was no longer with him.

"So Pete…."

"He is a thing of the past." Sylvia was evasive and careful with her answers.

No one told Seven about the marriage, not being sure how it would affect him. Somehow though, the news made its way to him behind bars, and it crushed him to pieces. It ruined all hope. He'd begged her since they were young teenagers to marry him, but she never would. Now she'd gone off and married some guy she had just met. It lit a fire in him, to improve his own life, to move on, and put Sylvia into his past.

Luckily, he was given the opportunity to trade jail time for rehab, which he gladly excepted considering his incarceration would have been twenty years. It wouldn't be as easy as he thought either. The program was no picnic, and with its many strategic rules and regulations, Seven had a lot of issues to face and many decisions to make. He focused all his efforts, on getting better for his daughter. He dreamed of being a father she would be proud of.

Being in a rehab gave his family the opportunity to visit with him face to face. With every visit, he looked stronger and happier. On one trip to see him, Erik, Mary, Mae and Bella spent an hour with him. He explained to them how much his life had been wasted, and how he planned on turning it all around. His new goals included staying in Anniston and working with other drug addicts to come clean. The rehab program was so impressed with his change of character and determination to succeed; they had offered him a position on the staff, once he completed his required time.

Sylvia began have marital problems with her new husband within weeks of their "I do's". Timothy didn't like sharing her with her long list of necessary boyfriends. Danny Morey was still a fixture in her life, hanging out with her in Timothy's house.

"Timothy turned off our lights and is going to put my momma in jail."

Bella continued to share in her life with Aunt Mae, who kept trying to figure out what was going on.

Uncovering Sylvia's struggles were nearly impossible, she being so secretive and quiet concerning her life. Though at times, she could be quite talkative, it depended on what type mood she was in.

It was true though, her marriage was on the rocks, and Timothy would successfully have Sylvia put in jail several times at the beginning of 2005.

Danny continued to play a part in Sylvia's life as Bella would relish little details here and there.

"I like Danny and Timothy, but they both want to be with my momma."

Mae worried what was going on in the little one's mind? During a trip to the store with Aunt Mae, as Bella was sitting in the front of the buggy in the check-out line, she asked her Aunt a question.

"Do you steal Aunt Mae?" The inquiry was innocent enough, but took Mae off guard as she was taking items out of her buggy.

"No, I don't." Mae laughed to herself, but wondered What the almost four year old could possibly know about stealing. "Why?" She asked the innocent girl, whose piggy tails hung down the sides of her head.

"Danny does, he showed me how to do it. It's not hard Aunt Mae." Her green eyes were wide and dancing... "I put things inside my shirt for him all the time."

Aunt Mae looked in horror at the small girl smiling back at her.

"Sweetie, Aunt Mae doesn't steal, I pay for my things, and you shouldn't steal either." She tried to explain.

"But Danny does it all the time." Bella looked confused.

"I don't care. It's against the law honey, and he will end up going to jail, if they catch him doing it." Mae spoke with seriousness, looking over her little niece wondering if she'd stuck anything in her clothes when she wasn't looking.

"Oh..." Bella was chuckling. "They can't catch him!"

Chapter Thirty Six

After a year and a half in rehab, Seven continued to get better. His experience had changed his life completely, and sobriety cleared his mind, giving him the chance to really dig in, and make himself a better person. Throughout the time, he'd tried to put Sylvia into his past with his many other mistakes. It was impossible to cut her out entirely, with her being the mother of his only child.

Bella turned four at the beginning of January 2005, while her little brother Liam would turn one in March. Their mother remained in-between relationships, but Sylvia was well aware of the fact Seven would be getting out during the year. She'd started dropping in on him for some of his visitations. Slowly she worked her way back into his graces.

She never had any intentions of ever letting him go.

It was soon after Liam turned one that Sylvia turned to Rex and Mae for help. Rex had recently acquired an old trailer, and Sylvia asked to rent it, having nowhere else to go. He talked with Mae, and they agreed to help her, mostly for the well-being of the two children.

The trailer needed some work done before they could move in, and Sylvia offered to help fix it up. It didn't take long before Rex was fussing about the number of men who were hanging out with Sylvia at the trailer. Rex ended up running three men off in one day, Fabio Ranchez, Peter Roder, the father of Liam, and another guy named David Looney.

"Unless y'all intend on getting off your butts and helping me paint, then you'd best get the hell out of my way."

They had no intentions of working, so they'd come back when Rex went home.

Within this time, Sylvia became pregnant with her third child, and started insisting the baby belonged to Seven and that they procreated during a visitation she had with him.

Sylvia had a place to stay, but couldn't afford to keep the lights on. She'd decided to go to the Department of Human Resources for assistance. Once the Department found out she was living in a trailer with two children and no electricity, they immediately informed her they would have to take her children, putting them into a foster home, until she could prove she had her electricity on. Threatening to take her children always set Sylvia off, and she managed to get a ride away from the DHR office, keeping her kids. What she did next wasn't as much as of a surprise as who she got to come help her.

Seven had completed his rehab program and remained in Anniston with full intentions of never coming back to Chambly County. His decision had been a painful one to make, loving his family and home. He feared that he couldn't come back, that his past would be waiting to haunt him. In Anniston, he had an entirely new life ahead of him, helping others who suffered with addictions like he had.

"DHR is going to take the children from me."

All it took was one phone call from Sylvia, and he got a ride to come pick her and the two children up, and take them back to Anniston with him. He'd only been out of rehab for a couple of weeks and didn't really have the means to support the instant family, but Seven didn't care. He had fears of the DHR, things his father had told him, and he never wanted his children in the States care.

No one was more surprised than Seven's family by his act of heroism to save Sylvia from losing her kids. Why would he take Sylvia back, after all that she had done to him? Hadn't he learned his lesson? Apparently not, or it could have been he never stopped loving Sylvia. She had been the one to leave him time and again, he never left her, and he never would.

Seven had a job in Anniston, but it wasn't enough money for him to support Sylvia, Bella and Liam. For a couple of month's he tried really hard to make ends meet, while keeping a bored Sylvia housed. Unlike the past, Seven was finished with drug use, while Sylvia had never acknowledged herself as a drug addict. Seven hoped he could somehow manage to change Sylvia, and help her quit that lifestyle.

Maybe if he could have managed to afford to stay in Anniston, Seven wouldn't have moved back to Chambly County. He didn't want to, but once he got Sylvia back, everything started circling around her and what he needed to do to keep her happy. Once Seven spoke to his old boss Carl, and got his job back, he moved his family into Mary's house, back on the Baker property.

The family wasn't thrilled with Sylvia's return, but Seven's happiness outweighed their concerns. It had been almost five years that they had been enduring Sylvia's behavior, but what Seven saw was his opportunity to finally make things right. He looked at it as his second chance to be a father, and be a husband to Sylvia. Of course, she would have to get divorced from Timothy Muck first, but in the meantime, they could plan their own wedding and life together.

Baby Cassandra Sue Levine was born the same month Bella turned five, January 2006. Seven had no idea if Cassandra was his baby or not. Sylvia claimed they had conceived the baby while she visited Seven in rehab. Either way, Seven refused to sign the birth certificate, but he loved her as his own from the second of birth. Cassandra would become Seven's only chance of ever enjoying the blessings of being a father.

A wedding was planned for the late summer of that year, and Seven began working extra hard to save money. They planned on getting a trailer of their own, and putting it on the Baker property behind Mary's house. Sylvia got a job working at a Dollar Store, and they began dreaming of their future together.

Sylvia wanted a church wedding, and Seven pulled out no stops to make her dream day come true.

Mary had even begun to believe, that the two of them had grown up and were finally going to make it as a family. She helped them with the kids and making ends meet. She drove them around, dropping the kids off to school and day care. She took Seven and Sylvia to and from work. She helped them pay for and plan the wedding.

The big day finally arrived, and the Church wedding finally happened. Seven floated around all day long, so happy that he was marrying the girl of his dreams. Marrying Sylvia seemed to have been a life-long aspiration of his, and anyone who knew him would tell you, it was the happiest day of his life.

Sylvia on the other hand, was depressed, despite all the hard work Seven had done for her. Absent was her entire family, who still after all the years, hated Seven. No one showed up from Sylvia's side, for their big day. Her brother James, the only one who was Seven's friend, couldn't show up.

Regardless, Seven's family was there for him, and they knew he had loved Sylvia since he'd met her eight years before. Erik served as his brother best man, while Melina stood in as Sylvia's matron of honor. Bella performed the part of flower girl, while Liam was the ring bearer. Mae photographed the event, and one of her friends sang during the ceremony. The day ending as all wedding day's do, with the happy couple, riding off in a car covered in saving cream with tin cans tied to the bumper.

Chapter Thirty Seven

Right away the young married family got to work on saving money for their own trailer.

Seven's job required him to spend most of the week out of town, but with his good income, it was easier to pay all the bills. Sylvia got a management position with benefits, and the extra cash helped them save.

Mary helped any way she could with the kids and continued to let the young family live under her roof. Even though her third shift job made it more difficult to do more, Mary was unrelenting when it came to helping Seven and loving those three children.

The young couple would argue over the fact Seven was out of town so much. The marriage ceremony didn't magically erase the years of mistrust. With sheer determination, Seven dedicated himself to providing for his family, and hoped in time; Sylvia would find faith in him. By the early spring of 2007, they had managed to get their trailer, and had it put behind Mary's house. Everything was falling into place for the young family. Seven couldn't have ever been happier, having his family and living right there on the Baker land, another dream of his come true. He had wanted to put the trailer way back in his beloved woods, but having it behind his Momma's house would do just fine. Living there with his mother and grandmother, the three kids were spoiled rotten. Though he hadn't wanted to ever move back to Chambly County, he felt safest on the Baker property.

Loving Sylvia was one thing, but loving his children penetrated his very soul. Bella was somewhat set in her ways, but eager to adjust to life of having just one daddy. Liam didn't know his daddy, Peter Roder, so for him Seven became his only father figure. Seven remembered how his father had treated Erik after Ricky got out of prison. Liam would never be treated in such a way, Seven loved him as his own. From day one of baby Cassandra's life, Seven had taken the place as her daddy too. He couldn't shake the feeling, that she might not be his, but that certainly never stopped him from falling deeply in love with being her father. Having the opportunity to finally be a full time husband and father, he beamed with pride.

Mary described a daily ritual that she would observe with her son.

"On the afternoons he was due home, Seven's ride would drop him off at the end of the driveway. The three kids would have been watching and waiting for him, and the moment they spotted him they would run to greet him. Bella and Liam would race, while baby Cassandra would straggle behind, running as fast as she could to either keep up with her siblings, or get to her daddy as fast as she could. Seven would reach down and pick up all three, hugging them and holding onto them, while walking home."

It's one of the precious memories of a beautiful young man, experiencing the joys of being a father. He enjoyed it so much, that he began considering a regular 9 to 5 job that wouldn't take him out of town. With Sylvia working full time, Seven believed that he could serve his time better helping with the kids and house more.

Carl Pacer had been a loyal friend and employer to Seven for many years. He always was willing to help Seven any way he could, and when Seven told him he wouldn't be working for him anymore, Carl explained to Seven he had to do whatever was best for his new family. Seven took a local job, which meant his income wouldn't be as good, but he could spend more time at home, taking care of the kids. Sylvia's job came with benefits, they didn't need to lose. He figured that Sylvia wouldn't mind having him around more either, but it turned out he was wrong.

Sylvia had been up to her old tricks, and while her husband had been out of town, she'd been in contact with her former gang of boyfriends. It hadn't been hard for her to hide her affairs, with Mary working the third shift, Sylvia had all night long. She never intended to put her past to rest, and she continued to look for the next best thing. With Seven in town every day and night, it put a major crimp in her "free" time. Worse was when he started noticing her phone buzzing all night with messages, and they argued because she wouldn't let him read any of the text or tell him who was sending them. Sylvia couldn't stand his constant presence, and she started complaining about living near his family.

The summer was hot in the South in 2007, as June rolled around with Seven turning twenty-six years old. He would be entering his last year of life. No one had any inkling that his existence was coming to such a violent end, and he would never get to experience being twenty-seven, except for many tortuous hours laying in a coma.

Seven was sober minded, and when his wife began threatening to leave him, he told her to leave. He'd once again, done everything he could do to make her happy, and as before, it seemed he failed. Instead of fussing he ignored her, and continued working on their yard. He enjoyed being home and taking care of his kid's every day. To his dismay, she left him and her kids, at the beginning of July.

Handling her behavior differently, he stayed in their trailer, with their three kids, and tried to continue as if nothing was wrong. Supper was cooked every night, baths taken, bedtime stories read. Bella wasn't late for school, and Seven didn't miss a day of work. If Sylvia wasn't happy, wanted other men, or didn't come back, he didn't care anymore.

Within the two weeks she disappeared, he even started talking to another girl named Maye. Seven had never gone without a female friend for long, even during all those years he chased Sylvia around. He was a good looking young man, hard-working and highly dedicated to his family. Many young women would have done anything to have half of the love he had for Sylvia directed at them.

His behavior or lack of attention only made Sylvia crazier. Never before had she come across someone that didn't chase after her like a fool. Could Seven just move on and forget about her so fast? Well he didn't, but he wasn't going to play the same games by Sylvia's rules anymore.

On July 11, 2007, late that Friday night, Seven was home with his three kids. Having been alone for weeks, he had company over that night, his niece Melina and his close friend Jason Hanslin. While Sylvia had been gone, Seven had emptied all their moving boxes, putting things up and hanging pictures on the walls. He took pride in having his own trailer, and he wanted it to be comfortable for the kids. Melina was playing with baby Cassandra, Jason was playing a game on the game station and Seven was cooking supper. Suddenly the front door flew open and Sylvia rushed in. Instantly she flew into a rage when she saw how no one seemed to be missing her.

Melina began to take Cassandra to her mother, never before having a reason to fear her Aunt Sylvia, but without warning, Sylvia punched Melina full force in the face, causing her to fly backwards. Melina hit the floor, while she continued to hold onto the now screaming baby. In a flash, Sylvia grabbed one of the kitchen chairs, brought it up above her head, and crashed it down on top of Jason, who was as shocked by her violence as Melina. The chair broke as Jason crumpled to the floor, trying to protect himself from Sylvia's continued attack. Melina, still in shock, with blood oozing from her mouth, put the baby down, and ran outside.

Seven tried to grab hold of Sylvia, to give Jason time to escape before she killed him. Turning her anger on Seven, they struggled with each other. Sylvia punched, spit, slapped, and scratched at her beloved husband, while continually tearing apart the house. Ripping pictures off the wall, throwing garbage all over the place, pulling things out of the closets and drawers.

"How dare anyone decorate my house!" She proceeded to rip it apart.

Relationships can really become complicated when you involve the police. For Seven to have to file a report on Sylvia, it had to be something he felt was extremely dangerous and serious. He detested the police and most law enforcement, due to his childhood and young adult experiences. He wouldn't have ever gone for help, unless it was a traumatic event.

In the early morning hours of July 12, 2007, Seven went to the police for help. It was the first report he'd ever made against Sylvia. Mary had taken both him and Jason to the police station. The move Seven was making, by drawing a line in his marriage, would end up causing the biggest fire storm in the family's history. One year to the date, July 12, 2008, the family would be laying Seven in the ground to his eternal rest.

Chapter Thirty Eight

After the police report, Seven had hoped that things would calm down. He felt bad about it, and never went back to the police department to sign a warrant. He felt guilty for having to do such a horrible thing to Sylvia, as fill out a police report on her. Watching her violent attacks on both Melina and Jason had left him no choice. Wishing they could work it out, it was never going to happen. He couldn't figure out what had torn their love apart. Sylvia had left him, as she had so many times before. Though he pretended he didn't know where she was, she never hid it from him. Unlike the days when drugs ruled his mind and reactions, she couldn't figure out how to provoke him, but she never stopped trying.

Commitment had never been one of Sylvia's best traits, and in all honesty marriage was something Seven had wanted, not his wife. He'd been so busy since they had gotten their new trailer in place, trying his best to fix it up and make it a permanent home for his children. He had grown up on the Baker property, playing, running and exploring. Now he had the joy of watching his three little ones as they delighted themselves with the same childhood bliss. Having taken the in-town job, he had anticipated his wife being pleased. After all, he wouldn't be traveling out of town anymore. He could help more with the kids and house; they would have more time together as a family. Yet as they moved into their new home, before the boxes were ever fully emptied, the marriage in its ninth month completely crumbled.

The two had years of experience with each other, but Seven had changed. His twenty four months of rehabilitation had made him into a new and improved, drug free person. Years back, whenever Seven was on drugs, it wasn't a pretty sight to see when he got mad. Losing his temper had been easier too. What Sylvia didn't realize, because she'd never elected to change or seek help, was that she couldn't push his sober buttons anymore.

It's hard to look at a person like Seven, and think his wife was the violent, abusing one. He wasn't someone you could easily shove around. He didn't back down or run away. If you wanted him, you'd get him. So it's difficult for most people to grasp the reality that Seven was the victim, and Sylvia was the aggressor.

Every day after he changed jobs, Sylvia grew more and more hateful towards him, and his "nosey family".

"You're a sorry piece of shit!"

This would become one of Sylvia's favorite expressions, for her husband. She'd freely tell him, in front of his children, mother or friends. She wouldn't hide her displeasure from him, and she hated him being home all the time. She began to really detest his family.

Mary continued to provide the couple with rides. Before that, she had opened her house to Seven and his family. At no time had Mary ever nosed herself in their life. She would take Bella to school, Seven to work, Liam and Cassandra to daycare and drop Sylvia off at work. In the afternoon she would pick Seven up and the two at day care. Bella rode the bus home. After the Dollar Store closed, Mary would drive Seven and the kids to pick Sylvia up. Mary did this every day, whether she had to work or not. It wasn't until Sylvia got her van, that she decided Mary and her family were meddlesome.

The arguing got so bad, Seven would end up sleeping on either his mother's or grandmother's couch to escape the belittling. He was confused as to what he was doing wrong. He worked and would come straight home every day. He took care of his kids, maintained things around the house and worked in the yard to give the kids plenty of safe room to play. He cooked. He cleaned. He tried to please his wife every day. The more he tried to do for his wife, the madder she seemed to get.

Why couldn't he make her happy? Why was she acting this way? Why had it started after he took the in town job? Why did she suddenly turn on his entire family? She became hateful to him at all times, and soon was physically slapping at him so much he would have to leave.

What happened next urgently worried him until the end of his life. He had been run out of his house, which had become the daily drill. Seven still had to go to work every day. He needed his sleep, so he'd crashed on Thulah's couch.

It was after two in the morning when Thulah thought she heard knocking at her back door, but she figured it was just Sylvia, trying to get Seven back home to continue with their fight. She paid the noise little attention as she turned herself over and tried to fall back to sleep.

Seven didn't hear anything, usually if he got to sleep, it was very deep.

Mary happened to be home that night also, and she too was awakened by knocking at her front door. Opening it there stood Bella and Liam, both crying and terrified.

"I can't find Momma!" Bella cried, holding tightly to her brother's hand.

Liam had awoken Bella in full crisis mode, because their mother was missing. Both small children had bravely walked together in the dark, making their way to their grandmothers' homes.

Mary called Thulah, who woke Seven up.

Until that night, no one had a clue; Sylvia had been leaving her children home alone. Seven couldn't deny what was happening, but he didn't know what to do about it either, except file another police report.

Unlike the years before, Seven stayed calm and determined that no matter what, Sylvia wouldn't provoke him. The more composed he became, the more ruffled it made her. His concentration wasn't on her demands as much as it remained on their children's needs. No one was allowed to take his attention from her, not even her own three kids.

Sylvia was an expert manipulator for sure, but no one would have ever been able to predict what would result from her husband trying to get help for her violent behavior. To the public she portrayed herself as a sweet and vulnerable young mother. She didn't want people to actually be aware of how smart, clever and cunning she really was. Though she pushed Seven away, and continued to entertain her long list of male friends, she violently refused anyone else near Seven, including his own mother and kids. Certain things really offended Sylvia, and one of them was when someone tried to stop her behavior with the law. Once that first police report was made, she became determined to make Seven pay severely. Nearly obsessed with hurting him, Sylvia wasted no time in planning a way to pay him back.

Seven continued his loving pursuits with his siblings. When Sylvia would run him off on a Friday evening, he would find his way to one of his three sister's homes. He was with Terri Lynn and her husband Leonard on the Saturday his wife put her plan into action.

Sylvia continued to hold her management position, and was at work when she called for Seven over at his sister's house.

"Hey, do you mind coming by the store for a minute, so we can talk?"

Seven told his sister what Sylvia wanted, and Terri Lynn agreed she could give him a ride over to the store. She needed to pick up a few things herself. Seven didn't really want to talk, but he did think it best to do it in a public place, as a precaution to trouble.

Walking in, other store employees witnessed him with his hands in his pockets and a smile on his face. He questioned where Sylvia was and was informed she was in the back of the store.

Leonard later explained that within less than a minute, Seven was slowly, and still with his hands in his pockets, walking back out of the store, with Sylvia hot on his trail.

"I'm calling the police on all of you!" Sylvia was dramatically screaming at the top of her lungs. "You people come to my place of employment and try to cause trouble!"

Leonard looked over at his wife Terri Lynn, who appeared as surprised as he was.

Customers and other employees were witnessing the big performance.

Seven never said one word; he ignored her and continued back out to the car.

Sylvia wasn't blowing off steam, she had already dialed 911.

The police department was around the block. They eagerly believed every false accusation Sylvia made about both her husband and his family.

Now when Seven and Jason had made their earlier reports to the police on Sylvia, neither one signed them, so no warrants were ever put out on Sylvia. She wouldn't show the same mercy to Seven, she wanted him arrested for harassing her, assaulting her and causing a scene at her job. Even though there wasn't one eyewitness to back her report, a warrant was issued and Seven was arrested.

She wasn't finished with him, far, far from it.

August sixth, Seven ended up having to file another domestic violence report on his wife, but again, he didn't sign it. He didn't want to put her in jail, like she wanted to do to him; he just wanted her to stop physically attacking him. She tried her best to provoke him to hit her back, and maybe in the past he would have knocked her lights out. If he'd been under those old influences, he would have killed her. The thing is, he just loved her, and wanted her to just love him back. She wanted him under her control, one way or the other. He had to permanently move out of his trailer in order to keep some peace

Something inside Sylvia had snapped. Her attack and manipulation wouldn't be reserved for only Seven. He had too many people on his side, and living right there on the Baker property posed some problems for her. Her next target was Mary. How better to go after Seven, than to attack his own Momma?

Sylvia had managed to befriend a handful of police officers in Lanyard. One of them was an Investigator named Woody Muck. Investigator Muck seemed to take a personal and special interest in Sylvia.

Mary continued to work on the third shift, and would sleep during the day. August 12, would be no different for her, as she lay down after getting home. Just about the time she got to sleep, the phone started ringing. Despite trying to ignore it, the caller kept calling. So she got up and answered to Sylvia on the other end.

"I want my things, and I'm going to be coming with the police to get it."

Mary gave it some thought. Her son's family had moved out months before, and had gotten the majority of their belongings moved into their own trailer, sitting right in Mary's back yard. Many times, Mary has asked both Seven and Sylvia to come in and get the rest of their things. Neither seemed interested, yet now Sylvia was demanding it. It wasn't that Mary minded Sylvia getting the last of her things out, but she was fatigued, and not up to

Sylvia marching around with the unnecessary law enforcement in her house. She definitely didn't appreciate her daughter-in-laws approach.

"No, you'll have to wait until later." Mary's reply was dry.

"Bitch, you can't stop me from getting my things, the cops have done told me I can." Sylvia bit back.

"I don't care what the cops have told you, you'll just have to wait until it's a more convenient time for me." Mary hung up the phone, and marched back to bed. "The nerve of that girl!" She remarked to her dog Max, as she pulled the covers over her head.

Sylvia wasn't done, she continued to call, and she wasn't joking about the cops helping her.

Investigator Muck had taken it upon himself to assist poor mistreated Sylvia. He hadn't ever seemed to like Seven, much less his mother.

"Because you lived in the house, you have every legal right to retrieve your belongings."

His support gave Sylvia the power she needed to feel vindicated over Mary, Seven and every other member of his family. After his help and personal assistance, Sylvia believed that she could do just about anything she wanted, legal or not.

The phone's non-stop ringing had ticked Mary off. She wasn't going to let Sylvia run her life. She got up, put her clothes on and went to a friend's house, where she could at least get some sleep.

Investigator Muck showed up and observed the house being empty.

"Well, you can break into the house and retrieve your belongings if you want." He sat in his car and watched as Sylvia and one of her friends Amy, went through a window and proceeded to go through Mary's house, and remove anything she claimed was hers.

Now before the local law started helping Sylvia by condoning her running over Seven and his family, she was only a small time monster. After they started supporting her though, it gave her the supposed authorization she needed to persist in victimizing them. The local law was feeding a dangerously burning fire, one which would soon blaze out of control.

Mary was beside herself with annoyance, finding her home broken into. She called 911, and waited all day for a patrol car to come by. She called the next morning, and again, waited all day. She called the police chief, Freddy Corgis, whom was immediately defensive of his department. She went straight to the police and was put into Investigator Muck's care. It was very convenient that he would be the one to fill out the report made by Mary and be the supervisor to sign it.

"Levine reported that between listed dates and times Amy Wheeler and Sylvia Levine entered her residence and removed some of Sylvia's personal belongings. Sylvia and Seven Levine, Ms. Levine's son, moved into a trailer behind Ms. Levine's residence. Since then no effort has been made for her to come and get her property. On the 20th of August, Sylvia called Levine and advised that she wanted to get her things. Levine advised her that it would have to be another day because she was lying down before having to go to work third shift. Sylvia called again, wanting to get her things and said that she was coming with the police to stand by while she got her property. This was left on Levine's answering machine. After hearing the message, Levine left the residence to go to a friend's house to lie down and get some sleep. At some point Sylvia arrived at the residence with Lanyard police escort. Sylvia had a friend with her named Amy. Her last name may be Wheeler. Sylvia and Amy gained entry to the home through a rear window. They removed some of Sylvia's belongings and left. Levine wishes to sign a warrant on Sylvia and Amy for Criminal Trespass 1st."

This report never made it to the local paper, and was filled out with the wrong date to start with. Woody had no intentions of it going anywhere. He found the entire episode humorous. Seven Levine had no friends at the Lanyard Police Department, not like his wife did.

Chapter Thirty Nine

Feelings of any kind had become quite unbearable. I didn't want to spend the rest of my life experiencing the frozen sensations of being emotionally dead.

With murder, it's nearly impossible to allow much in without the rushing torrent of death's brutal victory. This was worse than death, far worse.

Every living thing faces death, but murder only touches certain ones, without any segregated views to stop it. Like death, it has no limits. Unlike death, it's not natural. The opposite of death is life, and without one you can't understand the other. Murder has no flip side, and there is no comprehension to find. Your mind has a hard enough time wrapping around death, but the thought of homicide isn't allowed to even pierce your perception.

In the morning I'd wake up, and the fact was always there to greet me. In the weeks and months after laying him to rest, everything felt unreal. I would have to learn to live each day without him. Once he could be seen, felt, touched and heard. Now his being has been replaced by silence while the numbness has become necessary to survive.

I never realized how tenacious I could be, until the murder. I'd moved into a strange world where everything that had once been washed with sunshine was suddenly shadowed in eternal black.

wasn't prepared for what murder would do to my life, or how my mind and heart would receive the trauma. My soul sought a cure for the pain. My mind began to analyze who I really was and what I was capable of withstanding. If I let it completely penetrate my mind, I have a fear it will literally burn me from inside out. I can feel the embers glowing in my gut, waiting for the truth to ignite every molecule in my being. While living in a world, that twirls, twist and shakes all around us, surrounded by images, sounds, and smells of human indifference.

The draw-back of lacking reactions though is missing out on the obvious greater good. Even though I can plainly see precious miracles all around me at all times, if I can't let feelings in, I miss out on all that I do have. What you get with murder is a double edge sword, no matter which way you move, it's going to cut you wide open.

My days were filled with a constant flow of tears. They just wouldn't stop. The tears would continue to flow, every day, for well over a year, and I'm sure for decades to come. Though the flood has slowly damned up with time, unexpected surges and leaks bring them randomly, with the intensity of spasms, similar to the muscle contractions of giving birth.

Water creates and sustains life. My tears created a large part of what I've become since losing Seven. They loosened locks and bolts on dark secrets my soul held tightly. At the time, while going through the mind-numbing event, I cried the deepest well of water. I had no ability to understand the profound and powerful effect of the simple strands of wet trails down my face.

If anything kept me sane throughout the experience, it was allowing myself to cry. I still do. It's a reminder that I'm only human. To attempt to hide from my tears prevents my soul from healing.

Acknowledging the tears, in all the eyes of those who loved Seven, helped build up my compassion to an unbelievable level, which enabled my heart to continue beating despite its ruptured walls. I can't give you the number of tears I've shed throughout these pages yet they have helped carry my soul onward.

Tears are pure. During times of great struggle and pain, their wet presence protects you, like a shield. Our wholeness is enhanced each time we openly acknowledge our feelings and share our many secrets.

CRY! CRY! CRY! Always allow your soul to cry.

Chapter Forty

The misery had just started for Seven and his family. They had no idea of the inferno, blistering in their direction. Certainly, they had their share of drama, in the past, but nothing could have prepared them for the anguish Sylvia would unleash.

Mae had a life outside the circle of Seven. Both of her daughters were mothers, making her a grandmother. Her son was a teen providing her with plenty of non-stop excitement. As a matter of fact she felt her life was running out of control. She had her own issues and daily demands. Her husband had inherited the business from his father that had passed away. That summer, Mae had been planning a large surprise birthday for her grandmother Thulah's eightieth birthday, coming up at the end of August. She cleaned houses for a few elderly couples every week. She had only heard a little about what was going on with her brother since his marriage. It saddened her, but it didn't surprise her too much.

Sylvia had started having her own run-ins with Mae though. The first occurrence took place the night after Seven made his first police report on July 13th. That night, around nine thirty, Mae's phone rang and the caller id showed it as Mary's number. Dressed for bed, and looking forward to winding down, Mae wondered what her mother had to tell her so late. Usually, Mary would be working, but Mae had never been able to keep up with her mothers work schedule.

"Hello."

At first there was nothing but silence, but then Sylvia inquired. "Who is this?"

Mae wasn't sure what the game was, but she played along with it. "I'm Mae…" She couldn't help but grin.

"Bitch, I'll whip your ass! You f*#!ing bitch!" Sylvia's voice surged through the phone-line. "Don't you ever call this f*#!ing number again!"

Mae lost her grin. "I'll call the number any damn time I want!" Mae could feel the storm coming through the phone.

"Oh, my God, bitch, I will f*#!ing kill you!" The phone went dead.

Mae looked at her phone, half way believing the conversation hadn't really occurred.

Rex was laying on the bed, already watching one of his favorite programs on TV. He glanced over at his wife, who continued to stand there holding the phone with a funny look on her face.

"I'm going to Momma's." Mae began pulling out some pants.

"What? Why?" Rex knew it took something major for Mae to drive after dark.

"Sylvia just cussed me out…" She'd gotten her pants on, and was pulling a jogging shirt over her t-shirt. "And she said she was going to whip my ass."

"Well, she ain't worth all that." Rex didn't like the sound of it.

"No, she isn't, but Sylvia is in my Momma's house, which she shouldn't be, and I'd just like to take a visual of the situation." Mae was dressed and already leaning in to give Rex a goodbye kiss. "I'll be right back."

"Well, be careful. Do you want me to come too?"

His offer was kind, but Mae knew he didn't really want to. She shook her head no.

Behind the wheel, her mind began playing out the threatening confrontation she might have with her sister-in-law. It wouldn't be easy, but if she had to defend herself, she would. One thing was for certain, Sylvia wasn't going to tell her she couldn't talk to her own mother.

Driving up, she could see both Seven and Mary standing outside by Mary's car. The both of them had been forewarned by Melina. She had been sitting on Mary's couch when Sylvia had stormed inside and made the phone call to Mae. Once Sylvia threw the phone down and stomped out of Mary's house, Melina ran outside, hysterically informing her grandmother and uncle.

"I don't know why, but I think Sylvia just called my mom and cussed her out!"

Melina remained terrified of Sylvia ever since being punched in the face by her. With her broadcast, Seven and Mary were both wondering what was about to happen.

Seven had never seen his oldest sister freak out on anybody, well he had no memory of it, but he'd heard enough from his own father to know it wasn't a good thing. The scarce event had him and his mother nervous with concern.

"Where is she?" Mae was marching toward her mother and brother.

Without any hesitation, they both pointed toward the married couple's trailer.

Mae started for the front door, with Seven walking behind her. He had his hands in his pockets, and his head down. He opened the door for Mae, but stayed outside.

In an instant, Sylvia was approaching, but as soon as she saw her sister-in-law walk in, both of her eyes opened wide, like she was seeing a ghost. Her complexion turned paste white, as her hands went up to her opened mouth. Sylvia had made a mistake.

"I, I…" Completely stunned, Sylvia stammered. "I'm sorry, I didn't know, I thought…" She started crying really hard, backing away. "I thought you were…" Moving into the kitchen, she went to work putting hamburger helper on the three kids' plates. They were all sitting at the table, waiting for supper.

Instantly Mae calmed down with their presence and with Sylvia's startled reaction.

"I think I'm losing my mind. I didn't know it was you, I heard your name, and that's her name." She continued sobbing really hard as she glanced over at Mae.

Mae stood in the living room, listening intently to the clarification Sylvia was giving while she finished putting supper on her kid's plates.

The three little ones were paying attention to the present situation, but happy to finally be eating.

Sylvia walked on down the hallway leading to her bedroom, a bath and the back door. She opened the door leading to her back yard and sat down.

Mae made her way through the kitchen, smiling at the babes eating. As she got to the slouched over and crying girl, she squeezed herself in the door frame, and sat next to Sylvia.

"I'm sorry I hit Melina, I can't believe I lost it like that." Sylvia dabbed at the tears rolling down her face and lit a cigarette.

Mae listened, and wondered what she was talking about, having heard the story from her mother, but still finding it hard to believe herself. Why would Sylvia attack Melina, especially if she was holding baby Cassandra? Mae wondered to herself, while listening to Sylvia, who continued.

"I can still see her flying across the room after I punched her. I'm sorry; I don't know why I did that, I guess it just upset me to see them all in my house, with pictures on the walls." She paused to puff on her cigarette. "He don't love me anymore, he doesn't care about us." In an instant the conversation changed.

"Why would you think that?" Mae quietly asked her, not wanting the children to listen to the conversation.

"He has a new girlfriend, named Maye." Sylvia sobbed the name out.

"OH!" Now things were making some sense. No wonder Sylvia was so upset. The light bulb went off finally in Mae's mind.

"I doubt he has a girlfriend." Mae tried to offer. She knew how much Seven loved Sylvia. It hadn't been a year that she'd photographed the etched happiness on his face the day of their marriage.

Sylvia wouldn't be consoled, and Mae was now feeling really sorry for her. Listening to her for a while longer, Mae played with the kids briefly, and headed out the door to go home.

Outside, Seven stood, leaned up against his mother's car.

"She says you have a girlfriend named Maye." She'd marched right over to him to find out if it was true or not.

Seven looked down at his feet. He had never been able to lie to his oldest sister. Seven couldn't tell lies to anyone without them being able to see right through them. His reaction was all Mae needed to confirm it.

"Well, that's what her problem is." With her eyes squinting at her him, he looked away, unable to look back at her.

Seven didn't try to explain to her why there was another girl named Maye, and that the two of them had done nothing wrong. He had befriended her during the first week after Sylvia left him. Maye's husband was in jail at the time. The both of them knew that just being together was wrong, but they were desperately hurting and lonely at the time. It felt good, just to have someone to talk to. They longed for their spouses, but neither had access to them. Seven had invited her over to Mary's house and she showed up. They talked, but with Seven's three children running around playing, they kept their distance. Mary came home, finding them sitting in her living room. She knew immediately what was going on, and called the both of them on it.

"How is your wife doing Seven?"

Her words hit their mark.

Maye got up to leave and Seven didn't stop her.

The reality of what was happening hit him. He was married, something he had always wanted to be with Sylvia, and here he was in less than a year, picking up another woman. He'd felt guilty for it ever since, realizing he was no better than Sylvia by doing it. He knew how bad it hurt to be cheated on, and he didn't want to cause his wife such pain. Though he'd done nothing wrong physically, in his heart he felt he'd already committed adultery.

When Mae had first showed up, in a fire ball of anger, and went into Seven's trailer, he had looked over at Mary and remarked.

"Sylvia will twist things around, and have Mae feeling sorry for her in no time."

He had been right.

As Mae went home, she thought about what was going on at the Baker property, but she didn't see anything happening to indicate what Sylvia had in store for her.

Chapter Forty One

"Hey, look, this Friendly Rental guy just donated a refrigerator for me and the kids."

Mae listened to Sylvia, who had called for a favor. It had been about a month since the phone cussing.

"I don't have any way to get it to the trailer though, and I was wondering if Rex would mind using his truck to do it? I hate to ask, but the kids really need a refrigerator."

Mae sat in deep thought; things had been pretty bad over on the Baker property. Not only had Seven been arrested for beating Sylvia up on her job, but Mary's house had been broke into by Sylvia with the police's help. There was even a rumor going around, Sylvia had tried to hire two brothers to beat up both Seven and his friend Jason. The assault on Melina hadn't been overlooked either. Despite all the drama, Sylvia had no problem asking Mae for help, knowing full well she was easy to operate.

"I seriously hate to ask, and wouldn't if we didn't need it so bad."

The three children reached into Mae's thoughts, and like putty in her hands, Mae reluctantly, but politely told her it would be no problem. She knew she would more than likely tick Mary off for helping Sylvia, but it was for the children. They did need a refrigerator. She hung up and looked over at Rex.

"Someone gave Sylvia a refrigerator, and those babies need that." She let that sink in for a second. "The problem is she has no way to get it to her house."

Rex looked over at her and rolled his eyes, he knew he was being reeled in. "Where is it?" He got into his truck, and went by one of his employees Ennis Davis's, offering to pay him a little to come help him move the object.

Mae felt good to know the kids would have proper food storage again, and let the subject drop from her mind. She hoped her mother wasn't home during the delivery, to evade any trouble that might bring.

Mary did notice Rex's truck out in her back yard, but she didn't know what he was doing, and was irritated that anyone would do anything for Sylvia, after all the harm she was purposely causing Seven. Mary was adamant that there was no way Sylvia was going to use those three babies as a manipulation tool against her.

Sylvia knew having Rex helping her would unnerve Mary, and she shared the experience with Mae one afternoon a couple of weeks later. She'd stopped over with the three kids, and showed off her recently acquired conversion van.

"You're Momma was pissed off because Rex helped me with the refrigerator! That woman got mad because someone wants to help my kids..."

Mae and Rex stood outside in their driveway, listening to Sylvia, and playing around with the kids.

"I'm sick of it. I know everybody has been talking about me, and wondering where I stayed while I had left Seven. Everyone thinks I was out drugging and drinking, but the truth of the matter is I was at a cop's house."

Her words half-way intrigued Mae, and half-way irritated her.

"Officer William Billing happened to let me stay with him at his house. I helped him get his Haunted Trail ready for Halloween. So whatever anybody says about me, I know I was at a cop's house, with his family." Sylvia laughed, pleased with herself.

It bothered Mae, but she had other things on her mind than Sylvia. She had begun to notice something different with her husband's behavior and attitude toward her. Quite sensitive to subtle changes, Mae began watching his every move very closely. She quickly detected that every night, when she got into the shower, he would go outside. She figured he was talking on his phone, but couldn't figure out why he had to go outside every night at that particular time to do it. She suspected he was having an affair, and she gave it a few more nights to play out, giving Rex all the rope he would need to hang himself. She hoped she was wrong.

It was Labor Day and Rex stayed busy running errands and talking on his phone most of the day. Late that night whenever Mae got into the shower, as his new custom, he headed outside. This time though, Mae took a faster than normal shower. Getting out, she made her way to the side entrance of their house, and could easily see him talking on his phone.

Rex wasn't using his personal phone; he was using his extra phone line that he kept in his work truck. He noticed the movement Mae made while looking, and he hastily threw the phone into the vehicle and came inside.

Mae waited, lying there beside him in bed. She had caught him, but she wasn't sure of what. After all he could have been talking to a customer. Maybe he hadn't even been on the phone. She had to be sure.

"Dang, I've got to go out to the van and get my extra bottle of aspirin." Mae held up the empty bottle from her night stand.

Rex looked over, halfway listening, still thinking about the person on the phone. He wasn't aware of his wife's suspicions.

She went outside, glancing in the trucks window, before retrieving her bottle. Sure enough, a phone lay in the seat, but the door was locked. Going back inside and lying back down with the new bottle, she went ahead and took two pills, thinking she would need them. After five minutes, she couldn't stand it any longer.

"So, if I go out to your truck, and get your phone sitting in the seat, you won't mind me pushing the redial?" Mae's question came out of left field, and Rex's reaction was all Mae needed to confirm her dreaded fears.

"What? Umm, what do you mean?" He smiled at her, but it wasn't a happy smile.

Mae had already started getting up. "Give me your keys!" She demanded holding her hand out.

Rex got up, grabbing the keys to prevent her from discovering his secret.

They both headed outside with Rex in the lead. He opened the truck door, with Mae pushing herself inside first, trying to grab the phone that Rex was attempting to hide. She struggled with him to get it in her hand.

"Give it to me now!" She growled, taking it and walking back to the house. Pushing redial, she turned to her husband. "You can either tell me who she is, or I'll find out myself." She showed him the phone that was dialing the last number called. They were both now standing in the kitchen.

"OK! I'll tell you who it is!" Rex offered, with a sick look on his face. "It's Sylvia."

As if he'd shot her with a 12-guage rifle, she could feel the impact and hole left right through her chest. The air left her lungs, as Sylvia's name targeted her heart and mind.

"What?" She couldn't believe her ears. "What? Sylvia? Why?" The blood was leaving her face, as the room began to spin around her.

"It's for the kids." Rex began to explain. "I was doing it for the kids."

"YOU SHUT UP! Don't you dare blame those babies for your disgusting actions!"

Mae had to get away; she ran to her room, grabbed her purse and headed out the door. Jumping in her vehicle, she took off, not really sure where she was going. She still had his phone in her hand. Pushing redial again, she waited, but Sylvia's answering service picked up.

"You have messed up now!" Mae left a message to Sylvia. She didn't know that after she left, Rex had given Sylvia a call, warning her that his wife had found out about them. Whatever she did to him or for him, she'd managed to completely blind him to the pain he was causing his wife.

Mae had driven to a Waffle King parking lot, and was sitting there, crying her eyes out. Never in a million years, would she have suspected Sylvia as being the one who was sleeping with Rex. There was no doubt, he had someone else, but she couldn't have ever anticipated the designation of Sylvia. Why would this happen now? After all the years, why would the two of them choose this time and place to do something so despicable? Mae drove back home, decided it wasn't in her best interest to confront Sylvia at that time. She cried to her husband that he had done the worst thing ever! Not just to her, but to her entire family!

The affair had started the day Sylvia asked for help moving the refrigerator. When Rex was at her house is when she made her move. She wanted to exchange phone numbers, which Rex willfully and eagerly agreed too. They had been meeting on dirt roads, and started sexting dozens of messages to each other.

Mae considered the two people involved in hurting her, Rex and Sylvia. Mae realized that Sylvia was always looking for the next best thing; even if it permanently affected deep family bonds. Rex wasn't the first family member Sylvia got her clutches into, nor was he the first man she outright decided to cheat on Seven with. She thrived on people "feeling sorry for her", and she would go to no ends to obtain that pity. What boggled Mae's mind was why

Sylvia would want to hurt the very people who had done nothing but try to love and accept her.

Ten days after the affair was discovered, Mae was out early in the morning on her way to go clean a house, when she passed Sylvia's vehicle on the side of the road. The rage Mae began to feel flowed out of every hair on her body, like an electrical current. She had a split second of thought to stop and just slap the hell out of her, but her next consideration was to just drive by and let her sit there with no assistance.

"Take that!" Mae barked as she rode past without stopping. Normally she'd have given some aid, but not since the bitch got her clutches in Rex. Within seconds though, she was turning around, believing that if only one of those three children were stuck in that vehicle, she couldn't drive past them. Heaven forbid if they had watched her go past. As Mae pulled in behind her, the back door opened and Liam started running toward her. Terrified that he could possible run sideways into the street, she popped out of her van, and darted over to him.

"Aunt Mae! Aunt Mae! Hey, Aunt Mae!" He was yelling as he ran into his Aunt's legs.

"Hey there Liam!" She smiled at him, and helped him back to his seat in their vehicle. She looked into the front seat at Sylvia, who gave her a sly, sideways glance.

"Hey Aunt Mae!" Both Bella and Cassandra chimed in unison.

"Hey you guys!" She spoke while keeping a close eye on Sylvia.

"I've got no money, and no gas." Sylvia explained holding her phone up. "And I have no time on any of my phones." Sylvia tossed the object down, and retrieved another one off the floorboard, giving it a try.

"You want me to take Bella to school?" Mae asked, knowing Bella would already be tardy.

"If you don't mind." Sylvia had no choice if she wanted Bella in school. Bella eagerly jumped out, while both Liam and Cassandra were left behind to Mae's dismay. She dropped off her niece, and then stopped at the convenience store across the street. Buying a gas container, she filled it with gas and delivered it back to Sylvia. There was no way; she could just leave those two babies stuck.

Chapter Forty Two

JULY 2007:

4th - Sylvia left her house, husband and children for seven days. She proclaimed to stay at a Lanyard Police Officer's home, William Billing, with his family. They worked on a Halloween themed trail.

11th - Sylvia returned home, attacked and assaulted her niece Melina while she was holding onto baby Cassandra. She then proceeded to attack Seven and his friend Jason.

12th - Seven and Jason made an early morning police report concerning the attack by Sylvia. Melina had outstanding checks and was afraid to file a police report. The two police reports were in the local paper, but neither Seven nor Jason ever went back to sign a warrant.

13th - The evening Sylvia went into Mary's house and pushed the redial button. She proceeded to cuss Mae out due to mistaken identification.

Two more events occurred in July, but the exact dates are not known. (1) Seven went to the police to report his wife for leaving the kids alone, after the night that Bella and Liam were walking around in the dark, trying to find their momma. (2) At some point in July after the initial report made by Seven on the 12th, Sylvia made the false report about Seven and Jason at the Dollar Store. She signed the warrants and both were arrested.

ONE more event occurred, sometime in between July and August, when Sylvia was at work, running the cash register. Two individuals who were common acquaintances of Seven and Sylvia's were shopping in the store she worked at. The guys were known as cousins, and when they were checking out they were offered a proposition from Sylvia. She didn't hide what she was attempting; she figured everyone wanted the same thing she did. She offered the cousins $500.00 to "hurt" both Seven and his friend Jason. Luckily, the cousins were offended and informed Jason about the hit offer. They were worried that somebody else might take that offer, and they warned both Seven and Jason to watch their backs.

AUGUST 2007:

6th - Seven made his second domestic violence police report, and was forced to move out of his house. The report was in the local paper, but again, he never signed the warrant. Though he wanted Sylvia to stop physically, mentally and verbally abusing him, he didn't really want her arrested.

12th - With the assistance of Investigator Woody Muck, Sylvia and her friend Amy Wheeler, broke into Mary's house, to legally retrieve what Sylvia insisted were things she needed immediately.

16th - Sylvia called Mae to ask if Rex could bring his truck to pick up a refrigerator, and deliver it to her trailer. They exchanged phone numbers, and began sneaking around with each other for the next two weeks.

21st - Mary made a police report on Sylvia and Amy for breaking into her house on the 12th. Mary only made the report because after Sylvia got away with it, she started harassing Mary every single day. Not only did Sylvia start verbally harassing Mary, but the long list of visitors Sylvia had at her trailer, joined in with her. The report was conveniently made by the same law officer that abetted Sylvia, Investigator Woody Muck, who happened to be the supervisor to sign off on it too.

Toward the end of August, Thulah was turning eighty-years-old, and a large surprise birthday party had been planned by Mae. Family from as far as Texas was in attendance, but her three great-grandchildren that lived right in her back yard, were forbidden to attend. Mae had called and asked Sylvia if it would be okay for the kids to come to the party, if only for a little while.

"No, there's gonna be some people there that I just don't want my three children to be subjected too."

Mae didn't comment, but she wondered who Sylvia was referring too.

"It's not safe. Like Lewis, Erik and right now, I don't want Seven near them, with his history, I'm just concerned with their safety. There are a lot of weird people in your family." She laughed.

"Well, I'll watch over them." Mae tried, feeling ill that Sylvia felt her family to be weird, when within the same year; she'd happily married into it.

"Oh, well, I'll think on it."

Mae hung up, and looked out the trucks window. She was riding with Rex to price some work. "She won't let the kids come to Maw Maw's party." It was disappointing; she'd wanted to gather as many of Thulah's children together that she could.

"Why?" Rex wondered out loud.

"She says it's because she doesn't want them subjected to Lewis, Erik or their own daddy."

Mae didn't know at that time, Rex and Sylvia's affair was in full bloom.

Rex did talk to his girlfriend and managed to arrange for Bella to spend the night August 31.

By the beginning of September, the Baker property had become populated with a hoard of Sylvia's family, friends, and followers. Her brother James and his pregnant girlfriend Tina had moved in once Seven was forced out. Her sister Beverly visited with her three children, nearly every day. A few girls, Robin and Tiffany Bass, Amber Lorne, (the daughter of one of Sylvia's old male friends, Uncle Mac) would frequent late at night. Amy Wheeler brazenly walked about the property, proudly boasting how she and Sylvia broke into Mary's house with police assistance. Also, Leesa and Maggie Morey, who were related to Danny Morey; Leesa was his sister and Maggie his teenage daughter.

The list would include a host of male companions too. Some were old boyfriends and others were just hanging out. Charles Wheeler, who was Amy's brother. Campbell Collier, Abe Markesan, and a pair of brothers named Paul and Chris Douglas. Danny Morey visited the property one time, but didn't get out of his car.

SEPTEMBER 2007:

3rd - Mae uncovered the brief affair between Sylvia and Rex.

19th - Wednesday, Mary took Cassandra and Liam to DHR. She then returned the children to Sylvia at the police department. Sylvia threatened to kill Mary in the presence of Lanyard Police Officer Sage.

24th - Monday, Sylvia punched Mary in the face. A report was made by the reporting officer, who informed Mary, he would personally sign the warrant.

27th - Thursday, Mary had endured two full days of jeers, taunts and threats from Sylvia, as well as the many occupants of her trailer. Mary went to the police department, to ask if a warrant had been made, concerning her being assaulted by Sylvia.

28th - Friday, after midnight and within hours of Sylvia getting out of jail, most of the windows in Mary's house were smashed. Mary filed another police report, concerning her vandalized home.

September also marked the month of the one year wedding anniversary of Seven and Sylvia.

Chapter Forty Three

It was the beginning of September on Labor Day, that Mae uncovered the affair between Rex and Sylvia.

Before the affair was uncovered, and while it was going on, Mary and Sylvia had become arch enemies. It wasn't that Mary was trying to protect Seven, as much as she was concerned over her three innocent grandchildren, who happened to be smack dead in the middle of a major struggle between adults.

Seven had been forced to move out of his trailer at the beginning of August. He'd started sleeping at Thulah's. If he tried to stay at his mother's, Sylvia wouldn't let him have one hour of peace. He felt that if he was still on the property, he would be there for his kids, even if Sylvia refused to let him see them.

Through the end of the hot summer, the three kids were not allowed to leave their trailer. The days of running and playing on the Bakers land were over. Sylvia wouldn't let them step foot outside, and gave stern warnings to the baby sitter.

Many new faces were being seen every day going into Sylvia's place. They were not complete strangers, but never before had any of them ever graced the property with complete abandonment.

Sylvia's brother, James, who had run into a string of bad luck, had moved in to help his little sister.

The babysitter, Maggie, was the daughter of one of Sylvia's old boyfriends, Danny. Maggie's boyfriends would hang out during the day, and party late into the night.

Sylvia worked full time, so the kids were left to Maggie or James.

Mary wouldn't get up every time a vehicle drove up in her yard, but it didn't help her get much rest. One early evening she got a knock at the door. It was baby Cassandra, who had somehow escaped the babysitter, and made her way to her grandma's house. One thing for certain, Cassandra loved her grandma, and couldn't understand being forbidden to see her. Mary opened her screen, to let the baby in. She smiled to see the little one who was filthy, with her diaper dragging the ground. Someone had doodled all over her with a permanent marker, if she hadn't done it herself. She had a nasty black eye, from falling out the front door, a few days before. Mary was enraged. Luckily the baby hadn't wondered out into Highway 51.

"Cassandra, you are a mess!" Mary reached down and picked up her beloved granddaughter. "Let's see, if I have any more diapers left here." She began looking around whenever she heard another knock; it was Liam, who was already letting himself in. "Hey, Liam, can you go get me one of Cassandra's diapers?"

He shook his head up and down, looking nervous for being at his grandma's house, and went back out the door.

Suddenly there was banging at the door. It was Maggie.

"Get your damn hands off that baby, bitch!" Maggie had opened the door, but Mary quickly chased her back out.

"You get out of my house and off my property!" Mary blew the words out like a dragon blowing fire. She continued holding Cassandra.

The girl continued back around, cussing at Mary. "Bitch, Sylvia is going to kick your ass!"

Mary had had enough. She still had car seats sitting in her car, and she put Cassandra into one, and told Liam to get in to the other. She backed out, with Maggie still threatening her with vulgarity. Thulah had heard the commotion and was standing in her back yard. She got into Mary's car as it was leaving the property.

"What is happening?" Thulah's worried expression made Mary start crying. She glanced back at the two wide eyed children. "What's happened to that baby's face?" The black eye and scribble across Cassandra's face frightened Thulah, thinking the baby had been beat.

"I'm getting her a clean diaper."

Mary's mind was racing, and she was in shock with the sudden surge of fury. She'd had it with Sylvia and her friend's behavior; it was costing the innocent children too much. Quickly she drove to the nearest store, and purchased a bag of Luv's. The thought struck her that she needed to get proof, once and for all, that Sylvia was negligent of the children. Instead of changing the diaper, she headed for the DHR

After they observed Cassandra's filthiness, and even before Mary could get the diaper changed, they explained they could not help her or the kids. She decided to drive over to Mae's, and ask her to take some photographs for evidence.

While Mary and Thulah were riding from place to place, Maggie had notified Sylvia. Immediately Sylvia called on her certain Lanyard cop friends. Next she began riding around in her conversion van, looking for Mary's car. Stopping at Mae's, she banged loudly on her front door.

Mae opened up to a hostile sister-in-law.

"Where's my f*#!ing kids? You got them?" She started to push herself past, but Mae took a quick step toward her.

"No." Sylvia being a mistress of her husbands, she had the inclination to surprise the girl with an iron frying pan to her head.

"Your damn Momma has done gone and crossed the damn line. Whenever I find her, I am going to f*#!ing kill her!" Sylvia threatened while running back to her van. Squealing her tires, she took off.

Mae watched and wondered what was happening, and began to worry for her mother's safety. She rushed to call Mary but no one answered. That's when she noticed Mary's car pulling up in the driveway. Running out to both greet and warn her, Mary already had Cassandra out, holding her in her arms.

"Momma, did you go nuts and steal the kids?" Mae always had a tendency to try to ease tension with humor.

Mary was in no amusing mood. "No, I want you to take pictures of what these babies look like."

"Mom, they probably have an APB out on you for kidnapping them. Sylvia just drove off; you can see her tire tracks. Please take them to the police department, don't return them to her yourself."

Mae reasoned with her mother, who didn't know Sylvia was out searching for her.

"Well, at least take a few photos." Mary looked nervous, but determined.

Mae quickly retrieved her camera, terrified that any minute, Sylvia could drive by again. She snapped several shots of both kids, and watched as her mother left her yard, heading for the police department. Mae knew Sylvia couldn't hurt her mother with law enforcement present but unfortunately Sylvia happened to live only thirty feet behind Mary.

As Mary arrived with the kids at the police department, Officer Sage was outside waiting.

"Ms. Levine, could you tell me why you decided to take these children from their home?" He stood tall and looked down at her.

"Look at them! Tell me, if these were your grandchildren, would you be happy to see them in this condition?" Desperately Mary tried to reason with the ridged officer. "I went to buy the baby diapers." Mary clung to the bag, holding it up to show it as evidence.

"Well, you can't just take other people's children."

Mary looked up into his eyes and realized the man already had his mind made up. The law was the law.

"I took them by the DHR also, to show them their condition."

"If the condition bothered you so much, why didn't you just clean them up?" He crossed his arms, looking at the conversion van barreling into the parking lot.

"Because, if they were cleaned up, what would there have been to show the DHR?" Mary felt like she was walking around in circles, when all she wanted was to be able to take care of her grandchildren.

"Bitch I'm going to f*#!ing kill you!" Sylvia was making her way to them.

"Sylvia!" Officer Sage was putting his hands up to block Sylvia, but wasn't encouraging her to calm down.

"No, that mother f*#!ing bitch kidnapped my children. She's a child molester, and should be arrested, or I'm going to f*#!ing kill her with my own two hands." She began lunging at Mary, who continued to stand behind the cop. "Yeah, you wait bitch! I'm going to make you f*#!ing pay!"

Mary resigned and walked away, leaving Sylvia's threats behind her. Getting into her car, Thulah sat wondering what the police were going to do to them for taking the kids. Before Mary could back the car out, Sylvia had ran over and spit on the windshield.

"They aren't going to help us." Mary watched the irate girl walk away and knew the battle had just begun.

Chapter Forty Four

Seven was no longer in town throughout the week. With the disintegration of his marriage, he'd went back to work with Carl Pacer. He had really loved being at home more, near the children, but he wasn't allowed to see them anymore. His home was now a twenty-four hour party house, and it pained every single cell in his body to watch his dream's blowing away with the hurricane winds called Sylvia. The long list of rowdy and often time's irate visitors, traipsing across the once quiet and serene Baker land, made his blood boil, as Sylvia took complete control of everybody's sanity. Anywhere Seven tried to rest while at home, whether at his mother's or grandmother's, Sylvia would literally break the door down to get inside to him, or keep the phone line occupied calling. He reasoned that if he was gone, Sylvia wouldn't cause as much commotion at Mary's and Thulah's. He figured while his marriage was breaking apart, he could stay busy and make some money.

Sometimes, when he was in town, James would let Seven come in and see the three kids. James could only do so, if the trailer was empty of Sylvia's friends. Seven and James had always gotten along. James had always seen straight through his sister's multitude of ploys over the years.

"Everything is going to be okay, I've just been working." Seven would attempt to reassure his little ones that everything would be okay. Their eyes would display the undeniable traces of confusion and fear. Once they were free to roam every square inch of the Baker land. Freely they'd travel back and forth to their grandmother's houses, anytime they felt like it. Now those two spots were off limits. For most of the summer, they were sequestered inside their house. Even as the foliage on the trees started changing colors with the Fall season's approach, they were still forbidden to go outside.

It was hard for Seven to look them in the eyes and promise them anything, when he himself was so unsure of how things were going to turn out. It started plaguing him; the marriage might be beyond repair. His fears focused on Sylvia's attempt's to get him in trouble with the law. He was still on parole and Sylvia seemed determined to send him back to prison.

"Seven, that woman is trying her best to get you locked up for good."

His parole officer warned him sternly after he was arrested for the false accusations of beating Sylvia up on her job. The seasoned officer had gotten to know Seven really well. He was absolutely convinced Sylvia had the Lanyard Police Department wrapped around her fingers and with their help, put her husband away.

There had been a court date set for the incident at the Dollar Store, the first of many more court dates to come. DA Holly Bass would get her first opportunity to meet both Sylvia and Seven.

Sylvia was sitting at a table in the front of the court room when Seven and Mary arrived. Mary took a fast seat, while Seven walked over to his wife. He greeted her and started to sit down next to her, but she refused him the seat. Deflated in the presence of the growing crowd of people, he slumped around to sit across from her.

A Lanyard Officer walked up behind Sylvia and proceeded to softly whisper into her ear, while massaging her shoulders.

Sylvia was giggling with the breathe in her ear, and didn't mind having some stress kneaded out of her shoulders either.

Seven watched this display of another man putting his hands on his wife, and could feel the weight of the room on him as he tried to push the images out of his mind.

When their case was called before the judge, they both moved to the front of the room.

"I have something to say…" Sylvia introduced her dilemma. "I made it up."

DA Bass looked hard at the assumed victim, and began shaking her head back and forth.

"You did what?" Judge Millen looked down at her and frowned.

"I made it up; Seven never attacked me at work." She gave the court her sweetest look.

Officers that lined the wall, wiggled about as they eyed Seven with disgust.

The room got quiet for a second, but then it erupted with opinions flowing through the spectators.

"You're aware that falsifying a police report is a crime?" The judge didn't look entertained.

Sylvia was arrested and taken behind closed doors, while Seven was let go.

The DA smacked her armful of folders down and marched out of the room following Sylvia.

Seven made his way to the back of the room where Mary sat. He could feel the weight of the law enforcers glaring at him from around the room. He never expected his wife to tell the truth. Having on multiple pairs of underwear, t-shirts and socks, he'd come to court fully prepared to go to jail. He wanted to tell her thank-you, and let her know he would get her out.

"Mom, I'll meet you at the car, I've got to talk to Sylvia."

He made his way back where they had taken her, finding her in a room, surrounded by cop's who were consoling her. The assistant DA Bass was scolding her for letting Seven get by with what he'd done.

"Why would you do this? Why would you let him get away with putting his hands on you? Why protect someone like that? Did he force you to do this?" The DA had her back to Seven, not seeing him open the door.

The same officer who had been favoring Sylvia in the courtroom stood up straight from talking to her. He'd noticed Seven's entrance, and was already sending visual messages that he wasn't going to let Seven get away with hurting Sylvia.

DA Bass turned around to greet him. "You are nothing but a sorry piece of crap to make your victimized wife take the blame for your crime!" She was walking right up to him, and nearly smacking his face with her finger. "You're one sorry man, husband and father!"

Seven's head dropped as he looked down at the floor. The words hit him, making his guts twist up on the inside. He did feel bad for Sylvia having to be arrested, he hated it, but he hadn't done anything to her to start with. She'd done it to herself. He could easily see Sylvia didn't need his help, and he rushed out as fast as he could. It was raining outside and he was soaked by the time he got into his mother's car.

"Sylvia has got not only the police on her side, but the DA hates me too." He described what happened to his mother.

It was only one more event to add to Mary's growing list of legitimate complaints concerning the local law and judicial system. As upsetting as it was to know the police were against them, Mary had been feeling more agony and despair concerning the events happening in her own back yard. Her mind stayed on the three children, locked up, and segregated from their own family.

Bella had started to develop her own opinions. Being only six, she was easily convinced her daddy was a monster for putting her momma in jail. She was also told her grandmother was a child molester. Bella had no idea what that was, but she heard how Mary had tried to get Liam and Cassandra.

"You're a nasty child molester! You are a bitch!"

The words would come out as a song. Such hurtful expression's flowing out of the mouth of a six year old, followed by obscene hand jesters. It would be the only conversation Mary had with her beloved granddaughter.

Mary developed a twenty-four hour fear that her house would be burned down, maybe even with her in it.

Sylvia not only threatened it, but some of her house guest promised to do it too.

Chapter Forty Five

The days and weeks would blur and blend together as the month's started adding up for Seven and his family. So many things were happening it was difficult to keep up with.

September 24th fell on a Monday that year and it was late in the evening when Sylvia's screams broke through the air. Seven had just gone out to get his bag from Mary's car. His boss would be showing up shortly to pick him up to go out of town for work.

Mary's head was already aching, and she contemplated calling in sick from her third shift. Instead she grabbed her keys and purse, deciding she'd rather go to work then stay home with Sylvia outside raving mad. She walked out to her car, and could see Sylvia putting the kids into her van, while Seven stood off to the side, struggling to reason with her.

"Sylvia, you can leave them here, I will watch them. Sylvia, don't drive, you're in no condition."

"Shut the f*#! up! You're no one to me…you don't give one flipping f*#! about my children!"

The words coming out of his wife's mouth were incoherent, as she staggered around.

"You're drunk Sylvia…"

"And that ain't all bitch!" Tittering as she slammed the vehicle door, and continued cussing at him from behind the closed glass. "You're not nothing but a piece of f*#!ing shit." The van began pulling off.

As all this was happening, Mary watched, waiting for the safest moment to leave.

Seven was now looking at the van's back tail lights and in a moment of panic, he bent over, picking up a handful of gravel, and threw it at the back of the vehicle.

Brake lights glowed as the van abruptly slid to a halt.

"What the f*#!, you're scaring your children!" Sylvia got out slurring at him.

"I'm sorry." Seven was so grateful that the vehicle stopped, he began apologizing to her while he opened the side door on the van. Looking back at his three children with terrified looks in their eyes, he felt remorseful for scaring them. "I'm sorry you guys, I just wanted your momma to stop."

"You mother f*#!er, you scared them!"

"Well you don't need to be driving around with them drunk!" Seven tried to remain calm, as he tightened up anticipating her slap.

"They like it when I drive them around drunk! It doesn't scare them, you scare them! We go driving all the time, you go to f*#!ing work, we have fun too!"

Sylvia abruptly stopped talking, noticing Mary standing by her car, holding her cell phone.

Just about the time Sylvia stopped the van, Mary had pulled her cell phone out. At first she thought about calling the police, but immediately felt that would be a bad idea. Next she considered video-taping the episode playing out in her front yard. No one seemed to believe Sylvia was the instigator, so she could possibly get some physical evidence to support their claims. She had a problem though; she'd never used any of her phones features, and had no clue how to get the device to work.

Sylvia noticed Mary opening her phone, and she took off toward her.

"You f*#!ing skank bitch! You tried to steal my kids!"

Seven realized he wouldn't ever get to Sylvia before Sylvia got to Mary.

Mary's attention was still on her phone, as she desperately tried to figure out how to make the video turn on.

Sylvia tightened up her ring encrusted fist. "Bitch, you ain't gonna make me lose my kids!"

"No one will have to make you lose them Sylvia, because you'll do that all on your own!" Mary glanced up, not realizing Sylvia was so close, too close. Sylvia's fist pounded her right in the face, nearly knocking her to the ground.

Within seconds, Seven had his arm around Sylvia, pulling her off his mother. He continued to pull her back to the van, but had a hard time restraining her. She wasn't finished with Mary, and screamed she wanted to kill her. Seven pushed her into the van, and jumped in himself, driving the van down Highway 51.

Mary was left shocked and bleeding in her front yard. The blow had slashed open her eyebrow. Without wanting to, she reluctantly placed a phone call to 911. The officer filled out the report, and made a note on it, that he would be signing the warrant himself.

Believing herself to be in physical danger, Mary assumed Sylvia would be arrested without haste. She waited two full days. During that forty eight hour period, Mary would call the police station every so often, after being threatened by Sylvia personally, or by one of her friends. Somehow, she'd become known as a "nasty child molester". Everyone that went into Sylvia's trailer would yell it or shoot birds at Mary and her friends.

Sevens world was crashing in around him, and he had no idea how to make it stop. He took the punch his mother withstood personal, and didn't know why he'd reacted the way he did. He was beginning to get scared, that something bad was going to happen. Someone could eventually get hurt, but he couldn't control Sylvia. Every day she was up to something new. He wanted to protect the ones he loved, but wasn't able to choose between the two most important woman in his life. He knew both women well, and he knew neither would give one inch.

Mary decided after she was physically attacked, and her son left with the attacker, that she couldn't help him anymore. This caused her unbelievable pain. She loved Seven, he was her baby, and his children meant the world to her, but Sylvia was uncontrollably treacherous, and growing dangerously meaner every day.

Thursday morning Mary decided to go down to the police department, and find out why they wouldn't arrest Sylvia. At first they couldn't find the report, much less a warrant. Mary still had a nasty open wound above her swollen and blackened eye.

"Well I know there was a report, and the officer promised me he would be signing the warrant himself. But I tell you what, if he hasn't signed a warrant, I'm here to sign it right now."

The lady behind the thick glass looked blankly at Mary.

Mary folded her arms.

Within seconds the report was found, but they had bad news. "We can't locate Sylvia."

Mary wasn't amused with their unprofessional attitudes. "She works right around the corner from the police department, every single day...." She could feel her blood pressure rising. "Not to mention you people know she lives right behind me!"

By the time Mary got home, Sylvia was finally apprehended at work, and placed under arrest. Mary was content, that finally, she'd gotten some justice. Even though she had a horrible black eye, she went to work that night.

Later that night while Mary was at work and within an hour of Sylvia getting out of jail; nearly every window in Mary's house was bashed in. Seven called while she was at work to inform her. As she drove up, her house looked like a bomb had gone off and blown out all her windows. Through her tears, she tried to reason what her eyes were seeing.

Seven told Lanyard Officer Hale he knew Sylvia did it, but wasn't there to witness it being done.

"Now Seven, look over there at your mother. You know she doesn't deserve this. We all know your wife did this."

"Oh I know she did this, no doubt about it, but I wasn't here. I didn't see her do it."

One of Sylvia's friends, Robin Bass, had provided her a ride home from jail. Both of them were bragging about their vandalism the next day. Sylvia used an old metal chair to break the glass, while her friend Robin threw rocks.

They also had someone else to blame. Sylvia claimed the husband of Seven's "girlfriend" Maye, did it because he found out Seven was the man sleeping with his wife.

Mary was left with replacing all her broken windows, and cleaning up the mess of broken shards of glass throughout her house. Because there were no eye witnesses, there was nothing else she could do.

Seven's depression was returning, and his life felt like it was starting to spin out of control again. Watching as Sylvia not only attacked him, but his mother, he was feeling the effects, and was becoming more worried by the day. He knew his siblings were highly upset, with Mary being physically attacked, and he felt tremendous grief for what his wife had done. He felt like he was stuck in the middle of hell, with absolutely no escape out. Like the shattered glass covering his mother' house and yard, there was no way to pick up the thousands of little pieces and put them back. Whichever way he went, it would hurt someone and without a doubt, hurt himself.

Chapter Forty Six

That fall season would bring more than a sudden chill in the air. It would pass about some serious accusations, to both mother and son. By the end of October, Sylvia would have managed to have both Seven and Mary put in jail. All based on her concoction of lies.

OCTOBER 2007

6th - Sylvia received her first eviction notice from Mary. The eviction was solely for Sylvia Dean Myers Muck Levine, and it meant to put her off the Baker land for good.

20th - Sylvia took her daughter, Cassandra, to the local emergency room. Seven was allowed to go with her. Sylvia's friend, Leesa Morey, accompanied them also. The baby was treated for a serious Staphylococcal infection on her leg.

23rd - A report was made by a local emergency room nurse, that her cell phone had been stolen.

26th - Sylvia broke into, burglarized and trashed Mary's house. Sylvia called Seven, while inside Mary's house, from Mary's home phone. Seven was spending the night at Jason's parent's house. Seven and Jason, rode over to Mary's house. Once he checked his mother's house, he walked back to his own home. A domestic violence police report was made by Lanyard Police, for Seven nearly beating Sylvia to death.

27th – In the early morning hours, a drunken Sylvia is pulled over by the

Lanyard police. She was beaten and claimed to be trying to escape being killed by her violent and aggressive husband. She was placed under arrest, for an old 2005 domestic warrant, by the Lanyard Police Department, to prevent her from driving and being arrested for DUI.

28th - Mary filed a report on Sylvia's breaking into and burglarizing her home on the 26th.

29th - Sylvia was telling her co-workers and customers that the reason she had a black eye, was because Seven tried to kill her. She gave many different versions of what happened. She accused that Seven used a crow bar and his steel toed boots. She was also spreading it around her fellow employees that her six year old daughter, had started her period.

30th - DHR showed up at Sylvia's trailer. They had concerns over the six year old bleeding at school.

31st -Mary was placed under arrest for stealing a cell phone, from an emergency room nurse.

At the beginning of October, Seven was losing hope that he would be able to fix the damage done by his wife. Once Sylvia physically assaulted Mary, things would never be the same again.

For one thing Mary wanted the girl off the Baker property. Maybe she couldn't control Sylvia or her friends, but she would regain control on what use to be a peaceful place. She'd grown tired of worrying if her house would be burned down. It had gotten to be a hassle to wash her car windows every day, in order to see through all the spit produced by Sylvia as she'd purposely walk past it as many times she could just to spray it. The cold air blew straight threw her windowless home. One thing for certain, Sylvia had to be removed.

This put a hurting on Seven, and a bond between mother and son was effectively broken. He was torn between what his heart told him, and what everyone else was saying.

"SAVE YOURSELF, LEAVE SYLVIA!" The voice inside his head screamed.

"I love my kids, and I love her too!" Screamed Seven's heart and soul.

The eviction became a personal slap to Sylvia from Mary. That's how Sylvia saw it and she vowed.

"I will never have to leave this land, as a matter of fact, I have witnesses that will vouch they heard Mary give it to me! This is my land now, and I'll kill that bitch before she kicks me off it!"

All the while, Seven just tried to keep the peace one day at a time. Whenever he got a chance to be with the kids, he would try to make light of the situation and hope they could hang on until their mother calmed down. They couldn't comprehend why their mother wanted to be with other men. Nor, did they understand how their daddy had become the bad guy, or why they weren't supposed to be around him anymore. He would work as much as he could, and in between he would hang out at his siblings or friends.

None of them realized though, they were walking in the last sad days of Seven's life. It was precious and ticking time for the kids to spend with their father, but instead, he was banned from their lives.

October 20th was on a Saturday and baby Cassandra was extremely unwell. The baby was in need of medical attention. She was running a fever and had a sore on her leg oozing green pus. Listlessly she cried with intense pain.

Seven arrived back in town that afternoon, and after seeing his daughter so ill he insisted Sylvia take the baby to the hospital.

Sylvia wouldn't go unless one of her friends went with her, so Leesa Morey traveled with the parents to the emergency room.

Once inside a room, Seven tried to comfort his daughter, who wasn't thrilled with the sights and sounds around her. While he busied himself with Cassandra, he attempted to ignore Leesa, who searched the room's interior for anything she might want to keep. It bugged him that she was along for the ride, and Sylvia refused to come without her. Glancing out the door into the hallway he noticed one of Lanyards police officers talking to Sylvia. Looking back down at the baby, he felt trapped in Sylvia's world.

The nurse came in followed by Sylvia, and it was the first moment that he felt Cassandra was in safe hands. Excusing himself, he went outside to smoke a cigarette. He looked around cautiously for the same officer he'd just seen Sylvia talking to, but the guy was gone. Finishing his cigarette, he considered calling someone to come pick him up, but he wanted to know about Cassandra. He lit another cigarette, mostly to pass some more time. Checking his pants pocket he found enough change for a can drink and made his way to the snack machines.

Back inside the room with the baby, Sylvia and Leesa had already checked around the entire room for knick knacks to steal. The baby rested while they covertly moved about. The nurse walked back in and laid her pink cell phone down on the cabinet, along with the baby's file. Checking Cassandra's temperature, she rubbed the fevered babies face.

"It's going to be okay sweetie."

Cassandra only opened her eyes and closed them. The pain from her infection had exhausted her.

The nurse then walked back to the chart, made her notes and walked out of the room. She forgot to pick up her phone.

Most hospitals have video surveillance. Inside the room with Cassandra, a camera recorded the nurse leaving her personal pink cell phone on the counter, while she tended to the sick baby. When the nurse left the room, she forgot to pick up her phone. Two people, who did notice the nice cell phone being left, were Sylvia and Leesa.

Sylvia couldn't have possibly have planned that the nurse would leave the phone, but her mind went to work immediately on how to take advantage of the situation.

Leesa picked the phone up and slid it into her pants pocket.

The nurse came back in with some forms for Sylvia to fill out. It was at this time that Sylvia introduced Leesa as the baby's grandmother, Mary Kay Levine. On the forms, Sylvia listed Mary Kay Levine as the responsible party for the bill, listing her name, birthdate, address and place of occupation. Leesa signed the forms, Mary Kay Levine.

The ER nurse would later state that's what information Sylvia and Leesa gave her. Once the police report was made, Mary Kay Levine would be the one who would have a warrant put out for her arrest.

Sylvia liked putting Seven in jail, but now she was going to teach Mary a lesson also. From her perception, Mary had her put in jail, and now she was going to return the favor. She wasn't above making false accusations, and she didn't seem all that concerned if she got caught. With the police and DA on her side, she was like a kid in a candy store, dreaming up ways to get back at the family she now despised.

With her husband locked up in prison, he would have no life, and it would prevent all those who did love him, from getting to him. If she couldn't have him, no one could. She believed she had every right to control Seven's fate and that of his family's.

Seven had never hidden his personal loves of life, family and home. That's exactly what she was going after, his bliss. If his life and love had been centered on a red mustang, she would have wrecked it. She went straight to the things he loved and held close to his heart. Just like a common thief, she wanted to rob Seven of his life, while he was still alive to live it.

October 26th, Friday after Cassandra's trip to the emergency room, Seven got back in town from work early. He was eager to check on her, having worried all week. The warnings about her condition from the hospital staff had been serious. Luckily, he got in before Sylvia got off work, and he rushed on down to his trailer. His brother-in-law James opened the door and welcomed him in.

The past week had been rough for James, being left with caring for the highly contagious and sick child. Her painfully infected wound required cleaning and changing the dressing every so many hours, and it wasn't a pleasant experience for either the baby or the person forced to cause her the pain of washing it.

"Please no, no, no. Please no touch." The baby would beg and cry, while the wound continued to ooze and had a very bad smell.

James had asked Mary to come over many times, to change the dressing for him.

Mary didn't mind taking care of her granddaughter, even though it wasn't a pleasant experience. The biggest worry for Mary was if Sylvia showed up, and found her inside the home

Seven found his daughter lying on the couch and excited to see him. She continued to be in pain, and was very protective of her boo-boo. They were each enjoying the other's company, when Sylvia walked in the door, home early from work too. She was overeager to confront her husband.

"You're nothing but a sorry piece of shit!"

It didn't take long before she had run him completely off the land. He figured she must have plans for the night, some of which she didn't want him around to see. Deciding to sleep over at Jason's parents, he figured he was far enough away; she would leave him alone.

Jim and Brenda Tiller, Jason's parents, never minded Seven sleeping over. They felt really bad about his situation, and both had personal experience dealing with Sylvia. Anyone who tried to love or help Seven became a target of hate for her. Whenever he stayed with Jason, Sylvia would burn up the phone line calling him. This night would be no different than the rest. What Seven didn't anticipate was the phone call coming from his mother's house number. He knew his mother was at work, and he wondered why she was at home. He worried Sylvia had done something again. When he answered it, the receiving end didn't have Mary on it, instead it was his wife. Sylvia didn't need to break into Mary's house for a phone. She had several lines herself, as well as a number of her friends who had phones also.

"You ain't shit!" She was slurring her slang.

"What are you doing in my momma's house?'

"She ain't shit either, and you know what, f*#!-you mother f*#!er! There ain't a damn thing you or your skank momma can do about me being here. This is my f*#!ing house bitch! The cops know y'all ain't nothing but drugged up child molesters!"

"Sylvia, get out of that house!"

"Oh I've been in here a while, been finding me some stuff, my stuff, and what I want."

Seven panicked and was worried what was going on at Mary's. He couldn't call the police for fear of them, and he knew Sylvia had no rights in Mary's house, no matter how many Investigators claimed she did. Brenda agreed he needed to go check it out, and she gave her son and Seven a ride over. The two quickly went into Mary's, could tell it had been ransacked, but was empty of people. They headed down toward Sylvia's.

"Seven came into the trailer, threatening everyone. He had a pipe in his hands, and he told everyone to get the f&#! out of his house. When I tried to stop him from hitting people, he attacked me with the pipe. He kept beating me, over and over, in the face and head. He punched me, slapped me and pushed me all around. I thought he was going to beat me to death. He was throwing things, cussing everyone and putting his fist into the walls. I don't know why he did it. I had no choice but to leave, even though I knew I had been drinking. He was trying to kill me and he would not stop hurting me. I had to get out of there."

Sylvia's first version sounded rough, but in future versions she'd claim he also beat her with a crow bar and kicked her violently with his steel toed boots. (Seven owned no such boots, they hurt his feet.)

Her husband's description that he gave Mae in the early morning hours after it had happened, were no indication, he meant to hurt Sylvia, but he had no doubts that he did.

"I've done gone and messed things up!" The words choked out in between bitter sobs.

"What's happened?" Mae was worried immediately, sitting up in her bed.

"I hurt her, I know I did. I pushed her really hard; I know it had to hurt her." It was difficult to understand what he was trying to explain. "She went back into a table…" Seven paused. "It broke. So I know it hurt her."

"Seven; why did you push her?" Mae worried her brother had finally snapped.

"She was in the bed with Campbell, which doesn't make sense, because Campbell is Maggie's boyfriend. But Maggie was having sex on the couch with that Abe Markesan." His explanation was making things more confusing for Mae.

"Okay, you came home, found Sylvia in bed with Campbell, and you pushed her?"

"Yeah and I know it hurt her." Seven was more than upset, he had been set up, and he didn't even realize it. Once he calmed down the next day, he explained it again.

"I got a phone call from Sylvia, while I was at Jason's. She was calling from Momma's phone number. It worried me, and so Jason and I drove over. We both checked Momma's house, and Sylvia wasn't there anymore. We walked back to my trailer, and went inside. I felt like she was up to something, so I picked up a pipe for my own protection, not sure what might happen. When I walked in, Maggie was on the couch, having sex with Abe.

It bugged me, because my kids were in the next room, and could easily come out and catch the sex show going on in the living room. I walked back to my bedroom, opened the door, and there was Sylvia with another man, in our bed. Both were undressed. I'd only come inside my home to tell Sylvia to stop breaking into my Momma's house. Then I find my wife in bed, having sex with Campbell Collier. He is only a kid and I scared him to death standing there with a pipe, but I would never hurt that boy, hell he's only sixteen. All the blood had run out of the boy's face, when he saw me walk in though. I pointed the pipe at him and told him to get the f&#! out of my bed and house. He jumped up in an instant, but Sylvia wasn't happy. She jumped right in between us, and told me no, Campbell was staying, and I was the one going. The next thing I know, she is attacking me. All I could do was back away, but she kept coming at me. I tried to get out, but she wouldn't stop. I pushed her back, but she continued. Next thing she had a big metal candle holder, and she's smacking me with it, in my head. After the second time, I snapped. It really hurt, and I turned around and pushed her. I pushed her really, really hard. Hard enough that I'd have time to get away. I know I hurt her though. It had to. She went back, right into the table, breaking it. I left her like that, and I know she had to be hurt."

Seven's friend Jason would have a view of the dispute also. He'd followed Seven down to the other trailer, and stood in the living room, while Seven had headed down the hall with the pipe.

"Seven came back down the hall, with Sylvia all over him. I was scared, because she already broke a chair over my head, so I backed over to the front door. Seven was trying to get out from under her, but she was all over him. Slapping and scratching, punching and spitting all over the place. She wanted him to hit her back, but he was holding his hands over his head, while trying to get out, but she wouldn't stop hitting him. He pushed her back finally, but she picked up a candle holder, one of those big ones. She smacked him in the back of the head really hard. She held it up over her head, and smashed it back down again. Pop. He turned on her then, and as she went to hit him again, he just shoved her backwards off her feet. She fell back into the kitchen table, and crashed through it. Seven started for the door, but she got up, still cussing and threatening him. She stumbled forward, and fell face first into the gas heater on the wall. We left right away, because Seven knew she would be calling the police. He knew they wouldn't believe what really happened."

Campbell Collier would eventually get his rendering of events to Seven's family. Embarrassed for being the naked boy in Seven's bed, he'd always felt guilty about what really went down.

"I don't know why, but she all of the sudden wanted to have sex with me. She was all over me, begging me. So, we went back to the bed. Not long after that, Seven opens the bedroom door, and he is holding a pipe. I thought I was a dead man; he scared the shit out of me. He pointed the pipe at me, and told me to get the f*#! out of his damn bed. He told me to leave, and I got up, telling him I was sorry. I don't know why, but I had a feeling he wasn't going to hurt me. Next thing I know, Sylvia has done jumped right in between Seven and me. She starts telling him he has to leave. All of a sudden she attacked him. When I say attacked, I mean, like I'd never seen anyone get attacked before. I'd never believe it, but she was whipping his ass, really bad. She was hitting him with her fist, and picking things up, smacking him really hard across the head. Next thing, he pushes her into a table and he gets out the door and leaves. She got the best of him that night."

When asked if he knew that Sylvia had just called Seven, he looked surprised, and shook his head no. Campbell was informed that Sylvia had broken into Mary's house, and called her husband. When asked if he knew about that, again he shook his head no.

"If I'd known Seven was coming home, I'd never have got into that bed. The girl was really messed up on pills and she was drunk too. One day after that, we was in my truck, and the police pulled us over. Sylvia had prescription pills and other drugs on her, which the police found. I figured she was going to jail, and probably me too. They let us go. I couldn't believe it."

It was an unfortunate night, that would leave a community divided on who was and who wasn't telling the true story.

After Seven left, Sylvia got into her van, highly intoxicated, and drove just far enough to find a cop to pull her over. She was ready to go to jail for DUI, but pleaded she had no choice but to drive in an attempt to save her life.

"Seven came home with a pipe and did this to me."

The Lanyard officers were highly offended to think Seven beat Sylvia so horribly. They were not about to arrest her for DUI, when she had no other choice but to get away. In order to get her off the street though, they apprehended her on an outstanding warrant from two years back. They took her to jail in the early morning hours of Saturday, October 27.

Chapter Forty Seven

Mary came home the morning after Sylvia's break-in and battle with Seven, to a ran-sacked home. She spent the day debating whether or not she even wanted to go to the police department. Once she got some of the mess cleaned up, she began to realize, Sylvia had robbed her. Several things were missing, like the telephone and all of her family photo albums. From her jewelry box, a gold nugget ring, that Seven had bought her out of the blue. Tears blinded her eyes as she looked at the plastic she'd hung up over the broken windows. Sylvia had easily pushed it aside. Mary measured the fact it might be easier to just move.

The next day she'd made her mind up. Even though she had the feeling it was a waste of time, Mary knew this time she could prove Sylvia broke into her home. The phone call Sylvia made from her house to the Tidwell's, looking for Seven. Mary felt for certain, with such evidence, the police would have no choice but to listen.

The same Monday morning that Mary walked into the Lanyard Police Department to file a report on Sylvia; Sylvia was at work around the block, showing off her badly bruised and battered face to the public. Working at the Dollar Store, she had plenty of puzzled and inquiring citizens to impress with her harrowing story, of her husband's attempt to kill her. It had many people talking and most was not happy with Seven Levine and what he did to the mother of his three kids.

Sylvia was also informing her fellow employee's that she was worried because her six year old daughter had started her period.

A few days later, on October 30th, DHR showed up at Sylvia's trailer. They had received a phone call from Bella's school. Seems Bella was bleeding, profusely, and needed medical attention. What really shocked Sylvia was the announcement her condition would be under investigation, because she was too young to start her menstrual cycle. It was suspected the girl had been molested.

Another warrant was making its way through the system. On October 30, it was signed and apparently passed out to all the local police stations. It was the very first warrant of her fifty-eight-year old life. Mary didn't know she had accomplished such an exciting thing, but she certainly would be finding out.

October 31st, had its late evening trick or treater's running from house to house as the sun went down on the Halloween night. Mae and Mary were on the telephone, and were discussing mother-daughter stuff.

"You're not going to believe this, but that crazy girl is driving her van around my house." Mary broke through the conversation.

"Do what?"

"Yeah, she's honking her horn, and cussing. She's actually riding around and around my house." Mary watched out the front as Sylvia's van barely missed hitting her car. "I can't believe this; she is driving around my house!"

"Momma, call the police!" Mae knew about her mother's dislike of the police, but still, the girl was going to end up hurting someone, if not seriously injuring herself.

"For what…They won't do a damn thing to help me!" Mary was hurt by the local law. She had never caused any problems for them since she was born.

It bugged Mae that things were turning out this way for her mother. Getting off the phone, she debated going over there. It was obvious; Sylvia was looking for trouble. Fearful for her mother, she tried to picture what Mary was claiming. It was a crazy thing to do. Why would Sylvia drive her van around Mary's house, unless she'd completely lost her mind?

Sylvia had a plan in motion; all she needed was for Mary to come into contact with the police. She'd been tipped off about the warrant being signed concerning the stolen cell phone. Now she just had to entice Mary to call for help. She drove around and around, screaming, honking, cussing and every so often, coming close to striking Mary's car.

Mary watched from her windows for over two hours, but eventually went outside. Fearfully she got into her car to pull it closer to her house. Sylvia took the prime opportunity to try to hit Mary with her van. Narrowly Mary got back inside her house, and finally picked up her phone and dialed 911.

"911, what's your emergency?"

Mary slammed the phone down. "This is ridiculous!" Mumbling to herself, she didn't know if she wanted to cry or scream. The phone started ringing.

"This is 911, we just received a phone call from you that was disconnected, is everything okay?"

"NO! No it's not okay, this is Ms. Mary Levine, and my daughter-in-law has been circling around and around my house in her van now for two straight hours. I'd like someone to tell her to stop!" Mary rubbed her forehead. "But I know y'all have no intentions of doing anything about it, so never mind!"

"Oh, no ma'am, we are going to take care of this tonight, once and for all." The operator stated matter of fact.

Both Mae and Rex heard the signals go out over their scanner, that Ms. Levine was being harassed by her daughter-in-law, Sylvia Levine. The very next thing they heard was a police officer explaining that Mary Levine had an active warrant out of Westwood. Mae and Rex looked at each other, puzzled if they had heard it correctly. They both jumped up, and started out the door. Mae debated calling her mother back, and warning her of what was fixing to happen.

Mary wasn't thrilled to see the police, but she was relieved that Sylvia would have to stop for the night. She allowed the officer inside.

"Ms. Levine, I hate to inform you of this, but you're under arrest." The officer informed, pulling out his hand-cuffs.

"Arrest who? Arrest me? For what? What have I done?" Mary laughed at the thought.

"Theft of a cell phone..."

"I stole a cell phone? When did I ever do that?"

They had no explanations. That would be for the judge to figure out. They just had to do their job. They allowed her to call Mae, who already knew, and assured her mother they would get her out.

With Mary's arrest it took things up another notch for Seven's family and realizing how far Sylvia would go to hurt them. In order for her to have pulled this stunt off, she had to know that night that she could get Mary arrested. Someone had to let her know.

Mae became quite unnerved by the entire episode. What was the limit of Sylvia's power to manipulate? Where did her sovereignty come from? How was she getting away with so much? When would it end? Why did she want to destroy, humiliate and hurt Seven so bad?

Chapter Forty Eight

As November rolled around, Mary was more determined than ever to get Sylvia off the land. Angry about being handcuffed, booked, and fingerprinted; she was seeing red. Being innocent, she didn't understand how Sylvia had managed to pull off such a stunt. She went down to the Westwood Police Department, and asked if she could at least see the surveillance tape, so she could easily prove it wasn't her. The police sent her to the hospital security, who said they had already sent the video to the police. Returning to Westwood PD, she was told if she wanted to see the evidence, she would need to go get an attorney.

The next morning, she got an early morning phone call from a Lanyard Detective. He had some interesting news for her.

"Ms. Levine, you placed a report stating Sylvia Levine burglarized your home, the night of October 26."

"Yes I did." Mary held her breath wondering what was happening.

"Well, it's impossible for it to be Sylvia Levine, because our records indicate she was in jail, under arrest for an old 2005 domestic warrant. Being that she was in jail, she couldn't have been the one to break into your home."

Mary couldn't believe her ears, but then she already knew the Lanyard Force was on Sylvia's side.

By now, everyone knew about the events of October 26th. Seven had an arrest warrant out on him for domestic violence. The District Attorney's office was hot on catching him. They possessed physical photographic evidence of Sylvia's severe injuries.

Mary argued with the detective. "Oh really, because if that's fact, then the warrant Sylvia has out on my son, for beating her, wouldn't be legitimate. If she was in jail during my break in, then I know she was in jail during the time she claims Seven beat her up, because the burglary happened just before the domestic occurrence."

The detective grew quiet, as if he'd been corrected, and he couldn't figure out a way to fix the scam they were now attempting to pull for Sylvia.

"As a matter of fact, I can prove she was in my house, because she used my home telephone to call Seven at Jim and Brenda Tillers house. You can call them and confirm that, or you can easily subpoena the telephone records, I don't really care. The girl broke into my home and stole my belongings, and the fact isn't going to change, just because you people want to sleep with the girl." Mary slammed the phone down, growing more ill by the hour.

The next day, Seven turned himself into his parole officer, and was put in jail overnight for the domestic violence. It angered the police to find out he walked so quickly. They didn't know Seven's parole officer was privy to Sylvia's behavior.

Mae wrote an article for the local paper, complaining about how her mother was set up and arrested.

TO THE EDITOR: This is a story about a mother, something we all have. Let's say this mother is near the age of 60. She is at home alone, one late evening, getting some rest before her third shift starts at work. Suddenly a vehicle drives around and around her house, recklessly circling and honking. The thoughtless and irate driver screams vulgar obscenities out the window aimed at the older mother, who is now watching the scene from inside her home. Fearfully, she wonders what is happening. The driver is the same girl who had already physically attacked her in her own front yard weeks before. Nervously, she fumbles with the phone to dial 911. Frustrated though, she hangs up.

The phone rings, its 911 calling back. As calmly as she can, she explains the situation and the police arrive. Instead of assistance, she discovers a warrant has been issued for her arrest. They handcuffed her, read her rights, and took her fingerprints and picture. In her entire life, she has never committed one crime. Our community has essential laws to protect us from aggressive animals. Who or what law is there to defend us from belligerent human's intent on hurting innocent people, causing needless pain and suffering?

Adding some dimension; what if this older mother also took care of her 80 year old mother, who lived on the same property. Some would call her

Grandma. What if some girl, hurting you mother, harassed your grandmother too, constantly calling her at all hours, using offensive language to degrade her daughter?

This twenty something year old girl has friends or followers who are as hateful, hurtful and hostile as she is. They too like to victimize your mother, even though she has never wronged them in anyway. In less than two months, this mother has been verbally attacked too many times to count. She spent a month with a black eye after being physically assaulted by the same girl. The mother's home has been continually broken into, not to mention burglarized and also vandalized. Her mail has been thrown into the street, and even her family and friends attacked. On top of all that, she's been arrested for nothing, handcuffed, mug shot, and fingerprinted.

Her trust and confidence in our city govt. system has been shattered, and will never be the same again. Evidently, this young girl has nothing better to do than pick on and hurt our older generation. Perhaps it's the "in" thing to do. All her followers and accomplices must be amazed or astonished at her ability to manipulate the system to work to her advantage. Some would find it sickening to know how easy it is for certain people to use our system to hurt innocent people; victims with no assistance.

Assault, menacing, criminal trespass, burglary, criminal mischief, harassing communication, defamation, and criminal impersonation, the mother has endured within two months' time. If this was your mother, how would you feel? How would you help her? If you knew the people hurting your mother, and watched as their actions were looked over, for whatever reasons, what reaction would you have? What reaction should you have? Well, what if it was your mother? If all this can happen to this one mother, who's going to prevent it from happening to yours?

I certainly have no intentions of provoking anyone, but it is disturbing to witness as it all happens to this mother. Being a mother and grandmother myself, I wonder who I'd call for help - Ghostbusters. Judgment is supposed to be done by a judge. I implore those hurting this mother to stop. Sometimes actions have far-reaching consequences, and that one lonely mother suddenly isn't alone anymore. Your actions and behavior have not, nor will not, go unnoticed or ignored by all.

Marion Mae Smithfield, Lanyard

The same day the article appeared in the paper, Mae got a visit from a Lanyard Detective. She didn't hear the knock at the door, but she did manage to catch the unmarked car leaving her yard. Picking up her purse, she wondered what the cop had to say to her. Did it concern the article she wrote? Curious, she rode over to the police department.

She was reaching her limit concerning the actions of her sister-in-law.

Everyday Sylvia would come up with a new way to get to her family. Driving to the Lanyard Police Department, she worried if perhaps Sylvia hadn't somehow arranged for a warrant to be out for her, too. It could be a set up. Mae didn't know how many cops Sylvia had won over, but she had heard from both Mary and Seven it was enough. Judging from her mother's subsequent arrest, it was hard to be able to trust anyone connected with the law or court system.

Sitting in the parking lot, Mae had to center herself, and breath to get the nerve up to go inside. She wasn't sure what to expect. Fearful, she might run into that one cop her mother had been complaining about ever since he helped Sylvia break into her house. Going inside, she told the lady behind the glass who she was, and that she believed a cop just came by her house. Within minutes, Woody Muck stepped out from behind the locked door.

"Mrs. Smithfield?" The rather short and balding investigator had big eyes. Smiling he used his hand to issue Mae into the back where he led her to a small office. Sitting across from each other, he thanked her for stopping by and began.

"We're under an active investigation, concerning a harassing communication phone call." He put his two hands together, with the fingertips touching.

Mae realized the smile on his face was phony. They looked back and forth without speaking. Mae had no idea what was going on, still worrying that, like her mother and brother, she was being set up. No doubt this investigator was pals with Sylvia. The leather chair she was sitting in was uncomfortable and made continuous noises, even though she didn't move.

"This call was made to my wife." He paused still smiling and now slightly twisting his swirling office chair around. "Two months ago."

Still Mae made no reply, but she watched him as closely as he was observing her.

"It was made on a pre-paid phone."

"Really?" Mae finally responded, trying to act like she was proud of him for doing such a good job. There was something about his smile, that rang a bell of familiarity in Mae's memory banks.

"Yeah and it seems that phone hasn't been turned on since that phone call to my wife was made."

His entire investigator training was being used to track down a horrible prank caller, Mae thought to herself.

Woody was getting ready to deliver the punch line.

"I got a court order for the phone records and they came back to a Rex Smithfield."

Mae's eyes squinted at him, as he continued to smile at her. A long pause made the room feel uncomfortably small as they both shifted around in their seats. His words were not making any sense. Why would her husband call this guy's wife? As if he was reading her mind he added.

"The phone call to my wife was made by a woman, who warned my wife that I was seeing Sylvia Myers." He stopped talking again, watching Mae's every reaction or lack of response.

Mae's mind was churning all around, still trying to figure out, what was happening. Was Sylvia behind this?

"The number is ***-***-****." He sat watching to see how Mae would behave with each word he spoke.

Mae was thinking she knew Rex had two phone lines, and that he had been using one to talk with Sylvia. The number he called out didn't sound familiar. Something told her Woody couldn't possible get records for a pre-paid phone. Suddenly she was struck with a realization that maybe Rex had a prepaid phone too. What if the number he was talking to Sylvia was on a prepaid line? Either way, the only way that Woody would be able to find out would be through Sylvia. Mae smiled back at him; they were trying to set Rex and her up.

"I know your husband has many phones, and I'm sure his crew members have phones too."

"Yes Rex has two phones that I know about, but I don't know about his crew members." Mae agreed, but held back her concern over how Muck seemed to know so much about Rex from a pre-paid phone bill he'd pretexted a court order for.

They smiled back and forth.

"Well this is my phone number; would you have your husband call me?" He handed her his card.

Mae unexpectedly had to know if Rex and Sylvia had their own private prepaid line. That would make sense, and be a good enough reason for Sylvia's number to not show up on his bill.

"I can't wait to get home and ask my husband about it." Taking the card, Mae grinned back at the investigator who looked like he might have let a cat out of a bag.

That funky smirk on his face, suddenly sent a shiver down Mae's back, she remembered where she had seen that smile before. It had been on that day Seven tried to kill himself, and that patrol cop was standing around beaming, despite the morbid situation. This was the same guy, only he'd worked himself up to detective. She'd not made the connection like her mother had, though Mary had actually worked with him when he was fresh out of high school.

Woody stood up, and ushered Mae out of the room, telling her he appreciated her coming down and talking to him. As they got into the hallway Mae returned the politeness, but she wasn't finished with him.

"Well, it wasn't a problem; I was concerned it was over my news article about Sylvia." Woody's eyes opened wide, and his arms folded.

"Let me ask you, just how is it that you know Sylvia? I mean I'm just wondering?" His shoulders shrugged.

"She is married to my brother, Seven Levine."

As if Mae had slapped him, his head went back. "Seven is your…and Mary is your…Can you come back in here and let me figure this out?" He was ushering her back into the little room. Both taking their seat, Woody looked harder at her. "Oh, now I can see the resemblance to your mother."

Mae made no reply as he continued.

"I don't know Sylvia all that well. I mean, I know her, but I knew her when she was a Myers, not a Levine."

Mae thought to herself it didn't matter what her last name was, it didn't change her DNA.

"I know Mary doesn't like me very much." He laughed nervously. "Sylvia had every right to go into Mary's house to retrieve her belongings."

Mae listened, nodding her head up and down, smiling back at him.

"Your Momma has accused every single police officer of sleeping with Sylvia."

"Well that would be ridiculous huh?" Mae sarcastically laughed back at the man.

She left with a head full of thoughts. So Sylvia and Rex had their own personal prepaid thing going? That explained why she'd been unable to find Sylvia's number on Rex's phone bill. It was apparent that Woody was seeing Sylvia, because Sylvia would have been the only person to know about Rex's extra number. She was certainly going to confront Rex. If he had another phone, she would be retrieving it.

Once Rex came home, he tried to call Woody Muck, but Woody wouldn't answer or return Rex's attempts. It was true; he and Sylvia had been talking on that secret prepaid phone.

Mae warned Rex. "Well, your whore is turning on you, so I hope you're watching your back."

The remainder of November, the last one of Seven's life, was relatively tame. Sylvia continued to harass his family with phone calls and spit, but other than that it grew uncomfortably quiet, similar to the eye of a storm passing by.

Mae did a little investigation over the stolen cell phone at the ER, going to the hospital and talking to the victimized nurse. The nurse listened to what Mae tried to explain, but it sounded so farfetched, she had a hard time believing the wrong woman had been arrested.

Mary went through the eviction processes, and at the end of November, Sylvia would receive her second eviction notice to vacate the property.

Chapter Forty Nine

Forgiveness has become something many assume I should get straight to working on after Seven's murder. It's something many wish I'd do, or maybe something they think I need to do. Trust me; forgiveness has been a burning issue since I can remember. Incidentally I believe what goes around comes around. So do victims deserve being victimized? No, but there will come a moment when I myself will have to ask for forgiveness. Yet I can't have something, I'm not willing or able to give.

So far, since his murder, no one involved has requested forgiveness or acknowledged their wrongs. No one has said, "Please forgive me!", or confessed any crime.

The lessons I'd learned before the murder were simply. I offered forgiveness in order to erase the control the other person had over me, with the hate I had for them. That hate will consume massive amounts of energy. Energy I desired to use in better areas of my life, in a positive direction. In order to transfer that energy, I had to let go of the hate, replacing it with love.

Compassion is an act you do to get closer to God. Though I can't comprehend what happened to Seven, I can know that I trust God. Instead of using the anger and rage for hate, I'll use it to get even CLOSER to God. If and when I offer it, that's between God and me. I will forgive all those involved with hurting not only Seven, but his entire family and county full of friends. This will come in time.

Forgiveness is as intimate of any other emotions. It's always between God and You. Its effects are penetrating and far reaching. The benefits out weight the pain, and you shouldn't expect it, if you're unwilling to give it. It's done for your own life, soul and spirits sake. To hold onto forgiveness, is like a deadly slow suicide. You're holding onto intense pain, confusion and fire red rage. It sounds simple, especially being reduced to ink on paper. Let me point out, without forgiveness, you're an alien to Love. Some people are more easily able to forgive than others. Some have to learn how and some are gifted. The important part of forgiveness is to begin and to continue, giving your life to learning more about it.

By the time of Seven's murder, I hadn't gotten to the place where I could forgive Sylvia for the pain and agony she caused by seducing Rex. I was in the middle of trying to forgive my husband. It had my mind and heart pretty wrapped up. My marriage, not Seven's, was my top priority.

I was too busy trying to learn to turn the other cheek as she continued attacking our family. I wasn't taught to fight back, instead I was taught to take it. Brought up to be polite, respectful and only speak when spoken to, etc...Trying to be good, orderly, and compliant in the face of inner or outer danger, cuts a person from knowing; it cuts them from being able to act. Sometimes when you're being nice, your eyes are closed to everything damaging around you, and it forces you to just live with it.

Never take your own revenge, beloved, but leave room for the wrath of God, for it is written, "VENGEANCE IS MINE, I WILL REPAY," Says the Lord. Romans 12:19

Do not be overcome by evil, but overcome evil with good. Romans 12:21

Well what about self-defense?

There exists a law, not written down anywhere, but inborn in our hearts; a law which comes to us not by training or custom or reading…a law which has come to us not from theory but from practice, not by instruction but by natural intuition. I refer to the law which lays down that, if our lives are endangered by plots or violence or armed robbers or enemies, any and every method of protecting ourselves is morally right. –Marcus Tullius Cicero, 44 BC

I've had to fight back, but I call it self-defense. Those that have hurt me in life purposely and accidentally created opportunities of experience. Instead of looking at them as curses, I'd made them tools of a higher learning capacity. The monsters would assume they held the control, yet, I was actually using them. They were teaching me more about myself. I'd like to believe, with my reactions and behavior towards them, that they were learning something themselves, through me.

How easily it would be to behave like them! I can hit back. That's what they wanted me to do. That's what they expected me to do. I wonder what lessons they learned from hurting someone who refused to sting back.

This book has been my way of dealing with the demon that took my baby brother from me. I intend on swallowing it and taking its power from it. The greater our life's pain; the greater our life's reply. I won't fight my enemies the way they want me to fight; I'll choose my own path, thus taking their power from them. How do you love your enemy without condoning what the enemy does? Without accepting their aggression?

Chapter Fifty

The last Christmas season of Seven's life would not be a merry one. He fought demons of depression and loneliness, hanging on with only the grace of experience. Despite those believing him to be a monster, he prayed Sylvia would stop trying to make him into a monstrosity.

DECEMBER 2007:

2nd - On a Sunday afternoon, Sylvia was in a truck that had been pulled over on four separate occasions,by the police; all on the same day. Three times by Lanyard, who let the driver and Sylvia go, but the one time in Westwood she was pulled over they found thirty prescription pills, which were not prescribed to Sylvia. She was arrested, but not jailed.

Later that night, moving into the early morning hours of December 3rd, Sylvia busted out more of Mary's windows, and accused Seven of stabbing her with his knife, after she accused him of raping his own daughter, Bella. She also assaulted Mae.

3rd - One police officer from Lanyard, that had become more aware of Sylvia's unlawful actions toward Seven and his family, Officer Hank Hale, informed Seven that Sylvia made a report over being stabbed. He also told Seven about Sylvia being pulled over so many times the day before.

4th - Sylvia was arrested for assault and criminal mischief over the events that occurred at Mary's house on Dec. 2.

14th - Mary went to court with Sylvia over the punch in the face. The District Attorney, Holly Bass, called Mary a bogus liar, and court was continued until further notice.

14 - 16th - Through the weekend, Sylvia was arrested in Westwood over the three counts of possession of a controlled substance. She attempted to get Seven involved and arrested too. He hadn't even been in town.

18th - Mary and Sylvia appeared in Eviction court. Sylvia lied to the judge when she claimed she hadn't gotten into any trouble concerning drugs. (She'd just been arrested over the previous weekend.)

21st - 23rd - Over the weekend, Sylvia was arrested by a state trooper for DUI. The Lanyard police being the first on the scene were unable to help her get away with it, because she had wrecked and caused property damage. The Lanyard officers had to call a state trooper. The police knew she would be arrested, and they informed her how to behave and act in front of the trooper. They gave her gum, to cover up her alcoholic breath.

27th - Seven moved back into his trailer.

By the beginning of December the storm's eye had moved on over, and the full force of the damaging winds of Hurricane Sylvia returned. For Mary it had been six months of hell dealing with her daughter-in-law. She wondered anew every morning when would it end?

She was called home from work by Seven, in the late hours of Sunday, December 2. When she got home, it was a bloody mess. Sylvia had taken it upon herself to bash in more windows. Seven described to her what had taken place in the glass filled home.

"James had come over because he wanted me to know what Sylvia was up to next. Right after he got here, Sylvia showed up, walking right into the house. She started screaming at me, that I was nothing but a sorry child molesting rapist. She said I put semen into her daughter's vagina. She was accusing me of raping my own daughter. I lost it instantly, and was going to knock her head off. That's why James had come over; he knew what Sylvia was fixing to do. She wanted to make me mad enough to hit her. I didn't know Bella had been hurt, so I was immediately made as hell, and she knew I would be. James grabbed his sister, and pushed her back outside. That's when she lost it, and just started smashing her hands up against the glass door. Both James and I were trying to keep her from breaking more windows, but she kept coming."

Seven's hands were cut up, but not nearly as severely as James'. Both boys were terrified, that the police would be coming to arrest them, because James knew that was his sister's intentions. With the past six month's chronicle with the Lanyard police, Mary agreed to take the boys over to Jason's parent's house before she called the law. She also made a call to her daughter, who got up and went straight over. When she arrived, Mae was shocked by the amount of glass and blood covering the living room and spilling out onto the front porch and yard. Mary felt like she was going to have a nervous breakdown. She cried while trying to make sense of the mess. Two police officers were writing down the report, as Mae tried to console her mother. The officers left the two of them alone, as they counted up the amount of new broken windows. It was frigidly cold, and Mary knew she wouldn't be able to stay in her home until the glass was cleaned and replaced in the windowsills.

"Momma, you don't need to go back to work. I think you need to just go to Maw Maw's and get some sleep. I'll come over tomorrow and help you clean this up." Mae tried to comfort her mother. Mary agreed, and they started walking toward Thulah's house. As they got to Thulah's, a vehicle pulled in, and went down towards Sylvia's trailer. Mary pulled out her cell phone. She wanted Sylvia arrested immediately, and she dialed 911, while walking back down to her vandalized house. Mae thought seriously about just leaving, but if Sylvia was around, she couldn't leave her mother until she knew it would be safe to do so. Slowly, she walked back to her mother's house. Mary had gotten inside her car, so Mae stood outside the car's door, watching her talking on the phone. Sylvia, who had been in the vehicle that brought her home, got out and made a beeline straight towards them.

"Have y'all got a problem or something?" She slurred, getting right up in Mae's face. Mae looked over at the vandalized home and thought to herself that sure she had a problem with her mother's house being trashed, but she said nothing.

"My friends need to get by please." She staggered as she pointed toward her friend's car. "Without you people stalking, staring or taking pictures."

She was swinging her arms all around for a dramatic effect. Mae just wanted to slap the crap out of her.

"Your friends have plenty of room, if they need to get by." Mae looked Sylvia in the eyes. Just like looking into the eyes of an irrational and vicious dog, Sylvia began moving in closer to Mae.

"You got a problem or something?" Sylvia put her arms up in the air, getting too close for Mae's comfort.

"Yes I do, I sure do, with my mother's house being van…" But before Mae could finish, Sylvia screamed.

"Seven and James beat me up!" As if on a movie set, she began crying hysterically into her hands on cue.

"Sylvia, go home; just take your drunken ass home!" Mae insisted, while rolling her eyes.

"Make me bitch!" The dramatics changed paced from crying to rabid raccoon, taking a step closer to Mae.

"The police will make you." Mae took a step back away from the aggressive girl.

"Bitch; what you waiting for the police for?" Sylvia was getting braver, as she slurred at Mae.

Mary opened the car door, seeing that Sylvia was getting ready to attack her daughter. Sylvia's attention was immediately diverted to her mother-in-law.

"All of this is your f*#!ing fault, you nasty ass skank bitch!" Sylvia attempted to get to Mary, but Mae blocked the way, preventing Sylvia from attacking her.

"Hit me bitch!" Mae wanted to keep the attention on her, trying to protect her mother.

Sylvia jumped toward Mae. "Bitch you hit me!"

As Mae quickly glance toward her mother, who was still communicating with 911 on the phone, and just as she started to turn her head back toward Sylvia, a warm and gooey ball of spit hit Mae right in the face. Sylvia darted off toward her trailer, escaping any retaliation from Mae, who now was figuring out how to get the nasty off her face without touching it.

While this was happening, the vehicle that had dropped Sylvia off hadn't moved. A female voice could be heard yelling to Mae.

"Mrs. Mae, Mrs. Mae!" The driver was yelling out the passenger's window at Mae, but Mae continued to keep her eyes on Sylvia.

"Mrs. Mae, you don't remember me?" The girl's voice was carrying itself through the bitter night air. Mae looked toward the car, and walked over to it carefully. As she began to peer into the window, she recognized the driver, but before she could reply, Sylvia had run over, shoving her away from the vehicle. Nearly falling off her feet, Mae caught herself. She remembered the driver as a youth from her church.

"You stay away from my friends bitch!" Sylvia stood her spinning ground.

"I know your friends!"

"No, you don't know them!"

Mae couldn't help but laugh. "Her names Anna, her little sister's name is Tessa, and their mothers name is Elizabeth Bidden." Mae had gotten her cell phone and was dialing the police herself. Being shoved was one thing, but being spit on was another.

"Your names Anna?" Sylvia was asking the driver, not even knowing the girl herself. The male passenger was the father of the driver's baby. He was also an old boyfriend of Sylvia's, Charles Wheeler.

Mae went back to her mother, who was still sitting inside her car on the phone. She looked down and realized she had 911 on the line also.

"LOOK, the girl just spit in my face, my mother is on the phone with you now, send us some help before somebody gets hurt!" Mae wasn't sure how much more she could withstand before she lost it too, like the incredible hulk waking up inside David Banner, the old warrior Liz was cracking open her eyes inside Mae.

Sylvia had started walking toward her trailer. She knew the cops were on the way. Yet she felt she still had time to provoke Mae a little more. She was pulling out all stops to trigger an attack

"Your phone records will prove you called that wife and you're going to jail. You're so stupid and sorry you can't keep your man. He had to f*#! me cause you're no damn good." She was rubbing herself. "He couldn't keep his hands off me. Bitch he has several girlfriends, one 21 year old nurse in Valley Point. You ain't nothing but a stupid skank." Sylvia had started walking slowing toward Mae, pointing her finger. She was laughing one second, and then the next she started screaming and sobbing.

"Your brother's sperm is in my six year olds vagina, you sick child molesting people!" Sylvia was hell bent to get Mary or Mae arrested for whipping her ass and shutting her mouth with force.

"Where is your proof on such a horrible lie? Who have I ever molested?" Mary having heard the sick accusation about Seven and the horrid words spoken to Mae, had stepped out of her car again.

"You let him molest you kids for years. All your family and kids are drug, pill popping..."

Sylvia stopped abruptly as blue lights began swirling all around in the cold darkness, and took off running toward her trailer.

Two cops ran past Mary and Mae, while a third one waited with them.

Soon one of the two came back outside and made his way over to mother and daughter. The officer gave them some news, while Mae took notice of his name tag.

"She says that Seven stabbed her in the arm with his knife." He gave both women a serious look.

Mae looked over at Mary, who gave her the same confused expression.

"Or, Officer Hale, could it be a wound from when she was running her arms through my mother's now broken glass windows." Mae pointed to all the glass and blood.

He motioned his head up and down, like he could see that happening.

The other officer, who had stayed longer with Sylvia, came outside. Walking past the two women, he made a comment.

"I remember her; she's the one who was nearly beaten to death by Seven Levine. Now he's done gone and stabbed her."

Nothing was done to Sylvia over the turbulence of destruction she'd been involved with that evening. Reports were made against her, but nothing would be done until a judge sat to observe it.

One warrant was made that night though, and issued for Seven Scott Levine. He was being charged with stabbing his wife in the arm with his pocket knife.

As Mae drove home, she thought about the ugly things Sylvia had disclosed about Rex. Also, she thought it interesting that Sylvia mentioned the police officers wife being called. Mae had told no one about that meeting, except Rex, and she wondered how Sylvia could possibly know such information. Sylvia had to find out either through Muck or her husband.

Chapter Fifty One

Eventually the predicaments would end up in a court of law.

Mary had been looking forward to that day when she could finally receive some type of justice for being punched in the face by Sylvia. As she sat in the packed room, she hoped she'd not be spending the entire day waiting for her case to be called. She sat anxiously waiting with her notebook of evidence needed to prove her case. Her daughter and mother, along with her friends Peggy and Dessa, surrounded her for support.

The Lanyard city court was full, but as the day wore on, it began to empty, until finally Sylvia's case was called. Mary made her way to the Prosecutor's side, while Sylvia had a court appointed attorney to represent her.

Before the case started, District Attorney Holly Bass requested to speak with Mary in private. Everyone watched as they left the court room through an adjoining door that connected the courtroom to the Lanyard PD. No one could really make out what was being said, but there was no doubt that a yelling and screaming match was going on behind the closed metal door.

Bass had immediately confronted Mary, as soon as the door shut. "The only reason you are accusing Sylvia of hitting you is because she has reported Seven for domestic violence!"

At first Mary said nothing, she was completely shocked, but then she stood her ground. "That's not true!"

"Yes Ms. Levine, you only filed a report on Sylvia, because she has filed one on your son."

Mary held up her notebook of proof, but the DA put her hand up, blocking it.

"I don't want to see your crap." She refused to look at the evidence right before her eyes.

"You are wrong!" Mary pointed her finger at the red faced DA.

"The only reason you are here is for revenge over what has happened to your son, Seven! You're nothing but a BOGUS LIAR!" Holly Bass pushed her finger back at Mary.

Mary felt dizzy, this couldn't be really happening to her. Yet it was, and she could suddenly feel the fire growing inside her.

The public defender for Sylvia, McNally, stood off to the side, listening as the two women argued.

Mary pointed at the man. "Sylvia has an attorney to represent her, but the State is representing her too. Who's supposed to be here to represent me?" Mary paused, pointing at Bass. "You won't be representing me, because you've already made your mind up!"

With that said, Judge Millen was forced to set the case for a later date.

There would be another Lanyard civil court hearing taking place within the next week though, concerning the eviction.

Sylvia sat in the room, crying to the judge and lying to him. Somehow, she was able to get the court to believe her every word. She told the judge that she wasn't doing any drugs, even though she'd just gotten arrested the weekend before in Westwood with prescription pills.

The next weekend after the eviction court, (Which effectively was progressing to have her removed, but the process took time.) Sylvia was arrested by a Alabama state trooper after she crashed her van and damaged some property. She would receive a DUI, and proceeded to bragged about the experience.

"The Lanyard police would have let me go if they didn't have to call the

State Trooper. They helped me by giving me gum to mask the vodka smell, and told me how to behave in the Trooper's presence."

Once the eviction process started, and Sylvia wasn't going to be allowed to continue live on the Baker property, she took a different approach. She'd began to believe that all the things she'd done could just be forgiven and forgotten. Somewhere in that brain of hers, she believed that if she just apologized, everything would magically bounce back like it had been before.

By the end of December, Mary had a restraining order on Sylvia, stating she couldn't come in Mary's house or anywhere within so many feet of it. There's no way Sylvia was frightened of some piece of paper, and for the last week of December, she would show up at Mary's front door, begging her to accept her apology. She was shocked that Mary never wanted to speak to her again.

Seven hadn't been able to mend the rip either. He didn't believe Sylvia could have gotten Mary arrested over the stolen cell phone, but then again, he'd spent two trips to jail for nothing too. He would forever be caught right in the middle, never being able to have his family and Sylvia at the same time again.

Sylvia had attempted to file another false report on Seven, accusing him of stabbing her that December 2nd night. When Seven went to his parole officer, he was surprised when the officer pulled the warrant out, and pushed it to him across the desk. Seven figured the time had come, that Sylvia had finally succeeded in getting him locked away. It really surprised him when the parole officer pulled it off the desk.

"It doesn't exist anymore." The experienced officer couldn't help but to crack a smile at Seven's response. "I've made it go away." He tossed it into the trash.

Incredulously Seven looked at him. He had always assumed the man had it out for him, when in reality; the man had been harder than usual on Seven because he could recognize a good guy when he saw one. There was no smoke screen blowing in his eyes, he could see straight through Sylvia's intentions. He was impressed with how the seemingly vulnerable woman had managed to wrap an entire police department and DA office right around her fingers.

"I tell you what though; I'm not going to be able to keep doing this. You're going to have to get away from that woman. It's obvious she isn't going to stop until she gets you put up for good."

Seven left the office feeling good, but knowing the parole officers actions could have repercussions with the local law who were making it obvious he'd better watch his back.

Despite everything Sylvia had done, whenever she asked Seven to come back, he nearly tripped trying to get in the door. At the end of December,

Seven would begin making decisions that some would later say, cost him his life.

It wasn't because she suddenly loved him again, but because she'd got herself into a mess of trouble over the past six months. She had nearly ten warrants out on her. Her friends had deserted her not long after the letter written by Mae hit the paper. They realized they were contributing to everything Sylvia decided to do in order to torture Seven and his family.

While Mary waited for her next opportunity for court, she stayed in her vandalized home. She'd covered the windows with plastic, but was afraid to replace the glass. She still noticed things going missing every day. Crazy things like toilet paper that she was sure she'd just bought, along with food, towels, washing powders and even shampoo. Such things only made her feel like she was losing her mind.

Seven's troubles wouldn't be ending. Whatever he decided to do, someone would end up hurt and angry at him. If he tried to please his wife, it angered his mother, and vice versa. Neither woman would allow the other in his life. He tried to make the best decision, believing his larger responsibility was his wife and kids. Though Seven's desperate need for his family caused him horrible heartbreak, he made the ultimate choice to sacrifice his own bonds in order to make Sylvia happy, and protect his children.

Chapter Fifty Two

Seven's life was slipping out from underneath him, and his wife had made it clear that she wouldn't share him with any member of his family.

"If I can't have him, no one can."

Mae tried to give her brother the benefit of the doubt. Going back to Sylvia after everything she had put him, the children and his family through, had to be for a good reason. She also reasoned that, she had stayed with Rex after what he did with Sylvia. Who was she to tell her brother he had to leave his wife, when she herself had chosen to work it out with Rex? If Seven wanted to work on his marriage, then that was his God given right and business. Mae hadn't resolved anything with Sylvia, and she never intended on having to deal with her again if she could help it.

Sylvia's life was out of control, and without Seven around to protect her and their kids, she was losing everything fast. While she'd spent months tearing their lives apart, the bills went unpaid. Without electricity, it would only be a matter of time before DHR was called. All of Sylvia's houseguests had either grown bored or indifferent to her behavior and stunts. She had gotten caught with prescription pills and now faced jail time or fines. Seven moved back in, because she was about to lose it all. Thus he was continuing down the predictable path of a victim of domestic violence. Breaking up with a woman like Sylvia, was no easy task to do.

Mary didn't care one way or the other what her son's reasons were for going back to Sylvia. She continued with her push to have her daughter-in-law evicted from the property. She couldn't protect her son. With Sylvia on the property, Mary had a hard enough time defending herself. It did bother her to know how much it hurt Seven to have to choose between Sylvia and his family, but she wasn't the one forcing him to make that decision. She figured Seven believed if he moved back into his trailer, perhaps she would change her mind about evicting Sylvia.

There were three innocent children's lives at stake. No doubt Sylvia couldn't be trusted to keep them safe, and Seven desperately loved his three kids. He wasn't allowed to have anything to do with his family without the wrath of his wife coming down on him, but the state of their finances had Seven grasping at ways to get things under control. Having his momma to lean on his entire life, he continued to ask her for help. Grudgingly she would take him to the store to buy groceries for his family. He hated having to ask his momma for anything, but because of the past six month's crap Sylvia had put them through, they were in deep debt.

Things had gotten much quieter on the Baker property. Once Seven moved back into his trailer, there were no more late night police calls.

As the second week in January 2008 rolled around, Mary had her first Westwood city court case concerning the stolen cell phone. It was a plea hearing and her plea was "innocent".

District Attorney Bass was the one pursuing Mary, and there was no doubt in Mary's mind that Bass actually believed she had stolen the phone and was merely trying to set Sylvia up for it. The situation was bad enough for Mary that she was forced to hire herself an attorney.

The attorney made attempts at viewing the hospital's security video. Mysteriously it had disappeared.

Mary began to worry she could actually lose her job.

Seven still had a hard time believing Sylvia was involved with his mother being arrested. He'd been at the hospital with the baby that night; he hadn't noticed his wife being malicious, vengeful, vindictive or nasty. Had she been? Could she possibly pull such a stunt off without a hitch?

The next Lanyard city court date was something Mary wasn't looking forward too. Usually victims want their day in court, but the last time Mary had hers, the District Attorney had called her a bogus liar. She feared what she might be accused of next. Perhaps she was not only a lying thief, maybe she'd robbed a bank or kidnapped somebody? All of her family and friends were outraged at how the police department and DA's office had treated her. So on her day of court, she had a group of people there to support her.

All the past Lanyard cases were going to be presented to the judge at one time. (Absent the civil eviction cases and the Westwood city, stolen cell phone fiasco.) 1. The broken windows. 2. The assaults on both Mary and Mae. 3. The domestic violence case concerning October 26th, which Seven was accused of nearly killing his wife.

Because Mary had refused the state's prosecutor, Holly Bass, another DA sat to the side most of the day, waiting on the Levine case. Chief Deputy District Attorney Lewis Gold patiently watched as the day unfolded.

Bass had brought pictures of a badly beaten Sylvia to present to the court. She would present the state's many cases for that day, but she had only one on her mind.

Sylvia's badly beaten face could be seen on 8x10 glossy pictures that Bass had placed on a table used by the prosecutors. DA Gold sat at the table, and at one point, picked up the pictures to take a close look. He was puzzled as to why he would have to stand in on one of Bass's cases, especially one she was so impassioned over.

Before Judge Millen called any case numbers or names, he requested that anyone who wanted to plead guilty to come up front. Seven would be one of a dozen that went to the front to plea. Persistently he waited his turn. Once he stood before the judge, he asked him a question.

"Yes sir, if someone is hitting you, and you push them back, is that against the law?"

"In this state, it is considered domestic violence." The judge answered, looking down at Seven.

Judge Millen had been dealing with Sylvia, Mary and Seven for six months. The escapades that started in the summer of 2007 were well known in the court house. Sylvia had cases against Seven, while Mary had cases against Sylvia, and Mae had a case of being pushed and spit on. Judge Millen had presided over all the cases, including Mary's eviction of Sylvia, as well as the stolen cell phone. He hoped that by putting as many as they could on this one day that most of the trouble would end once and for all.

"Well then I am guilty, but I have pictures to show what she did to me. The only reason I pushed her, was because she was attacking me." Seven put several pictures of himself down before the judge. Mae had taken the photos at his request the day after the Oct.26th incident happened. He had scratches all over his face, torso and both arms. His face displayed several black bruises, from where the large candle holder had made contact.

The judge quickly dismissed the case, and moved on to other business.

Mae sat watching as one usually does in a court room. Her focus stayed on Holly Bass, who bounced around the chamber. The look on Bass's face at one point was priceless for Mae.

As the judge went through his case numbers, Sylvia's domestic violence case against Seven was called. Bass ran over, having been eagerly anticipating this moment, and grabbed Sylvia's 8x10 pictures. She motioned for Sylvia to come up front. For month's she had been chasing down Seven Levine, and now she would be sending him to prison. Once she found out the judge had already dismissed the case, you could see the blood drain from her face. She hadn't noticed Seven go up earlier. Just like that, her chance was over.

DA Gold would have to wait all day. Once the court room was emptied of all other cases, the chance for justice would come for Mary. In front of Judge Millen, Mary, Mae, Seven and Sylvia stood. Thulah stood behind her daughter and Sylvia had a court appointed attorney, Donnie McNally. DA Gold would stand in for the case involving Mary's assault; otherwise Bass continues her verbal onslaught against Seven and his mother.

The first case Judge Millen listened to was concerning Mary's windows being bashed out on two separate occasions.

Seven had to testify for his mother and against his wife. He hadn't seen her the first time she did it, but he did the second. At one point Sylvia said something to him, and he made a loud reply that got everyone's amused attention.

"I won't lie for you Sylvia, you know what you did. Get over it!"

Sylvia was found guilty of breaking Mary's windows, on the second occasion but got away with the first.

Next the case of Mary being assaulted by Sylvia was called. Finally DA Gold would stand in for DA Bass. Mary had her own pictures to show the court. Still, she had to endure questions from Sylvia's attorney. His questions insinuated Mary had purposely gone after Sylvia.

"Ms. Levine, can you explain to me why you felt the need to go outside while Seven and Sylvia were fussing."

"Because…" Mary looked at the man like he was the devil. "I was giving Seven a ride." In her mind she was screaming at him. "It's my damn yard you fool, and if I want to go outside, I can anytime I want!"

"You decided to video the fight?" McNally continued his quest, ignoring her hateful glances.

"That's right!"

"Why would you do something like that?"

"Evidence of the hell she was causing." Mary had had just about enough of the public defender.

Regardless of the discomfort caused by Bass and her constant coughing noises and grunts, and along with McNally's further victimizing the victim, the judge found Sylvia guilty.

After that came the case over Sylvia spitting and pushing on Mae.

"Yeah I spit on her, but I didn't push her." Sylvia offered while looking over at Mae half laughing.

McNally got his opportunity to drill Mae also, giving her a long stare before he started. "Why were you at your mother's house so late at night?" He looked down at his folder of papers, flipping through them quickly, before he looked back over to her.

"I was in bed asleep, until my mother called me concerning her house being vandalized."

"What I mean is, why didn't you go home, when you saw Sylvia come home? Why did you go down to her house?"

"I didn't go to her house; I was at my mother's." Mae was trying to restrain her sarcastically hostile feelings for the public defender.

In the background Sylvia was talking out loud, making comments for everyone in the court room to hear.

"She's calling all the police officers wives and telling them I'm sleeping with their husbands, and she's writing newspaper articles, talking about how I hurt people."

Some of the officers leaning up against the walls of the room smiled and folded their arms.

Mae glanced at all them all watching from the sides of the courtroom. Everyone in the room was entranced by the case playing out in front of them. She worried that they actually believed what Sylvia was saying.

"Well Sylvia, spitting on people in malice is a form of assault, so I find you guilty." The Judge pushed that file aside, happy to have another case done.

Nothing really become of the day. Sylvia got into no real trouble, and if she was court ordered to pay restitution, she never did. It really was an entire day wasted and had served no real feeling of justice.

Seven didn't win any points from his mother even though he testified against his wife.

Sylvia certainly wasn't happy he wouldn't take her side and lie against Mary to prove his love and devotion to her.

What no one in that court room realized, was to the day, Seven only had five month's left to be alive. Though the day had been a rough one for him, it would be the very last time he would ever have to stand in a court of law.

The "system" believed and protected Sylvia. The same "system" pampered Sylvia. The "system" whose responsibility is to invoke law, allowed Sylvia to get away with her crimes, and as a result, it would cost the family unspeakable pain. While turning the other check for Sylvia's crimes, the "system" chased

Seven and his mother down. They provided Sylvia support to continue her victimizing, and in doing so, created a monster. The refusal to allow her to be punished for anything, led to tragedy for Seven and all those who loved him. The "system" he went to for help, provided him none, while supporting his aggressor.

Chapter Fifty Three

During the same day of the Lanyard court cases, someone called DHR, concerning Seven and Sylvia's home having no electricity.

Seven quickly moved his family off the property, and into a motel in Valley Point. It became urgent for them to get their trailer moved.

Mary's eviction of Sylvia from the Baker property sealed the fate of her ever returning to the family's fold.

Everyone still had hopes that Seven would wise up, but he just couldn't stand the thought of his children being removed from their mother. In his mind and from his experience a mother was the leading necessity for a child. He believed that he was the only one who could save Sylvia. Love is to blame, and what a horrible crime he was committing in loving her.

Sylvia hadn't magically changed back into a good wife overnight. She continued to drink and start fights. Her obsession to manipulate and control wouldn't ever stop. Seven would try to take care of the kids, while his wife tried to find ways of hurting herself. One night, Seven visited Thulah's, very upset because Sylvia was threatening suicide.

"She visited her mother's grave today, and she told me that her mother told her it would be okay for her to leave me and the kids." This had him unnerved and sick with worry. She was burning and cutting herself. He had caught her trying to stick objects into the electrical sockets. She threatened to throw herself in front of moving cars.

"I don't know what to do." He hoped his grandmother would have the magical answer, but there was nothing anyone could tell him.

Her luck had run completely out. She still had her fans at the police department, but she'd used them so much, they were leery of her. The job she had was lost. Without employment, Sylvia was completely dependent on her husband's income. DHR continually checked in on them, to Sylvia's displeasure. She was feeling the consequences of some of her actions. Yet, her husband never left her, despite all the hell she put him through.

Seven's last month's on earth would be sorrowful and heartbreaking. Despite the brave front he displayed, beneath the surface his soul was torn in half. He walked about in a constant battle with his own heart tugging him in too many directions. Guilt ate at his spirit. He missed having his family around, and would cry himself to sleep many nights, unable to find a way to fix the damage done by his true love. As lost as he felt over losing Sylvia and the kids, he felt just as shallow on the inside without his family's love and support.

Mae went on with her life while her brother endured his hell. Her daughter, Melina, had gotten into some trouble with the law, and was due to give birth of her second child. Cameron was a married young mother herself, and things weren't going well for her. Mae and Rex were trying to help find a place for her family to live. Both girls were demanding for their time and attention. Then there was her son James Robert, who had moved out and was trying to make it on his own. During the last months of Seven's life, he would go over to where James R. was living, and briefly visit his nephew. Essentially Seven had special bonds with each member of his family, but he claimed James R. as being the one who "calmed" him.

What was difficult for Mae was the guilt she felt for putting Seven and his children aside. It wasn't them; it was their direct connection to Sylvia. The affair's effects were very raw and Mae couldn't bring herself to just forget, and would have preferred to walk through fire, than to allow that back into her life.

After the last day in Lanyard court, Mae wouldn't talk to Seven ever again. She had no clue about that though. Eventually, she figured, the commotion would eventually calm down, and Seven's perceptions would come around.

What hurt as bad as the isolation of Seven's presence, was the loss caused by being kept from his kids. It was like they had no family anymore.

Mary continued to be vigilant about taking back her life and sanity. Watching her son follow Sylvia was like watching him jump from a cliff. She continued with the things she had been doing before Sylvia's rampage. Work and friends filled in, while she enjoyed the quiet and tranquility of having Sylvia off the property for good. Still, she missed Seven and the children. Mary hoped her son would come to his senses and leave Sylvia.

Seven on the other hand was confused as to why no one would excuse his wife's behaviors. He still didn't believe Sylvia could have had anything to do with Mary's arrest.

That was until she confessed to doing it.

On the date of the Westwood city court hearing, concerning the stolen cell phone, Mary was like a nervous cat in fear of being drowned. She didn't know what to expect.

The victimized ER nurse sat in the court room, and was confused as to why Mary was there, because she wasn't the same woman who had been in the room with the baby's mother.

It would be another entire day of waiting for Mary. Her daughter, mother and loyal friends sat with her.

At the end of the day, DA Holly Bass casually informed Mary's attorney that Sylvia had called the District Attorney's office the day before and confessed to lying to the nurse. Sylvia confessed that she gave the hospital Mary's information.

Bass could have easily let Mary go earlier in the day. Yet Bass was still under the impression that Seven's family was forcing Sylvia to make all these confessions, and that Sylvia was the victim. She detested Mary, and anything she could do to make the poor woman's life hell she would. Assistant District Attorney Bass was no doubt an impassioned attorney for the State, maybe a good person to have on your side, but the worst demon to have against you. If she disliked anyone more than Seven Levine, it was his mother, whom she continued to believe was nothing more than a bogus liar.

Nothing was done to Sylvia for all the trouble she put everyone through, including the ER nurse.

Leesa Morey, Sylvia's partner in the crime, was never charged or troubled.

After Seven found out his wife had effectively put his mother in jail, something inside him shattered. His view of his wife changed, and he could no longer be intimate with her. Who had he married? Were there any limits to what she would do to hurt him?

Chapter Fifty Four

Seven was smart, clever, handsome, considerately kind and infinitely amusing. There was energy, a vibrancy that surrounded him. Despite everything Sylvia did to him, he forgave her. If anyone has lost the best thing to ever happen to them, it is Sylvia. To have had that kind of love, and then throw it away for nothing, must bring tremendous regret.

He would continue to drop in on his grandmother, Thulah. It wasn't anything unusual the last time he walked into her back door. Through his entire life, his feet had carried him across that land, and into the Baker home. He was always welcomed to come home.

Thulah described her last encounter with her grandson. He was her seventh of eight grandchildren. Having lived with her or near her the majority of his life, the two shared a unique relationship. She had her share of commotion with him over the years, but it had never affected her devoted love for him.

"He came into the back door like he always did, and found me sitting in my chair. He stood there for a minute and then looked down at me."

"I love you Maw Maw."

"That's all he said, then he kissed me on my forehead." She breaks off in tears at this point, and then continues. "I patted him on the butt, as he turned to leave, and I told him. 'I love you too boy'."

Thulah said he was acting funny, and he stood in the kitchen like he wanted to tell her something else. He had his hands up on his head, looking out the back door, just standing there. And then he was gone.

On the same day he walked into his mother's house with some news, he was excited about.

"My parole officer told me I would be getting off parole early!" His face beamed.

Mary wanted to be happy for her son. He had been through so much and deserved to be a free man. Yet she couldn't help but worry what the news would do to his wife.

"I wouldn't tell Sylvia."

His teeth flashed with a wide smile. "Well why not?" Her question had instantly puzzled him.

"Because if she knows, then she won't rest until she puts you back in jail. If you tell her, then you're going to end up back behind bars or dead."

He just couldn't comprehend how dangerous Sylvia was, or to what extremes she would go to in order to keep her complete control over him.

By March, Seven had his trailer moved from the Baker property. It would be place in Focus Trailer Park, which would turn out to be his final address. The trailer park was an older one, and was full of families. Seven didn't intend on it being their permanent dwelling, he planned on finding land to put it on. His main objective was to get Sylvia away from Mary, and try to hold his family together.

Mary had begged her son. "Seven, you don't have to move the trailer, you and the kids can stay."

"The kids need their mother mom." He looked across Highway 51, where Sylvia sat watching.

"No son, they need security, something that woman will never provide them." Mary's words went on deaf ears.

It was a quiet time for Seven's family; everyone felt that the worst of it all was behind them. No one knew what was going on with Seven and Sylvia; it had grown quiet concerning them. Seven continued to work with Carl and spent most of the week out of town. His neighbors never got much of a chance to get to know him. While he was home, he could be seen cleaning up his yard, or playing with his kids. He would walk with Bella to school when he wasn't out of town.

Sylvia continued with desires to share her life with her friends. Around Easter Maggie Morey stopped by the trailer, wanting to take the kids to an egg-hunt. Seven put his foot down, and refused to allow his kids around Sylvia's friends, considering his family was barred from their life.

An old boyfriend, Nathaniel Walker, the man who believed Bella was his daughter, dropped in to visit one weekday. He was as surprised to see Seven at home, as Seven was to see him at his front door. Nathan lived right around the corner, and explained to Seven he'd heard they'd moved there. Seven invited him in, having at one time been good friends. Nathan didn't stay long, but his impromptu visit had Seven wondering what might be going on while he was out of town.

There was one man Seven did somewhat befriend. Ennis Dorsey, who didn't live in Focus Park, but daily, frequented it. His trailer sat in another trailer park, and a small wooded trail joined the two mobile home parks. The distance between their homes was less than a five minute walk.

Ennis happened to be an employee of Seven's brother-in-law, Rex. He'd worked for the company since he was a teenager, year's before Rex inherited the business. Ennis' mother, Angie, was married to Rex's uncle, Luke Smithfield. So, when Ennis befriended Seven, he had been working with Rex for many years. He lived and shared two children with his girlfriend Sissy. They were a volatile couple who couldn't seem to get on their feet. He and Seven had known each other for years but weren't close friends. After Seven moved into Focus Park, they would get their families together for cookouts. Seven had only lived there four months before he was attacked, so they didn't have a lot of time to become best friends. Ennis is the only one that Mae personally knew that Seven hung around in the trailer park. She heard Ennis talking about her brother every so often. From what she gathered, he didn't like Seven that much.

"That son of a bitch set me up, I know he did."

What Ennis Dorsey was referring to was a particular night when law enforcement surged his property. It was true, that it appeared a little suspicious the way things went down, but Seven was as clueless as Ennis when the cops jumped out of the woods.

It was a late Friday night, and Ennis was sitting outside his trailer, next to a bon-fire he had blazing. Seven showed up, for nothing more, then to sit and talk a few minutes. Ennis offered him a cold beer, as Seven took a seat. Out of nowhere, the yard was stampeded by law enforcement; that had been hiding all around Ennis's trailer already, unseen in the thickets.

"Freeze, put your hands up! Both of you put your hands up!" Both young men stood up with their arms up.

Within minutes, they allowed to Seven go. Unfortunately for Ennis though, they searched his house, removing guns and paraphernalia. They also forced his wife and kids to leave the house for the night. This had Ennis furious, and he would continue to complain and fuss about it to anyone that would listen.

Lanyard Officer Hank Hale would later comment to Mary, how angry Ennis Dorsey had been that night.

"I want to know why y'all let Seven go? That boy should be arrested too! That punk is a snitch."

Though Seven was polite and respectful towards Ennis, he wasn't that fond of him. He'd observed Ennis physically assaulting Sissy, and it bugged him, but not as bad as witnessing Ennis abuse his kids.

After a cookout, Ennis had stayed over at Seven's past the party hour. Sissy had gone home with one of their children, and left the infant with Ennis. The baby was in a car seat, and when Ennis decided to walk home, he grabbed the seat. Seven was concerned about the baby, and he offered to walk Ennis home.

"When we got close to the top of the trail, all of the sudden, he tossed the baby, just tossed the car seat up into the air. I couldn't believe it. I ran to check on the baby, she was crying some, but appeared okay. Ennis reached down and grabbed the seat again. He wanted to wake the baby up so Sissy would have to get up and take care of her."

Seven was disturbed to the core and couldn't help feeling guilty if he didn't try to help those kids. Of course, Seven wasn't thrilled with the prospect of calling DHR.

A few weeks before the homicidal attack, during one of the cookouts in Seven's yard, Ennis and he were involved in a physical fight with each other. No one knows what it concerned.

Toward the end of the month, Rex's mother Jenny unexpectedly passed away. Without warning, Rex's family was sent reeling from the loss. It became something else to keep Mae preoccupied and too busy to know what was happening with her brother. Ennis Dorsey would serve as a pall bearer at Jenny's funeral. He was after all, a family member.

The last time Mae saw her brother alive was when he was walking on the side of the road. She observed him at first from a distance as she was driving by. As she neared the individual, and surveyed him walking with his hands in his pockets, she knew it was his trademark walk. Immediately pangs of guilt could be felt going across her heart muscles. She knew she should stop and at least say "hi" to him, but as she drove past, her anger over Sylvia kept her foot on the pedal. Looking at him in her mirror, she prayed he didn't notice her van go by, fearing it would have hurt his feelings. Mae knew her brother still needed his family despite his wife's disposition. Something about the occurrence unnerved Mae, as if she'd really made a mistake. It haunted her from that day on.

Chapter Fifty Five

As the spring turned into summer, the war between family members seemed to be finally cooling down. A stand-off of sorts was occurring. Seven hadn't lost his family. He continued to talk to his mother, grandmother, brother, nieces and nephews. Sure his siblings were angered over what had been done to Mary, but as long as the violent attacks stopped, they were content. Never did Seven leave their thoughts or prayers. They all worried about how he was doing and what his wife was doing to him.

As mentioned earlier, Mae and Rex had tried to get their daughter Cameron set up in a place of her own. The found a trailer that sat in the same park where Ennis's trailer was located. Being she was so close to Seven, Cameron started visiting her Uncle's home every day.

Seven was thrilled to have her company. She had her own trailer, but she hated staying there alone. She'd lost custody of her two children and was suffering from it. Seven, ever protective of Mae's children, welcomed her to stay with them.

Sylvia didn't mind it at first, having Cameron around, but it didn't take her long before she began to feel "watched" by Cameron. She was, after all, a family member of Seven's, and she didn't like sharing Seven with anyone.

Mary would still receive calls from Seven. One day he called and asked her for a ride to the grocery store. Though she was still hurt and angry over the past months, she picked her son up and took him to the store. She pulled into the parking lot, and removed her keys.

"I'll wait for you."

"What? You're not going in with me?" Seven had opened his door, but shut it back.

"You said you needed a ride. You didn't say I had to go in." Mary looked over at Seven.

"Well, how am I supposed to buy food?" It pained him to have to ask, much less keep asking.

"Seven, I've already told you, I can't help you as long as you are with her! Anything I do for you, or my grandchildren benefits Sylvia. I am not buying food for her to put in her mouth!"

"Well, then take me home. I'll find the money." Seven folded his arms.

Mary started the car and drove nearly all the way back before she turned the car around and went back towards the store. Her son and her grandchildren needed food; she wasn't going to let them go hungry. It wasn't fair that she couldn't help her own without it benefiting Sylvia. They drove back to the grocery store in silence most of the ride. Seven loved his mother with all his heart, and nothing would ever change that. She purchased a few bags of groceries and took him back home. She watched as her son happily unloaded the food.

"Thanks, Momma."

Mary was still upset with the thought of Sylvia eating the food she had provided.

"You tell that wife of yours, every time she puts a bite of food in her mouth, that your mother bought it. Me, the woman she called a child molester, the woman she assaulted, the woman she had put in jail, the woman, whose house was destroyed and robbed. Sylvia is the one who said she wouldn't ever accept nor need my help; so tell her who it is that is feeding her!"

"Okay…" He smiled at his mother, but he had no intentions of saying one word to his wife. "I will."

Mary's last contact with her son was when he showed up to retrieve the electricity pole from where his trailer had sat behind his mother's. Mary didn't want him taking the power poll; they stood outside arguing about it. In reality, it wasn't the power pole she didn't want removed from the property, it was her son Seven. In the end, she allowed him to take it, but Seven left the yard crying. He hated the thought of his mother being hurt and angry with him.

The last conversation with her son was an 'out of the blue' phone call from him. He wanted her to know he had a new way of making some extra money. Mary was concerned with that, and asked him if what he was doing was legal.

"Oh yes Momma, you don't have to worry about that. This is *very* legal. I can't tell you what it is, but I can promise you, it's extremely legal."

Mary had no inkling that she was carrying on the last conversation to be had with her son.

At the end of May, Seven arranged a cook-out for his niece Melina. She'd been down on her luck, and had given birth to a baby she couldn't keep. This had Seven very upset and he hoped to raise her spirits some. Seven loved parties and cooking out. He also loved spending quality time with his family, and on that evening he had the last chance. Melina, Cameron and their brother James Robert, all three spent the evening with their Uncle's family. For Seven it was the closet he'd been to being happy in well over a year.

Despite how much his wife hated her husband's family, she tolerated them. After they ate barbecue chicken, they sat down and watched a scary movie, another one of his favorite things.

June rolled around, and his time on earth was ticking away. Two weeks before he was attacked, Sylvia was put in jail. She hadn't been paying on her fines, and a warrant had been put out for her. Seven was upset because he didn't have enough money to get her out. He asked Cameron to stay in his trailer with the kids while he went out of town to earn the money required to get Sylvia out of jail.

Cameron's husband, George Rowe, was back in the picture, so he had moved into Seven's home also.

Seven hated having to leave Sylvia in jail for any amount of time. He was well aware of how she hated being locked up.

With every second that she was incarcerated, she envisioned the fun her husband must be having. She was enraged Seven didn't get her out faster. It bugged her to know his family was in her home. By the end of the week, Seven got back in town, and went straight to get his wife out of jail. It took every single penny he had. She wasn't happy with him for that either. He had some nerve making her sit in jail so long.

What he was, was a wonderful human. He served as a charming, sweet and warm hearted son. A simple man who was a honestly loyal and devoted husband. Seven knew he was blessed and was eternally devoted to his children. A direct blessing and answered prayer to his siblings. He took great pride in his family and functioned as a dedicated friend. His desire was to help people, to relate to their pain. He loved nature and noticed the miracles in God's work. Every moment that he isn't around is noticed

WHY I MUST CONTINUE TO WRITE

By: Mae

As I attempted to carry myself through the last days of Seven's life, knowing there was no other choice, I moved about each day in deep pain and nearly paralyzing fear.

When you are going through a tragedy, you're in such a state of numbing shock; it's tough to understand the profound grief you're in. How humans find the strength to walk through such days boggles the mind.

Murder colors your world in the blackest black you've ever seen. You're trapped in it, with no way out. With its effects, it is nearly impossible to find the hope or courage to fight your way out of the darkness. Rage finds itself simmering and filling your entire being with fire. It leaves you feeling empty and believing life to be a meaningless journey of pain. Nothing about the life you had before the murder equals what your life has become. You see the world in a completely new somber tone.

Seven was gone, but his healthy young body continued to reflexively fight to live. Mechanically machines kept him alive. Sedated he lay lifeless, never to open his eyes again. Still we could see him waking up, and asking us what happened. Prayerfully we put all the recent drama behind us, and pulled together in hopes of encouraging him to come back to us. As he labored to live, we worried he was being tortured by the procedures being done to preserve his life. To this second, I ask myself question that plague my heart with the knowledge that I'll never know the answers.

Certain issues were still ongoing. No resolutions had been made with Sylvia, at least not from my vantage point. Being in shock and numb with incomprehensible grief brought a temporary cease fire.

Homicide creates a person within you that you would never have known to exist. My new persona was making me a sister of a murdered brother.

PART TWO

THE LAST DAYS WITH BABY BROTHER

Chapter Fifty Six

Erik Tripp was Seven's best friend in the whole world. The two simple boys had survived their shared experiences of both joy and pain. Both boys had grown into handsome, brawny men. Neither was short or tall, though Erik did stand an inch taller than his baby brother.

He would be the first to receive the phone call that fateful day. It came around 4:30 am and woke him from a restless sleep. His niece, Cameron, was on the line.

"Seven's been hurt really bad. They are putting him on a helicopter. He was beat with an axe in the head."

With his mind racing and as if running on an auto-pilot, Erik telephoned Mary at work.

"Momma, Seven's been hurt bad, with an axe. They are putting him on a helicopter." Hanging up with his mother, his heart was beating fast. He couldn't wait, he had to know. He ran out to his truck and sped towards his brother's home. 'This can't be happening…I just saw him…He has to be okay'. He drove with unbearable thoughts trying to reach into his mind. He needed to see Seven, he had to see Seven, and he couldn't get there fast enough! The words helicopter and axe pushed him to drive faster.

An elementary school, sat across the road from the Focus Trailer Park. It had a large ball-field where Erik could plainly see the ready chopper. An ambulance and dozens of police vehicle lights flashed red and blue all around. As if in a nightmare that he couldn't wake up from, Erik found himself running towards the body being pushed towards the trauma helicopter. Police appeared, trying to block him.

"He's my brother." Erik's mouth moved, but his entire focus was on the body.

"Well, let's go this way." The officer pointed to the hovering blades above their heads. "We don't need you getting hurt too." The officer led Erik around the spinning metal. "Now Seven is trying to talk, don't talk to him, he needs all his energy." The officer's words could be heard, but Erik wasn't able to get past all the blood covering his brother's face.

Gone was the handsome man he had known, replaced by a battered victim. So much blood covered his entire head. It oozed and dripped from multiple wounds. Seven was wiggling around a bit.

'He's not going to make it'. Erik's heart dropped as his mind raced with every second he looked upon his struggling brother.

Seven was babbling and incoherent, as he struggled to speak to his big brother.

"You're going to be okay Seven; it's going to be okay!" Erik tried to assure Seven, and tried to appear strong. "It's me Seven, Erik; you're going to be okay!"

Erik stepped back. While in the shock of his life, he watched as the helicopter flew away with what was left of his little brother. He couldn't take in what he'd just seen, yet at the same time, it was pounding in his head to make sense. The sound of Sylvia's voice brought him back. Unlike Erik, she seemed to be running all around, talking about Seven's wallet, and needing a ride back across the street.

"Can you give me a ride home?" She stood in front of him.

"No, I've got to go get Momma." Erik backed away from her. The images were caught in his head. He had to hurry. They were taking Seven to Birmingham, but Erik just couldn't see his brother surviving the journey. What would he tell his mother? Calling her while driving back, he told her what the police told him; where they were sending Seven and who it was that had attacked him, Ennis Dorsey and Kendall Martin.

"It doesn't look good momma, they messed him up bad." It was all he could say.

He wouldn't have to talk about it; his mother was on her cell phone most of the ride to Birmingham. In silence he rushed, praying Seven would still be alive when they got to him.

Mary had put the phone receiver down after Erik gave her the news. Something in her heart told her, her worst fears concerning Seven were coming true. Making her way home, police cars roared past her, and turned on the road leading to Seven's home. She knew they were heading to her son. Instinctively she wanted to follow them. Yet Erik was waiting for her, so she continued on home. When she got home, she found the place empty. She knew where Erik was. Picking up the phone, she called Mae.

Mae was awakened by her phone, and the thought that such early morning calls generally never brought good news. Turning over, she reached for the obnoxious instrument, and tried to make her eyes focus on the number. She didn't recognize it. 'Figures', she thought to herself, 'wrong number'. Immediately she flipped back over, reasoning she might be able to fall back asleep.

The police scanner, which normally couldn't be heard over the noise of the daytime environment, was easily discernable at night.

"Transporting female from Muller Elementary to Focus Park."

Mae sat up, wide awake. Something told her that female was Sylvia. Something told her it had to do with Seven. Grabbing her phone, she listened to the message left from the strange number. It turned out to be her mother's new cell number which she hadn't had the chance to get. Her mother had left her an urgent message.

"Mae, this is your mom, I am waiting on Erik at the house. Somebody beat the crap out of Seven…with an axe handle. Thank God it wasn't the other end, but Erik said his head was messed up, that he was purely messed up. They are airlifting him right now from Muller School to Birmingham. I guess I'll call you, I'm waiting on Erik, and we're going to Birmingham. I don't even know where the hospital is in Birmingham, but I'm fixing to find it. If you get this message, how about calling me. I might try to call you again in just a minute. I'm supposed to take momma Monday, to get her… well I'll worry about that later. Well I'll talk to you later."

With her fingers shaking, she pushed to redial the last number that called. Something didn't feel right. 'This can't be happening' Mae was thinking to herself with the word axe handle slicing its way through her mind. Mary answered and explained again what she knew, that Ennis Dorsey and Kendall Martin had both attacked him. Hanging up the phone, Mae looked over at Rex who was awake and listening to the events playing out.

"They say Ennis did it, with an axe handle."

Rex couldn't comprehend exactly what she was telling him.

She repeated the words, trying to understand them herself. "Ennis and Kendall Martin beat my brother in the head with an axe handle." The slower she spoke the words, the more confusing they sounded.

They both sat looking back in forth in shock. Rex had fired Ennis the previous week from his job. Ennis's work ethic and personal behavior over the past months had deteriorated to the point that Rex had no other choice but to let him go. Did Ennis beat Seven because Rex fired him? That would be a crazy thing to do. Seven had nothing to do with Ennis's employment.

Kendall Martin was another subject all together. There was an ugly and brief history with Martin. Ten years before, he had coincidently attacked Erik from behind tossing a brick across the back of Erik's head. It was an unprovoked attack which left Erik bleeding from the ear for a week.

As Mae quickly got herself up and ready to go, the questions began bubbling in her mind. Again the scanner caught her attention, the police had the suspect in his house, and a warning was given that the suspect had a 10-32, code talk for gun. Mae considered the fact that they might already have Ennis in custody. What about Kendall?

Rex had recently purchased a GPS, so Mae felt confident to make the journey to Birmingham alone. Though she didn't know which hospital, she figured she could call her mother again, and get better directions. She stopped at a local gas station to fill her van up. Going in to pay, one of Seven's closest friends, Ava Burnside, stood behind the counter. Mae wondered if she had heard the horrible news.

"I'm on my way to Birmingham, Seven's been attacked by an axe handle, and was flown by helicopter..." Mae had started explaining but was immediately interrupted.

"What?! Seven?! I just talked to him early this morning; he called me wanting a ride. He said he was with Kendall Martin, and he'd caught him with Sylvia. I told him I would give him a ride, but not Martin, I can't stand Martin." Ava was trying to remember the early morning call, the last time she'd heard his voice.

"Well, it was Ennis Dorsey and Kendall Martin who beat him." Mae didn't have time to talk.

"What?! No, this can't be happening; I just talked to him a few hours ago!!" Ava began to sob, shaking her head back and forth. "This can't be happening!"

Mae left Ava with the tragic news, determined to get to her brother as fast as she possible could drive, while in constant prayer that Seven be okay when she reached him. She did call her mother on the way hoping to get the correct hospital. Birmingham had many medical centers, yet UAB would more than likely be the one. Mary confirmed UAB, and she had a little more information.

"His head has been nearly beaten off!" Mary could hardly speak with grief. "They were fighting over a video game or something. Seven had been fighting with Kendall Martin, and a disturbance was videoed with three boys at the local convenience store."

Mae picked up the pace, putting the address into the GPS. It began giving her the directions she needed. The images playing in her mind made her start crying. Imagining an axe handle hitting her baby brother in the head made her cringe. How could anyone do such a violent thing to another human? Over a video game none the less. She wouldn't allow herself to think he wouldn't survive. Of course he would survive. Seven was one of the strongest people she knew. Everything would be okay. He would be okay.

Arriving, Mae took no time running toward the emergency room door. She could see the helicopter sitting to the side. Poor Seven had the ride of his life, and probably had no clue about it. Then again, maybe he did. Maybe he was seriously injured, but there was no way he wouldn't survive. He had pulled through so many close calls through the years. Certainly no dumb jerks like Ennis and Kendall had the ability to take their loved one away from them.

Reaching for the door, Mae began to touch the handle, when suddenly she saw a picture in her head. Crystal clear, she could see a body, lying on the ground, surrounded by a group of people, and they were hurting him, like a disturbed mob. Shaking the sickening image out of her mind, she pulled the door open. Looking around for anyone familiar, she walked over to the nurse sitting behind a glass window. Once she mentioned Seven's name, the nurse pointed her toward a closed door. Looking at the door, Mae became fearful to open it. What news hid behind it?

Suddenly it opened, and Sylvia stepped out. The two stood facing each other. Neither knew exactly what to do or say. Nothing had been settled; no declarations had been made, and now they were force, to confront each other.

Chapter Fifty Seven

Sylvia stood frozen for a moment with Mae looking at her. Bella, Liam and Cassandra came walking out from behind her, followed by Cameron and her husband, George. They all stood looking at Mae with the same transfixed silence that had Sylvia paralyzed. Mae's knees began to go weak from the look on Sylvia's pale face. Fearing the worst, Mae braced herself for the news.

"He was awake, he moved, he started jerking…" Sylvia wasn't able to articulate what she was experiencing. "They have rushed him back for emergency surgery. They are going to do all they can do to save him."

Mae looked down at the three babes, whose eyes betrayed their confused distress. Not only was their daddy hurt really bad, they were being confronted by family members such as Mae, whom they hadn't been allowed to interact with for months. They didn't know if they could even look at their Aunt Mae, but you could tell, they longed desperately to be reunited with those that loved them.

Looking at her daughter Cameron, Mae inquired. "Where are momma and Erik?"

Cameron pointed to the same closed metal door that the nurse had originally directed her towards.

Unable to find any words to speak to Sylvia, Mae pushed passed the crowd, and made her way behind the door. It merely opened to a hallway, with more doors. Luckily, Mary, Erik and Thulah stepped out of a room, so Mae didn't have to search any longer. They all were as white as ghosts. Mary had been crying, while Erik looked as if he would pass out any minute.

"What's happening?" Mae urgently quizzed them.

Mary explained they had taken him into emergency surgery, as the four made their way to the waiting area. Arriving in the large room with chairs, they sat down as Mae listened to what Erik had begun to explain.

"Seven called me early, sometime after two in the morning, which woke me up. Not long after that call, he showed up. He was driving Cameron's car and he had both Kendall and Ennis in the car with him. It was 2:37 am, because I looked at the clock as I answered the door. Seven looked serious, yet he reached over and gave me a big hug. He wished me happy birthday and told me he loved me. Seven explained he needed some back up, and asked if I would ride with him. We walked down to the car, because he wanted to show me who he had with him. It was Kendall Martin sitting in the front seat, and Ennis Dorsey was passed out drunk in the back seat. Seven wanted me to go with him, but I didn't want to ride around with Kendall or Ennis."

Mae listened. Then she explained to her mother and brother how Ava told her that Seven had called her, asking for a ride also. Just like Erik, she had declined, because she didn't like Kendall Martin. Mae thought silently to herself, why would Seven want to get a ride away? What was Seven doing, hanging around someone like Kendall Martin? What did a video game have to do with anything? The more answers, the more questions. Numbly, they sat in silence until Sylvia showed up.

The three children made their way into the large waiting room. Following their mother, they all took seats, and began looking around at the family longing to hold them. They were afraid to cross their mother; it was no secret how she felt about Seven's family. The entire room was uncomfortably thick with confusion and fear.

Bella was itching to get to her Aunt Mae, and she was the first to ask her mother.

"Can I go sit by Aunt Mae?"

Sylvia eyed the family looking back at her, and told her daughter she could. All three jumped up. The permission to return to the family's fold had been a long desperate need. Cassandra ran over to Mary, her beloved grandma, while Liam grabbed Thulah's walker and began pushing it around the room. Bella, sat in her Aunt's lap, letting Mae hold tight to Seven's oldest child.

Other than the three children running around, everyone else sat in stunned silence with their morbid thoughts. This just couldn't be the way things would end; it just couldn't be the end of Seven's life.

Cameron acted like she wanted to talk to her mother, and the two went to the other side of the room to converse. From what Mae could tell, her daughter was in shock.

"By the time we got outside, there were police cars blocking the road. We were told if we went past them they would arrest us. We didn't know if it was Seven that was hurt, but we had a feeling it was. I could see a body lying on the ground in the neighbor's yard. Detective Muck had Kendall Martin in his car, and they were driving around looking for Kendall's necklace he had lost. Sylvia was talking to another Lanyard cop, Officer Billing. The EMS was working on the body lying on the ground, while other cops were taking pictures. I kept asking neighbors standing around who it was that was hurt. It wasn't until they were picking the body up off the ground, that we found out it was definitely Seven."

Cameron had to stop talking for a few seconds as her emotions started flowing.

"I didn't care at that point if they arrested me or not, I was going to him. They had already pushed him into the ambulance. Through the little window I could see him, his body jerking and blood flying out of his mouth." Sobbing now, she was choking down her tears. "I had to turn away; I just couldn't see him like that."

Mae tried to change the subject slightly. "What was Sylvia doing?" She glanced over at her sister-in-law to make sure she wasn't listening.

"Well they wouldn't let us leave until they spoke to us, but when Kendall got out of Muck's car, Sylvia got into the car with him. After about five minutes, she got out and said we were free to leave. The police never spoke to us."

They had to stop talking as Bella pulled on Mae's hand, wanting to keep her Aunt's attention.

Like all waiting rooms do, they gobble up time, with minutes fading into hours.

Erik continued to verbally dwell on the last moments he had with his brother.

"I just talked to him, he told me happy birthday and that he loved me...I should have went with him." Erik was feeling the intense pangs of guilt.

Mary and Mae reasoned with him that it was more than likely best he didn't go with Seven, or he too, could be lying in surgery.

"NO!" Erik refused. "This would never have happened if I had just gone with him."

Sylvia sat in stone silence for most of the time, occasionally glancing at Mary and Mae. The turn of events hadn't been in her continued battle plans. Without Seven, what would she have to fight over with his family?

No one wanted to think Seven wouldn't make it. There was just no way to believe it.

Mae watched the kids playing around, unconscious to what their daddy was going through. It was a special day to them, being able to interact with Thulah, Mary, and Mae. Looking over at Sylvia, Mae realized that if Sylvia didn't want her to see Seven, being his wife, she'd have the power to forbid it.

Mae decided she would try her very best to be nice. Then again, she couldn't think of one time she hadn't been to start with.

Erik nonstop allowed guilt to eat at him. "He was just standing on the porch. I should have gone with him. I wish I'd gone with him." He stood up, sat down, and stood up again shaking his head back and forth. "This wouldn't be happening if I'd just got in the car with him. I know him, he was anxious and nervous acting. Seven looked like he knew something was going on and he needed my back up."

No one could change his mind, nor could anyone help him. Everyone was sitting and thinking about the last conversations and opportunities they'd had. Every family member felt they'd not loved Seven like they should have. They had let him go, when he decided to take care of his wife and kids. It hadn't been his fault that his wife had acted like she did. But he willingly chose to take Sylvia's side.

"I fussed at Cameron." Sylvia started conversing. "When I came in and found out she'd let Seven go in her car with those two. I jumped all over her! I cussed her out. I told her, if something happened to Seven, it would be her fault for letting him go." She paused to help Cassandra open a bag of chips. "I slapped Ennis really hard more than once. I kicked Kendall in the head. He was on top of Seven, and I ran up and just kicked him in the head, and told him to get the f*#! off my husband."

They all sat listening to Sylvia, trying to comprehend what she was explaining. She'd finished, and the room had gotten quiet again, except for the three kids bouncing about. Mae took the opportunity to explain to Mary how she was acquainted with Ennis Dorsey.

"He worked for Rex, until last week. He had been working with the family business for years before Lawson passed away. For the past few months his work ethics had started deteriorating, as well as his attitude. Rex hated to fire him, but had no choice." Mae sat thinking, and then added. "His momma, Angie, is married to Rex's dads, youngest brother Luke." Mae continued. "I took pictures of Ennis's entire family during a birthday party for his little boy. Ennis, served at Rex's mothers funeral as a pall bearer a few months ago." Growing quiet, Mae's mind continued spinning with thoughts. Of all the people in the world to attack her brother, she'd never have imagined Ennis to be the one. Kendall would, but Ennis just didn't seem to be a dangerous person. Thank God they'd failed to kill him, but they certainly tried their best.

No other family would share the waiting room that morning. Other surgeries were scheduled, but Seven's had been put first. In between giant moments of awkward silence, the kids kept everyone occupied. Anytime the door opened, everyone looked. The surgery was going on three hours.

Cameron and George strangely were trying to sleep, leaning up against each other, and it struck Mae odd they were able to. Then again, Mae considered, whose to know how one would or should act in such moments of torture.

Without warning a doctor walked in, and looked the entire room over. After realizing Seven's family was the only people in the room, he made his way toward Sylvia.

"Are you Seven's wife?" He asked her while sitting down in the empty chair beside her. He glanced at the rest of the curious and worried looks coming from the family. "I've repaired the damage done to his skull as best as I can, repairing the crushed temporal bone as best as we could." He paused. "The shattered bone in his face was taken out, it was beyond repair, but will grow back over time."

Mae began feeling nauseous, with the stinging reality of his face being shattered. Tears started rolling down her face, as the doctor continued.

"He is still unstable and in critical condition. We have him paralyzed and sedated. He is on a respirator, which is breathing for him. We will just have to wait and see from this point, I've done all I can do, it's entirely up to Seven now." The unnerving silence made him wiggle around in his seat a bit. "He is in recovery, holding on, and the next twenty-four hours will be touch and go. They will be moving him up to the seventh floor ICU."

"Can we see him?" Sylvia asked in a scratchy voice.

"Well, Seven must not have any stimulation at all." He answered while scratching the side of his face.

"What's that mean? I can't even touch him?" Sylvia moaned.

"No! You can't and you can't speak to him or make any noise. We do not want him agitated in any way!" The doctor stood up to go. "We don't know what the extent of the damage that has been done to the brain. It's like Jell-O, and when you hit one side, the other side is slammed up against the skull. Each injury has multiple traumas, and he had multiple injuries to his brain, that appear to show he was struck from behind. We have to keep him as still as possible, and as calm as possible. He has received traumatic injuries, we just have to wait and see."

His words had caused everyone in the room tremendous pain. Seven had been beaten nearly to death, then left to bleed in the dirt, all alone. The family wanted to assure him, he was no longer all alone. Now that they could be with him, they couldn't even let him know he wasn't abandoned. They couldn't touch him, or tell him they loved him.

The doctor looked at Mary. "We have inserted an ICP (Intracranial Pressure monitor) which will help us keep check on his brain pressure. The normal numbers rang between seven to fifteen. Right now, Seven's is extremely high, as to be expected." He took the continued moment of silence to leave the room.

Everyone had the seconds after to think of their own disturbing thoughts. Though he was still alive, Seven was not ever going to be the same. Hence he was gone, and everyone feared it. Looking into each other's eyes, no one could hide the anguish. Everyone was scared to death.

Chapter Fifty Eight

Fear is as confusing an emotion as love can be. Like love, it holds many levels, creates different reactions, teaches many lessons, and constitutes great change. To be without fear, is to be without love.

We were so fearful of losing Seven. We feared what could possibly be left of his brain. Our minds were racing with somber fears of what he must have gone through, being hit from behind; without any warning. These fears were no illusions, they were very real.

What horrifying fear he must have faced. Did he know? Did he think about his kids, and missing out on their entire lives? Did he wish to be back with his family? Did he feel the hands of the medics working on him, lifting him and carrying him? Could he hear the noises all around him? Police radios, sirens, the talking of onlookers, and the screaming of his wife? Did he know it was his time to die?

I prayed he couldn't possibly have any memory of what happened to him. I feared he would.

These were brand new fears that I'd never imagined facing.

As the doctor had informed, Seven had received multiple injuries to his head. A fact I didn't know. I already knew he'd been hit, but not repeatedly. With each hit his head took, he received two injuries in one whack, as his brain slammed into the skull on the other side of the impact.

Any assailant who aims for the head of a human being is intent on killing that person.

Miraculously Seven was still alive. He'd made it through intricate brain surgery. Yet the fear of the unknown had taken over my heart. What was the extent of the damage to his brain? The brain can easily begin to die. What if he didn't survive after all?

My soul was torn open. Throughout the entire day, I'd stayed in a constant state of pleading with God. Just like every other fear in my life, I could do nothing more, but hold onto God's Love, and trust in His Wisdom. No matter how painful, desperate or dismal, I'd pull through, without any ability to comprehend how or why. The experience had to be felt.

You never know if the last time you see somebody, that it could possibly be the very last time you will ever see them alive. Life's fragility can open you up to things you'd never have noticed before. That the one thing you can count on is that nothing is permanent. Temporary pains, fleeting emotions, momentary dreams; our lives are brief, like the mist in the air.

He was so beautiful to me. I wish I could explain in words how much I loved him. What his murder had done to me, how it's made me into a person I'm so unfamiliar with. At one time strong, stubborn, determined and always looking for the blessings in life. I now can hardly comprehend the point of existence. I am broken.

Sylvia loved to hurt him. No doubt about it. I've never seen anyone so hell bent on destroying another human's dignity, happiness and well-being. She knew how much he loved his family, and that's the one thing she refused him. She wanted him all to herself, though when she had him, she treated him worse than any other human alive ever would.

Seven believed me when I told him to love and live, and everything would come out okay. To be grateful for the things you do have, and not to take life for granted. He listened to me, and deep within his heart and soul, he believed his love for Sylvia would fix her. He had high hopes that in time, everything would work itself out for the best. He didn't know how limited his time on earth would be, though.

What's so painful is that he will never have the chance to prove them wrong.

All those who so freely took potshots at Seven's reputation; and so easily believed the horrible lies told about him. Perhaps some believe with his death, the truth will never make its way to light. Or better than that, maybe they are in a daily fear, it will.

Either way, I owe him. I won't rest until Seven's truth is known. It's not something I'm doing in spite. It's being done for the love I'll eternally have for him.

I am so grateful and proud that I got to be his sister. No one can rob me of that honor. I know he was a boy full of affection. I witnessed that pure love, and I experienced its radiant power. Go ahead, ask anybody that loved him, and you will hear the same. Seven was a man devoted to those he held dear. Those traits and characteristics were there from the start of his life, and very much there at the end.

Chapter Fifty Nine

Eagerly they all made their way up to the seventh floor of the hospital, where the ICU was located. Each family member was as frantic as the other to have the opportunity to see Seven, even if they couldn't talk to him or touch him. Even if they couldn't do anything but see him, they were anxious to do so.

Seven was a victim of a crime. Someone had attempted to murder him.

So the nurses in the ICU were well aware of his pending arrival. They met the family as they all emptied out of the elevator. From the first moment with the nurse, it became apparent that they were extremely protective of their charge. Seven's life was now in their hands. They didn't care who you were. To get to Seven, you'd have to first get through them. She informed them he hadn't been moved yet but would be very shortly. His room number was 712. Once he arrived, they would have to get him settled in. Once that happened, she would let only two people at a time visit him briefly.

Bella had become adamant that she intended on seeing her daddy. There was no way she could go back into the ICU, so Mae tried to explain that to her. She promised Bella that when they brought him off the elevator, she could possible catch a glimpse of him then. They both lingered in the hallway with Erik.

The elevator opened and closed several times before Seven was finally brought out of it. Mae picked Bella up as the team of medical staff wheeled him by quickly. Though it was only a fleeting sight, it was enough to nearly make Mae sick at her stomach.

Erik grew paler than he'd already been, and backed himself up against the wall for support.

Mary and Sylvia showed up just in time to see them wheel him on into the big metal door of the unit.

Everyone stood silently watching Seven disappear.

The brief foretaste of his head broke Mae's heart as she imagined the brutal attack all over again.

Why would Ennis do this? Who was this Kendall guy?

Through talking to Cameron, Mae found out Seven's attack had occurred in the neighbor's yard. Her version of what happened was as perplexing as Sylvia's, but for Mae, finding answers was all her mind could focus on. As soon as she got the chance, she inquired about the entire evenings events.

Both of Cameron's eyes were swollen and red. Tears continued to flow as she tried to recall to her mother the last hours of her Uncles life.

"Seven got home around five. He had roman candles that someone gave him for his birthday. We all went into the back yard and he shot them off. The kids wanted to do his birthday, so we sang Happy Birthday, and then everyone ate some cake. Seven and Sylvia got dressed and went out to eat at San Juan's Mexican. He wanted to go out for his birthday. They left around six thirty to seven. They were gone one and a half to two hours tops. They came in, drank, and then left. Came back, and then left again. They had some weird beer. Later I was fixing to take a shower. They were going to Opella to get some alcohol for Sunday."

Mae wanted to ask questions, but as long as Cameron rambled, she sat silent, rubbing her daughter's hands.

"Sylvia got mad because George wanted to go with them, and Seven didn't care. Sylvia started fussing at Seven that he didn't love her or want to spend time with just her. They both started arguing with each other. Sylvia left out the front door, and Seven went out the back. George followed Seven out into the back yard. Then George started to clean out the back seat of the car, so he could ride with them. Sylvia came back, and wanted to know where Seven went. Seven came in, and wanted Sylvia to tell him where she went. They argued again, and both leave again. George went out to look for Sylvia. Seven came back, and asked where Sylvia was. When I told him I didn't know, he started out the back door. Frustrated, he punched the picture by the back door. Sylvia walked back in the front door, and she said she had been sitting in the car the entire time. She wanted me to run her up to the store so she could call her brother. I went into the store and got some cigarettes, came out and Sylvia told me she wanted to stay at the store. When I got back to the trailer, Kendall and Ennis were there. Ennis kept trying to show George and me a card trick."

She looked over at her mother with a puzzled look on her face. "I mean he really wanted us to watch him." Taking her hands she attempted to rub her face of all the wetness, then continued. "Later they decided they needed cigarettes. I told them George and I would go, but Kendall didn't want to give us his money. Seven asked if he could drive them, that 'they would go straight to the store and back'. They left, and Sylvia came in, cussing and fussing at me for giving Seven my car keys."

Mae listened closely to her daughter. It had been fortunate that Cameron had been in Seven's house. Without at least one family member there, it's possible that no one would have ever known the events of that night.

"Later, Seven ran inside the trailer, asked George to help him keep the fight fair. Seven was looking for his stick." Cameron stopped, remembering something that had happened earlier, when Seven had gone out of the trailer, the very first time when they started arguing. George had followed Seven out the back door. Cameron tried to keep her memories straight, but everything was so confusing.

"Seven had told George, 'if Sylvia hits me, take me down, I don't want to even accidentally push her'." Nothing Cameron said made much sense to Mae, but she allowed her daughter to talk freely, not wanting to disrupt her train of thought.

"Ennis said they were fighting because it 'was just a man thing, something to get the frustrations out'."

Mother and daughter sat outside the hospital, where a large water fountain was displayed. The mist from the massive fountain cooled them from the hot sun making its way to the top of the noon day sky. Luckily, Mae had this opportunity to talk to her daughter in private. Usually either George or Sylvia was with her. Mae wanted to get back up to the ICU waiting room, but she wanted to know about a particular individual.

"Who is this Kendall?" She inquired while looking at the hospitals front door.

"Seven was gone, Wednesday, Thursday, Friday and Saturday. I can't remember if it was Thursday or Friday, but Bob brought him over. George was trying to sell his necklace, and Bob said he knew somebody that might buy it."

She paused, looking sharply at the front entrance. Like Mae, she was watching it.

"Well, before that though, I'd met him one other time, the first time." Cameron explained while Mae tried to keep up. "I was at the store, getting some gas. When I go in to pay, Ennis was inside with Kendall. Kendall asked me who I was, and if I was interested in hanging with them. I told him no, that I was married. Well, when I went home, I was telling George about the guy with Ennis that had hit on me at the store. Seven asked me what the guy with Ennis looked like. I told him, that one side of his face was messed up. Both Seven and Sylvia knew who it was. Seven told Sylvia right then that he did not want Kendall Martin anywhere near his family, home, or even in his yard."

Cameron paused as her face exposed the pain of her recollect. "He warned me that Kendall was a dangerous boy, and it was best to stay far away from him."

Both Mae and Cameron seemed nervous and uneasy. Knowing the outcome of Seven's moments with Kendall, his words echoed the wise truth he had somehow known.

George was making his way towards them with the three kids in tow. Cameron wanted to tell Mae more, hurrying before her husband and the kids got to them.

"Sylvia and Kendall was friend's, they had been neighbors when Sylvia was a baby." Pausing, she finished with something Mae found really interesting. "She called the cops on Seven, while we were in Ennis's yard. She told the cops that some doped up boys were outside, and she didn't want a fight to break out. She didn't want the drama at her house, but told the police 'there is going to be a fight'."

Mae was stunned. How did Sylvia know there would be a fight? It irked her to know Sylvia had been lifelong friends with Kendall. She didn't have too much time to think about what all her mind was taking in.

As George and the kids got to them, Mae gave the three little ones handfuls of pennies to throw into the fountain. They all three began tossing their change into the water, that was already littered with previous wishes. Each one wished to see their daddy again, alive and well.

After waiting another long two hours, the family was finally allowed to briefly visit Seven, but only two at a time. Sylvia and Mary walked toward the two large metal doors. They had to wait until they unlocked and mechanically opened.

Erik and Mae stood watching as the two alpha females in Seven's life walked together. It wasn't something anyone believed could ever have happened after the entire previous year of traumatizing drama Sylvia provided.

"If Seven open's his eyes, and sees Sylvia and Momma together, he's going to think hell has frozen over." Erik joked mostly to himself without smiling, but Mae heard him and worried Seven really might think he was already dead.

Mary left the ICU first, leaving Sylvia with her husband. While Mae tended to her mother, Erik bolted for the opened doors. Mae held her mother, and listened while she sobbed.

"I can't make any sense of this! I can't believe this is happening to Seven! How could someone beat him like that? Beat him so severely?!" Mary cried as Mae cried with her.

Seven's three children sat very still and quiet, taking in everything that was happening. It would become nightmarish memories for them to have for the rest of their lives. There was nothing anyone could do to stop what was happening.

Erik didn't stay very long with Seven. He exited the ICU, white as snow, with tears rolling down his strong face. He looked sick and dizzy.

Mae let Mary tend to Erik while she made her way toward Seven. Entering the doors, she went to the left, and looked above the doorways at the room numbers. 712 loomed before her, with grim faced nurses and doctors coming and going out of his little room. Mae looked around, suddenly terrified to see what had been done to her brother. As eager as she was to see him, she was as scared to go beyond the curtain. Holding her breathe, she went in.

There is nothing in the universe that could or would have prepared her for the sight of what a piece of wood could do to the human skull of someone she loved.

Seven's entire head and down to his throat was covered in a turbine of gauze. Tubes of every sort and size came from all parts of his body, in every direction.

Silently Mae sobbed, not wanting to produce any noise. She searched in vain for any familiarity of what had once been a beautiful boy. Hidden, was the severe damage and anything left for view was black and bloody.

The nurses moved about, squeezing around Sylvia and Mae, as well as the number of large machines that were keeping him alive. All kinds of beeps and sounds were coming from all the gadgets that were plugged up.

The smell of human pain overwhelmed Mae. Still she moved closer, working her way around to Seven's right side.

Sylvia stood as if in a horrified trance, shifting herself back and forth on her feet.

His right eye was a mixture of deep purple, red and black. Looking at his hand, Mae could see a few scratches on his knuckles. She just wanted to touch him, and let him know she was there. His entire family was. She cried, looking down at his lifeless body. She wanted to tell him she loved him. That she was sorry for not being there for him. She wanted to apologize for not being a better sister to him. Though she wanted to just sit and stay with him, Mae knew others would want their chance to be with him. With great pain, she left him, praying it wouldn't be the last time she'd ever see him alive again.

Chapter Sixty

Driving back home, Mae's mind raced with questions. The main one was "why"? She had a hard time believing Ennis was the assailant. What little she could grasp of Seven's wounds, resembled a gang beating. Seven had survived several close calls over the years, but the massive damage done this time made Mae shake with trepidation.

Why was he attacked in the neighbor's yard? Why would Ennis want to kill Seven? Why would Ennis hit Seven from behind? Seven had no injuries on his arms. If he had seen an axe handle coming at him, he certainly would have reflexively tried to stop it. Seven would never turn his back on someone threatening to hit him, much less with a weapon such as the one used.

As Mae arrived home, she demanded Rex take her to the crime scene. She had to see for herself, where it took place. She had no plan to talk to any of the neighbors; she just wanted to see the location of the attack.

Rex was well acquainted with the neighbors, and he didn't mind taking his wife to their yard. As they made their way over to Focus Trailer Park, Mae cried with shame.

"I've never even visited Seven or his kids over here!"

Outside standing on their front porch was David and Sue Smith, Seven's neighbors. Other people were walking around in the yard, but Rex didn't recognize them. The reason Rex was acquainted with the Smith's was because he had almost married their daughter, Candy, who also resided with her parents. Though their relationship fizzled out over a decade before, there were no hard feelings between them.

Coincidently, Mae had had the opportunity to get to know Candy a few weeks before the attack on Seven. Melina had given birth three weeks before, and while Melina was in the maternity ward, Candy had given birth to her own baby, and her room sat across the hall from Melina's. Mae and Candy had spoken with each other on a few occasions while they were in the hospital. Mae had even sat in Candy's room and rocked her newborn baby.

Getting out of the truck, Mae scanned the yard, looking for clues of a crime. Immediately her eyes were drawn to a triangular outline in hard orange clay dirt. A white car was parked right next to the disturbed dirt. The only trace of blood was a circle, about twelve inches across. Mae had the instinct to put her hands in the bloody dirt. It was, after all, her family's blood that had been spilt. Candy, stepping outside holding her infant, made Mae refrain from doing the morbid act.

Candy was the person who found Seven lying in their front yard. She made the first 911 call for the police. She was eager it seemed to talk to Mae. First she asked what Seven's condition was, and then she began giving her details of what happened. While pointing at the blood circle on the ground she began.

"That's where I found him lying, there were two bloody circles, and his head was laying in that one."

Mae looked toward the ground, but could only see one obvious wet spot. She didn't interrupt Candy, who hadn't stopped talking.

"He was lying face up, and blood was splattered all over momma's white car, from the front to the back, all over the side. We washed the blood off though, and daddy has been trying to cover the spots on the ground with dirt, to dry it up. I heard some yelling outside. That's why I came out. Momma handed me the telephone, and I practically tossed the baby at her. I called 911. Momma called them back after ten or fifteen minutes, cussing and fussing. I'm sure it's recorded, momma was yelling 'He's gonna die out here!'"

"Was he making any noise?" Mae interrupted with a morbid question.

"Yes, he was gurgling and gasping, but I didn't go down to him. I was afraid, not knowing what had happened, or even really who he was. He could have been anybody. There were two blood puddles, and blood was everywhere, and I heard that Ennis's trailer is covered in blood."

Mae listened closely, but her attention remained on the dirty wet circle. The entire day had been an intensely hot one, with temperatures in the high nineties. There must have been a large amount of blood for a wet circle to still remain.

Candy continued. "All of our vehicles were searched by the police, our yard and trailer. They were looking for the weapon used on Seven. Kendall had a lot of blood on his shoe; so much blood the police noticed it and questioned him about it. Kendall told them he must have been cut, and the officer said he must have a bad injury, with so much blood. They took his shoe and tested it, but he didn't have one single drop of blood on him anywhere else. Sylvia and Seven had been fighting; she had already called the cops on him, trying to send them to that other trailer park. That skinny boy (referring to Cameron's husband, George) was yelling while Seven lay there, 'That's all our money; Seven had all our money on him.' Sylvia wanted Seven's wallet; she screamed it over and over. They wouldn't give it to her. The EMS worked on Seven for at least forty five minutes before they moved him."

Still Mae continued to look at the blood circle that the sun couldn't dry up. Candy noticed what Mae was looking at.

"Daddy has been trying to cover the blood with dirt all day. I don't like seeing the blood. It was the worst thing I have ever seen. I can still see him lying there. I just can't forget it. They had to clean all that blood off momma's car."

Mae was half grateful and half disturbed at the neighbor's behavior. The spot where the attack occurred should be respected, and these people couldn't get it covered up and over fast enough. She'd seen and heard enough. She thanked them for their time, and returned to the truck. Quickly Mae grabbed her notebook, and through her pouring tears, she noted everything she'd been told. She drew a diagram of what she had seen. Over and over in her mind, loomed a big question.

What was Seven doing in the neighbor's yard? It was a simple question, with no simple answer.

It would become the first question of hundreds. She had a new mission for life. She was numb from the inside out, while a disturbing pain pounded to make its way into her heart. She didn't seek this mission for answers. It found her.

She wasn't finished with Focus Trailer Park. Through her tears, she jotted down a rough diagram of what the crime scene looked like, or what was left of it. It troubled her not to see crime scene tape of some sort. 'A serious crime had occurred, you'd figured they could wrap something,' Mae thought to herself.

"Take me to the trail, the back trail that Ennis used to walk to Seven's." Mae ordered through sniffles.

Rex looked over at her, but didn't comment. He drove on past Seven's trailer, and around the curve of the dirt road. Passing a couple of trailers, he pulled over to the side of the small road. Mae got out with her notebook, looking around, taking mental notes here and there. She followed her husband up the short wooded trail, which wound through a small patch of pine trees, over grown kudzu and weeds.

"Who is this Kendall boy?" Mae questioned her husband while they walked.

"I don't know." Rex shrugged his shoulders.

They walked up to a clearing, which brought them right behind Ennis's trailer. Mae looked over at the home, the place which was supposed to be covered with her brother's blood. She wondered if it was true, wanting to check it out.

"I've seen that axe handle before." Rex was in a state of shock also. He just couldn't wrap his mind around what had transpired. "He's been toting it around for months." He pointed at the trailer next door to Ennis's. "He's even threatened that old woman in that trailer right there with it."

"Why?" Mae asked her husband as she started to follow him back down the trail to the truck.

"I don't know, something about the grandson owed him, but he walked around her trailer beating on it with that axe handle." Rex's long legs made Mae have to jog to keep up with him. They were back beside his truck in less than a minute. Mae considered how close Ennis's home was to Seven's, even though their homes sat in two separate parks.

"Well why didn't she call the police on him?" Mae was beginning to wonder how many people Ennis had gotten away with threatening with his axe handle.

"I guess it's because it involved her teenage grandson that lives there with her. That's who Ennis was after." Rex got into the truck, starting it up before his wife insisted they go talk to Ennis's neighbor.

"Either way, why didn't…" Before Mae could finish, Rex cut her off.

"I don't know."

The two sat in silence as they circled around to make their way back out of Focus Park. As they drove, a man came out from underneath his garage, attempting to flag them down. Rex pulled the truck over again.

"That shit pisses me off! Everyone knows a whole gang of them did it! Robbed him! Had it planned!" Mae put her pen to work, taking notes, but she didn't let the man notice her doing it. He appeared a little intoxicated, but his topic of conversation intrigued her.

"That boy did not deserve that, he was a damn good boy. He didn't do anything but work and stay to his family." He paused while glancing over at Seven's trailer. He rubbed at his forehead. "But them boys knew he had worked all week. They knew it!" He noticed Mae was listening to him very closely, causing him to look down at the ground. "He would sometimes come down and sit outside with me. Smart boy, loved his family, and didn't mind helping." He looked back up at Mae. "He didn't deserve that."

Mae wanted to start firing questions, but she somehow knew, he wouldn't give her the answers she needed to hear. Still she tried.

"What boys knew he had worked all week?"

He smiled at her with a toothless grin. "Hell, all of them."

Chapter Sixty One

That day that started with the early morning phone call of traumatic news, would also be a day that ended with the phone in hand. It was every type of phone call that could be imagined. From sympathy, curiosity, shock, grief, and anger, the calls came in.

Rex's phone hadn't stopped ringing , all day. His family was a large one. Rex's daddy had a dozen siblings, and with Ennis being one of those siblings step son's, the entire family was seeking answers. Stories were flying around town, like a wild fire out of control.

Late that evening, Mae's mind was overloaded, and physically she was exhausted. Mixed with the inability to relax and a constant fear of not knowing, she was a nervous wreck. Rex insisted she lay down, if only for a few minutes. She tried, but once she got still, the pain became far too intense. Rex sat down beside her, and turned the television on. Mae wasn't in the mood to look at the stupid box of insanity, and luckily her phone's ringing gave her excuse to get up. It was her mother who had just gotten home.

Mary was far worse off than Mae with her shock and grief. She didn't want to leave him. She wanted to stay with him. Every second that went by was agony. She didn't want to leave Seven alone with Sylvia.

Neither had Angel, who was terrified Sylvia would finish him off.

No one in the family knew how to help the other, with each one going through the hell themselves.

Rex's phone began to ring also, which made him get up and leave the room. Mae continued to listen to her mother, lying in bed with her eyes closed, she could feel a tremendous headache making itself at home inside her skull. Rex walked back in quickly.

"Bob just called me, wanted to know if I had a job opening. I told him no. Then Bob asked me how Seven was doing, and told me he didn't know what happened last night. Bob said he passed out earlier, and was sound asleep. I asked Bob if he knew where Kendall Martin was, and Bob said he would try to find him." Rex stopped talking, and looked at his wife to wait for her reply.

Mae remembered Cameron mentioning a Bob, and it was Bob who brought Kendall to Seven's trailer. She tried to explain what Rex had told her to Mary who was still talking to Mae on the phone.

Suddenly Rex's phone rang. Immediately he started asking Kendall what happened.

Mae told Mary that Rex was putting the call on speaker phone, so she could listen in on it too. Mary got Erik to pick up another house line so he could listen also. Putting her phone next to Rex's, they all listened as Kendall gave his fast paced account of the attack.

"We couldn't believe it, that he was actually beating him in the head. After he had hit him three or four times, Seven went down, and Ennis straddled over him and kept on beating him. We were all in shock that he was hitting him with the stick. I was like 'somebody's got to stop him or he's gonna kill him'. I jumped down off the porch. I told Candy to call the police. Ennis took the handle and ran away."

"Where did the axe handle go?" Rex questioned, while grinning at his wife. He could play detective too.

"I don't know what he did with it, after I leaned it up against the porch." Kendall's conversation then turned to the moments when Seven had driven them to the store. "While we were at the gas station, I went inside to get some cigarettes; Ennis started arguing with someone in another car outside. The clerk was calling the police, and when I looked outside and saw what was going on, I just handed the clerk five dollars, and told him 'I had to go'."

Mae wasn't content with the boy's answers; she prodded Rex to ask him what Ennis was arguing over with Seven.

"They were fighting about a video game." The conversation ended with him having to go.

Mae was no closer to finding the truth to what happened. Why would anyone kill someone over a video game?

She wasn't happy with the boy's version of events either. Candy had claimed to have been inside her house. No one imparted they were watching the fight. From what Kendall stated, there was an audience watching her brother be beat to death. Why didn't anyone try to help? Why would they lie and say they didn't see the fight?

Looking over at her husband, Mae gave him one demand. "I want you to go out tomorrow and find that axe handle."

Rex agreed to go looking, assuring her he had seen the handle before.

Day two would be the start of Mae's new routine, with everything centering on Seven. Waking up, her first thoughts were questions of if he'd survived the night. She'd gone to sleep trying to chase the thoughts of axe handles coming at her head. Every second felt like it rushed to a pending fate. The sorrow was heavy in her heart. It was such needless and senseless violence.

Mae got to the hospital early, but Seven lay just as she had left him.

His condition hadn't changed. All the specialists, doctors and nurses agreed that his brain needed to have adequate time to heal. They still couldn't tell what the extent of the damage was.

Helplessly, Mae watched the machines do everything for her brother. She wondered in silent tears if he woke up what would be left of the boy she once knew? He could be blind, deaf or both. What if he never woke up? She chased the bad thoughts out of her head. Seven had held on for over twenty four hours after the horrible beating and emergency surgery. He wanted to live. Making no changes was both good and bad, but Mae refused to believe he wouldn't make it. The inability to touch him or even whisper to him was hard, but just having him alive was good enough.

Sylvia hadn't left the hospital all night, sleeping in the waiting room. She refused to leave her husband. She sat beside him in silence, with all her attention on his face, pleading with him telepathically to just open his eyes.

Mae made her way around to the back of Sylvia, and somehow found the strength needed to wrap her arms around her sister-in-law. Mae was making the gesture for her brother's sake.

"I'm sorry for all that has been said and done between us in the past year. I'm here for you and your kids." As Mae whispered into her ear, Sylvia shook with tears. Mae held onto her for a minute or so. She needed her brother back. His kids needed their daddy. Mary needed her son. Mae was attempting to put the past drama to rest, in hopes it might bring Seven back.

Though Mae was willing to try to forgive, her close friends were not so soon to let her forget. Everyone warned Mae to watch her back as far as Sylvia was concerned. They had seen the damage Sylvia had caused for Mae, and they feared Sylvia was somehow connected to Seven's attack. Mae tried to assure them that she didn't trust Sylvia any further than she could throw her. That Sylvia had separated from Seven many times before, but she'd been one of Seven's lifetime keepers. Loving Sylvia or hating her was of no concern; Seven's life was all Mae was worried about. She forced her growing doubts about her sister-in-law out of her head. Positive energy, good thoughts, and pure love were the only things that Seven needed around him.

The second day fell on Monday. With Seven being in the guarded walls of the ICU unit, time with him was limited by their strict rules and hours. At all times, someone had their eyes on him. Sitting silently with him, watching him just lay there, with his head all beat to pieces, was almost too painful to bear. The long ride to the hospital gave up hours of waiting in little rooms filled with other families in fear of losing their loved ones too.

Mary, Mae, Sylvia and Mary's friend Peggy, all sat together in between hours of ICU visitation. Big open windows, looking out on the hustle and bustle of Birmingham, gave them all something to look at. Mae's phone rang with some astonishing news from Rex.

"I found the axe handle!"

"What?!" Mae sat up, motioning to Mary and Sylvia. She mouthed to them the news.

"Yeah, it's lying on Ennis's burn pile."

"You didn't touch it did you?" Mae was excited, with the grim news.

"NO!" Rex sounded amused. "No way! What should I do?"

"Call the police!" Mae thanked her husband for finding the weapon, and hung up the phone.

Sylvia and Mary were amazed that Rex had found it. Mae explained to them how Rex had told her he had seen Ennis with that axe handle before, on many occasions.

Mary fussed how the same local law that hated Seven, hadn't been able to find that weapon. She would never rely on or have any faith in their local law again.

Sylvia looked uncomfortable at Mary's topic of conversation; she excused herself to go smoke outside by the fountain. Mae decided to go with her, and as they took their seats across from the misting water, Sylvia began talking immediately.

"I just don't understand where all his money went. There was only sixty two dollars inside his wallet, folded up and put separate. It was our water bill money, but I know he had some money in his pants pocket. He had bought cigarettes, beer and we ate out. Then those drum sticks he bought for James Robert." Sylvia looked at Mae for instruction, but Mae didn't know what to tell her.

"You need to tell the police if he was robbed." Mae offered. "If he was, they need to know."

Mae left the hospital soon after talking to Sylvia outside. She was eager to find answers to her growing list of questions. There was nothing she could do for Seven, except pray really hard. She could however, start looking for answers. Her very first question was why did the attack occur in the neighbor's yard?

The Smith's had claimed to have been inside their house. Kendall on the other hand, stated they were outside during the attack, watching it with him. His statements of "we" were all surprised, "somebody's" got to stop him and "I told Candy to call the police". Versus what Candy had revealed, which was they were in bed asleep and were awakened; to "find" Seven's body and saw no one else.

Mae decided she would ask Candy and her parents one more time what had exactly happened to Seven in the early morning hours. Which account was the true version of the events occurring in their front yard?

With the shock of what happened to Seven, Mae's long drives back and forth from the hospital were filled with plenty of time to think. Though his mortal body lay motionless, she could still see him in her mind, remembering all their good and bad times together. She could still hear his vigorous laughter, strumming through her head. As she drove through the world, in her standstill nightmare, everything continued to rush all around her, oblivious to her family's desperate pain.

As soon as she got home, Rex began explaining how he had happened upon the bloody weapon.

"It was just lying there on top of Ennis's burn pile. It wasn't the first place I looked; I'd figured he had tossed it along the route he ran home. Once I found it, I backed away, and called you. Then I called the police, and I walked back to the spot with the detective. I watched the detective put it into a brown paper bag. He took another axe handle out of his trunk, one they had found the previous day, and tossed it out. Detective Ridge found another piece of evidence, the bloody red t-shirt Ennis had on during the attack."

While Rex and Detective Ridge were outside of Ennis' trailer, Ennis's wife Sissy was standing on the back porch watching. As the detective walked back holding the red t-shirt, he questioned Sissy.

"Do you recognize this shirt?"

"Yes, it's my shirt." She tried to appear calm.

As the detective put his evidence into the trunk of his patrol car, he spoke openly to Rex.

"Well, this case is all but solved. Ennis has already made a complete confession." Detective Ridge smiled at Rex while slamming his vehicles trunk.

The words of the detective ticked Mae off. How could the case be closed, when it was so obvious so many more were involved? She wanted every last one of them punished for what had been done to Seven. The local law wouldn't do anything to help. It seemed odd to Mae that for almost a year, anytime Sylvia called the police, they were right there to help. Strangely, the very night Seven was attacked and Sylvia had called, they didn't seem to show up at all. Now they were going to be the heroes of the day for solving Seven's murder attempt. In spite of that they had neglected to protect his life. Did they neglect to show up because they were tired of Sylvia after she took her husband back?

When Mae read the day's local paper, she nearly threw up. There was no mention of what happened to her brother. Yet in the police reports it read: Seven Levine made a report that a first degree assault had happened to him. WHAT? How could Seven have made any reports? His head was nearly beaten off his shoulders. The way it appeared in the paper, Seven was just fine. Well enough to make his very own report.

Chapter Sixty Two

So the fact that there were people in the Smith's yard, right up until the attack, was now no secret to Mae. One of the first instincts she had, even before she saw her brother was that he had been attacked by a group of people. Looking at him, Mae felt his spirit had been crushed; his feelings hurt and his heart broken with confused pain.

Seven was just too strong for someone like Ennis to be able to just come along and take him down all by himself.

Mae returned with Rex to the Focus Trailer Park. She wanted to listen to what was being said and talked about. The story in the park was that everyone knew Seven had money on him and it was a planned robbery. They ganged up on him. The other buzz in the tightly knit trailer park was how Sissy had moved in with Ennis's two children into Kendall Martins trailer. One more version was that it was a drug deal gone badly. The most painful story Mae heard, was how Seven was doing just fine in the hospital, sitting up eating and talking.

As Mae listened to all the different stories, she failed to hear anyone explain just exactly what happened. Someone wanted to kill Seven, and she wanted to find out just exactly who and why.

Upon visiting the Smith's for a second time, Mae quickly informed Candy and her parents, David and Sue, that Seven's condition was unchanged. She then decided to run Kendall's version of events by them. She was curious to see their response.

"Kendall told me that this yard was full of people, including you three." Eagerly she waited to see their reactions. Her information did seem to unnerve each one of them.

David started shaking his head back and forth, while Sue and Candy gave each other awkward glances. Candy was the only one to respond with a similar version of the day before. She repeated what she told of finding Seven, but instead of being awakened by the sound of yelling, she heard three loud pops.

"I thought it was a gun or something." She explained. She also gave some information concerning the video game that nearly cost Seven his life.

"That game was among many items stolen from several trailers in the Focus Park, weeks ago. Out of all the items taken during the burglary spree, only the stolen game had provided finger prints on the cabinet it was taken from and had a police report on it. It was stolen from our trailer." Candy happily informed.

Mae had heard enough, and had already come to her own conclusions. If there was no honor among thieves, there was even less among murderers. This family was telling lies, and she couldn't figure out why. Why would anyone want to lie about being a witness to an attempted murder? Mae believed they only had two reasons to lie. One, they were involved, and the second reason would be to protect somebody. Either way, no doubt, they were not being honest, and she had no urge to ever speak to them again until they were ready to tell her the truth.

The third day brought absolutely no improvement in Seven's condition. He continued to lie in the same motionless position. The only movement came from the respirator that made his chest move up and down. The numerous nurses had different opinions and views of Seven's condition. Some worked tirelessly, determined they were going to bring him back to life, while others were less optimistic. Most of the doctors avoided Seven's family as much as possible. Without having anything positive to say, they would go and come while the visiting hours were closed. Seven's continued fight for life amazed every one of the medical staff involved.

Mae and Sylvia had plenty of time to talk between visits. Mae would mostly listen as Sylvia talked about her life with Seven. Sylvia spoke about their dreams and future plans. She just couldn't imagine what she would do without Seven; they had so much more life to live together. She apologized for all the drama she'd caused the previous year. She admitted that Seven had never done anything to her, except love her and take good care of her.

"Well, he tried, despite my behavior." She smiled while revealing something that Mae already knew. She wished she had a recorder, but felt guilty for thinking it. Seven would need every single member of his family.

"He loved Erik to death." Sylvia's voice cracked. "He talked about Erik all the time. He just loved his big brother Erik so much."

Mae could only imagine her brother's love for each other, having spent years observing the two of them growing up together. Immediately, she felt sorry for Erik's loss, and joined Sylvia in uncontrollable tears.

In those first few days, the waiting area would become home for the family. Over those days, Sylvia would seldom discuss the last hours of Seven's life before the attack. When she did talk, it was difficult to articulate what she was saying. She seemed to feel a lot of guilt about her own actions.

"It was supposed to be a perfect birthday evening. We planned on kicking Cameron and George out of the trailer that night. Instead they babysat while we went out. I love him more than anyone else in the world! I can't live without him."

Mae didn't interject anything Sylvia had to say, but she certainly listened. It was hard for her to imagine Seven, kicking Cameron out. He had an unusual soft spot in his heart for his nieces and nephews. Sylvia wouldn't have minded it, because she hated Seven's family taking his attention from her. She was far too jealous to share him.

On the other hand, Mae could easily see why Seven would want to kick George out. George wasn't an ideal husband for Cameron, and not too many people, except Sylvia, liked him. Mae had not believed Cameron's stay at Seven's would last long anyway. Seven was a vigorously friendly individual, and loving to most. Yet he was very protective of his home, and he felt it to be his only safe place. He was always willing to help his nieces and nephews, though he did have limits to that hospitality after a point. Regardless, he didn't kick Cameron out, and she had no clue that he had plans to do so. From her perspective, Seven wanted her to look after the kids, so he could take Sylvia out to eat at San Juan's for his birthday.

Sylvia described Seven's last meal, which consisted of Nachos and Cheese, with a pitcher of Margarita. She cried when she repeated the last words she spoke to him.

"If you're in, you're in, if you're out, you're out."

She added. "Kendall called Seven's name, and though he started to come in, he turned around, and followed Kendall. I slammed the door closed. I then went to my bedroom, sat on my bed and smoked a cigarette. I went into the bathroom after that. All the lights were off in the trailer, and I noticed the blue lights, flashing through the window. I ran into the living room and made George go see what was happening to make sure it wasn't Seven."

Sylvia had started letting Seven's family know, in an unobtrusive way, she needed help. She had a local church that had immediately jumped into action, helping her in any way possible. The children had a multitude of people to look after them, including Cameron and George, who stayed at the trailer in Focus Park. Without Seven's weekly income, Sylvia was faced with needing a way to continue supporting herself and the three kids, while watching Seven die before her eyes.

Seven's family acknowledged this need from the start. They did what they could, while they themselves were going through the shock of their lives.

The time with Seven was silent and somber.

Mae looked upon her baby brother, feeling helpless, when suddenly she was struck with a terrorizing thought. 'Seven wouldn't have the opportunity to prove he wasn't the bad guy his wife had made him out to be'. On the third day as Sylvia sat beside her husband, Mae announced her decision, to both Seven and Sylvia. In a rather loud whisper Mae declared.

"I'm going to write. Seven, I'm going to tell the story, of what has been done to you. I'm going to set the record straight about all the lies told on you." Mae looked at Sylvia, not wanting to hurt her, but to make her understand her full intentions. That Seven at least deserved for his truth to be known. She continued while looking at Sylvia. "He wasn't the bad guy. He wasn't a monster. He wasn't a wife beating, child rapist, and I won't stop writing until I get that truth out! If he can't do it, it's the least I can do for him."

This proclamation was openly made, but it's doubtful that Sylvia could register the words coming at her. All of her energy was being consumed by the longing for Seven to open his eyes, and come back to her. She was wearing down, staying at the hospital all the time, sleeping on the hard concrete floor of the waiting room.

Later, before Mae left, they sat back outside looking at the many people enter and leave the massive hospital. They discussed some of the events of that fateful evening.

Sylvia was surprised to find out that Seven had visited Erik that night. It had been only one of Seven's many stops that night while he was driving around in Cameron's car. Sylvia continued to be concerned about the money Seven had on him. She informed Mae that the last purchase Seven made was to buy a pair of drum sticks for his nephew James Robert.

Inconsistencies stood out to Mae like stubbed toes. Sylvia was telling her Seven's last acquisition of drum sticks. If she didn't know Seven had made a trip to see Erik, then how did she know about the purchase he made for James Robert? How could she know? When did Seven have a chance to tell her?

Seven's last purchase of his life was made from a guy named Taylor Boyd. While Seven was driving around in Cameron's car, along with Kendall and Ennis, he had visited Erik. Sylvia didn't know about this visit, yet Seven had visited another house that night before he went to his brothers. Seven had made phone calls to Erik and Ava; these phone calls were made from Taylor Boyd's house phone.

Taylor Boyd is the one who Seven made the last purchase of his life from. Taylor carved what he called, "mini-bats". They favored drum sticks, and Seven purchased a set of them for James R., who was an avid drummer. Taylor Boyd was no friend of Seven's. When Seven visited his house that night, it was the first time he had ever met Taylor.

No, Taylor wasn't Seven's friend, but he did happen to be Kendall Martins best friend.

Regardless, if Sylvia didn't know Seven had visited Erik, how did she know that he purchased those drum sticks from Taylor? Sylvia also hadn't mentioned calling the police on Seven, or how she and Kendall were lifelong friends.

While these questions began forming in Mae's mind, she chased them away, trying to stay positive. Watching Sylvia hover over Seven's lifeless form, it was hard to imagine that she could be a part of what happened. On the other hand, it was as difficult to trust her. Mae refused to believe Sylvia could possibly want to have Seven killed, but then again, she'd promised if she couldn't have him, no one would. The seesaw of emotions felt like being pulled by a rip current in one direction and the other.

Chapter Sixty Three

By the fourth day, the family began to believe there was hope. Though Seven hadn't improved one bit, he continued to hold on to life. His only changes hadn't been improvements, but it seemed you could feel his will growing stronger every hour.

His lungs had developed double pneumonia, but the doctors and nurses insisted it was only a natural side effect. Basically, during the attack he had swallowed blood or even regurgitated back into his lungs. So even before he was put on the helicopter, he more than likely had the beginnings of pneumonia. Seven's tolerance to medicine was strong, due to his years of previous drug abuse. It meant, every day, sometimes by the hour, the amount of sedative had to be increased to prevent him from waking up. With sixteen intravenous infusions going into his body, he had started to plump up. The family was continually told everything happening was to be expected.

On the fourth day, they removed the turbine of gauze that had been wrapped around his head. It would be an eternally memorable event seeing the extreme damage done to his skull. As Mae made her way into room 712 that morning, Sylvia was sitting on his left side. Immediately Mae noticed the stitches going across his forehead, but was thrilled, to be able to finally see a glimpse of the brother she once knew. Going into the room, she slowly made her way around to the right side.

"Watch it, it looks bad." Sylvia began to warn her, but it was too late.

The words floated past Mae, as her eyes, beheld his damaged head. She wasn't anywhere close to being prepared to see the grisly remains. Her knees began to buckle out from underneath, while the room began to tilt sideways. She turned from the scene, grabbing hold of a cabinet for support.

Seven's right eye had been one of the many points of impact. Tears flowed while she tried to reason with what she was seeing. The brain surgery had left its own large hideous scar in the shape of a large question mark, behind his right ear. The surgeons cut was being held together by too many staples to even count. It had been the point of entry for the doctors to try to repair the smashed temporal bone and remove many crushed bones that were beyond repair around the eye. Ignoring all the explicit warnings to not speak to Seven, Mae leaned over, and whispered to her brother.

"I love you."

She was in a new kind of shock. Witnessing Seven's continued struggle caused unbelievable pain, and to know another human did the damage to him, twisted Mae up on her inside. Looking over at Sylvia, their eyes met, and they shared a moment of grief. It was easy for them both to love Seven now. Why couldn't such love be allowed while he was able to receive it?

The metal staples were grotesque looking, and Mae hated seeing them. She knew her brother wouldn't be happy with such a gruesome scar.

As if Sylvia was reading Mae's mind, she commented. "He won't like that scar." She paused to laugh slightly through her tears. "He knew he was pretty, but now?"

The family started talking to Seven once the gauze came off. Regardless if the hospital staff liked it or not, the family felt it could very well be the last chance they had to tell him they loved him. They hoped it would bring him back to them.

Mae just wanted to make sure he knew how much he meant to her, and how proud she was to have him as her brother.

Everyone studied his brain pressure machine which displayed numbers resting in the twenty's, a rather high number. The respirator had its own set of number, as did his heart monitor. The IV machine controlling all the fluids going in constantly beeped and had to be changed several times during each hour. Both of his legs had been put into massage balloons, to keep his circulation going in his motionless limbs. His temperature gauge showed that he continued to run a high fever.

Some nurses were treating him like a human being, while others not so much so. Pictures were not allowed in the ICU, yet Mae insisted they see the boy they were working on. Though he looked like a monster, he was their precious and priceless family member.

As painful as it was to sit and visit in silence with Seven, it was becoming apparent, that if one wanted to see him, they should take the opportunity.

Of Mae's three children, James Robert was the most difficult to talk into going to see his uncle. Driving to Birmingham that morning with his mother, she tried to prepare him for what he would see. Nothing could really prepare those who loved Seven to see him all beaten up. With his condition and all the machines, it was an impenetrable situation to comprehend.

Their visit that day with Seven wouldn't last long. It had become harder and harder for Mae to see her brother continue to lie in one position. Every day, he would look worse than the day before, with his body holding so much fluid. They rode back in near silence with their thoughts.

James Robert didn't want to face the reality. He wanted to believe Seven would pull through. He didn't look at his mother, but stared out the window and began describing the last opportunity he had to see his uncle alive. It had been during the cookout Seven had for Melina.

"Seven camped out in the living room all night with me." James R. spoke in a desolate tone. "We watched movies all night and talked a lot."

Like all the others, he was realizing his last moments with Seven.

"The next morning, his boss was knocking at the door, and I had to wake him up." He laughed. "He looked rough that morning, but got up real fast." James R. wouldn't allowed himself to doubt his time with Seven was through.

Every day would end with Mae on the phone. If not with numerous people, it was her mother.

Mary was living a parent's nightmare, and could hardly function properly. If she wasn't with her son at the hospital, she was under tremendous stress to get to him. Every moment of every second, she feared his pending death. She wanted to be with him just in case he did open his eyes. On this day, she was upset because she wouldn't be able to see Seven the next day.

Thulah had been scheduled in advance, before the attack on Seven, for a heart catheterization. Mary was torn; fearing her son would die while she was in another hospital, seeing to her mother's needed heart surgery. In between sobs, she revealed her desperate fears of losing her son.

"I won't be able to take it, if he dies. Oh dear, what if he dies? What if I'm not there with him?"

Just the fact she would be going through her mother having heart surgery terrified her too. Thulah had a bad heart, and had already suffered from a major heart attack. Mary felt her world falling in on her, and she just couldn't take much more pain or loss. She was scared to death.

Late that night, Sylvia called Mae to give her the evening's updates on Seven. Her long stay at the hospital was beginning to really grind her down mentally. Turns out, homeless people would sneak into the large hospital at night, and sleep in the various waiting rooms, because there was no security camera's in them. Sylvia was disturbed by one particular man, who started stalking her about the hospital, and wanted to share the waiting room with her. Still she refused to leave Seven.

Around midnight, the phone rang again. Mae had already closed her eyes, but hadn't fallen asleep. Her heart went into her throat as she noticed it was Sylvia calling back. With Seven's condition and clinging to life, the first thought Mae had wouldn't be a good one. She'd already begun to tear up before she could get her shaking fingers to answer, fearful her brother was already gone. Answering it, she could hear Sylvia crying really hard, which had Mae physically tensing up all over in anticipation for what Sylvia was going to tell her.

"They're going to arrest me!" She cried into the receiver.

The words didn't make sense to Mae, as she continued to hold her breath.

"I called the Lanyard Police and everything. They confirmed it to me when I called that I was going to be picked up in the morning."

Her words were swimming around in Mae's head. What would they be arresting Sylvia for? Did she have something to do with Seven's attack? Maybe it was something else; she had caused a bit of trouble for herself the last year.

"Please, please, please be here in the morning!" Sylvia pleaded. "I can't stand the thought of no one being here with him! Please promise me, you won't let Seven be alone!"

"I promise I will stay with Seven personally." Mae assured Sylvia.

"Do you think I had something to do with Seven's attack?" Sylvia outright questioned her sister-in-law.

"I can't believe how anyone who claimed to love Seven could do such a horrible thing to him." Mae answered her matter of fact.

How could anyone do such a thing, even to an animal, much less a living human? Sylvia hadn't displayed anything to indicate she had been involved.

"No, I don't believe you had anything to do with his attack." Mae tried to ease Sylvia's mind and agreed to take care of her brother.

Chapter Sixty Four

Getting out of bed early Thursday, Mae hadn't slept all night, after receiving the midnight phone call.

Sylvia was going to be arrested?

She couldn't believe it. After all the trouble Sylvia had caused the year before, it was just too difficult to imagine the police department she had wrapped around her fingers, would actually arrest her. Mae reasoned it had to do with something previous to Seven's attack, still finding it hard to fathom that someone who loved Seven could be behind nearly killing him.

Most of those in town, who knew about the previous year's events, believed Sylvia was involved somehow. Yet Mae just couldn't fathom Sylvia wanting Seven dead. How could she control him if he was dead? She had him jailed and beat up several times, but if he was dead, what would that get her? A monthly check from the state for Seven's children?

Mae drove to the hospital early, with Mary on her mind. She worried about her mother, sitting there alone while her mother was in heart surgery, and her son lay at death's door. Mae could imagine how her mother was torn up with guilt over not being with Seven and guilt for wanting to leave her mother all alone while having to endure a heart catheterization. Thulah felt guilty for even needing the procedure to start with. Everyone was over the edge with emotions. Mae hurried. If she could do nothing but sit with Seven, then she would get that done. She worried if she would make it to the hospital before the police arrived to pick Sylvia up.

While driving to the hospital, Mae decided to call the police herself. It wasn't something she enjoyed. Ever since Woody Muck had showed up at her house that day, she had been uneasy about the Lanyard Police Department, and all the officers that believed Sylvia's lies. Woody Muck acted like he didn't know Sylvia, yet he did. Sylvia had many officers believing Mae was calling their wives. At least that's what Sylvia had proclaimed that day in open court.

The day Rex found the axe handle, the detective that came by to pick it up, gave Rex his phone number. Mae felt comfortable to call him just to ask why Sylvia was being arrested. If it concerned her brother, she felt she had a right to know. The detective answered the phone with a friendly tone, yet when Mae told him who she was, his attitude turned irritated.

Mae needed answers, so she tried not to take his sudden and abrupt tone personal.

"Why is Sylvia being arrested?" She asked him as nicely as she could.

The man busted into laughter. "Wow, that's not true. She isn't being arrested!" Detective Ridge continued to chuckle.

Despite his weird reaction, Mae was relieved to know Sylvia was not being put in jail. It wouldn't have been something she could handle. Knowing Ennis Dorsey, it was hard enough to comprehend why or how he could do such a horrible thing. No matter what happened, two families were already destroyed, Seven's and Ennis's.

No, she didn't want Sylvia to have anything to do with Seven's attack. Those three children had been through so much, and now with their daddy clinging to life, the last thing they needed was for their mother to be in jail. It still troubled her to think the police believed Sylvia over them. Why? The detective's attitude wasn't all that blistery until he heard Mae's name. Then she could hear the obvious displeasure and the air of his tone changing in an instant.

Riding on the elevator to the seventh floor, Mae couldn't wait to tell Sylvia the good news, that she wasn't being arrested. Sylvia already believed people thought she was involved, but Mae didn't want her stressing over a pending arrest.

Already, Sylvia was manipulating Mae, making her believe in her sincerity concerning Seven. Mae had always wanted nothing more than to be sisters with Sylvia, and now with Seven's life in the balance, she wouldn't let the past effect the present.

Upon entering the room, Mae was pleased to see Seven having a bit of color to him. Anything but the pale grew hues he'd displayed for days. Sylvia stood beside him, and Mae gave her a smile. When visiting Seven for the first few minutes, it was silent communication, since speaking to him was frowned upon. Looking at him, Mae sent him messages of love. Tenderly she put her hand on top of his. Quietly she glanced over at Sylvia and informed her that she wasn't being arrested.

"Oh, I know." She answered while looking at Seven's blistering face. "Investigator Woody Muck called me a little earlier. He was laughing so hard when he called, because there was a rumor going around about me. He asked me if Mary had been the one to tell me I was being arrested." Sylvia looked at Mae; she was annoyed with Investigator Muck for insinuating Mary had anything to do with how she found out.

"I told him no, that Mary had nothing to do with it. That I had called myself, and was told by the dispatcher I had a warrant for my arrest." Sylvia looked down again at Seven. "I mean, why that Investigator would accuse Mary, it just ain't right. Her son is laying here fighting to live. It just isn't right to find humor in what is happening."

If Sylvia thought the Investigators behavior was wrong, mere words couldn't describe how the conduct was perceived by Mae. Looking down at Seven, Mae wouldn't allow the negative energy produced by the thought of the smart aleck cop to ruin her moments with her brother. She made herself smile, and think hard about the good times she had with her brother, and thanked God for those moments.

Poor Mary was torn to pieces, and then forced to choose between being with her son or Thulah. It had killed her to miss seeing Seven, yet she knew her mother needed her too. Her fear for that day was that her son could die while she was gone. The time she had with him could very well be limited hour by hour, so every second away from him felt like a knife slicing into her heart.

In the background of Mae's thoughts were the insistent beeps of his IV machine. One of his bags was nearly empty. A nurse squeezed into the cubicle to address the beep. Mae concentrated on Seven's right hand, wondering if it would ever move again. He had a large wart on his pointing finger. Suddenly and without warning, his finger lifted up, followed by his entire hand twitching twice.

"His hand just moved!" Mae exclaimed a little louder than she meant to. He wasn't sitting up and talking, but it was the first time she had seen any movement from him at all. Both the nurse and Sylvia stopped talking, and all three of them looked at Seven's hand. It didn't move anymore.

"It's probably because his sedation had run out." The nurse answered while she continued to carefully study her patient for any movement. She knew he shouldn't be moving at all.

"Does that mean he's trying to wake up?" Mae was desperate to see his eyes open.

"Yes, he was more than likely trying." She gave up watching, having replaced the empty bag; she left Sylvia and Mae alone to monitor him.

The family had wanted Seven to wake up, but the many specialist that were working on Seven all agreed, they needed to keep him sedated for as long as possible. His brain needed all his energy. Some doctors believed if they were to allow him to wake up, it could possible kill him instantly.

Worry over what was left of his brain, plagued the family. Yet to have him alive was better that to lose him. No matter what condition he might be in, they would gladly accept it. Some nurses told the family he could hear them, but he just couldn't respond. While other nurses didn't believe he was ever going to wake up. The family remained hopeful that Seven would come back to them.

Sitting outside in front of the water fountain, Mae ended her visit to the hospital that day talking to Sylvia..

Still holding tightly to the belief Seven was going to pull through; Sylvia wanted Mae to get some information about brain trauma.

Mae had already though about it from day one. One of her first tactics was to obtain as much information possible. She did this for any situation that might pop up in her life. For her to physically look at what her brother's prognosis was had been a difficult thing for her to study. His condition didn't give much hope, and Mae hadn't taken the time to look, fearful of what she might find. Mae assured Sylvia she would try to gather up as much information about TBI (Traumatic Brain Injury) as she could find.

The topic of conversation turned to the previous year of trouble Sylvia had produced for Seven and his family. Mae was uncomfortable talking about it, but she listened to Sylvia explain how she was sorry for it. Her apologies were never on the actual events, they were generally covering her bad treatment of her husband.

"He was the good one; he really was good to me."

Driving home with her thoughts, Mae considered the things Sylvia had said. It was bad memories that Mae wouldn't soon forgot. Then she remembered the phone call Woody Muck had made to Sylvia that morning. Within seconds she could feel her blood start boiling. 'The nerve of that jack ass! '. It proved her suspicions that the Lanyard Police were not on their side. Well, at least not Woody Muck. Just what had their family ever done to that stupid man? How could he be so hateful and rude to the mother of a victim? There were times and places to be a jackass, but while serving as a tax paid law enforcement officer, it wasn't what his job called for. Mary's son was clinging to life, the last thing she needed was an investigator starting rumors about her.

After she got home, she tried her best to forget Woody Muck, and she went to work on the internet looking up TBI information. Just as she suspected, it didn't look good for Seven. If he woke up, his outlook for any type of a normal life wasn't going to happen. From what she read, his chances of waking up were slim to none. If Seven did wake up, his grievous wound's would make him an invalid. The damage done to his head during the night of horrors would more than likely leave him visually impaired, deaf or mute. If he could ever sit up, he would be bound to a chair. There was only so much the doctors could do.

Chapter Sixty Five

Mae woke up on Friday morning after a restless night of tossing and turning. She couldn't figure out why the Lanyard police couldn't at least offer her brother's family a little condolence with their tragedy. They were being forced to endure a great heartbreak. As well as being forced to allow the same police that was poking fun at the victim's mother, to be in control of the investigation. Mae was one half her mother, but also one half her father. She wasn't about to let Muck shove her family around. First she would call him, and then she would call the mayor and inform him of how hateful Muck had been. She also considered writing an editorial about it in the paper. Then she could schedule an appointment with the city council. Maybe he'd gotten away with misusing his authority before, and believed himself invincible.

Mae wanted him to realize, she didn't respect *his* authority, and with her experienced knowledge, no one was unshakable.

She left him a message on his machine, asking him to please call her back. Not that she believed he would. She felt Muck at least owed Mary an apology. Mae figured he would never have suspected Sylvia of telling Seven's family what he said. Seems that Woody assumed the family would still be at odds, even with Seven's battered condition. She laughed to herself that if he actually trusted Sylvia, he was a bigger idiot than she originally believed. Maybe, calling him on his professionalism would help the next victimized family that came along.

Leaving a message on the mayor's answering machine, she figured that would be the end of that. At least she voiced some of her frustrations. She had watched Mary suffer the entire last year of Seven's life. Mary now had to watch him fight to live and endure the constant lingering fear that he could go at any second. It just didn't seem fair that the police wouldn't at least lay off of her while she was going through the worst nightmare of any mother's life.

What really surprised her was getting a return call from Muck so fast, but their conversation would do nothing to ease Mae's concerns.

"Yes, you made a comment to Sylvia yesterday on the phone concerning my mother. It was uncalled for, and frankly inappropriate and unprofessional. It hurt my mother's feelings, and she happens to be suffering enough." Mae attempted to stay calm as she voiced her complaint.

"I didn't know what kind of trouble your family was kicking up. Yeah I said it. That's from your perspective how you take it, considering you're the one who called my wife." Woody wasn't about to take the same crap his little friend Sylvia had been subjected to by Seven's family.

Mae certainly I wasn't prepared for his self-righteous demeanor, nor was she in the mood to deal with it anymore.

"You know, Woody…" He was now speaking to LIZ, and she wasn't one to hold any punches. "You can stop pretending like you don't know Sylvia, you look ridiculous doing it. You know and we know, she used to be married into your family." Her words hit the spot.

Sylvia's first marriage had been to Timothy Muck and when Sylvia conceived her third baby, she was still legally married to Timothy.

"You're out of line! Look, if you've got a complaint against me, you can follow the proper procedures." Woody was speaking law enforcement language, which lucky for him, she was raised speaking. It was second language, and she played along.

"Well why don't you tell me the procedure in dealing with someone like you?"

"You talk to the chief of police. Then it will be investigated." Dryly he answered, exuding his displeasure in having to speak to her.

Mae could envision him holding the phone with his finger-tips, holding it away from his face. She couldn't help but laugh at the prospect of calling the chief. Mary had already tried that approach the year before, and it had been a complete waste of time. It would make more sense to go outside and talk to a pine tree.

"Sure, I'll do just that." She hung up first, at least having won the 'who could hang up on the other faster' game.

The ride to Birmingham was traveled with eyes full of tears. Since talking to the rude Investigator, Mae had a crushing pressure in her chest. She had the sensation that Woody Muck was actually tickled at what had happened to Seven. His profession should make him slightly more empathic than most, yet it was obvious to Mae, his power had gone to his head. Mae rubbed her chest, trying to figure out a way of relieving the unbelievable pain. What was happening to her? Was her heart actually breaking? The shadow of death loomed about, waiting anxiously to grab Seven. It hurt to be conscious, it hurt to breathe, and it felt impossible to continue.

She thought about the crime scene, running the images through her mind. When it got to the part of watching another human brutally bludgeon a man from behind, the pain in her chest grew more intense. How could one human hit another living creature over and over in the head? For what reason? There just had to be more of a motive than a video game. Seven's injuries were so severe, it was obvious to Mae, rage had been behind the attack. It wasn't even an attack, it was overkill.

Mae had done a little investigating on the stolen game theory, and heard a hearsay story concerning it. Ennis ended up with the stolen game system, which he'd fenced it from the boy who stole it. Ennis had sold it, but before he managed to pawn it off, Seven saw it sitting on the floor of Ennis's house. Was that what cost Seven his life? It just didn't add up.

Edgily Mae made her way through the hospital maze to her brother's room. Mary was sitting in the room. Having been away from him the entire previous day, she wouldn't be leaving his side anytime soon. She looked exhausted, with eyes swollen from tears. Mae made her way to Seven's side, and rubbed the hand she had seen move the day before. She whispered in his ear and carefully kissed him. The scar on his head was difficult to look at. Dried blood still fell from his hair like little pieces of black dandruff. His right eye had started turning deep black.

Mae began studying the blisters going across his forehead. It looked similar to being out in the sun too long. They were odd, like something went across his face and burnt him. The wooden axe handle couldn't have caused such an injury. It was more like a burn from rubber sliding across his face. If wood had hit him, it would have broken the skin easily. Looking closer at his black eye, she had the same thought. If wood had hit the tender skin covering the eye, it would have split it wide open. Something else caused the black eye and blisters.

The answer became obvious to Mae; Kendall was kicking Seven while Ennis was hitting him with the stick. That was why his right shoe had been covered in blood. Knowing it and proving it were two separate things though.

Seven's condition remained unchanged from unstable-critical. The blisters going across his head were not the only ones on his body. With so much fluid going into him intravenously, he had giant blisters the size of softballs popping up over his torso. His body had bloated substantially. It was such a helpless feeling, not being able to comfort him. Because of the strict rule of only two visitors, Sylvia decided to go out and smoke a cigarette. Mae decided to go with her and allow Mary some needed alone time with her son.

Having looked up the TBI information Sylvia had requested, Mae didn't know how to tell her what she had uncovered. The life Sylvia had before the attack would never be the same. It was over. Mae didn't really want to talk about it herself, so she hoped Sylvia wouldn't ask. What Sylvia wanted was a ride to the store, which Mae was happy to provide. Sylvia explained that she had walked to the store a couple of times, in-between visitation. Mae knew being stuck in that hospital all day and night couldn't be a pleasant experience.

They rode around the block, and Mae told Sylvia about the conversation she'd had with Woody Muck. Sylvia said nothing about it; she was lost in her misery. She wanted to talk about Seven and how their relationship had just gotten back on track. As she cried over losing everything she had, Mae cried with her. They both agreed that there was just no way would they lose him. They would force themselves to believe he would come back to them.

The world continued to circle about Seven's family, ignorant of the tragedy that had changed their lives.

On Saturday morning Mae woke with a somewhat optimistic outlook and she willed good thoughts for most of her ride to Birmingham. When she got to Seven, she would get good news, he will have improved, maybe he would wake up today.

When she entered his cubicle, he was lying in the same position. Sylvia wasn't in the room, so Mae took advantage of the first chance she had to be alone with him. A fan was blowing on him. She touched his hand, and it was hot. He was running a high fever. Tears formed, and crying was all she could do. It hurt so bad to see him continue to suffer.

The charge nurse came in doing her hourly tasks of keeping him alive. Mae asked her about the fan, already figuring it to be fever, but she hoped the nurse would give her more information. His ICP numbers were in the twenty's. The nurse told Mae he had a fever while she began cleaning the respirator tubing going into his mouth and down his throat. Suddenly, Seven began having what looked like a full body seizure. He looked like he was trying to cough. The episode was harrowing to watch.

"I know sweetie, I'm sorry." The nurse continued to clean his mouth, while his body continued to spasm over and over.

Mae thought she was going to throw up and pass out all at the same time. He continued to convulse for a minute or two.

As the nurse left the room, Mae walked over to Seven, rubbing his hand. "It's okay brother."

Sobbing so hard, her heart began to tighten up even more. How much more could he possibly take? How much more could the family take watching him bear unimaginable pain?

Mae got back into her van to return home, she took a look at herself in the rearview mirror. Looking back at her was a complete stranger. Who had she become? Everything about life hurt, every second, of every day.

Chapter Sixty Six

Seven had spent his entire life defending himself. He hadn't hurt one single person in that trailer park. He'd done nothing wrong. Loving his family was his only crime, one for which he had already paid a high price. What was Ennis thinking? Why would he do such a thing? Then there was Kendall Martin. What was Seven doing around Kendall? That made no sense, because Seven knew how dangerous Kendall Martin was.

Kendall was a TBI survivor himself, having had someone pop him in the side of his face with a brick when he was a teen-ager. Mae heard a couple of different versions of what had happened to the boy's face. In one story he'd been kicked by a mule. Another was he went looking for trouble sitting on the back of a pick-up truck, when someone yanked him off. They hit him with a brick. He was a violently messed up individual. Seven had given explicit warnings not to let him around their home. He knew Kendall was not quite right.

Mae remembered the name, but had never seen him. Her memories of the boy had been from a decade before, when Erik had been attack by him.

Erik had been at a party, and his first encounter with Kendall was a sucker punch right in the side of his face.

"The group of us was just sitting there, and I didn't even see him. Wham! His fist hit me. I didn't fall, but when I turned to see what hit me, he just stood there. I didn't even know him, and hadn't ever seen him before. I just let it go; not knowing what the boy's problem was."

Erik was not a volatile person, laid back and mild tempered, but it wouldn't be his last incidence with the threatening boy.

"Again, I didn't even see him coming, and I hadn't done anything to him. I'd just got arrived at my friend's house, and wasn't going to stay long. One second I'm talking to Sheila and the next I've been slammed with a two by four. Bam! Like someone swinging a bat and using my head as the ball. I was dazed, and my ear was ringing. I didn't know what had happened. Then I turned around, and saw who it was. I thought 'oh no, you got away with it once, but not twice'. "

Erik was no push over. He and Seven had grown up tangling with each other. In their teen years, and with the assistance of Ricky Levine's lies, the two had many fierce battles. Seven highly respected his older brother, and that's because Erik earned it from him.

"I commenced to beating his stinking ass. I whipped him until her ran away."

Mae remembers seeing the damage done to Erik's head, and how his ear bled for a week. She'd heard who had done it, yet she had no idea of who her brother's friends and enemies were. They were a generation apart. Mae took the attack on her brother personally, and it upset her very badly. The name had stuck in her head ever since. Now, the next time Mae hears the boy's name, he has been hanging out with her other brother, who coincidently, was brutally attacked from behind. Like someone hitting at a baseball, except making an impact across the temporal bone over the ear of an oblivious victim. Being struck from behind

It had never left Seven's mind either. It had never stopped bothering him. What was Seven doing hanging around Kendall Martin? Was he using his technique for dealing with enemies? Was he getting close to him, in order to watch him? No doubt, Seven would know Kendall Martin would need to be watched at all times.

Why did Seven want Erik to ride with him that night? What did Erik need to back him up for? Why did Seven call Ava and ask her for a ride for him and Kendall? Why would he insist on taking Kendall? Both Erik and Ava would have helped Seven, yet neither wanted to have anything to do with Kendall. Was Seven trying to get Kendall away from his family? Had something been going on between Sylvia and Kendall?

Seven's life was Sylvia and those three children. That was all he cared about; having sacrificed every single thing he loved in order to keep them. They were why he got up in the morning, and the reason he worked a full time job to support them. Seven had to go out of town, and it must have worried him to have to leave his family in that trailer park. Yet they had to eat and pay for their trailer. The kids had needs. Sylvia had a long list of fines to pay.

No, Seven wouldn't normally have time for the likes of Kendall. He definitely wouldn't want him around his house while he was out of town. What other reason would Seven have to be physically fighting with Kendall? It had to concern something or someone he cared about, or he wouldn't have given Kendall the time of day. He had worked way too hard to come back from the bottom, and Seven had no intentions on going back there. Unlike Kendall and Ennis, Seven didn't have the luxury to roam about the trailer park all day; he had a family in need of his foundational support; a family that he would fight the devil himself to protect.

As he continued to lay motionless; a week after his attack, the decision to wake him still hadn't been made. It was an agonizing experience to see him lay there and deteriorate right before their eyes. The family continued to hold onto the hope he would wake up. Just open up those beautiful brown eyes. If anyone could do it, it would be Seven.

Mae was losing her hope though. Having read the information concerning TBI, she couldn't see him living. The facts were outweighing her wishes. No one who sat watching him would ever get over the experience of what their eyes, mind and heart had seen. His chest continued to heave up and down, with the rhythm of the machine. The air could be heard as it was being forced into his lungs. Mae cried as she sat wishing she could hear that loud laughter coming from those same organs that were now filling with fluid by the hour. Just the sound of his deep voice, which played like a broken record in her head. His infectious enthusiasm for life was a stark contrast to lifeless person he'd become. What would life be like without Seven in it? How would they manage?

Mary had always had a special bond with her boys. She'd never imagined one of them being so brutally hurt. Watching her watch her son was a painful experience in itself. The long intensity of the aftermath would make lasting scars for the rest of their lives.

Chapter Sixty Seven

The beginning of week two had Mae and Mary riding together to visit with Seven. Their conversation circled around Woody Muck, who they had found out was the lead investigator in Seven's attempted murder case. It was odd to them, that he would be the one to end up being put in charge of Seven's attack. There was no question in either Mary's or Mae's mind, that the man had antipathy towards their family. They shared the same feelings toward him.

Arriving at the hospital, they found Sylvia sitting outside by the fountain. She was crying and visibly shook up. They both hurried toward her, anticipating bad news. Listening to her try to talk between sobs, they braced themselves.

"That Nurse Lilly said she'd been working in the ICU for over twenty years..." She took a deep breath. "And in all her years of experience with patients similar to Seven, they never wake up."

Her words hit them all hard, and the reality of losing him struck a chord of pain. Mae's mind raced to the image of having to bury her brother, and she had to sit down next to Sylvia, or fall down from the lack of oxygen getting to her brain. The blood seemed to have drained out of Mary's face, as it took on a ghost white appearance.

"NO, NO, NO!" Sylvia started screaming, standing up, and shaking her head back and forth. "NO! He isn't dying! He will wake up! I don't give a damn what anybody says!" She walked away from Mary and Mae and then marched back towards them. "I am going to have that nurse kicked out of Seven's room; I don't want her anywhere near my husband!"

Both Mae and Mary agreed with her. If the nurse wasn't going to be optimistic, then Seven nor his family needed her around. They all made their way back up to the seventh floor. Mae and Mary watched as Sylvia took off toward the ICU where she intended on having it out with Nurse Lilly. They sat down in the waiting room taking in the sickening news.

"We need to take pictures of the damage done to Seven." Mae whispered to her mother. "We need to have proof of what has been done to him." Being a photographer, she'd taken hundreds of pictures of Seven since he was born. These pictures wouldn't be easy or fun to take. They would also be very difficult to get. The ICU nurses were protective of their patients, and no pictures were allowed to be taken of the them. If they were going to get them, they would have to sneak to do it.

Visiting him that day was difficult. The once beautiful boy was nothing but a lifeless, bloated, and badly beaten body. Seven had been long gone since the attack. Maybe the nurse was right. Yet those thoughts were quickly chased out of the mind.

Mae watched Sylvia and continued to have mixed emotions concerning her. These feelings made her feel guilty. Sylvia hadn't left Seven's side and she'd watched him very closely. It still pained Mae to think that the local law and DA's office were easily fooled by her. Obviously the girl was obsessed with Seven and controlling his life. She was so jealous of him she'd made him cut his own family out of his life so she wouldn't have to share him. Rumors were going around about her that the only reason she was staying with Seven was because she was worried he might wake up and tell everyone what really happened that night.

It wouldn't be hard to hate Sylvia, yet Mae considered what her brother would want and need for her to do for him. In his honor, Mae knew he would be concerned about his wife and kids. She actually derived a bit of comfort in tending to Sylvia, feeling her brother would most certainly appreciate it.

"He cried himself to sleep at night." Sylvia freely shared over and over, describing what Seven had gone through the last few weeks of his life.

Being estranged from his family had been such a very painful experience for him. Yet he'd hoped that with time everything would calm down and the problems would be worked out. What could he do to change what his wife had done to his own mother? Having Mary arrested had to have affected him negatively. Time was no longer on his side though, and it was steadily running out.

"Baby, please, just open your eyes, please don't leave me." Sylvia began to plead with Seven on that day, as if her own life depended on it. She never quite felt comfortable around Seven's family. She continued to feel paranoid about their actions.

Mae told Sylvia many times that the past had to be put aside, that Seven would need everyone who loved him to help take care of him.

Sylvia somehow knew that all the trouble she had caused could not be so easily forgiven, much less forgotten.

"He called you the counselor." Sylvia's words surprised Mae.

"He called me what?"

"The counselor…"

Mae smiled but tears also began pouring.

"We both felt that we could always come to you for advice or help." Sylvia looked away, rubbing her nose that ran like her tears.

The message was bittersweet. Mae didn't know her brother felt that way about her. She'd never realized he looked up to her like that. She also didn't realize Sylvia had similar feelings, it stunned Mae into silence.

On the way back from Birmingham, Mary was acting a lot like Sylvia. She was absolutely refusing to believe her son would die. Her mind wouldn't allow the thought.

Mae reassured her mother that Seven was a very strong boy. Of course he would make it.

"He's one of the most stubborn and strong people I know Momma. If anyone can pull through such a brutal attack, it's Seven." Mae's words helped Mary, but neither could chase away the realities they were facing.

Mary had been doing just fine, having to be around Sylvia. She seemed to except Sylvia again, yet you could tell she was worried whether Sylvia was being authentic or manipulative. With Sylvia sleeping on the concrete floor and pacing the halls of that hospital for over a week, you couldn't help but feel pride in her doing so much for Seven. Mary had started considering the idea of getting a motel room in Birmingham. She'd decided to take a leave from work and just stay near the hospital. That way, Sylvia could share the room, and at least they could take turns watching him, while the other got some rest.

Seven's other sister Angel had begun making the daily trip to Birmingham also. Just like Mae, she was living a nightmare.

Then there was Terri Lynn, who lived in north Alabama, and was desperately trying to find a ride to get to her injured brother.

Terri Lynn and Angel's mother, Alicia, managed a motel in Birmingham, and had offered a free room to Sylvia, who used it to take a needed shower and visit with her three kids. Sylvia refused to stay the night away from Seven though. She determined herself to be at the hospital when Seven opened his eyes.

"What would happen if he opened his eyes? He needs someone with him, he hated to be left all alone!"

It was no secret to the family; Seven did have a distinct fear of being alone.

Before Mae and Mary got back, Mae's cell phone rang. Looking at the number, she realized it was the Mayor of Lanyard calling her back finally. She pulled the van over to the side of the road. She wanted him to have her full attention.

Quickly she began explaining to the Mayor how his city's lead investigator, Woody Muck, was treating her family. She informed him of the comments Woody had made to her about her and her mother.

"He accused our family of kicking up trouble. I just don't think his amusement in our tragedy is appropriate or professional behavior."

The Mayor assured Mae that he would speak to the Police Chief concerning Woody's conduct.

As Mae pulled her van back onto the road, she was eager to continue fussing over Woody Muck, but when she glanced at her mother, she could see what was on her mind.

The remainder of the trip, Mary confided to her daughter how scared she was that Seven wouldn't ever be coming back home. His life hanging in the balance and not knowing if he would live or die was slowly ripping her soul apart. She'd confronted a doctor in the hallway one day, and he refused to give her any assurances. She couldn't work, finding it impossible to even function.

Their world had changed in an instant. Every emotion felt, was mind numbingly painful to experience. The ominous and heavy presence of lingering death stalked their every move.

Chapter Sixty Eight

Those who choose to serve and protect deserve the admiration and respect they work so hard for. I grew up wanting to be a police officer like my daddy. For me, it was the ultimate sacrifice to voluntarily put your life at risk in order to protect the innocent. I tried to understand my daddy, and believed his job to be the blame for his aggression towards me. He saw things that he couldn't deal with, and would bring it to my attention, not wanting me to make such mistakes when I grew older. I never feared the police because of my father; instead I felt I understood their positions better than most. I respected their authority as being God ordained. That lifetime of respect went down the tubes after Woody Muck entered into our family's lives.

My first impression of Woody was that he simply believed Sylvia's lies. If he was presented the facts, he wouldn't assist Sylvia in hurting our family anymore. Once personally meeting this individual, and experiencing his personal cause to protect Sylvia, I developed a new outlook, for the local 'good old boys'.

My mother had already taken notice of how several of the officers seemed to feel the need to coddle Sylvia. She pointing out their behavior toward Sylvia in the many court cases they had.

I didn't really believe my mother, figuring she was just overly agitated, yet I not only witnessed them rubbing Sylvia's shoulders and such, but experienced their top rate protection of her.

Woody had worked his way up to investigator, which in the department meant he was a boss. What the boss does, those beneath him rarely go against. If Woody was protecting Sylvia, so were his subordinates.

Facts remain, SEVEN was an obvious VICTIM. All those who shared in his life, were victims. If Woody held any grudge that was his God given right, yet using his power to hurt people, while on the tax payer's time clock is a shame. Nearly two years later, I still feel an unbelievable disgust for him and all those who are like him.

While a cop is on duty, they can get away with just about anything. Being the law, I always felt they should be examples of such law. It plagues our family that they wouldn't protect us, and yet they helped Sylvia get away with so many crimes, using their police discretion. At least that's the excuse used to allow Sylvia free reign on our sanity and life.

Since the murder, I've come to realize that officers who FAIL to arrest a person alleged to have committed a crime could well be charged with failing in their duty. Who knew? We've been thrust into this life of protecting ourselves, for years now. I am now claiming citizen's arrest on Woody, for failure to arrest. Yet it's a silly prospect to believe I could possibly be one to make a difference in the way things are being run around our town.

No one wants to alienate themselves from the law, least of all me. Though I've experienced the unjust judgment of Woody, I won't allow one rotten apple, to destroy my faith in the rest of those who serve and protect.

Momma's opinions wouldn't be the same as mine, and to this second, she despises the uniform more than ever. She called for help, and they laughed at her, made fun of her, and helped the assailant attack her. They arrested her. So while Sylvia was getting away with driving while intoxicated, burglary and assaulting people, Mary was being put in handcuffs, for doing absolutely nothing wrong. Her faith in the "system" is forever gone.

Being her daughter, and watching her pain, what else should I feel but anger that it has happened to the mother I love. If Woody or any other cop took offense to me wanting to protect my mother, then they can take that offense and shove it where the sun doesn't shine.

Perhaps I don't see the world the same way they do, and for that I am very glad. If the things done to my mother and brother had been done to one of their own, they would understand. Yet they don't care, so why should I care what they do, think or say?

It does speak volumes about their character to find any amusement in watching others in unbearable pain. It lets you know exactly what type of person you're dealing with.

But I wouldn't allow Woody or any other poor sap the power to control my reactions. I would not let the good or the bad behavior of another person determine my own behavior or lack of it. I choose who I want to be, and being in command of my own actions, all but erases the false power their behavior has given them. It's just a sad topic to know those who are in power to protect victims use that same power to create victims.

Our time with Seven was coming to an end. It's not that we didn't know it, we just couldn't face it. Looking back and having intensely studied his injuries, I have no doubt's, he was dead from the moment he received his first hit across his temporal bone, from behind. It had crushed it inwardly, smashing skull bone into his brain. The next hit would have killed him too, splitting the back of his head open. So though he would receive at least three or more hits to his head, the first two did enough damage.

We had hope, yet there was none.

No prospects were promised from the dozens of doctors, still we believed.

I'd been painfully reborn into a truth I was far from ever comprehending. I not only saw things differently, those looking at me saw me in a diverse way also. There's just so much discomfort involved, that those going through it can't be reached. Nothing can come close to fixing what's happened. Sure, we had to except it, but how?

I'm now on a quest to understand. Our world is full of problems, it always will be. It's what happening in our own back yards that we need to sit up and take notice of.

Chapter Sixty Nine

July had arrived without warning.

Every one of Seven's family members was stuck on the day of the attack.

Seven had only been twenty-seven for a little less than two days when he was attacked. His boss Carl had informed that Seven had been really eager to make it home in time for his birthday on Friday. It didn't work out, and they had to stay another night out of town. It had really upset Seven, because he knew Sylvia and his kids would have planned a family birthday celebration for him. He had tried to call Sylvia Thursday, to let her know he wouldn't be making it back until late Saturday. Sylvia didn't have any more time on her phone, so Seven had no way of reaching her. He'd called his friend's mother, Brenda Tiller, to ask her to "please go by and let Sylvia know I won't be able to come home until Saturday".

Unfortunately, Brenda didn't get the chance to go by, and so Sylvia had no idea Seven wouldn't be coming home. Sylvia didn't know if Seven had come back to town or not. Friday night, she just wasn't sure and didn't know what to think when he didn't show up. Having made him a strawberry cake, they ate it without him on his birthday, Friday night.

"He was very worried that Sylvia would be mad at him for not being home Friday. " Carl shared. "He fretted over it all day long Saturday, up until we pulled into his driveway. Then everyone came outside to greet him. His three kids were so happy to see him, and they all wrapped their arms around him. 'Happy Birthday Daddy!' they were telling him. I could see Seven beaming with pride, and all his worrying about being late left him. It sure was a beautiful scene, seeing Seven so happy." Carl loved Seven like a son, and he hadn't realized that when he dropped Seven off from work, it would be the last time to ever see him well and alive again. "Every man should be welcomed home like that."

Seven had an unlucky date, and it was July 4th. From his past history, the day had always brought bad luck. No matter how hard he'd tried to enjoy the day, it just wouldn't ever turn out like he planned. As if sensing the impending date, Seven's condition began to take a turn for the worse. His brain pressure began rising, managing to hang out in the low 40's. The respirator pressure had to be turned up, meaning he was having more difficulty breathing. Under Sylvia's watchful eye, she could tell he was suffering from pain, and they had to start giving him higher and more frequent doses of Fentanyl and Hydromorphone.

It tortured Mae to know that her brother was laying there paralyzed, sedated, feeling intense pain, and unable to move or make it stop. You could look at him and tell he was fighting the hardest battle he'd have fought in his life. With so much struggling to live, how could he die?

The odds were staking high against his surviving. His pneumonia was getting worse by the hour, and he wasn't responding to the antibiotics at all. If nothing else, he would suffocate to death.

Mae brought a picture of him and put it on the wall. The nurses didn't object, and were happy to finally see what the person looked like under all the damage.

Leaving him every day was difficult; the unshakable fear it could be the last time. Guilt twisted the insides up like a dish rag. The wanting him to wake up and wanting his pain to just stop, kept the heart dripping with pain.

Late that evening Mae stopped at a local gas station. She was deep in thought, handing the clerk the money, and didn't notice who the employee was.

"I don't know what Seven did to Ennis to get him to do whatever it was he did, but I'm sure Seven had it coming and deserved what he got."

It was, Anna Bidden, the same girl who had offered Sylvia a ride home the night Mae was spit on and shoved. The one yelling..."Mrs. Mae...Mrs. Mae..."

Her utterances came as she was handing Mae her change. The girl's lexical noises literally felt like slaps across Mae's face. Having learned to control her emotional reactions in life, Mae turned away and willed her feet to carry her back to the vehicle. Her heart was nearly beating out of her chest. The blood was running so hard and fast through her body, that Mae felt like she would explode before reaching the security of her van. Climbing inside and shutting the door, her ears were ringing loudly, everything was moving in slow motion around her, and then it would speed up making her dizzy while seated.

'How could someone say something like that?' Mae thought to herself with every muscle in her body beginning to tense up. 'My brother **deserved** to have his head beaten in'? Mae put her keys into the ignition. She forced the darkness from overcoming her and left the gas station. Crying as she worried how many more heartless assholes would say such things to her.

So many ugly rumors had surfaced. The biggest was how it had been a drug deal that had gone wrong. Other stories concern Sylvia and how she was calling people and telling them she observed the attack and was involved with the crime. Some tales had Seven catching Kendall and Sylvia together when he got home from work. There were stories about the video game and about a planned robbery. Even a story that Seven had become an informant for a certain cop, and was shut up by those he was informing about.

Mary had been carefully watching Sylvia and running the past year through her mind. Something wasn't right. Now, she had easily enough worked her way back into a family that had all but refused her forever. Mary worried about how Sylvia would behave if Seven survived, but wasn't able to be the same man he had been.

His words were haunting her now.

"I'll finally be free and clear!" Seven had bragged.

"I wouldn't tell Sylvia if I was you."

Seven's smiled. "Why?'

"You'll end up in prison or dead."

He laughed at her. "Why do you think that?"

"Because she won't ever let you be free."

Mae had wondered how the trauma of the past experience with Sylvia could ever be mended. The prospect of losing Seven had never been an imagined solution. Mae never had any intentions of staying away from Seven and his children for too long. She had just needed some time to calm down from the extramarital affair of her husband and Sylvia. Seven seemed to have gotten over it easily enough, but Mae figured Sylvia hadn't been completely honest with him about what actually went on between her and Rex.

Rex told Mae what happened, and Sylvia had proclaimed it to her that December night of spit and shoves.

The only thing Mae had cut out of her life was Sylvia. She wanted to show her sister-in-law that she couldn't be controlled by her using Seven and his kids.

Unbeknownst to Mae, Seven had told Mary, he knew exactly what Rex and Sylvia had done, but he didn't want Mae hurt.

"Mae wouldn't believe it, she doesn't want too."

Wednesday, July 2nd, rolled around without anything different than the day before. Depression was setting into every family member. Nothing they could do would help Seven.

He was surrounded by an array of women who loved him very much. Mary, Sylvia, Angel and Mae kept a vigil by his side, as much as the ICU rules would allow. They all began to witness the true horror of what the human body can be put through. His bloating had increased, and it gave him the appearance of being in constant pain. With all the pressure on his lungs, they had started collapsing. Just looking at him, you sensed he felt all alone in his slow torment.

One nurse assured them, that though he couldn't respond, he could more than likely feel them touch him and hear them talking to him. To what extent his traumatized brain could comprehend wasn't something she would elaborate on.

Later the same nurse shared some information with Mary and Sylvia, involving Seven's condition.

"I was concerned about how bad his lungs had gotten, so I went down to the emergency room and pulled his file. Seven had contusions up and down both sides of his torso. That type of bruising would indicate he was kicked repeatedly. He also had a very distinctive shoe shaped bruise imprint on his chest. A shoe size of nine & a half was written down. It indicates his chest was stomped on. That's why his lungs are in such bad shape. "

Her words stunned both women, who looked back at her with their mouths open.

She wasn't finished. "The toxicology report showed he had very little alcohol in his system, and nothing else."

For Mary it was a relief. Some rumors she'd heard had Seven out roaming the streets, drunken and disorderly. That Seven was looking for a fight. Now she had facts to support her son was sober when they attacked him.

When they told Mae, it didn't really surprise her. She already suspected Kendall was involved, and she was willing to bet his shoe size was nine & a half. Then there was the way the neighbors were lying about not being out in their yard during the attack. Mae had always felt Seven's spirit had been broken, and something like a yard full of people attacking him for no reason, but meanness, would do it. It confirmed to her she was on the right track, and that Ennis didn't act all alone.

There was one more piece of evidence Mae hadn't heard anything about, the gun. Ennis had a gun on him when the police found him. Nothing had been mentioned about the gun, but its presence had Mae wondering if they wanted Seven dead, why didn't they just shoot him? Why beat his head off?

Mae began putting together her own time line of events, starting when

Seven got home from work. She started her own witness list of the last people in contact with Seven during that last twelve hours home. She would fill in the blanks, and see what she could come up with herself.

It was like putting a jig-saw puzzle together with dozens of missing pieces.

She'd work with what she had and patiently search for the rest.

Chapter Seventy

On that Wednesday night, Sylvia decided to go home to her children, for one night. It was a hard decision, not one she was so sure about. She held onto to dread Seven would either wake up or die without her there with him.

Seven had always had a fear of being alone. Now every member of his family shared in that fear with him.

The children needed their parents. They were shadowed with their own uncertainties. Bella knew Seven had been hurt really bad, and she knew what was being said about it. While her younger siblings continued with their innocent pursuits, Bella continued to be adamant about seeing her daddy.

Having her own set of questions, Sylvia spent most of her time home running around asking questions, and letting off steam. The one person she wanted answers from was Kendall Martin.

Kendall had given many people his version of events. The detectives, Rex and Mae, and even Erik, who made his trip over to Kendall's house the day of the attack. Kendall told Erik, basically the same thing he had informed to Rex and Mae.

Now Sylvia wanted her answers, and she got George to take her to Kendall's trailer, which sat in the same park as Ennis's. She demanded to know what statement Kendall had given to the police. She insisted he get into the car with her and that they all go up to the police station and get a copy of his version of what happened. They left the police station empty handed, and Sylvia didn't accept anything Kendall was saying.

"If Seven dies, I will kill you!" She threatened him when they dropped him back off at his trailer.

Mae couldn't blame her for threatening. She felt the same way. Anger had become such a strong emotion to deal with. Nothing had ever made her angrier than what had been done to her brother. Mae used her charged up emotions to propel her into finding the truth. The first question had always been, why in the neighbors "empty" yard? Why was such an easy question so hard to find the answer for? The complexity of it grew worse every day.

On Thursday morning, with Sylvia home, Mary and Mae decided to take the opportunity to all go to the police department and ask the lead detective a few questions. As they sat in the waiting area of the police department, Mae recollected a few months prior, and the scene with the three women would have been ugly. Now they were all working together, for the same purpose.

It continued to annoy Mary and Mae to know that Woody Muck was the one they would be forced to talk to.

The wait was intense. Mary looked as uncomfortable as Mae while Sylvia sat looking at the floor. One officer came out and went straight to Sylvia. He was one of her coddlers, and his concern for her being forced to sit with us must have urged him to see to her safety.

"Hey girl, what do you need?" He smiled widely while talking to her, but it quickly faded with her angered expression and curt answer.

"I won't to know what you're going to do about those who attacked my husband?!" She didn't hold back any emotion with her demand.

"OH! Well, I guess the investigator will be out to talk with you." He backed away and disappeared into a doorway.

Investigator Muck took his sweet time coming out to talk to the strange trio.

Mae figured he was having a hard time working up the nerve.

Mary wouldn't claim to dislike Woody; she went straight forward with hating him. She most definitely didn't trust him or any other law enforcement officer. She believed the entire system was against her, and after her experiences, no one could blame her. Sitting in the department's front waiting room, she felt like a cat being forced to sit in a bathtub.

The wait continued but finally Muck stepped out. In appearance he looked a little nervous being in the same room with Mary and Mae, who looked at him with contempt.

"I heard the case is closed!" Sylvia jumped right in with rumors she'd heard.

Muck took a seat across from the three women. "It remains open. We have a confessed perpetrator sitting in jail, but that's it." He smiled.

"Well, Seven has a size nine and a half shoe imprint on his chest, and contusions up and down both sides of his chest! Seven's toxicology showed he only had a small amount of alcohol in his system."

Muck looked slightly surprised with that, but only replied by nodding his head up and down. After a few moments of uncomfortable silence Muck spoke up.

"We were short-handed that night, so the crime scene wasn't secured. When I arrived on the scene, the neighbor whose yard Seven was attacked in, had a shovel out there, covering all the blood up so his dogs wouldn't get in it."

His words set all three women on fire, while he seemed slightly amused with the information he was providing.

He continued talking though, oblivious to the heat. "I personally took the evidence collected to Montgomery, where forensic testing will be performed."

"Are you planning on taking any pictures of the damage done to my brother?" Mae tossed in a question, making his head snap in her direction.

He looked at her, smiling and shook his head no. Standing up he insinuated the meeting over.

"I tell you what; I'll just take care of it myself!" Sylvia stood up and continued facing him directly.

"You are all to stay away from both Ennis and Kendall!" His warning went on mute ears.

All three left the department in separate vehicles to meet back up later at the hospital.

Seven was doing much better that day, or as his nurse informed, he had a slight hair of improvement. To the family, it was a mile. His body had accepted some of the antibiotic's healing. The sixteen IV tubes had been replaced with one main central line directly inserted into his chest. They hoped with the one line, his body would stop bloating so badly.

Mae ended her visit sitting outside with Sylvia. They were both floating with the good news of his tiny improvement. Sylvia began talking about the night of the attack. She was informing Mae of the first fight between Kendall and Seven which occurred within the hour of Seven's murder attempt.

"Ennis was involved too, and George witnessed them all fighting. George was there because Seven had asked him to 'come out and keep it a fair fight'. It was around three forty in the morning. George had already taken the axe handle away from Ennis. George said Ennis made the comment 'Yeah your right, man on man', then George said Ennis pushed the axe handle back into his shorts. By the time I got there Kendall was sitting on top of Seven. I just ran right over to Kendall, and kicked him in the head and told him to 'get the f*#! off my husband'. After the fight, Kendall remarked to Seven, 'if your old lady hadn't helped you, I'd have killed you then!'."

Sylvia also relayed a strange story about a dark shadow that had started following Seven around.

"One night he fell asleep on the couch, and I just let him sleep. During the night, I was awakened by a loud noise, like someone had slammed into something. Suddenly, Seven ran into the bedroom, turning with both of his fist in the air, like something was coming up behind him. I asked him what was wrong, and he jumped into the bed and told me he'd seen a black shadow. It had scared the color out of him, and he wouldn't get back out of the bed to go look."

Terrified, he described what happened to his wife. "I was sleeping, and I dreamed there was a dark shadow, looking down at me, I woke myself up swinging at it, and my arm hit the coffee table. Being awake, I looked around, thinking it was only a dream, but then there it was again, across the room. I jumped up, and ran into the kitchen table, trying to get away from it. It headed down the hall, towards the kids rooms!" Seven's descriptions disturbed Sylvia.

"I told him to go check on the kids, but he was so terrified, he wouldn't budge. After that night, we both would hear noises, like something being drug across gravel."

Mae was glad that Sylvia was finally sharing some of her witness view of that night. Knowing how private and paranoid Sylvia could be, Mae wondered if she'd ever tell exactly what went down.

For once Mae drove back home from the hospital without crying. She thanked God for Seven's hair of improvement. With her optimism she had more energy to focus on finding out what exactly had happened to him.

She'd started focusing on the last twelve hours of his life. She took a close look at every hour and who he'd encountered. She continued to look at the neighbor's lies and odd behavior. How could they be so cruel? She put herself in their place, and their behavior seemed all the more awkward. Shoveling up blood on a crime scene didn't sit well with Mae or any other person for that matter. Again, she imagined what her reaction would have been if she'd been "awakened" to find a victim clinging to life in her front yard. Many different reactions, but to save her life, she couldn't imagine thinking about going to get a shovel.

Then there was the tiny fact the police seemed so nonchalant about their crime scene being tampered with. Muck almost looked amused.

Mae's mind hummed like a computer, trying to put all the different information into one giant file.

She centered her thoughts on Kendall, why would he be fighting Seven? Mae could think of only one reason Seven would have to be at odds with Kendall. Sylvia. Seven was no friend of Kendall's; they had never been friends or enemies. Kendall had only been around town for a few weeks. The first and only encounter he has with Seven ended with Seven's attempted murder?

Mae's list of questions grew. 1. Why in the 'empty' neighbor's yard? 2. Why were the neighbors lying about being witnesses? 3. If Seven was fighting, where were his defense wounds? (An axe handle is coming at you, wouldn't your reflexes react? Shouldn't his arms or hands display wounds?) 4. Why did

Seven go by and ask Erik to ride with him and help back him up? Why did he call Ava asking her for a ride for him and Kendall? He was inside a car when he called. Why would he need a ride? Why would Seven want to bring Kendall along with him anyway? Ava wouldn't provide a ride, because Seven wanted a ride for Kendall too. Seven was not friends with Kendall. So why is Seven trying to get Kendall out of Focus Trailer park that night? 5. Why did Ennis or Kendall want to beat Seven to death anyway? 6. Why didn't Ennis just use the gun he was carrying around? Why beat someone to death? 7. Despite the neighbors covering the crime scene, why wasn't it ever taped up and secured? 8. Why was the blood really being covered over?

Questions and more questions filled Mae's mind to over capacity. It was driving her crazy to find the answers, or least find something that made sense. The one thing that bugged her the most was Kendall fighting with Seven to start with. Why? It had to be because of Sylvia. Mae intended to get to the bottom of it

There were neighbors in Focus Park that worked for Rex, and they would keep Mae abreast of any new stories about the attack. That evening, the new rumor floating around Focus Trailer Park had Kendall bragging about taking Seven‘s hard earned money during the attack.

It was true, Seven had money missing, but the police didn't seem to care to follow that story.

Mae rode around with her husband while he took care of some errands. While she was sitting inside his truck, a vehicle pulled up. Mae didn't pay it too much attention until she noticed Ennis's wife/girlfriend, Sissy, getting out.

Sissy made her way over to the passenger door, where Mae had put the window down. Sissy was eager to speak to Mae, apologizing and asking how Seven was doing. When Mae informed her that he wasn't doing well, Sissy paled and started crying.

"I can't believe he did that to Seven. I would never in a million years have thought that he could do something so horrible. I won't ever talk to him again; I don't want to ever see him." As Sissy spoke, she tried to evade looking into Mae's eyes. "He only needs a land owner to sign his bond, and he can get out. I don't want him out. I'm terrified he might get out."

Sissy's waist length strawberry blond hair floated around in the breeze. Her fingers pulled at it, keeping it from blowing across her face.

"Around three o'clock in the morning, I heard some screaming outside in our yard." Sissy had started to explain what she experienced the night of the attack on Seven.

Mae's ears were burning for the information, but she tried to stay nonchalant. She carefully gave Sissy all her attention.

"It sounded like a female yelling, so I got up out of the bed, and went outside on the back porch. As soon as I stepped outside, Ennis yelled at me to 'get my ass back in the house', which I did." She paused, putting her cigarette out. "Later he came inside, acting funny. He went into the bathroom, and passed out on the toilet."

With that Sissy was finished. The police were supposed to have found him passed out. She left Mae, apologizing for what had happened.

As Sissy drove off, Mae continued to go over facts in her mind.

Sissy had moved herself and her two children in with Kendall the day of the attack. It was an odd move and made everyone start talking about Sissy being involved too. Sissy hadn't mentioned one word about her husband being covered in Seven's blood. With every answer, always came more questions.

Chapter Seventy One

Independence Day was upon them and Mae just couldn't help worrying about the infamous day for Seven. In the past he hadn't had good luck on July 4th, and he was always happy to get through one without incident.

With every passing day that he survived, the family grew in confidence that he would wake up.

Mae got out of bed, trying to put happy thoughts into her head. Seven had made a hair of improvement, and who knows, maybe today would be the day he finally woke up.

She had friends that she hadn't been able to keep up with for the past two weeks. They had volunteered to take her to Birmingham for the day. Mae was looking forward to spending time with them, even if it was on a trip to the hospital to see her critically injured brother. Before they arrived that morning, the telephone rang. It was the telephone call Mae had feared for weeks. It was her momma.

"Seven stopped improving. He's unresponsive to the treatments, and his vital signs are deteriorating. He has started to decline. The doctors said he wouldn't make it through the weekend, probably not even through the night." Mary was hoarse and strangely calm.

Mae could feel the same numbness working down through her body. The tears were automatic. Her baby brother was going to die.

As her friends arrived, they could do little to comfort Mae so they followed in their car behind her fast drive to Birmingham. Over and over in her mind, the reality of Seven dying made her unable to function. Driving wasn't a great idea, yet she couldn't get to Seven fast enough if she let someone else do it.

"No, no, no, no, he just can't die. No, no, no, this can't be happening."

Going into his room, it was quickly obvious that the staff had changed the rules concerning Seven's visitor number. The room was full of family.

Angel sat beside him reading the Bible to him. Her three sons, Simon, Bruce and Clark, all stood looking at their once strong and powerful Uncle Seven. The brutality of the crime wasn't easy for them to take in.

Mary sat in silence watching her son.

Sylvia was nearly hysterical. She refused to believe her husband's fate.

Seven had started to really blow up. His body had swollen up to grotesque proportions. His head was doubled in size. His struggle to hold on was apparent, as his body glistened with sweat. Every so often, his swollen closed eyes, leaked trails of wet tears down both sides of his face. The respirator forcing air into his collapsing lungs sounded like it was ripping him apart. It was a nightmare that he couldn't wake up from.

Twenty-seven years old, and they had to just sit there and watch him die. Some stupid idiots decided to beat him to death, and now he was just going to die. Their beloved and precious family member was going to suffer and die for a video game.

Sylvia was informed, that if she wanted her children to see their daddy one last time, she needed to get them to the hospital.

Allowing the children in ICU further pushed home the inevitable. For the past two weeks, everything had moved in a slow motion circle. Now time seemed to be speeding up.

Sylvia and Mae discussed letting Bella see Seven, but because Seven looked so distorted, she didn't want the two younger ones to see him like that. Everyone knew if Bella didn't get to see her daddy, she wouldn't ever let them forget it. She had been demanding to see him since day one. Mae agreed to go get Bella and bring her to see her daddy for the very last time.

Rex drove Mae and Bella back to Birmingham that evening. When they had arrived to pick Bella up, she was so excited about being allowed to finally see her daddy. She was oblivious to the pain that was in store in her. They traveled to the hospital, listening to Bella go on and on about her wonderful daddy.

She laughed and spoke about all the fun things they had done together. She talked about all the things they still had planned to do together.

"When daddy gets well, we are going to go camping. I've never been camping, and I want my daddy to be the one to take me first." She believed as most little girls do, that her daddy was larger than life, and that nothing could take him away from her. "When daddy gets better, he's going to take us all to Six Flags." Perhaps it had been a plan of theirs, and she held firmly to her daddy's promises. Her daddy was her protector, and since the attack, she'd felt afraid of everything. She was wearing a dress he had bought for her a few months back for Easter. "Daddy will like to see me in this dress; he said I look so pretty in it."

Mae listened to her niece, giggling and chattering away. Tears constantly flowed, but she kept them hidden from Bella, not wanting to upset the little one more than she already had ahead of her.

Bella couldn't wait to see Seven, and she could imagine her daddy sitting up in bed with his two big arms wide open to grab and hold her tight. The moment arrived to take her back past the two ICU doors that had forbidden her from entering. Sylvia held to one hand while Mae held the other. They walked together towards room 712. Bella immediately began taking in all that her young eyes could see. She'd wondered what it looked like past the metal doors. As they stood outside Seven's cubicle, Sylvia leaned down to try to prepare Bella for what she was about to see. There were no words to describe the scene of a battered daddy to his seven year old daughter. Sylvia picked Bella up and stepped behind the curtain with her.

"Woahhh!" was all that Bella could say. She couldn't grasp what had become of the daddy she always had. He was gone, never to return. As she looked at the man she'd expected to see her through her life, Bella realized she no longer had a daddy. He would never speak her name again or hold her tightly in his arms.

Mae couldn't handle the scene, and she asked Rex to take her home. She couldn't stay in the hospital for one more moment. She wanted to get away from her life, entirely. She wanted to run away, but there was no place that she could go to escape the pain she was feeling.

Rex tried to help and insisted they go see fireworks. Watching them, Mae cried and cried, nothing would ever be the same, and as she tried to continue, every move she made filled her with guilt. While she lived, her brother was lying in a hospital bed suffering and dying.

As always the day would end with more rumor mill stories, to which Mae added to her immensely growing collection. Apparently, Seven had left his house to walk to the store. He was supposed to be going back to the convenience store for a pack of cigarettes, and Kendall decided to walk with him. As they were walking past the neighbor's house, Seven was called to come into the yard. Ennis attacked Seven over a stereo, and the crowd of people in the neighbor's yard egged the violence on. Then the neighbor, David Smith, was cleaning up the blood with a shovel.

Lying in bed that night, she couldn't sleep. Images of Seven as a young boy, running and playing, laughing and living, circled through her mind. Tossing and turning, she'd doze off and woke up thinking she heard the phone. Finally, she just got up, made some coffee, and began putting pen to paper. At first, he words flowed with no set course, making no sense, but the more she wrote, the better she felt.

Arriving the next day, after spending the entire night on pins and needles, Mae was confronted with a nearly impossible scene.

Seven continued to lie in the same stationary position, but his looks had drastically changed, with his body inflated even more than the day before. So badly, it gave him the appearance of being a balloon. Hopefully, she prayed that God would stop Seven's suffering. How much more could the human body take? How much more could the family's hearts withstand?

Ricky Levine and Terri Lynn had arrived in town late the previous evening.

Mae hadn't seen Ricky in over a decade and felt nothing at all for the man, good or bad. Watching him as he looked upon his dying son, Mae considered the tremendous pain he must be feeling. The worst a parent could ever fear to experience.

Terri Lynn was beside herself with grief. She wouldn't allow herself to believe her brother was going to die, regardless of what he looked like or what the doctors said. Over the years, Terri Lynn hadn't changed all that much. She continued to be crazier than hell.

Mae couldn't help but laugh at Terri Lynn's unique character. Most people wouldn't know the extreme tragedy of her childhood, but Mae was well acquainted with it.

The family hung around the hospital all day long, in and out of the ICU. Hour upon hour, they watched as his body continue to blow up way out of proportion. It twisted everyone up to see him suffering so much and be completely powerless to do anything about it. Frantically it seemed that Seven was desperately trying to hold onto his life. He wanted so badly to come back to all those who needed him and beckoned for him to wake up.

Outside by the fountain, Sylvia and Mae sat numbly watching as some children played inside the fountain. Eagerly the kids were picking up the change that had been thrown into it. It reminded Mae of the day Seven's three threw handfuls of change in with wishes for their daddy. Both Sylvia and Mae were slightly irritated by the carefree children playing and splashing in the cool water. It was so hot; Mae was considering getting in with the kids.

"I know Seven loved you Sylvia." Mae felt like Sylvia needed to know that no one doubted Seven's love for her.

"He would cry himself to sleep over missing his family and being put off the Baker land." Sylvia cried as she spoke. "He didn't know how to fix what I'd done to his family."

"It's in the past Sylvia; you know I'll help you. I know Seven has to be worried over what's going to happen to you and the kids." Mae was sincere, but she didn't know how the rest of the family felt. In the same token, Mae was highly emotionally, and like everyone else, exhausted.

"People believe I had something to do with Seven's attack." Sylvia eyed Mae for her reaction

"Sylvia, it's because of the previous year of crap, that's all. Don't worry about what people say." Mae felt like she'd managed to walk into the middle of a mind field. She didn't know what to say without it coming off accusatory.

In the evening, Seven's condition continued to deteriorate. His head continued to swell, until it dislodged the ICP, his brain pressure monitor. At first with the machine going to instant zero, it frightened everyone, believing he was brain dead. The nurse quickly assured the family of what had happened, but she didn't seem happy about it happening.

The day would end with Mae realizing her wallet had been stolen out of her purse. When she had arrived that morning, she'd been so eager to see Seven; she'd left her purse in the waiting room. Sadly, there were people roaming the hospital, making a living on robbing patients and visitors. The security guard told Mae that it was more than likely a crack addict and she could kiss her wallet goodbye. Mae would search high and low, in every trash can sitting inside the many waiting rooms, and even some outside the hospital. She considered making a report, but was tired and drained; she decided to put it off until after the weekend when she could just go to the police department.

Mae drove home in tears again. She blamed herself for leaving her purse, and losing her wallet. Even so, it had only seemed to make her feel worse than ever. Nothing about life was fair, not that it ever had been. She could feel her deep dark friend coming back, Mr. Depression. Its darkness covered her, and the prospect of living such a horrible life just didn't seem like a good idea anymore. She couldn't take anymore, it just hurt so badly. She missed the plain old crazy life she'd had before Seven's attack. Mae could feel her entire persona changing and her outlook for life becoming drizzled with hopelessness. The more you loved people, the worst it felt. Was that the purpose of life? To uncover how the true nature of love was death and pain?

Chapter Seventy Two

Sunday morning was a bright and sunny day. For two straight weeks, it had rained every day. Mae had gotten up early and headed to the hospital first thing. She'd been surprised that the phone had not rung all night. She stopped at a Dunkin' Donuts for coffee and a dozen of the pastries. Almost cheerfully, she made her way up to the seventh floor.

Seven had pulled through two days longer than the doctors had expected. He could still pull through. He could still make it. What do doctors know? They are wrong all the time.

The moment she saw him, she was filled with even more jubilation. Mary and Sylvia sat in the quiet room, while Seven lay in his same position. He was still grotesquely bloated, but the swelling seemed to have slowed down. Mae's eyes were drawn to his catheter tubing, which had a nice yellow urine color.

"He's peeing!" Mae exclaimed with joy.

Both Mary and Sylvia nodded their heads and smiled.

"Of course he's peeing." Sylvia had a wash cloth, carefully rubbing at the glistening beads of sweat covering his face and body. "We're peeing and breathing, ain't we baby."

She was talking to him, and it would seem he was absolutely listening. He seemed to be concentrating really hard, with intensity to his breathing. The yellow urine was a welcome to see after weeks of cloudy, dark green/ black color.

Mae worked her way closer, taking her own wash cloth; she dabbed at his dripping wet sweat. Something was different, he was trying. You could not just see it but feel it. They had him back!

He seemed to know they were there, even though he hadn't moved a muscle. He looked horribly bloated, but that could go back down. The antibiotics could continue to work. He could wake up. He could pull through. Though he was at death's door, he could turn around and come back to his family, who desperately needed him. Even though a yard full of people tried to kill him with their redneck hate, his family's true love could pull him through.

The three women left the ICU room together giving Seven's nurse's time to work on him in peace. Happily they walked and talked, believing the worst was behind them. Together, they talked about how happy he would be to have his family back together. They joked about Seven's rebellious nature, and how he only seemed to succeed with tremendous challenges before him. No doubt this had been the challenge of his life. No matter what condition he was in, they would love him and take care of him.

Mary teased about how much work her son had obviously put his guardian angels through during his short lifetime.

Not wanting to leave his side for too long, they made their way back up, and continued to talk softly while walking through the ICU hallway. Abruptly, all three stopped, looking in complete horror at the bloody mess Seven was in. To their horror, in the short time they had left him, the doctors had decided to re-insert the ICP. Ignorantly they had all assumed the tube would be simply put back in where it had pulled loose from his head. Never would they imagine that the doctors would come in with a drill and bore a new hole down into his skull, right there on his forehead. The new tube was circled in dripping bloody gauze.

"Why did they do this? Hadn't his head already been battered enough? They told us he could feel and hear us, so they just decide to take a drill and put a new hole into his already swollen brain?"

Mae was beside herself with grief. Her brother had been told that they would be right back. He lay there waiting, peeing and breathing, and then he gets a drill bit put into his forehead? She walked in to her brother. Both of his eye sockets were puddles of tears that flowed continuously down both sides of his face. In all the hours he had lain in that bed, he had never cried tears like that. Mae's heart dropped. Just by looking at Seven, she could tell he'd had enough. The pain was just too much to bear. You could see the confusion all over his swollen face, as the tears continued down their path.

With his newly placed tube, his brain pressure could be read again. The number showed 45, a terrible number, considering normal was 7-15.

Tears soaked Mae's face, as she told him over and over she loved him.

Mary had gone silent, while Sylvia hysterically fussed to the nurse's over what they had done to him.

"Why did they do this to him? Look at him! Why?!"

It killed Mae to think he could comprehend, and then again, it hurt not knowing for sure. Either way, it just wasn't fair for him to have to continue to be tortured. He no longer was sweating with concentration, but he was crying plenty of tears.

They had him, and now within minutes, they had lost him again. How many times were they going to lose him?

It was obvious he was in agony, and it hurt to the bone to witness.

Overcome with emotion, Mae made her way out of the room. She couldn't take it. How Mary and Sylvia could, Mae didn't know, but it was literally killing her. Around her, people moved about, but she only saw blurry images. The air was evaporating, nothing felt real, and the pain was like thousands of needles, puncturing her soul. She wanted to find a dark isolated room, yet every square inch seemed to be lit with extremely bright light. If she couldn't find a safe place, she was going to blow up! She ran to her van, opening the door with shaking hands, slamming the door shut, she let out a deep wail.

When Seven had his first ICP inserted, he had been under the sedation of surgery. Lying there, medically paralyzed, unable to respond or react in any way, they torturously drilled a hole into his forehead! It sounded so barbaric and cruel. First it's an axe handle from behind, then surgery to remove skull from his brain, two weeks of blowing up from fluid retentions, suffocation from collapsing lungs filling with fluid, heck why not drill a hole into his forehead? Mae feared her anger could be contagious if she didn't keep it retained.

She cried, and cried, a good river of tears, sitting right there in the parking lot, sweating in the hot sun. She felt more alone than ever in the seclusion of her van. Everyone in their town was acting like Seven had only received a good whack on his head. No one could possibly conceive of the damage done. The paper only reported Seven had been, 'struck in the head'. That gave Seven's true struggle for life a slap in the face. Nothing made any sense at all. She felt terrified to exist in such a good old boy world. The effects were so intense, she felt like she had received a shot of sedation herself. If Seven died, she believed it would kill her. It would prove that the local system had won. They successfully had let Seven be victimized by his wife, which ultimately put him off the Baker property he'd treasure so much. He had told everyone that coming back to Chambly County would kill him. That's why he wanted to stay on the Baker land, in the one place he'd felt safe, but Sylvia had taken that from him too. Why?

After calming down, Mae forced herself to go back upstairs. After only a few minutes, she was fired back up with many confusing emotions. As difficult as it was to watch Seven lie there, crying and shaking with pain, witnessing Mary's and Sylvia's grief made her head pound with pressure. The blood flowing from her breaking heart pumped through, making every moment intensify with agonizing grief. He was dying before their eyes, and there was nothing anyone could do to stop it. Mae apologized to the two women and told them she had to go. Looking at Seven, Mae cried as she kissed his bloody face.

"I love you brother, now and forever." She felt guilty for leaving, but she feared staying, she might end up in the hospital ICU herself. She worried that she might be having a heart attack, as her heart pumped painful beats that felt like rips and tares.

For two weeks, Seven had laid lifeless in room 712 of the ICU. He had blown up ten times his normal body weight, with fluid retention, medically called Edema. His kidneys had shut down completely. He was unable to breath with double pneumonia that had all but collapsed both of his lungs. The oxygen level on his respirator was set up to 100%, which would normally, and painfully, blow up most lungs. The liver had taken all it could take, and his vascular system had started breaking down. Regardless, his big loving heart continued to beat despite all it had been through. His will to live wasn't something he would give up easily. If anyone loved life, it was Seven.

Mae had gotten home and called her mother right away. Not one minute went by that Mae wasn't thinking about what Seven continued to agonizingly go through. She felt horrible for not having the strength to endure watching him suffer.

Mary told Mae that the doctors had tried to give Seven a last minute blood transfusion, in hopes it would help him.

Mae laid her head down to close her eyes, he head still pounding in beat with her heart. It was before midnight, and she couldn't believe her mother hadn't called her before now. That's when the phone rang, and Mae knew it was time.

"It won't be long. The blood transfusion did nothing but cause him to urinate blood."

Mary didn't ask Mae to come, but she got dressed, overwhelmed with the sensation, Seven would want her there with him.

Chapter Seventy Three

During the first am hour on Monday, they sat and watched, while Seven continued to linger with the irreversible damage done. While watching Seven die, he continued to urinate pure blood from the earlier transfusion. Mary, Sylvia, Terri Lynn and Mae all sat watching him hold onto life with all he had. Silent tears fell from all four women, with only the sound of the oxygen being forced into his lungs, to prevent Seven from suffocating to death.

He too shed silent tears, in testimony to his own suffering, pain and loss.

His nurses knew, having seen the scene dozens of times. One came in and let one side rail down on his bed. A gesture that was bittersweet. They'd never let the rail down before, so it seemed to be a way for the end to come.

All of them wanted to wrap their arms around him, but Sylvia lay down beside her husband, pushing her arm underneath him, so she could hold and hug him gently.

Terri Lynn left the room having just as hard of a time as anyone else. Seven had been so much more than her brother; he had been her confidante and friend. He had been one of a few men on the planet, that didn't want anything more from her than her love. Seven was able to understand Terri Lynn, and he knew why her life had been so difficult. They shared Ricky Levine.

As she left, the nurse stepped back into the room.

Mae, who was sitting at Sevens feet, asked her point blank. "What's the kindest thing we can do for him?"

Silently she stood for a few moments, looking at Seven as he shook from the force of the oxygen being forced into his body.

"When he goes into Cardiac Arrest, letting him go would be the best thing you could do for him."

She looked around the room at the three women looking at her, pleading with their eyes for a miracle. "All we could hope for, after the pounding and shocking of trying to resuscitate him, would be to make his heart beat again, but it wouldn't make him better. That's if we could even get him to resuscitate." She went silent, and they all looked at the battered and bloated boy. "His condition cannot be reversed." She finished and left them with their morbid thoughts.

Mae didn't want him being pounded and shocked. She didn't want to almost lose him, to get him back, to just lost him again. They had been losing him for fifteen days straight. Before she opened her mouth, Sylvia spoke up.

"No more beating on him, he has had enough of being beat on!" She was sobbing, while looking at him closely. She was still holding him.

Mae nodded her head up and down, slowly agreeing. What they were deciding felt like electricity going through their veins. They were electing to let him die and not try to stop it.

The united decision to let Seven go had been made. Still, his heart beat was steady. The beeping noise had amplified since the nurse mentioned Cardiac Arrest.

He had started sweating again, and both Mae and Sylvia dabbed at the beads forming all over his exposed upper body. Even though the nurse let the side rail down and allowed them to touch and talk to him, it was hard. What made it difficult were all the wires and tubes hooked to him and keeping him alive. If one wire came lose, then it would set off a couple warning beeps and buzzing noises.

Mary made her way to her son's side, rubbing his swollen arm, her tears making a constant flow down her checks. In her mind, she missed her once beautiful boy, and she couldn't manage to make it fit into her head that she was going to have to say a permanent goodbye.

Mae cried watching her baby brother. She had a screaming voice in her head saying, "YOU CAN'T MAKE ME SAY GOODBYE!" The pain was intense knowing she wouldn't have him around. The reality made her heart crush under the pressure. She wanted to take his place. She pleaded with God in her head to please let her take his place. His little ones needed him! His wife needed him! His mother, brother, sisters, cousins, extended family and friends, needed him! Knowing his heart would explode in his chest, right before her eyes, she could feel her soul being ripped into pieces.

Over and over they repeated to him that they loved him.

Mary sat down while Mae took her place standing beside him.

Sylvia lifted her head off his swollen chest.

They both glanced up at his heart beat on the monitor at the same time. It suddenly took an abrupt dip down. With so much sweat covering his body, they both assumed one of his taped on monitors had come loose. They tapped each one, and both began to realize what was happening.

"Check his monitors, one of them could have worked loose." Mary had stood up, her eyes staring at Seven's heart-beat.

Frantically, both Mae and Sylvia pushed at all his monitors on his upper torso, over and over.

Mae stopped and took two steps back, taking in what was occurring right before her eyes. Two nurses, followed by Terri Lynn, stepped into the small area.

"Okay, it's time, what is the decision?" His nurse questioned anxiously, while the other stood silently looking at Seven's heart beat going up and down.

No one spoke, except for Sylvia, who was begging Seven. "Please Seven, stay with me, please just stay."

Mary said nothing, sobbing so hard her body shook, the time had come to say goodbye to her youngest child.

Without an answer, the nurse spoke up with authority. "EVERYONE GET OUT!"

Mae's vocal cords let loose. "NO!" She was telling the nurse she wasn't going to leave her brother. They'd have to call the National Guard in to remove her. He had been all alone in that yard full of people that killed him. There was no way she was leaving him while he was being forced to leave them forever!

"Well, what do you want then?" The nurse pushed for a decision to be made. Their patient was having a heart attack. Mary, Mae, and Sylvia couldn't say what the nurses needed to hear, 'let him die'.

"So y'all are just going to let him die?" Terri Lynn was now screaming at the others. She hadn't been in the room when Mae had asked the nurse what was the kindest thing they could do.

"NO! NO! NO! No more pounding and beating on him! Let him go!" Sylvia found the voice to speak. "I don't want him beat on anymore!"

Mary backed her daughter-in-law. "Let him go." Sobbing was all they could do now.

"Well, I can't just watch him die!" Terri Lynn cried out loud, backing out of the room and disappearing down the hall. The two nurses left, closing the curtain behind them.

Sylvia, Mary and Mae held to Seven, crying together and watching as his heart finally gave out.

Lingering with him, looking at the flat line going across the screen, they couldn't speak. His chest continued to go up and down with the rhythm of the respirator giving him the appearance of still being alive.

Terri Lynn came back into the room and looked upon her dead brother. "I'm sorry, I understand why you had to let him go, I just…" She trailed off, leaving the room again, crying hysterically.

Once the nurse came in and turned the respirator off, they thought they would finally get a chance to hold him with all the gadgets removed. They were informed that nothing could be removed, that Seven's body would be sent as it was, to the coroner. His was not a normal death, and there was no room for the normal kind of grief. Seven Scott Levine had become a coroner's case with a full autopsy waiting.

It was done. Seven would never spend one more second in pain. Yet for those left behind, they would have to adjust to a life of permanent pain.

Mae couldn't get out of the hospital fast enough after the respirator was turned off, though she had no memory of leaving. Everything around her was blurry. Outside it was not only dark and drizzly, but a thick fog had set in over the city. Mae climbed into the seclusion of her van. Shutting the door her emotions broke free from the controlled parts of herself. Within the shelter of the metal walls and glass, she screamed at the top of her lungs.

"NOOOOOOOOOOOO!"

Her two hands slammed into the vehicles interior. Her heart was pounding out of her chest. Mae couldn't accept what was happening.

"WHAT HAVE YOU DONE? WHY? WHY? WHY?"

She was in agony wanting her brother back, and she couldn't go anywhere else but to God with her pain and anger. The images of what had been done to him hung heavily within her cognizance. Watching him suffer and experience such evil. The torture his injuries produced. All the while he grotesquely deteriorated right before her eyes.

"YOU PUT HIM BACK! YOU GIVE HIM BACK NOW! TAKE ME! PLEASE DON'T LET THIS BE TRUE, PLEASE DEAR GOD, PLEASE!!!"

She couldn't breathe and wished to be dead then to endure the truth of what had happened. Her bleeding heart felt just like it would rupture with the pressure.

"YOU DON"T CARE! YOU CAN'T CARE!"

WHY I WILL NOT STOP WRITING
By: Mae

Seven's death erased my personality and altered me forever. My psyche was disturbed by murders violent approach into our lives. Before I was polite and timid to speak about what bothered me. Now I was willing to be split wide open. I use to try to control my moments with sunny happiness, I could easily meditate on. Now I was fighting the battle of my life trying not to get stuck in my new dark world of wrath and destruction. I didn't want to live without Seven, or with the horrid memories of what he went through.

I didn't start writing because of the dark forces circling around our lives. My pen started flowing with the love I had for Seven, and being willing to let it take me wherever that may be. With my new found rage, the scary parts of life no longer had holds on me. I let the energy of fire produced in my spirit; invigorate me, to keep me going until I could find a way to calm and quite my enraged soul.

Since the beginning I was willing to let my memories come, many, I had long time forgotten about. Pain filled moments I had no intention of revisiting. Seven's love would carry me through them, and the love I had for him, returned blessings I could never have imagined. I wanted you to know the plain truth about Seven. How deeply I loved him, long before he was even born. Losing him has brought me to my knees, and completely blinded me to reason.

Healing after a murder is by no means an easy task to accomplish. There is no way to get through grief, than to go through it. It's an ugly monster to have to look at for the rest of your life, one that never goes away. You can't run away from it. This hideous creature doesn't fight fair either, and it's quiet demanding. You can look at it as if you're trapped with it, or you've chosen to live with it, either way, it's there every morning and every night. Learning to live with it takes extreme patience with others, but mostly with yourself.

I was told, within the first year. "Oh, you'll never write a book, and besides if you did, who would want to read it? It's harder than you think to write a book."

Losing what we've lost, now that's harder than you'd think. Luckily I believe in myself enough to see beyond anyone's limited vision for me. My only failure in writing would be if I stopped doing it.

I want to be able to remember the sweetest part of loving Seven, not the heartache of losing him. Missing him causes a constant flow of blurring tears. This new person I've become isn't something easy to be. I still feel insulted by what Sylvia and the system did to our family. We didn't start this, but I'm determined like you wouldn't believe, to finish it.

PART THREE

THE GRIEF

Chapter Seventy Four

Murder is an extremely violent way of learning lessons. It's common to man, and as Mae continued to write, it was becoming more ordinary by the day. Those like her are eternally marked by its demonist signature. In its wake, Mae had been born again as a complete stranger to herself. She didn't know who or what she'd been made into by the experience of watching Seven die. His death hadn't been natural in any respect of the word. It was preventable, yet it happened. Every day, she felt anger and hatred, flowing through her. Revenge fantasies began popping into her head. So graphic and horrifying, Mae feared she was losing her sanity.

In the blurry and numb days after the death, Mae shuffled her feet, but had no reason to live. Still there was business to attend to, a funeral to plan, and justice to seek. Hope had faded when his heart stopped, and there would be no waking up from the nightmare. Emotions that Mae had never known seeped out of every pore in her body. She felt isolated and alone. Her heart and mind felt different and damaged. Her family had been violently robbed of what could have been what should have been, but never would be.

The intense pain was fueled by anger. The anger absorbed so much energy; Mae elected to seek immediate therapy. Her new obsessions included fixing her brothers ruined reputation, seeking justice, and bringing to light mistakes the system made. She had to find the harmony her mind needed; the peace that the axe handle had bashed away. Embracing such pain was like trying to harness a bucking bull.

Mae didn't go out looking for this story; it found her. Unfortunately for those who found so much pleasure in victimizing her immediate family, they didn't realize Mae was a story teller. It has given her great pride to have had Seven as her baby brother for twenty-seven years. His memory deserved consideration and rectitude. It's funny to consider him an angel. He was by no means that. Being a victim hasn't caused him to magically turn into a saint either. Yet during the last year of his life, he was attempting with his best effort to be a good father and husband, with all the odds against him. Seven wanted nothing more than to protect his children from their mentally ill mother who he had to financially and emotionally support also. He believed his love for Sylvia could fix all their problems, and he hoped with time everything would work itself out.

The family had elected to have a private memorial service. Seven would be cremated, and his remains would be placed on the Baker property. It was Sylvia's idea to put Seven on his beloved home land. Only those close to the family and friends of Seven's were invited to attend.

Sylvia's experience with Seven's death didn't mystically change her into a better person. Certainly it transformed her, but it wouldn't be to the benefit of Seven's family or his children. Before Seven was even buried, she'd started attempting to manipulate and control the family again. Sylvia wasn't doing well at all. No one could expect her too, but the way she decided to mourn wouldn't be helpful to her three children who had lost their daddy.

Mae listened while Sylvia cried over her torment.

"I don't want this life! I don't want these kids who constantly remind me of him! I hate them! We finally had the happy life we both wanted. All I want is to be in that ground, our spot, right beside him. Nothing will make me happy! Nobody cares! What about me and my kid's pain? Our emptiness? No one gives a f*#!. He was our heart!"

Mae listened, and that was about all she had the energy and strength for. She wasn't going to judge Sylvia's agony and despair. Patiently she let Sylvia vent, and tried to comfort her any way she could. At the same time, she remembered all the needless grief her sister-in-law had caused Seven, trying her best to have him put in jail or beat up. Hurting him and controlling him couldn't be done from the grave. For years, her ambition was to control Seven Levine, and she had looked forward to a lifetime of it.

"Sylvia, we will help you with the kids and anything else you need." Mae tried to calm Sylvia.

"I NEED SEVEN!" She shot back at Mae, and hung up the phone crying.

Sylvia called Mae back a short time later. "I just found out that Ava Burnside was invited to attend Seven's service."

Mae knew about Sylvia's dislike for Ava, and how they had had a bitter rivalry over Seven years back. "Really? Well, she was Seven's friend." Mae tried to soothe the apparent trouble brewing.

"Who the hell invited that whore? He hated that bitch! He couldn't stand her!"

"I don't know Sylvia." Mae's nerves couldn't take too much, and she was beginning to worry about how she was going to control her anger once it started flowing out of her mouth.

"I heard something about Seven calling her on the night of his attack." Sylvia's tone wasn't friendly or kind.

"Yes, he called her around 2:30 am. He asked her for a ride for Kendall and him. You didn't know that?" Mae thought she had told Sylvia about the phone call. She recollected telling the entire family in the surgery waiting area on the morning of the attack.

"No, I didn't know he called her. Why hasn't anybody told me about it? You would figure that you people would tell me something like that!"

"I seriously thought I did." Mae became defensive.

Sylvia was quiet for a few seconds.

"I tell you what, if that bitch is going to be at the memorial service, then we won't be. You tell everybody that I refuse to go, and neither my children, nor Seven's remains will be there either! Seven hated that bitch! I can't believe you people want to disrespect me like that!"

"Sylvia, we've had enough too. We are not fighting with you over Seven anymore. Seven is dead, and you can't use him to control us any longer. You can do whatever you feel like doing with his remains, pour them out and roll around in them if you want. You can't use my brother anymore."

Mae's bluntness stunned Sylvia silent.

After two weeks of kindness, Mae had made it clear. The days of being manipulated were over for her.

Hanging up the phone, Mae felt the troubled past catching back up with them. She called Mary and told her what Sylvia had warned.

It upset Mary because the only people invited were those who loved Seven. Having lost her youngest child, Mary wasn't capable of much more than to sit and cry. Sylvia's demands didn't ease her discomfort. It pained Mary to have to call Ava and ask her not to come.

Sylvia decided to handle things her way. She had Cameron and George go inside the store where Ave worked, and warned her to stay away from Seven's family and his memorial service. Out of respect, Ava didn't come. (Cameron claimed to not know that Ava actually was a friend of Seven's.)

It wasn't a nice thing. Seven had loved his friendship with Ava, and Ava was mourning the loss of her longtime close friend. What upset Mary the most about the situation, and not allowing Ava to come, was a certain person that was invited by Sylvia.

Beverly, Sylvia's sister, was there assisting her. The thing about Beverly was that she had always despised Seven with a passion. She'd never accepted Seven as good enough for her family.

Seven's feelings for Beverly had been mutual. When Beverly didn't show up at their wedding, it had been the last straw for Seven. He'd tried to make the wedding day perfect, but the acceptance of her family was beyond his control. He would go into the ground never figuring out why Beverly hated him so much.

Two preachers and a version of "It's so hard to say goodbye to yesterday", was sung. Family members got up to speak. Mae read a letter Seven had mailed her from Mount Harper year's back, Angel read some words of peace, while Ricky spoke, but his words wouldn't be coherent.

Mary had purchased a safe to be used as a vault for Seven's ashes, and when it came time to lock them up, Sylvia cried holding onto the plastic container. It took a long time for her to be able to let them go. The children put pictures in the safe, while Sylvia place a long lock of her hair. Seven had cherished her long hair.

At the end of the service, when most had left, Mae watched as Seven's children shoveled dirt over what was left of their daddy. The three babes were performing the last thing they could ever possibly do for the young father, brutally taken from them.

Concrete would be laid over the site until a stone could be made. Molded prints of Bella's, Liam's and Cassandra's hands eternally protect the ashes of their daddy.

In those first few weeks without Seven, everyone that loved him was getting their first taste of life without him.

Sylvia was ridden with the guilt of having made him out to be something he wasn't. Soon it would become obvious that the previous year of drama hadn't been overlooked or forgotten.

Chapter Seventy Five

Everyone tried to overlook Sylvia's manipulative behaviors. She was, after all, the widow of a murdered husband. It would be expected for her to lash out. Burying a murdered love one produced plenty of discomfort, and everyone was in their own deep wells of sorrow.

It was the day after the memorial, that Sylvia would have her chance to verbalize her displeasure of Ava. Mary had informed Ava that she was welcomed to pay her respects, but it would be best to wait until Sylvia wasn't there. When Ava showed up with her two teenage daughters the day after the service, she didn't realize Sylvia was inside Mary's house.

Sylvia had been dropped off by Beverly. She was having a hard time being away from Seven, and was looking through Mary's pictures, while also sharing the new rumor going around in Focus Trailer Park.

"I've been told that David Smith was holding Seven down on the ground by stepping on his chest, while they beat on him." Sylvia was explaining while looking at Seven's baby pictures.

Before Mary could respond over the new rumor of David's participation, Ava's car was pulling into the driveway.

At first when Ava showed up, Mary quickly went outside in an attempt to advert an argument. Then she walked with Ava and her daughters down the wooded trail to Seven's gravesite. While they were down in the woods, Sylvia called Mae, beside herself with rage.

"That f*#!ing whore is down there with my husband!" Sylvia was spitting mad.

Mae listened and told Sylvia to just let them pay their respects. While Mae was talking to her, she didn't know that Sylvia had gotten a knife and was walking down the trail herself.

"I want to kill all of them!" Sylvia hung up with Mae and proceeded to make her presence known to Ava. While Mary stood talking to Ava, Sylvia stood over to the side showing the knife and carving into a tree.

Ava had noticed Sylvia approaching , and she told Mary that she'd better go. So as Sylvia started carving, Ava decided to leave the intensifying and dangerous situation. Ava said nothing to Sylvia, and was mostly concerned about getting her daughters safely away.

As they left, Sylvia walked behind Mary fussing.

"I don't want that woman down there visiting my husband!" Sylvia was accustomed to getting her way, and she was already reconsidering her decision to put Seven on his family's land. It seemed her control was far too limited on the Baker property.

"Well, she's gone, she just wanted to pay her respects." Mary didn't have the energy to argue, and she was glad that all Sylvia did was carve into a tree.

Sylvia was a single woman again, after less than two years of marriage. She still voiced her loyalty to Seven, yet the night she buried him she had three men to keep her company. That same night a van load showed up at Ennis Dorsey's parent's house. It was Sylvia accompanied by three men. They were brandishing shotguns and threats.

"Somebody's going to have to pay!"

Angie and Luke Smithfield called the police. The rioting group left before the cops arrived.

Within the first week after the memorial, Sylvia wanted to kick Cameron and George out of her house. In all reality, she couldn't afford to keep them up, no matter how much they helped out. She appealed to Mae and Rex to help her get the young married couple out of her home. George wasn't one of Mae's favorite people, and she didn't want Cameron hanging around Sylvia either, so she easily told the two to 'get out'.

George wouldn't listen to Mae though, he undermined his mother-in-law at every turn. He had grown protective of Sylvia, just like everyone else had the year before. He believed Seven's family was now bullying poor Sylvia.

Back on July 4th, Sylvia had asked Mae go get Bella in order for her to see her daddy for the last time. Sylvia didn't want the younger children to view Seven in such a grotesque condition. When Mae stopped by to pick Bella up, George accused Mae of playing favorites between the children.

"Sylvia doesn't want Liam and Cassandra to see Seven." Mae tried to explain to the questioning George. On that day, and under the circumstances, Mae didn't have the right frame of mind to deal with the jerk.

"Really? Well, I know Sylvia would want all three." George argued with defiance.

"Well, fine George, do what you want." Mae didn't like the punk trying to delegate her family's personal business.

While Seven had lain in the hospital, Mae had tried to stay away from anyone or anything that could possibly cause her to lose the little bit of control she did have. Her emotions and nerves were raw. Her patience was spread tissue paper thin. After the death, Mae found it easier to explode on George, and anyone else like him.

Not only was Sylvia having problems with Cameron and George, her neighbors were having disputes with her also. It wasn't easy to continue to live next door, to the yard where Seven had been beat to death. Animosity between the two homes was thick with vengeful anger. Even Seven's dog Coop had gotten involved with blood shed.

While Seven had lain motionless in ICU, his Bulldog Coop, attacked David and Sue Smith's little Chihuahua Rambo and almost killed it. Cooper had never attacked anything before, but he was loyal to his best friend Seven. No doubt David Smith's dog was walking around in Seven's blood, and Coop could easily smell it on him.

Sylvia claimed her neighbors were yelling at her and the kids on a daily basis.

Mae was still putting together witness statements and a time line of events. She kept her ears open and her eyes watching what was being done around her. Another neighbor had been telling people she'd seen and heard things. They lived up the road, outside the trailer park, but because they were talking, Mae decided to knock on their door. The husband and wife were willing to talk, but the wife did most of the informing.

"We've already given a statement to Investigator Woody Muck. He came by yesterday to ask us if we had seen or maybe heard something that night. I'm sorry to hear about your brother, but we didn't hear or see anything."

Mae looked around their front yard and could see their view would have been obstructed by an eight foot privacy fence that sat above the Smith's front yard. There would be no way that they could have seen the attack.

She thanked the couple and left, discouraged that she couldn't just find the answers her soul needed. Why had this happened?

Faltering with exhaustion, Mae couldn't sleep for feeling so powerless to help fix the situation her family was in. Still she refused to give up. Her mind circled around and around the murder and its participants. Then she got another tip that Seven had called a third party that night for help. Mae knew about Seven calling Ava and Erik, but she didn't know he had called another number asking for help.

Brenda Tiller had received several early morning calls from Seven. Mae quickly called her, wanting to know what puzzle piece she could add to the growing pile.

"He called five times and left a message that he 'needed help'. I answered on the fifth call and he said that 'Sylvia was messing with Kendall'. He said he had 'already made a police report and needed some help'. To 'please come get me, I need help, help me, I need help'."

Brenda was sickened as much as Erik and Ava that she hadn't assisted Seven when he called.

"I told him I wouldn't ride Kendall around, but I'd come get him." Brenda could only wonder what could have been prevented if she had given him a ride.

"Brenda, what's the phone number that Seven was calling from?" Mae's mind was working overtime, and she hoped Brenda had saved it on her caller id. Luckily she had, and Mae quickly jotted it down. It was the same number that had been called from when Ava and Erik got their phone calls, and around the same time. It was Taylor Boyd's number.

Brenda's information had Mae realizing Seven had known that Kendall was up to something that night. Why would Seven file a police report? On who? She remembered seeing the police report in the Monday paper, that Seven had filed a first degree assault report, but she'd believed it concerned his attempted murder. Seven had gone to the police that night, before he was murdered. Why? Who had assaulted him? It was an unusual move on Seven's part, almost unheard of. Who had assaulted him before he was murdered?

Another growing obstacle was the fact everyone had started remarking on Seven's disorderly and drunken behavior that night. If Seven had been drunk or disorderly, he would never have gone to the Lanyard Police Department. Heck, if he had been stone cold sober, it would still be a miraculous event. Kendall had been up to something, and Seven had known it. Was Kendall Martin or Ennis Dorsey's name on that police report?

Seven's way of dealing with problems was to jump right into finding the solutions. If he had an enemy, Seven would be his enemy's best friend. One of his favorite quotes was, "you keep your friends close, but your enemies closer".

Why was Seven hanging around with Kendall, especially if Kendall was messing around with Sylvia?

Mae still wasn't 100% sure if Sylvia had known Kendall Martin her entire life, but she was going to find out.

Chapter Seventy Six

Mary went to work finding out who her son had filed a police report on that night. It's public record, so she could easily go in and ask for a copy. Yet, she absolutely hated the police department, and decided to call an attorney for advice on getting the report her son made the night of his murder.

Mae called Sylvia and went to work trying to decipher the version of events from the one who had the absolute most to lose from the murder. She had a few minutes of small talk, then she went straight into questions.

"So I guess Seven hated Kendall. Do you know why?" She invited Sylvia's opinions.

"The day before Seven got home, Kendall had hit on me. I'd commented on how fat I'd gotten, and he said something like I could go with him to his trailer for a beer anytime. George told Seven what Kendall had said to me."

Mae could see why that would have Seven angry. While he was out of town earning a living, this creep was up in his house, trying to put the moves on his wife.

Sylvia continued, ignorant of the gears turning in Mae's head. "Seven didn't like Kendall at all. When they were fighting, it had me really upset, but he claimed that they were just rough housing and playing around. I told him it didn't look like playing to me and that I just wanted to go to bed. Ennis was mad that I'd slapped him. He was threatening me, and then he said he would just go get his wife Sissy, to whip my ass."

Mae was writing down every word Sylvia uttered, not thinking so much about what was being said, but just listening for the in between morsels of truth.

"Kendall had told Seven that he'd better be 'glad his old lady kicked him off, or he would have killed him then'. I'd called the cops. I just wanted them out of my yard, and I put Ennis out. Kendall was inside our trailer, and then Seven said he was 'going to get his sawed off and kill Kendall'. I went inside and forced Kendall outside. Seven was yelling, 'Sylvia leave him alone!'."

Mae decided to switch the topic slightly. "How well did Seven know the neighbors where he was attacked?"

"He'd only been over there maybe three times since we moved here. Seven liked David. He said David reminded him of his father Ricky. One day David had a little bitty radio outside playing, and Seven had a stereo that Cameron had given him. Because he had just gotten that big new stereo that he was so proud of, he offered David the little one given to him by Cameron. David wouldn't accept it, so they traded for it, and Seven came home with an electric weed eater. A day or so later George found out, and he went down to David's and got the stereo back, claiming it belonged to Cameron, not Seven, and that Seven had no right giving it away."

Mae wondered if this was the stereo that had been mentioned in one of the reasons Seven was in the yard that night. She didn't intersect Sylvia, allowing her to continue talking.

"Seven wasn't happy with Cameron and George staying with us. He didn't mind Cameron, but George got on Seven's nerves following him around everywhere like a puppy. He no longer had any privacy and would have to go to his bedroom to get away from George. We had started arguing over them living with us." She paused and then began crying. "He cried himself to sleep every night over being separated from his family. But we were finally happy, we were finally happy." She'd started sobbing harder.

Mae had heard about how her brother cried himself to sleep, many, many, times.

"It's not fair, that he is gone! After all the trouble I caused for him." Sylvia cried with her guilt ridden grief. "He was so crazy!" She was now laughing. "He use to chase after thunderstorms just so he could watch. I'm so sorry what I did to him the last year. It wasn't him, it was me!" Sylvia had apologized over and over for her criminal behavior towards Seven.

It made no difference now, he was dead and gone, Mae thought to herself, but she tried to assure Sylvia it would be okay.

Since the memorial, Sylvia had been as usual, surrounded by male friends.

It bothered Seven's family, but Sylvia wasn't married anymore, and so they just wanted to keep things civil as possible for the children's sake.

Sylvia was suicidal, but Mae felt the same sensations running through her own veins. Luckily, Mae had the sanity of mind to prevent herself from doing anything to her-self. Sylvia on the other hand didn't. She cut herself up and down both arms and ingested many household cleaning products, but she didn't manage to complete the job. The next morning she called Mae, hysterical.

"Bella has gotten a pair of scissors and cut herself! She says she wants to be with her daddy!" Sylvia didn't realize, Bella was watching her own mother's reactions to the murder.

Mae offered to take Bella for a weekend trip. Rex's niece was getting married, and Mae figured it would do Bella and her good to get out of town for a few days. That wasn't soon enough for Sylvia, and before the day was through, she'd called back.

"I hate these kids!" She was screaming at them. "I don't want them anymore, I hate them, I want them dead and gone!"

Within minutes Mae drove up into the front yard and picked up the three terrified children. Sylvia was apologizing for her outburst and explaining she really loved her kids, but that she just couldn't handle the fact she was stuck with them, all by herself, for life. Mae felt like she was being split into two separate people. One wanted to help Sylvia, or least the children. The other, hadn't gotten over anything, and after his heart stopped, things grew beyond human imagination to contain. Mae didn't know what to do or say. So many rumors were flying around town, and Sylvia had no shortage of help from her long list of friends. Why would she be screaming such hatred towards her three children? It didn't make any sense. She decided to comfort herself with the situation by considering what Seven would want her to do. How would he treat his children if their mother had been the one to be murdered?

Though the kids were going through hell, they took it like most kids do and continued to exist in a world they already knew they had no control over. Bella had taken on the little mommy routine, looking after her two rambunctious and tiresome siblings. She also felt the need to take care of her momma and hardly said anything about Seven's murder. Liam on the other hand, had lost his beloved daddy. Having had such a big and powerful parent, it shook Liam to his core to know his daddy was beat to death. His eyes had lost their sparkle, and he seldom smiled. Little Cassandra, knowing what everyone was saying, had no clue what had happened. Her daddy would leave, sometimes for weeks at a time, to go to work. She didn't see his body in the ICU, and only knew he was gone, just not forever.

Chapter Seventy Seven

Once Mae spoke to Brenda Tiller about how Seven had been asking for help, she decided to find out who Taylor Boyd was. All she knew, was that he carved mini bats, which Seven purchased two of, as drumsticks for his nephew. One of the two drumsticks was missing. Cameron had found that one in her car.

There was only one way to find out what he had to say, and that was to call him. As she waited for an answer, she debated hanging up. Before she could a man answered.

"Yes, my name is Marion Mae Smithfield, and I'd like to speak to Taylor Boyd if possible."

"You got him, what can I do for you?" Taylor didn't seem shy.

"Taylor, I'm Seven Scott Levine's sister, and I wondered if I may ask you a few questions?" Mae already had a pad and pen ready.

"Hey, I'm really sorry about what happened to him. That's messed up."

"Yes, it was messed up." Mae had plenty of memories of how mess up it had been.

"I can tell you what I know. I had never met him before that night. Seemed to be a alright guy. He acted really drunk."

"When did Seven come by? It was late. Why did he stop by your house so late? Drunk? Was he mad, happy or what?" Mae started shooting out questions.

"Like I said, I just met him, and didn't really know him. I was carving mini bats for him. It was around two am, and I had my front door open. I guess that's why they stopped by. Seven gave me twenty dollars for the sticks, though I had only one finished."

While he talked, Mae was forming new questions, but she didn't want to go overboard and have him hang up on her. If it was the first time he met Seven, then why was he making drum sticks for him? Had they talked before? He'd continued to explain what he witnessed.

"Seven was drinking, and to me, appeared drunk acting. He wasn't as drunk as Ennis. I had to tell Ennis to be quite a few times. My kids were sleeping, and I didn't want him waking them up. Ennis kept on wanting to go to a trailer and get his gun. He kept saying, 'We need to go back to that trailer where I left my gun. I need my gun'."

The gun again, it was interesting to Mae that not much had been discussed concerning Ennis's gun. Mae was writing down what he was saying, and trying to write her new questions at the same time.

"I know Kendall. We just got out of prison together. I've known him my entire life. Killing Seven is something he just would not do. I really hate what happened."

Mae got chills as he spoke. She'd never insinuated Kendall did anything. Why would he just come right out and say Kendall wouldn't kill Seven? Oddly, Seven didn't know Taylor, and wasn't friends with Kendall. Why would he be hanging out in the middle of the night with these two friends? Seven had never hung out with Kendall before, so why that night in particular? The same night Seven was beaten and killed? She wanted to start screaming at the guy on the phone, but instead she stayed calm.

"How long was Seven at your house?" Mae asked, and was going to inquire about the phone calls, but he answered her.

"They were here about thirty minutes, and Seven made some phone calls."

"I know. That's how I got your number." Mae couldn't believe this guy was life-long best friends with Kendall. They'd just gotten out of prison together. "I appreciate you talking to me."

"Oh, it's no problem, I know how you feel."

Mae's brow furrowed. "Really?"

"Yes, my brother was murdered too. Had his throat slit by his friend, while he was sleeping. Stole his wallet from him." Taylor answered matter of fact.

"I'm sorry to hear that." Mae felt strange to know that he did know exactly how she felt.

"You know, Ennis won't serve much time, the guy that murdered and robbed my brother only got twenty years. I told my momma, to let him out; I can't kill him if he is locked up."

Taylor laughed, but Mae knew he was serious. Her stomach went into knots thinking about Ennis walking free after taking Seven's entire life from him. She thanked the guy for talking to her. Hanging up, she cried and cried. The more she uncovered, the worse she felt. She was hurting to know how Seven was surrounded that night by so many people who didn't know him. They killed him because he wasn't like them.

Seven wasn't a stay out and party all night boy anymore. Being a full time parent and husband had changed that about him. His work ethics were supreme, and taking pride in his job helped keep his employer very happy. So after working all week, to support his family, he came home and spent the night 'hanging' with Kendall Martin and Ennis Dorsey? Why? They were not his friends. Ennis had a wife and two children. What was he doing out? What did Kendall have in common with either guy? Kendall and Ennis were both unemployed, but other than that, what was there common beef with Seven? What could Seven have possible done to either boy? He'd been out of town working, so how could he have looked for the trouble they were offering him that night?

The anger inside Mae scared her to death. She feared she was going to lose control. How she wished it was the wild west days. Then her family could just take care of it. Instead, it really wasn't their problem. It belonged to the state of Alabama now. Why did that upset Mae so much too? No one knew Seven like his family and friends. How could what happened to him be the state's problem? How would they promise to offer justice? She didn't trust anyone to take care of what had happened to her family. The more they offered to trust the system, the more the system victimized them.

Chapter Seventy Eight

I felt obliterated. Everywhere I looked, every place I visited, I'd catch glimpses of Seven that would leave me shaken and crying. I wanted to feel pain. My old demons awoke within me. In my mind, I envisioned ripping the skin off my arms. The feelings were so intense, they kept my skin tingling for months. With every bit of new information I got, the feelings grew more penetrating and unbearable.

They were exhausting too. All I wanted to do was sleep. I began reading into so many different topics. From crime and justice all the way to anatomy of the brain. Every question I had gave birth to two of four more issues of uncertainty. Every word I heard from witnesses, and every bit of speculation and rumor, would fill my tank of rage over the top. By the end of the first month, the numbness of shock, started to wear off slightly, and the agony really began to set in.

There is not a county or state in America, that hasn't endured the evil of murder. I now was beginning to realize that there were so many out there suffering, just like my family. That in itself was overwhelming to take in.

I had the crushing desire to hunt his other killers down and decimate them. Sure they had one of the attackers in jail, but I felt it in my bones that Kendall had a major part in the murder. The damage his foot did to Seven's face gave me nightmares. David Smith's boot stomped into Seven's chest, forcing him to lay down and be beaten. I could obsess on ways of killing, or I could fixate on ways of finding out the truth. Seeking professional help was something I had the presence of mind to know I needed to do immediately. I'd let the professional help me with the killing parts inside me, while I would deal with the unpromising preoccupation to find the truth.

Seeking the honest truth would take years though, and still it may never be fully known.

Regardless, the images my mind was showing me, of the things I wanted to do to those that had hurt my family were so graphically sadistic. I tried to study the topic of forgiveness, but my wounds were so extreme and raw. Somehow, with Seven's murder, all my previous distresses and scars were ripped back open. I wanted to scream, cry and hit something constantly. All the while, I walked around with a somber face and calm demeanor. I worried, that if Ennis had snapped over a video game, how easily I could over Seven's homicide. My therapist would calmly explain it wasn't in my character. I didn't have the nature to be a violent person. If that was the case, then why was I feeling such a strong desire to reach out and smack someone?

A "Homicide Survivor" was what I'd become. No amount of justice, restitution, prayer or compassion would bring my brother back. Nothing could be done or said that would return his life to him. There could never be anything done about the violent nature of Seven's death.

As much as I wished to just move on, it wasn't over.

We still had a lot of work before us, and many obstacles and hurdles to get through. Working with the criminal justice system and years of court proceedings, trying to obtain a word they call justice. There is no way to move forward and past such a crime. You have to learn to live with it. Closure is elusive with murder, if you're lucky to have any kind at all.

There is no peace to be found with a murder. Many good things can come from the revolting event though. From the people you'll cross paths with, to the conscious awareness of how you view life. I want to have good memories in honor of my brother, and to survive, I've learned just how strong I really can be. If I was going to be in so much pain, I was going to learn how to use it. I would somehow learn from it, and not allow it to control my life. Master it, and demand more from myself, to understand its presence.

I will share my experience, and give my life to helping those who shall be forced to endure the same.

Chapter Seventy Nine

Within the first month without Seven around, the silence continued to give testimony to his absence.

Mae continued to ask questions of the people who had been involved with Seven during his last twelve hours alive. He'd arrived home around five to five thirty and twelve hours later he was on a trauma helicopter flying towards brain surgery.

Having heard more of what Sylvia had to say about Kendall, Mae decided she would need to call Cameron and see if she would elaborate more on what happened. She needed to know why George would have told Seven that Kendall was hitting on Sylvia. What was Kendall's deal with Sylvia? What was Kendall even doing at Seven's house? Obviously, if Seven found out that Kendall was hitting on his wife, in his own house while he was out of town, that would be something that would have upset Seven. Most husbands would find it rather irritating.

Cameron was still with George, but the two of them constantly had problems. When Mae got the chance to talk to her daughter, Cameron was always busy with her strained marriage. Many things were happening in her life, and that's partly why she was staying at her Uncle Seven's house. Sylvia had put the couple out with the help of some of her friends. Because Cameron was angry at Sylvia, she was more forthcoming about what was going on in the trailer while she was there. One day while visiting her mother, she brought out many conflicting facts.

"I talked to Seven a lot, and he missed his family. Seven said Sylvia blamed Grandma and you for all the trouble they had in their marriage. He asked me not to tell y'all that they were not getting along. They hadn't been intimate with each other since February and Sylvia thought he was going through a mid-life crisis or something." Cameron laughed, but Mae was sickened to know Seven's life hadn't changed for the better.

"Did he ever say anything about seeing me drive past him?" Mae was still guilt ridden over driving past her last opportunity to speak to her baby brother.

"Well, yes, but I didn't know what he was talking about. Well actually, Sylvia is the one who was pissed off about it. She had made a comment about 'how his family didn't care about him, and wouldn't even stop to say hi or pick him up'."

Cameron's answer caused Mae more pain than she'd anticipated.

"I told him you said to tell him happy birthday, and he said, 'Oh, she'll tell me happy birthday, but she won't stop and pick me up off the side of the road'. I didn't know what he meant, but now I do."

Still she didn't realize how much extreme discomfort her words were causing her mother.

"Why did George feel the need to tell Seven about Kendall hitting on Sylvia?" Mae trudged on with her investigation despite the pain she was uncovering.

"George didn't tell Seven, Sylvia did." Cameron corrected matter of fact.

This little lie of Sylvia's is what made Mae begin to wonder about her sister-in-law even more.

Why lie?

Sure Sylvia was a professional, who actually believed her lies, but still, why? Was Sylvia involved?

"What's the deal with this Kendall?" Mae could feel her blood heating up.

"Sylvia told Seven that Kendall had hit on her. I know Seven didn't like Kendall. Bob brought Kendall over to the trailer earlier on Saturday, to buy a necklace from George." (Cameron and George had been pawning off most of their possessions for money.)

Mae noted that the earlier version Cameron gave her at the hospital, Cameron had said that Kendall had come over on Thursday, but in this version, he is over at the house on Saturday. As always, Mae refrained from correcting and continued listening.

"What time did Seven get home from work?" Mae persisted, asking Cameron questions she'd already answered before. She hoped to eventually get the entire story.

"Around five pm, he later ate out with Sylvia at San Juan's , and got home around seven. Later, Sylvia and I went to the gas station for cigarettes, when we left Seven and George was at the trailer alone with the kids. When I got back, Seven, Ennis, Kendall and George were there. Seven said they needed cigarettes and got my keys, Seven, Kendall and Ennis left. An hour and a half later, Sylvia and I walked up to Ennis's, to see if they were there. We heard a car door slam as we were walking up the trail, and we both knew it was my car door." Cameron laughed. "I mean I know the sound my car door makes."

Mae listened to her daughter, but wanted facts, not figures.

"Well, when we walked up into the yard, Ennis and Seven were having a heated argument, until Seven noticed us walking up. Then he started fussing at Sylvia for not trusting him. Sylvia and I got into my car and drove home. After about ten minutes, Seven ran inside and requested George come out, stating 'needs to be a fair fight'. George didn't hear him so he asked again, 'one more time, you going to keep it fair?'. Sylvia told me when they walked out that 'Seven was more than likely fixing to whip George's ass'. It upset me, and I was afraid for George, so I went outside. I could hear hitting sounds and walked over screaming, 'what the f*#! was going on?'. I was told by George to 'stay back!'. I saw Seven on the ground with Kendall on top. Later George told me that Ennis tried to hit Seven with his axe handle, but George told him 'no'. Ennis then pushed the axe handle back into his pants and said, 'you right, man on man'. Sylvia ran up and kicked Kendall in the head yelling, 'get off my husband', and then slapped Ennis twice, it pissed him off. Seven made up with Kendall and they started to look for Kendall's necklace that had fallen off in the fight. Ennis continued fussing at Sylvia and started to walk home, but then turned and walked down to the Smith's yard muttering 'motherf*#!er'. Kendall went inside the trailer, while Sylvia and Seven were fussing outside. Sylvia came in and pushed Kendall out. She told Seven, 'you're in or you're out!', but he wouldn't come in. Kendall called Seven and Sylvia slammed the door shut. She went and got a chair from the kitchen table, and sat it in front of the door, blocking it. She smoked a cigarette, about ten minutes, and then she went to the bathroom. In less than five minutes, she came running through the trailer, having seen the blue lights."

Cameron abruptly had to end her conversation, leaving Mae wondering even more about what exactly had occurred that evening. Sylvia hadn't been completely honest, and it made Mae wonder why.

Mary had grown angry with Sylvia, since the memorial. She blamed Sylvia for taking Seven away from her the last year of his life. It was a time she could never get back. She had loved her son so much, and knew it was because of Sylvia, that he'd been put off the land. She'd begged him to stay, and he just wouldn't leave Sylvia. Then there was a comment Mary heard Sylvia make concerning the three children that really hurt her feelings and opened the injuries of the past.

Sylvia was going to admit herself into a hospital for a seventy-two hour evaluation. Mae would be taking Bella out of town for a wedding. Mary assumed she'd keep the other two, but she found out they would be staying at their Aunt Beverly's. Sylvia was afraid that with her being in a mental hospital, Mary would attempt to take custody of her kids. When Mary heard what Sylvia had said, it started turning Mary against her.

Mary had had enough of Sylvia's paranoid delusions.

Mae continued to befriend Sylvia, though she felt like she was walking a thin line doing it. She wanted to find out as much as she could about what happened to Seven. Eventually, Sylvia would turn on them, but until then, Mae would play the sweet card. It worked, because Sylvia needed them. She couldn't afford to keep her family afloat without income. Her burdens were heavy, and there wasn't any way to fix what had happened. She talked to Mae, because she was worried about what the family was thinking about her.

"Melina told me that y'all don't believe Cassandra is Seven's baby, and that y'all think I just want money." Sylvia's words always upset Mae one way or the other.

"That's not true; I've heard no one say such a thing." Mae wondered why Melina would say something like that, and she figured that Sylvia could just be making it up to see how she would react.

"Why won't your momma call me back? I've called her and left her messaged." Sylvia was fishing for information. "Y'all haven't gone and looked at memorial stones yet have you? I want to go with y'all."

Mae had to be careful how she answered. Just as if she was in a mine field, one wrong move and boom!

"Well, Momma is tired and hasn't felt good. She's still working and sleeps a lot, I'm sure she will call eventually. No, we've not gone to look at any stones yet." Mae ended the conversation telling Sylvia when she would pick Bella up, and gave her information about where they would be staying.

"You know Seven didn't think y'all loved him anymore, and he knew how Thulah hated him."

Mae listened to Sylvia speak, but her words felt more like bullets hitting her. Why would she say such a thing now that nothing in the world could be done about it? Mae closed her eyes and tried to stay calm. "We all loved him, and I hope he knew that."

Every day was full of new stories going around, and as soon as Mae hung up with Sylvia, the phone rang again. It was somebody with some information about Sissy. They informed Mae, that Sissy was telling people that Ennis had beaten Seven over six hundred dollars that had been stolen. Sissy said that Ennis told her Seven had taken the money. So Sissy figured that might be why her husband beat Seven to death.

Sissy didn't know that Ennis had actually spent the money, and lied to her about it being stolen. He had spent it on a girl named Amanda, and they had spent the entire weekend together in a motel. An interesting twist to this is that Amanda happened to be Kendall Martin's girlfriend. Ennis had spent an entire weekend with Kendall's girlfriend, while Kendall was incarcerated.

Mae knew about the six hundred dollars, because Ennis told his employer Rex all about the scam, weeks before the murder. Ennis had explained to Rex that he had to come up with a good story to tell his wife, because he'd spent all their bill money on a girl. Rex had told his wife Mae all about it. What angered Mae now was knowing that Ennis had lied about it to his wife, blaming Seven, then he must have believed his own lie. He couldn't have murdered Seven over money that he himself spent, and lied about how he spent it. Or did he?

Chapter Eighty

Bella was certainly ready to get out of town with her Aunt Mae. The summer was almost over, and it had been the worst one for both of their lives. Mae wondered if it was as hard on Bella to hang out with her daddy's sister, as it was for his sister to hang out with his oldest daughter. Bella was so much like Seven, and looking into her eyes, you could see him. On the way, little Bella talked and talked about her daddy.

"Do you think he is in the van with us Aunt Mae?" She questioned from the back seat. Her question made Mae smile.

"I'd imagine he would be anywhere you are."

"Yeah, I think so too. Do you think he is sitting in the front seat?" Bella flipped her flip flops around on her feet.

"Well..." Mae looked over at the empty front seat. "I think he would be sitting closer to you." She looked back quickly at her niece and smiled.

"Yeah, I bet I am sitting on his lap right now!" Bella smiled and looked around her.

Mae could feel the tears forming, imagining him holding tightly to his daughter. It wasn't fair that he wouldn't ever get to hold her in his arms again. Poor Bella had lost her daddy forever. She wouldn't let Bella see her cry, and she spent most of the weekend wiping at her eyes.

They stayed at a motel, and drove around the small Georgia town looking around. They shopped some and ate out. Mae had picked a motel with a swimming pool, so Bella could get some swimming in. She sat and watched as Bella played around. Later that night, as they sat on the bed eating pizza and watching a Hannah Montana special, Bella decided to tell her Aunt something that had been bothering her.

"I knew that Ennis was going to kill my daddy."

Mae almost choked on her pepperoni. "What? How did you know that?" How indeed could a small child have known such a horrible thing? Mae lowered the volume on the television some, and gave her full attention to the youngster.

Though she was looking at the TV, she began talking. "Well whenever we had that cook out, and Ennis and Sissy came over, daddy and Ennis got into a fight, and were rolling around in the yard." Bella looked over at her Aunt Mae. "You know?"

"Yes, your daddy cooked chicken on the grill." Mae had already heard about the cookout that Seven had invited Ennis's family over, weeks before the murder, but not much concerning the fight.

"Yep, and daddy had scratches all over his back. When he came inside, Ennis came inside behind him. Ennis threw a gun on the kitchen table." With the most serious look Mae had ever seen, Bella explained. "That's when I knew he was going to kill my daddy. I just knew it." She put down her half eaten slice of pizza, having lost her appetite.

The two sat silently watching as Hannah danced and sang.

Mae was shocked and saddened by Bella's prophetic foreknowledge of the murder. She wondered what else Bella might have innocently witnessed. She tried to figure out a way to find out what she might know, without upsetting her in the process of revealing it.

"Bella, were you awake that night your daddy was attacked?" Mae looked over at her sweet niece and could already tell, she had been. Of course, when a child is put in bed and told to go to sleep, they are supposed to do what they are instructed to do.

"I was in bed, but I wasn't asleep." She glanced away from her Aunt, trying to not smile.

"Did you hear or see anything?"

"I could hear momma and daddy outside, and I thought I heard bottles or something."

"So you didn't see anything?" Mae was both grateful and disappointed.

"I didn't get out of bed." Bella looked like she wasn't about to get herself in any kind of trouble by revealing her secret.

"So you didn't see anything?" Again, Mae felt a wash of relief. If Bella had simply looked out of her bay window, she would have watched the mob attack and murder of her daddy.

"No, but I think I heard fighting. I didn't look. I pretended to be asleep, and I didn't get out of bed." Bella had had enough questions.

Mae understood and dropped the subject entirely.

The next day they attended the wedding, and even before they got to the church, they were both slipping into a memory depression. The wedding reminded them both of the last wedding they attended, which was Seven and Sylvia's. It had been the happiest day of Seven's life. Marrying Sylvia was all he'd ever wished for. Having secured his family, Seven beamed with such pride. His three children were a part of the wedding. They too were so happy, to have both of their parents commit to each other for life. Everything Seven wanted was so simple, yet it had been so hard for him to achieve.

Mae and Bella sat dressed up and watching the bride and groom smile and say the, 'I do's'. They both were ready to go as soon as the ceremony was finished. Neither wanted a slice of wedding cake or to watch anymore of the happy couple's day.

Riding back to the motel, Mae and Bella were silent in thought. The weekend trip was supposed to help them, but it was making it worse. Bella loved her Aunt, as Mae loved her niece, and they could sense in each other a need. Bella needed her daddy, and being near his sister was both calming and unnerving. Mae was desperate to feel her brother's presence, and being close to his daughter, filled that hole, but also made Seven's absence even more noticeable. No matter where they went, or what they ever chose to do with life, Seven wouldn't be there with them.

Mae couldn't get the images of him being beaten to death out of her head. What it must have felt like to be attacked by a gang of people set on causing him deadly harm. Certainly he had to have been terribly shocked and afraid. Not just afraid of the people attacking him for no reason, but terrified of dying all alone, lying in a yard of hard Alabama clay dirt.

Somebody had to pay. It was just a matter of figuring out exactly who did what and why.

Death had become her. Nothing mattered, after coming across the effects of murder. Life's meaning was muddled, like the pigment a painter gets when they mix one too many colors. She wanted to feel better, but the miracles of life eluded her. She couldn't get up from this event; it had knocked all the life out of her. She begged God for guidance, yet bitterly, she couldn't accept what had happened. It just wasn't fair.

Returning from the trip, Mae had dropped Bella off at her Aunt Beverly's home. Sylvia was still in the hospital. Beverly was told by the hospital staff that Sylvia needed to be committed.

Mae could understand why, feeling like she might need to find herself a dark rubber room to hide in too.

Beverly refused to sign her little sister into a mental therapy program. She was terrified of what her sister would do when she did eventually get out.

Again, Mae could understand that, having been on the other end of Sylvia's fury.

Mae wanted to do nothing but sleep. Exhausted, if her husband would have let her, she would have slept all day. Getting up and functioning was difficult, but it helped keep her from feeling guilty about the fact she didn't want to do anything at all.

The rest of the family wasn't faring any better than Mae. Mary, too, walked around like a zombie, void of any feelings. The pain was so intense, it was easier to feel nothing at all. She moved about her days performing her duties in between hour long sessions with seizures of tears and pain.

Erik couldn't accept losing his brother. The thought was so mind splittingly difficult, he couldn't think about it. It chase him around all day and night, the memory of what he saw pushed into a helicopter. How they had killed his life-long best friend. Erik had no memory of life without Seven in it. To continue, he pursued his new job and started looking for a new place to live. Staying with Mary wasn't necessary anymore, and everywhere he looked, memories of Seven haunted him.

Mae called him to check on him, still trying to adjust to having only one brother. Erik's and Mae's relationship was deeply rooted, but they were too much alike. Neither pushed themselves on others, and they ended up answering the phone far more than they ever dialed a number. Seven had insisted that you be involved in his life. When he called you, he wouldn't have stopped until you answered. Mae knew if she didn't call Erik, he would more than likely never call her.

He was more than happy to talk and apologized for not calling. Mae needed to ask him again what he could remember about his encounter with Seven. The day in the emergency room, Erik had said a little but was far too upset to give any statements. Still, like questioning Bella, Mae knew she had to be careful, because emotions were still raw. Before she asked him anything, she listened to his bit of intriguing information. A sister of one of Seven's old Jr. High friends, J.B., told Erik her brother had seen Seven and Sylvia the night of the attack.

"J.B. said Seven and Sylvia had come by his house that night looking for something."

"Really? What time? What were they looking for?" Mae started throwing questions.

"I don't know. I can only imagine what they were looking for. She didn't say what time just that it was earlier." Erik kind of laughed at his sister's tenacious energy.

"Well, where does this J.B. live?"

"I think he stays over at Fairfield. He and Seven weren't really good friends anymore, but J.B. was Sylvia's friend."

"Well, what exactly did he say to you when he visited you that night?" Mae pushed.

"He called first and left a message. That's what woke me up to start with. Not long after that he showed up. I looked at the clock as I was walking through to the front door. It said, 2:37 am. He was standing on the porch in a good mood, calling it a 'birthday visit'. He gave me a big hug. He wanted me to 'ride along with him, to back him up, and keep things even'. He remarked to me, 'look who I've got with me', meaning Kendall in the front seat. We walked down to the car, and I looked in and spoke to Kendall. I shook his hand. Ennis was acting like he was passed out, and he was muttering something, but Kendall told him to 'shut up, and keep your mouth shut'. When I stood back up straight, Seven joked with me, telling me he would, 'decimate him for me if I wanted him to'. He was talking about Kendall. I didn't want to ride around with or hang out with either Kendall or Ennis, so I turned down the offer to ride with him."

Mae listened and wrote down what her brother stated. Their conversation turned to matters of the living. He had found him a place to live in Auburn, near the campus. He spoke about how he could walk to dozens of eating places.

"Well that's what's important." Mae teased him.

The family had shared in the loss of Seven, but they all suffered in their grief separately. Everyone held him in different ways. Even his sisters had distinctly different relationships with him. So, though they all lost the same brother, they suffered separated losses.

Chapter Eighty One

George had witnessed a fight between Seven and Kendall, so Mae knew she needed to talk to him, even though she despised the boy. She also felt like

Cameron hadn't told her everything that happened that night either, and she needed more from her daughter.

"Okay, tell me what happened that night, again." Mae knew her daughter had already answered that question, but until she heard what she needed to hear, Mae never intended on letting it rest.

"Pretty much they were both gone after eating at San Juan's Mexican Restaurant. They came back, and they were drinking a weird beer. Seven was pouring his out the back door. They left to go look for something. Then they came back. Then they left again and came back, never finding what they were looking for."

As she talked, Mae wondered what Seven and Sylvia had been looking for that night. Erik had mentioned that they had gone over to a J.B.'s house, 'looking for something'. Another interesting point is that they were drinking weird beer. Many times it had been mentioned that Seven was drunk acting. Yet anyone who knew Seven knew he didn't even like beer, much less, weird beer. With his tolerance level, if he wanted to drink, his choice would have been Seagram's 7, with 7up. He called it, 7/7, and he loved it. Why was he drinking weird beer? Then again, why would he be pouring it out the back door?

"I took a shower, and when I got out they were fussing with each other. George wanted to ride along with them to go get some more alcohol for Sunday. Sylvia was upset about it and fussing at Seven, 'you don't want to spend time with just me, and you don't love me anymore'. Seven was in a really good birthday mood. He came home happy."

"Cam, were there any neighbors out in their yards?" Mae already knew there had been, despite the lies that were being told.

"Oh yes, a yard full. I noticed specifically two teens girls, David Smith and two young boys, but there were plenty of people in that yard, all night long."

"Okay, you mentioned Sylvia made a phone call to the police department concerning Seven. What time did she make that phone call?" Mae pushed on.

"Around three fifteen I guess. She wouldn't tell the police who she was or where she lived. Just that there was some doped up boys in the trailer park across from Muller Elementary School." Cameron had forgotten about that phone call, but before she could say anything else, Mae continued.

"How did you know Sylvia and Kendall were friends?"

"Well, when Sylvia came inside to make Kendall go outside, she put her hand out to him like she wanted to hold hands. When he put his hand in hers, she said to him, 'I've known you all my life, but now you've got to go'."

Mae meditated on the revelation that Sylvia had known Kendall so well.

Why hadn't she mentioned it before? Why had she called the police to report a fight? How did she know there was going to be a fight?

"So Sylvia was mad at you because you let Seven use your car?" Mae jumped about with her questions, wanting to keep Cameron on edge.

"Oh yes, she was furious, she told me that 'when Seven is hurt or arrested, it would be my fault, all my fault.'"

Concentrating on that, Mae was silent.

Cameron had had enough, she didn't like talking too much about it.

Mae asked her to put George on the phone.

George would eventually get on the phone with his mother-in-law. Since he and Cameron had moved into Seven's and Sylvia's trailer, he had turned into an elusive man. Mae didn't know if he would tell her anything, but he didn't seem concerned in the least.

"Seven came inside and asked me to 'come out and keep it a fair fight'. I didn't hear him and asked him what? He said, 'I'm going to ask you one more time to back me up. Keep it fair'. I followed him as he looked for his favorite stick in the yard, an oak stick that Sylvia had thrown at him earlier. He found it in the ditch, and started running down the road. He told me to 'not get involved in the fight, but keep the other one out'. I wasn't sure who he was referring to, Kendall or Ennis."

Mae was riveted to the phone. This was a portion of the night she hadn't heard one word about, and George had her full attention.

"He was running and then he swung his stick at Kendall's head, but Kendall blocked it with his arm, and it broke the stick into two pieces. Then Seven hit Kendall, knocking him down. When Seven reached down to grab Kendall up, Kendall kicked Seven in the groin, making him fall forward, with Kendall rolling over on top of Seven. At that time Ennis came up with the axe handle in the air, fixing to hit Seven, but I stopped him, pushing him back and telling him to stay back! Ennis said, 'You right, man on man' and shoved the axe handle back into his pants. Ennis then yelled to Kendall, 'Gun, F*#! it, use the gun, just shoot him with the gun!' , he just kept on saying it. Kendall didn't want to use the gun, saying he wanted to 'f*#! up this mother f*#!er, f*#! him up good!'."

Mae's pen was writing every detail down as quickly as she could keep up.

"Sylvia ran up and kicked Kendall in the head, saying, 'Get the f*#! off my husband!'. She then goes to Ennis and slaps him at least three times, really hard. Ennis got mad and told her he was 'Going to go get Sissy to whip her ass'. Sylvia told him, 'To go ahead, we'll sit down and have a wine cooler'. Meantime, Kendall and Seven were still fussing. Seven kept on asking Kendall, 'Why did you say that?'. Kendall told Seven, 'I'd whipped your ass, but I care about Sylvia and her kids and wouldn't want to kill their daddy'. Ennis went down to the Smith's yard. Kendall went into the trailer, sat on the couch and began playing the game Ten Thousand, one of Seven's favorites. Ennis had left, and Sylvia and Seven were talking in the yard. Soon you could hear Seven yelling from outside, 'I'm gonna kill that mother f*#!er.' Sylvia came in and went over to Kendall and said, 'I've known you all my life, since I was three, but now you gotta go!' Sylvia told Seven, 'The door is being shut, if you're in, you're in, if you're out, you're out!'".

"When was the first time Kendall and Ennis came over that night?" Mae wondered why the two boys initially even showed up at Seven's.

"They both showed up around ten thirty the first time, knocking on the door, and looking for Sylvia. I told them she was out with Seven. They wanted to come inside, but I wouldn't let them, because Seven had told me to not let anyone in his house. The next time they showed up it was around midnight."

Mae changed the topic some, and moved to the one night Sylvia had come home while Seven lay in ICU. George had driven Sylvia over to Kendall's house. Sylvia had forced Kendall to go with them to the police station, because she wanted a copy of the statement he had given to the police. Mae asked George what Kendall had told him during the course of that car ride and altercation with Sylvia.

"Kendall told me that Ennis and Seven were fighting over a video game. Kendall said that while they were in the Smith's yard, that Seven said, 'F*#! it, I'm going home'. He turned around and Ennis hit him the first time real good, but it took two or three more times to put Seven down. Kendall said that Ennis then rolled Seven over, straddled above him and kept hitting him in the head. Kendall explained how he jumped off the porch, wrestled with Ennis for the handle and put the axe handle against the porch. Kendall said that David, Sue, Candy and a whole party of people witnessed it."

George had a little more information. He had spoken to David Smith himself.

"David said he was in bed and heard three pops. He put his pants on and went outside."

With every new detail, the picture took more shape and form. Mae went over her brother's hour by hour, last encounters, with a fine tooth comb. Any element or factor was important to look at and mull over. The answer was there. She knew it. She could feel it. She would find it.

The gun wasn't a topic discussed until George mentioned it. Mae had almost forgotten about it herself. On the day of the attack Mae heard that the suspect had a gun on him. She'd wondered, morbidly, why Ennis hadn't just shot Seven? What had been left of his head wasn't viewable. If they hadn't cremated him, it would have been a closed casket. A gunshot would have saved them from enduring the agony of seeing his battered head. She'd keep her views about the gun quiet, for the time being.

Kendall certainly didn't mind sharing his version. Mae couldn't help but wonder how the boy had managed to keep Seven's blood off of his own hand. By his own statement, he had claimed to have wrestled the bloody axe handle, from the killers grip. Yet, by the time the police showed up, Kendall had not one drop of blood on him, except for his right shoe, which was covered. How did he manage to stay clean while attempting to man handle a murder weapon from a killer?

Ennis was supposed to be barely conscious drunk, yet he had enough presence of mind to pick the murder weapon up, and take it with him, and hide it.

Chapter Eighty Two

The District Attorney's Office was something Mae knew little about. The only time she'd had the opportunity to experience what their job consisted of, was while watching Assistant DA Bass victimize her mother. How could their family seriously trust them? Mae was concerned that, like Woody Muck, Bass would ultimately work her brother's murder, and in the process let all those who were involved get away with the brutal crime.

Fearful, Mae wrote a letter to the Attorney General's office begging for help. She informed the office of the entire previous year of events, and how Seven's murder was the ultimate crime after twelve months of enduring hell. How the police seemed to have assisted Sylvia and let her get away with so much. In doing so, certain police and district attorney's had created a monster that believed she couldn't be stopped.

Mae sent the Attorney General a copy of an email she had sent to the Local Elected District Attorney Paul Stuart, after Mary went to court over being accused of stealing a cell phone. Having been angry over Assistant DA Bass's behavior, Mae wanted to bring to light the mistakes his Assistant blatantly and so eagerly made. In the emailed letter to DA Paul Stuart, Mae pointed out certain facts before the murder occurred.

July 2007, Seven Levine made domestic violence report to the police against his wife. August 2007 he made another domestic violence report to the police against his wife. August 2007, Mary Levine reports her house being broken into by Sylvia Levine, with Investigator Muck's help. September 2007, Lanyard Police signed a warrant against Sylvia for physically assaulting Mary.

Before the month of September was finished, Mary's windows in her house were bashed in.

October 2007, Sylvia and a friend stole a cell phone from a nurse, and gave false information. Sylvia's friend pretended to be Mary Levine, and Sylvia gave them Mary's address, birth date and phone number. Toward the end of the month, Sylvia planned to have Seven arrested for domestic violence. She had broken into Mary's house, and called Seven from his mother's phone. Seven came home to find his wife in bed with a teenage boy. No one except Sylvia testified that Seven beat her nearly to death. All other eyewitnesses say Sylvia violently attacked Seven. Sylvia Levine had then gotten into her vehicle while intoxicated and the police arrested her for a two year old warrant instead of a DUI, after she was pulled over driving recklessly. Sylvia told the police she'd gotten in the vehicle despite her drunkenness, because her husband had tried to kill her. They believed she'd been beaten by Seven. The police then really turn against Seven, along with the Assistant DA Bass, who made it her mission to have Seven put in prison. On Halloween night, Sylvia had gotten into her vehicle and circled around and around Mary's house, driving over the lawn, trying her best to entice Mary to call the police. Why? Because somehow Sylvia knew Mary had a brand new warrant out for her arrest over stealing a cell phone. So before October is finished, Sylvia had both Seven and his mother arrested on FAKE charges. Both Mary and Seven were assaulted by Sylvia.

December 2007 in court, DA Bass accused Mary of being a bogus liar, and making up everything to hurt Sylvia and protect her son Seven. January 2008 in court, which had combined all the cases into one, basically was a waste of time, providing no justice for Sylvia's actions and crimes. February 2008, Mary had court over the stolen phone, with DA Bass going after her again. Sylvia had called the District Attorney's officer and admitted she'd made it all up and about Mary being at the hospital. Again, Sylvia got away with it. (Despite the fact Holly Bass knew Mary Levine was innocent, she let her sit in court the entire day, until her case was called.)

Mae was beginning to feel like a broken record playing the same old tune over and over. Why wouldn't anyone listen? Who could she go to for help? In writing the Attorney General, she was grasping at straws. What good would it do to bring up the past, now that Seven was gone? It mattered, because Mae felt it had everything to do with why he had been murdered to start with. A monster had been created when the police and DA assisted Sylvia over and over in humiliating Seven, Mary, and the entire family.

The letter she wrote to the Attorney General generated a fast response from the Chambly County DA Office. The DA victim's assistant, Maxine Kemp, called Mary and asked what her daughter had said to the Attorney

General. Mary told her she didn't know other than the facts of what happened the year leading up to the murder.

Maxine laughed, "Well whatever she told him, District Attorney Bass will not be working on Seven's case." She went on to explain to Mary that a Preliminary Hearing had been set in six weeks.

The news excited everyone in Seven's family, except Sylvia, who seemed concerned that they had already set a court date so soon.

Being unfamiliar with such procedures as the criminal justice system and how they seemed to take over Seven's case like it belonged to them, Mae started studying. How could they be trusted when the same office tried to destroy Seven's life? What exactly did the office do anyway, except vigorously pursue people? Just touching the service, Mae realized she'd need a Bachelor's Degree to comprehend America's political and judicial structure.

Prosecutors, as they are called, have the duty to protect the public from wrong doers and to see that criminals are punished for their crimes. It's also their responsibility to ensure that the police have done their jobs properly and lawfully. They do not present any case before they court that's without merit. After the police have completed their investigation, the officers present their case to the prosecutor. They provide the prosecutor with a copy of their case files and meet to discuss, in detail, all aspects of the case. It's the prosecutors job to compile the evidence that's been presented to them and bring about criminal charges and proceedings against the accused. Incidentally, the prosecutor is largely an American invention, one of the few governmental positions not inherit from England.

When presented with a case by the police, the prosecutor must decide first whether to file formal charges. He or She may (1) divert the matter out of the criminal justice system and turn it over to a social welfare agency; (2) dismiss the charges; (3) take the matter before a grand jury, which almost always follows the prosecutor's recommendation.

A prosecutor has "more control over life, liberty, and reputation than any other person in America." (Robert H. Jackson, Journal of the American Judicature Society, 1940.) Oh how well Seven's family knew it. With their experience this quote was all but true.

The US's chosen judicial and legal procedure's, put the responsibility for prosecuting criminals on the government. In most instances victims have no role, perhaps, other than as witnesses. The matter is strictly between the state, represented by the prosecutor, and the accused, represented by an attorney.

Mae had already begun the process before she was ready. She wasn't strong enough and she didn't know enough, but it was too late. Her thoughts and feelings had already started to take control and like thunder rumbling inside her, she grew determined to learn everything she could as fast as she could.

Seven's murder had brought out a response from her soul that she'd never felt before in her life. She didn't know the language and practice of the state and local judicial structure. She'd never taken any interest in politics. Yet before she looked for all the answers or learned exactly whom she would be speaking with, she began to make her voice known, along with her visions and values. Despite how lonely it felt, she knew she was not alone. There were others out there, suffering the same, and sadly they believed they were alone too.

It unnerved her to know her brother's murder case would be handled by those who cared so little for him and had absolutely no true idea who he had even been. Seven belonged to them, not some created judicial structure. Instead of letting her negative thoughts and emotions control her, she pushed to search for the truth. Having compiled her witness list, she began going over their statements. She felt like nobody had given her the whole story. They had given it in dribbles and half-truth's, with a few twists here and there.

Mae went back and forth, to recheck everything that could be checked. Then she would confront them with the inconsistencies in what they told her. After a while, the truth or at least the majority of it would surface to the top.

1. Carl Pacer - Seven's employer. "Seven was relieved when he got home, having been worried that Sylvia was going to be angry at him for having to work an extra day."

2. Sylvia Levine - Seven's wife. "All of the money Seven had in his front pocket, was gone." "The day before Seven got home, Kendall was hitting on me. He invited me to come to his trailer and drink a beer." "George told Seven that Kendall was hitting on me." All Seven and I argued over was his family." "If you're in, you're in, if you're out, you're out." "I sat on my bed and smoked a cigarette." "The Smith yard was full of people, all night long."

3. Bella Levine - Seven's daughter. "I knew Ennis was going to kill my daddy, when I saw that gun."

4. Cameron Jones Rowe - Seven's niece. "George didn't tell Seven that Kendall was hitting on Sylvia, Sylvia told Seven." "When I left Sylvia at the store and got back home at midnight, Kendall and Ennis, were in the trailer with Seven, with the axe handle." "Sylvia was yelling at me, that when something happened to Seven, it would be all my fault." "When Seven got home, he was happy." "Around 3:15 am, Sylvia called the police on Seven. She told them there were some doped up boys and she didn't want a fight to break out." "Sylvia held her hand out to Kendall, who put his into hers, and

then Sylvia said to him, I've known you my entire life, but now, you've got to go."

5. George Rowe - Cameron's husband, "Seven asked me to back him up, to help keep it a fair fight. Not to get involved, but to just keep the other one out." "When Kendall had Seven down on the ground, Ennis tried to hit Seven with the axe handle then, but I stopped him." " Ennis told Kendall to use the gun, to just shoot him. Ennis just kept on saying it." "Seven kept asking Kendall, why did you say that?" "Kendall told Seven that he was lucky he cared about Sylvia and the children, or he would have killed him right then."

6. Kendall Martin - Ennis's friend and Seven's enemy. "We was all in shock, that he was actually hitting him in the head with the stick. I said, somebody stop him! We all watched. I jumped down from the porch wrestled the axe handle from Ennis's hands, and propped it up against the porch. Ennis ran away, and I told Candy to call the police."

7. Ennis Dorsey - Confessed murderer of Seven. "He hit me first with the stick, I took it away from him and commenced to whipping his ass with it."

8. Taylor Boyd - Best friend of Kendall. "I just met Seven, I didn't know him." "He gave me twenty dollars for a set of mini bats I hand carved." "Seven was drunk acting." "Ennis kept saying over and over, that he wanted to go back to that trailer and get his gun." "Seven made several phone calls while he was here."

9. Erik Tripp - Seven's brother. "Seven was in a good mood and called the late night calling a birthday visit." "Seven gave me a hug, told me he loved me, and happy birthday." "He wanted me to ride with him to back him up." "Seven had Kendall and Ennis in the car with him. Ennis was passed out in the back seat. Ennis was mumbling something that Kendall told him to shut up about."

10. Brenda Tiller - Friend of Seven's. "Seven called my house five times, and left a message that he needed help." "He had caught Kendall and Sylvia messing around." "Seven told me that he had already made a police report earlier."

11. Ava Burnside - Friend of Seven's. "Seven wanted a ride. He told me he caught Kendall and Sylvia, messing around with each other."

12. Candy Whitefield - neighbor of Seven. "I came out, after hearing yelling, and found Seven's body. He was gasping and making awful gurgling sounds. There was two puddles of blood, and his head was laying in one of them, face up. Blood was splattered all over my momma's car." "Sylvia was yelling and screaming, concerned about Seven's wallet and money." "Kendall had not one single drop of blood on him anywhere, except for his shoe, which was covered in it."

13. David Smith - neighbor of Seven. "I got out of bed after I heard three loud pops."

14. Sue Smith - neighbor of Seven. "I made the second 911 call, I was afraid he would die before they got here."

15. Sissy Pasten - Ennis's girlfriend/wife. "I woke up at 3:00 am, when I heard a female voice yelling outside." "I think Ennis killed Seven over six hundred dollars, he believed Seven stole."

These were the people that had contact with Seven during the last hours of his life. Within their ranks, sat a killer or killers.

Chapter Eighty Three

Sylvia was having a hard time keeping her bills paid, so Mary assisted by paying her power bill to keep the electricity on. Though the relationship between the two was strained, Sylvia didn't mind asking Mary to help her, nor did Mary mind helping her son's children. Trusting and helping Sylvia was a rather difficult task for Mary. She couldn't break free from the feeling that Sylvia had something to do with Kendall, and that she used him to entice Seven. She believed that is what started the fussing that night. Mary also couldn't forgive Sylvia for taking Seven away from her the last year of his life. Mary knew Sylvia was telling people that she wanted to take the kids away from her.

Mae continued to help with the three children as much as she could. She tried to ignore the new rumors she was hearing about Sylvia. How she had some new guy living with her named Nathaniel Walker. That she was trying to convince people that Seven's family was against her. Also how she continued to tell some people she'd watched them beat Seven.

It plagued Mae as to why Sylvia had lied about where she was, after slamming the door on her husband that night. Sylvia claimed she went to her bedroom. Cameron stated Sylvia pushed a chair in front of the door and sat. What's the reason for such a stupid lie? Did she feel guilty for it? She didn't mind saying she slammed the door in his face, why would it matter where she sat and smoked a cigarette?

Mary had a theory on it. Having been inside Seven's trailer on many occasions, she knew if you were standing inside at the front door, you can look down the hall, and straight out the bay window in the kid's bedroom. If she was sitting in front of the door, she could have very well witnessed the attack..

Despite Sylvia's actions the last thing Mae or Mary wanted to do was push her away. All that was left of Seven was his children, and if Sylvia didn't want them to see the children, she had the power to prevent it.

The rumor mill went faster each new day. With so many people being involved with the murder, it was reasonable to assume many would be running their mouths.

Sylvia was out asking her own questions. She spoke to another neighbor who claimed to have seen Seven that night, right before the attack. He called himself Sid.

"Yep, they were having a birthday party at David's house, for his grandson. I was there until right before Seven showed up. I'd played softball that day and my shoulder was hurting. So I was walking home when I passed him on the dirt road. He asked me to come and drink a beer with him for his birthday. I told him my arm was hurting. I went home, and Bob was passed out sleeping. I went on to bed."

Another person who was working her connections was Terri Lynn. Just like Mae, she was Seven's sister, and she was searching for answers. Unlike Mae though, Terri Lynn had the right connections to her baby brother's world. She continued to hang around town after his funeral. Out of Seven's three sisters, Terri Lynn was the closet to Sylvia. One morning she had stopped by early to check on her. Knocking at the front door, Liam answered and let his Aunt inside. She didn't give it a second of thought that Sylvia was back in her bedroom, so she headed in that direction. Opening the door, she wasn't prepared to see Nathaniel Walker in the bed with Sylvia. It infuriated and nauseated her all at once. She left and drove right over to Mary's house, and stormed in the door. She cried as she explained what she found.

"I mean I walk in there, and this guy is laying where my brother use to..." She was suddenly furious. "Seven hasn't even been dead but a few months, and she's already got him replaced." Terri Lynn was beside herself with rage. "I'm going to prove what she did to him! I'm going to prove it!"

Mary wasn't surprised, because she had already met the guy. Sylvia had asked to borrow money because she had to go to court, and pay on a past due fine. The morning she'd given Sylvia the money to go to court, Sylvia had been with Nathaniel Walker, who was providing her a ride.

Sylvia's history with Nathaniel Walker was as extensive and long as the one she'd had with Seven. Walker had always believed he was Bella's daddy. Now he would be.

Neither Mary nor Mae made any comments to Sylvia over what Terri Lynn told them. Sylvia was no longer a married woman, as the vows state, till death do you part. She could do whatever she wanted, but still it didn't look like the behavior of a typical grieving widow of a young murdered husband.

Along with all the buzzes Sylvia produce, "the yard full of neighbors", who were witnesses to a murder, began bragging. Some of the girls that had been there were talking about 'getting their kicks in too'. Unlike Seven, who was the newest neighbor, the Smith's had lived in Focus Trailer Park for well over a decade. The murder had made them so uncomfortable, they moved out of the park.

Before the Preliminary Hearing, things between Seven's family and Sylvia had really started to disintegrate. Mary had tried her best to help Sylvia but was constantly informed how little Sylvia felt about her. Mae had become suspicious of the little lies Sylvia had told, and the tiny fact everyone seemed to think she had something to do with Kendall. Mae was beginning to believe that was half true/half false. Instead of the theory that Kendall was her boyfriend, Mae believed Sylvia was only using Kendall to entice Seven to get him in trouble, and she didn't care if Kendall or Ennis got in trouble either. Mae discerned Nathaniel and Sylvia were extremely eager to get together, and maybe, just maybe, they were having an affair. After all was said and done, and all three boys were in jail, she easily had Nathan to sweep right in and take care of her.

Once Terri Lynn had found Sylvia in bed with Walker, she told everyone. She and Sylvia started to be at odds with each other. To counter what Terri Lynn was saying, Sylvia started to tell people that Terri Lynn had stolen money and a cell phone from her. She even made a police report on Terri Lynn concerning it.

Then there was baby sister Angel, who had the hardest time hiding her disgust with Sylvia. Angel bumped into Sylvia in a store, and she told her no one in Seven's family liked her.

After this encounter, Sylvia decided she needed to move away. She started telling Mary and Mae that she was moving to Athens, Georgia, where her oldest half-brother Craig lived.

They completely understood why she would want to move. Living next door to the murder scene had to be difficult.

Chapter Eighty Four

It was difficult to depend on the DA's Office, but the Attorney General had explained that their family would have to trust the local Judicial System. Knowing that DA Bass wouldn't be around helped some.

The Preliminary Court Hearing, the looming "mini-trial", would be the first opportunity for the family to view Seven's murderer. Though a lot goes on with a Preliminary Hearing, all the family could think about was breathing the same air with the killer. Seven had been dead only one hundred and seven days, so the atmosphere was thick with gritty pain.

Ennis having been arrested for committing a felony, and formally arraigned, the preliminary hearing would be held to determine if there was sufficient evidence to take his case to trial. Both the prosecuting attorney and defense attorney would be making their arguments before a judge. Both trying to prove why he should or should not be tried. Witnesses could be called, and physical evidence could be introduced. Ennis would not be personally able to speak in his own defense at the preliminary hearing. He would just sit there. If the judge believed that there's sufficient probable cause, his case would move forward. On the other hand, if there wasn't sufficient probable cause, the case against him would be dropped. The DA would attempt to prove there was a murder and what evidence he/she has to substantiate the accusations. The defense attorney, public or private, would give reasons why his client is innocent.

It's a strange feeling to be excited about going to such an event, but Seven's family was eager to go after his killer.

For Mae, sitting in closed rooms with people she wanted to rip apart was laborious. It didn't feel good at all. It was difficult to even breathe.

All together for the first time since the murder, the preliminary hearing was a reunion of sorts. Only three witnesses had been subpoenaed, Investigator Woody Muck, Kendall Martin and David Smith.

Waiting for security to begin letting people through the metal detector, the family gathered on one side of the hallway, while the other's involved sat on a long wooden bench on the other side.

Mae hadn't ever seen Kendall Martin before, but she'd wanted to meet him a decade before when he physically assaulted Erik. Now he sat right across from her. It wasn't until that moment that she first set eyes on him that she felt it in her gut, that he was as guilty, if not more so than Ennis Dorsey, of attacking Seven.

His demeanor was cool, calm and collected, and every so often he would glance in the family's direction.

Sylvia was unable to sit still, and she paced inside and out. At one point she walked over to Investigator Muck. "What can I do to bring it forward that Seven was robbed? I calculated he had about $72.00 in his front right pocket, and it was missing."

"What more do you want? You already got murder." He gave her his famous grin, while shrugging his shoulders. He continued to remain snub and indifferent to the family.

Ennis Dorsey's mother and step father, Angie and Luke Smithfield pace up and down the hall.

Then there was Ennis's wife, Sissy; who was at odds with Angie and Luke. They'd wanted her to bring the children to visit Ennis in jail. She claimed she didn't ever want to see Ennis again, yet there she sat to go in and witness the hearing. Their children were bouncing all about.

The DA Victims Assistant, Maxine Kemp, made her way to Seven's family. She would be taking them through security first, and escorting the family into the courtroom. It was open court that day, so there were many people in the courthouse. Once everyone went through security, it was a packed courtroom. Maxine would stay with the family the entire day. They sat for hours, listening to other cases, waiting their turn.

At some point Sissy's children were noticed by Judge Millen.

"Excuse me..." He pointed in the direction of Ennis's son, climbing around and being a toddler. "Whoever's children...get them out of the court room." Sissy took them out, but came back in by herself shortly.

Finally the time arrived when Ennis was brought in with chains wrapped all around him. All the air seem to evaporate as he slid his feet across the front of the room. He was dressed in the typical jail fashion, with the issued orange jumpsuit on.

Sylvia had been jittery and nervous, but once Ennis walked in, she took on the appearance of a lioness stalking prey. Instead of physically attacking him; she began carving into the wood of the bench in front of her. Sylvia used the vault key she kept around her neck to score Seven's name into the nice cherry wood. The key was to the locked safe holding Seven's cremated remains.

Watching her, Mae figured if anyone would be able to get away with vandalizing the court, it would be Sylvia. Though Mae had instincts to stop her, or at least tell Maxine, Ennis's presence had her full attention transfixed to the back of his head. All kinds of thoughts were running through her mind; mostly bad ones. Every muscle in her body felt restrained, as the desire to smash in his skull, pulled at her. Mae's heart was beating so hard she had to push on her chest to prevent it from breaking through her rib cage. She glanced at her brother Erik who was squeezed up next to her on the front row, and he too was hypnotized to Ennis. Without warning, tears began flowing from her eyes like two broken damns. The pain of being so close, yet so far from 'making things right' or 'giving him what he had coming' made Mae feel nauseous and dizzy.

Mary had one of the two keys holding Seven's remains in the ground. She'd purchased the safe, and had put her key in her jewelry box. Within weeks of the funeral, someone broke into Mary's house, and stole nothing but that key. She was sitting right next to Sylvia, but she was hypnotized to her son's murderer. She'd brought Seven into the world. He had taken him out.

Many new facts were brought forward throughout the course of the next hour. DA Dan Dobbs presented the state's case by calling on witness number one, Investigator Woody Muck.

Mae turned her attention to the witness chair, holding a law enforcement officer that she had no respect in the world for.

As he sat on the stand, the Prosecution had him answering questions.

"Yes my name is Woodrow Lee Muck; I am an Investigator for the Lanyard Police Department."

"Where were you when you received the information concerning Seven Levine?" The Prosecution pushed through the easy inquiries.

"I was at home when I was contacted by dispatch. When I arrived on the scene, Levine was already in the ambulance."

"Who was the first officer on the scene?"

"Well, it was Officer David Crest and Officer William Billing."

Muck answered the next few questions with the same grin, but then the defense attorney, Lenard Paul, began his interrogation.

"Investigator Muck, when you arrived on scene, had the crime scene been compromised in anyway?"

"No."

"So the crime scene was or wasn't treated properly? Were there people with shovels running around covering blood?" Lenard Paul was a new attorney, and he had a reputation to build.

"No; but we were short-handed that night. The initial response to the call was for an assault, not attempted murder." Muck pulled at his tie slightly.

"Okay, so then what witnesses were on the scene when you arrived?"

"Kendall Martin, David Smith, Sue Smith and Candy Whitefield."

"Which one of them was covering the blood with dirt?"

"No one when I arrived, but David Smith had taken a shovel and tried to dry up the blood, to keep his dogs from walking around in it."

"Who handled the evidence?" Paul stood up holding his folder and pen.

"I've handled all the evidence, and am going to transfer it personally to Montgomery for Forensic Testing."

Woody's answer upset Mae, Mary and Sylvia; because he had told all three of them that he had already made that trip to Montgomery, before Seven died.

The defense attorney continued. "So who found the axe handle?"

"Rex Smithfield found it, and Investigator Ridge retrieved it along with Ennis's bloody red T-shirt."

"Rex Smithfield? Who is Rex Smithfield?" Lenard quizzed, while digging through his notes. No one answered, and the court room went silent.

A voice from the other side of the room bellowed. "Rex Smithfield is my nephew your honor." Luke Smithfield stood up, but quickly sat back down after the judge gave him a disgusted look.

"You will remain quiet in the court!" Judge Millen ordered, giving him a look of warning.

Lenard Paul thanked the Investigator and excused him from the witness seat.

The next witness called was Kendall Martin. He gave his name, age, address and employer's name. Mae had been attempting to keep up taking notes, but it was difficult with so many characters present in one room. She'd eyed Woody hard, listening to him make himself sound so professional. Now, with Kendall sitting in front of the room, she had all but put her pen down. Watching him wiggle around in the chair, Mae felt he was a bit nervous, considering that the District Attorney claimed he was their star witness.

Kendall Martin had been the only witness that came forward. Everyone else in the yard denied being there. He had been forthcoming with the police, eagerly giving them the information about the attack. He was after all, the one who pulled the axe handle from the killer's hands.

Though Mae tried to keep notes, it was difficult. She was transfixed, and so full of emotions. Both the prosecutor and defense were asking questions, but Mae's hands only wrote key statements. Facts she'd not heard.

He confessed that he'd had two fights that evening within the hour of Ennis attacking Seven. The first fight was in Ennis's yard after three am, not too long after Sylvia and Cameron left with the car. Once they left, Kendall admitted he said "something" to Seven that made Seven mad enough to physically attack him.

"WHAT DID YOU SAY TO MY BROTHER?" Mae wanted so much to scream. She had to fight the Liz inside her to stay seated and quiet.

Lenard did ask Kendall what it was he said, but Kendall completely succeeded in evading an answer to the court.

Kendall claimed that Seven picked him up, and tossed him down onto his head. Then Seven ran off, and it would have been at this time he showed up back at his trailer, asking George to come outside and back him up. He told the court that around 9:30pm, while he and Ennis were at the Smith's party, Ennis had asked David Smith to hold his gun for him. It was at this time, 9:30 that Seven and Sylvia made an appearance at the neighbors. Around 11:30 pm, Kendall said he went back to the Smith's yard, and retrieved Ennis' gun for him.

He stated that they showed up at Seven Levine's trailer that night because Sylvia had invited them over for a birthday party for her husband. In describing the second fight he had with Seven, Kendall claimed he had his hands wrapped around Seven's neck when Sylvia knocked him off of her husband. He stated that Sylvia attacked Ennis also. Kendall was adamant that the Smith's yard was full of people who witnessed the fight. He had one more fact to elaborate on, while grinning at Ennis. The day Ennis was put in jail; he moved Sissy and Ennis's kids into his trailer. They continued to live with him that day.

This admission stunned the entire court room silent, while Ennis shook his head back and forth.

David Smith wouldn't be called to the stand.

Mae figured it wouldn't do any good anyway, considering he was only going to lie about what really happened.

He'd sat slumped over during the majority of the day. Everyone looking at him with questions running through their minds. How could he be so worried about covering a bloody crime scene, when a boy had just been beat to near death in his front yard? What reasons did he have to lie?

Ennis was claiming self-defense and had pictures of bruises on his leg. His defense was that Seven attacked him with the axe handle first, then he took the handle away from Seven, and commenced to 'beating his ass'.

Mae wondered why it was Seven's skull bones that showed all the impact, and not Seven's pelvis bone.

Kendall would not back up Ennis's claims that Seven ever physically attacked or hit Ennis Dorsey.

The day left Seven's family exhausted with emotions.

Leaving the hearing, Mae's mind was swimming with theories. She was extremely angry with the way so many facts had been ignored, while lies were being allowed.

The DA didn't attempt in any way to defend Seven's actions. They agreed he shouldn't have been out at that time of night, running the roads, drinking and fighting. With all of the previous year's lies that Sylvia had produced, it wasn't hard for the DA to believe Seven was nothing but trouble.

The reason Seven had been out running the roads, was because two killers came knocking at his door around midnight, and he knew it. Seven was a working man, a husband and father. He hadn't been roaming the streets and kicking ass since before he was put into rehab. They showed up with an axe handle and gun, around midnight, for a "birthday party" that Sylvia had invited them too. Yet she wasn't even there. Seven had a clue in what the two were up to; he'd been around the block. He'd told his mother, if he moved back to Chambly County, they'd kill him. Seven wanted the two not only out of his trailer, off his land, but out of his trailer park. That's why he drove away with them in Cameron's car. He didn't want anything happening around his three kids. As soon as he got the two late night visitors out of his home, he started calling people for help. Seven was protecting his children.

No mention had been made that Seven had been robbed of his hard earned cash. The DA didn't care, and Muck thought it a waste of time. No one seemed to care that Seven was making frantic calls for help, and had made a police report. Sylvia had been arguing with her husband, but the DA wanted everyone to be under the impression she was sitting at home like Betty Crocker, baking cookies and cakes.

Mae tried not to get too emotional over things that didn't matter, but she couldn't get past the sensation that murder was something that mattered, no matter who or what the victim was perceived to be.

Chapter Eighty Five

The District Attorneys were having problems getting Seven's medical records released from the hospital. Mary was asked to help, and because Seven was married, Sylvia would be the one who would have to sign the paper.

Sylvia had been busy with her plans to move to Athens, Georgia to live with her oldest brother, Craig. She had Mae keep Bella one weekend while she traveled to Athens to prepare their trailer that sat on her brother's land. Mae's daughter Cameron had separated from her husband, and was planning to move to Athens with Sylvia.

This wasn't a comforting thing for Mae, who absolutely didn't like the idea of Cameron hanging around in Sylvia's circle of friends. Cameron felt the three children needed her to watch over them. She explained to her mother that Sylvia's didn't want Bella, Liam and Cassandra; announcing it all the time. Cameron was an adult, so Mae couldn't stop her.

Sylvia didn't hide the fact she was still crossing paths with the law. On the day Mary took her to get the medical records, they stopped and ate lunch at San Juan's Mexican Restaurant. While they sat there, Sylvia told Mary that she almost got arrested a few days before, but the police let her go. She was always eager to brag to Mary and Mae how the cops always let her go.

"Yeah, I was driving, but it was Willie's car. I'd thrown a small bag of pot out on the side of the road, and they said it was mine. Luckily, they got another call, and let us go. I'd told them my children needed me. I failed the sobriety test and had some prescription pills, but they let us go."

This didn't help ease Mae's concerns. Instead, it added fuel to her fire. She felt it was only a matter of time before someone else was seriously injured. Eventually, Sylvia or those innocent children could be harmed. The only reason Sylvia ever got away with the entire year of crimes, was because "someone" kept dropping the ball. Or, Sylvia had to be an informant. Mae intended to figure out who was to blame, and what she could do about bringing it to light. By letting Sylvia go constantly, they had made a monster, who believed she could do just about anything, and get away with it.

Who had Seven made the police report on? Sylvia and Kendall? How could she ever find out the truth? The bigger question was who would try to stop her? She felt the more she went over the events of Seven's last twelve hours, and studied his every move; something would reveal itself to her. Writing it down, over and over, sooner or later a common denominator was going to jump out at her. Her theories and thoughts circle around those involved.

Ennis owned the axe handle, and had been in possession of it all night. He'd used the handle to smash in the windows of his own car and terrorized the little old lady next door by denting in the sides of her trailer with it. Now he was claiming Seven had the axe handle and hit him first on the leg. They had pictures to support his claim.

Seven had pictures made also, of the bruising and broken bones that had been done exclusively to his head. Why would Seven hit Ennis? All night, Seven is fussing with Sylvia, and physically fighting Kendall over something Kendall said. So why all of the sudden would he attack Ennis? Then let's say he did, and Ennis took the weapon, how would he manage to hit Seven from behind? Seven isn't going to turn his back on a guy with an axe handle.

If Ennis was hitting out of self-defense, why would he need to turn Seven over once he had him down on the ground, and continue to bash in Seven's skull? What was Ennis's motive to do such a horrible thing? The pictures of Ennis's wounds was present, why wasn't the pictures of Seven's damaged head shown too? If all that was done to Seven was 'self-defense', then why had Seven's upper torso been covered with contusions and deep bruises, and a foot print?

Mae had experience with having to defend her own life. She couldn't believe Ennis was defending himself. Ennis had over killed a defenseless human. It's interesting to note that the gun was also Ennis's gun. So he had two weapons on the scene, not one. If he was so hell bent of defending himself, why wasn't Seven after him? Seven's attention had been on Kendall Martin. Ennis Dorsey was supposed to be a friend. The fight was supposed to be over a game, how could they have been fighting over such a stupid thing? Seven had no connection to that stolen system. The only one who was connected to that video game was Ennis who fenced it for the thief, who stole it from David Smith's house.

Seven loved his family deeply. Ricky Levine had told his son, Mary's family didn't accept him. For years, Seven feared his father's words were true. Once he found out the truth he'd decided then, to never take his family for granted. His love came from loss, and for the twenty seven year old young man, his family meant the world to him. Those would be the things he would fight for and over. In his mind at the time of the attack, he'd lost his family again, because of Sylvia's behavior. Seven only had a wife and three kids left to fight over. Those were the reasons he would have fought in the middle of the night, not over a stupid video game, stereo or any other crazy reason.

Kendall Martin was now the star witness. Surely the family of the murdered victim should be grateful to the young man for stopping Ennis from killing Seven in the Smith yard. He valiantly jumped down off the porch, and struggled with the killer, to take the weapon away. Then he returned to the scene to give his statement to the police. In his statement, he claimed Ennis hit Seven from behind, and that the yard was full of spectators.

The only blood Kendall had on him happened to be on his right shoe. Not one drop of blood was on him, anywhere else. His shoe was so saturated with blood; it brought the attention of the attending police officers. When asked how he managed to get so much blood on that shoe, he told the cops that he must have hurt himself, but his foot had no injuries on it. Then he explained that must have "accidentally" kicked Seven while struggling for the axe handle.

Seven was fighting that night, but not with Ennis Dorsey. His only concern with Ennis had been that Ennis would jump in and assist Kendall in the event of a fight. Seven had two physical fights with Kendall, within the hour of his murder.

Of all the people in those neighborhoods, Kendall Martin was the only one Seven had warned his wife about. The day before he left to go out of town to work, he had asked that Kendall Martin not be allowed around his house. Strange, when he got back, Kendall had not only been in his house, but the ex-con had made moves on his wife while there. He had said something to Seven that made Seven attack him. That something had to be about Sylvia or the kids.

Now during the second fight, when Kendall was on top of Seven, and George had stopped Ennis from joining in with his axe handle, Ennis made an interesting comment to Kendall.

"F*#! it, just shoot him!"

So during that second fight between Kendall and Seven, Kendall had the gun on him. During the preliminary hearing, Kendall had stated he'd gone back to the Smith's to retrieve the weapon. Why is this gun being moved around so much by the very people who ultimately killed Seven?

Kendall was fresh out of prison. Mae thought it odd, that out of all the experiences of her life, she'd never eye witnessed a murder. Yet the boy is only out of prison for a few weeks, and he is already a star witness for a homicide trial? Why was he after Seven? What was his motive? Did he just want to have sex with Sylvia? Or is he just a violent human? He incriminated Sylvia on the night when he claimed she had invited them over for Seven's birthday party.

Why would she do such a thing as invite Kendall Martin? After her husband's warnings? When was this party supposed to start? They showed up at 10:30 pm, according to George, and asked where Sylvia was. Then next time they stopped by was around midnight, after Sylvia had left to go to the store to make a phone call.

Yes, he is the star witness, because he blames everyone but himself. He claimed the Smiths were with him during the attack, along with a yard full of witnesses. He claimed Ennis hit Seven from behind, and that Seven never hit Ennis, or saw the axe handle as it was aimed at the back of his head. Yet, for some reason, Mae couldn't help but fully believe he was the mastermind behind the entire night. What had set him out for destruction was Sylvia's prompts. Both Sylvia and Kendall went out of their way to provoke Seven into thinking they were messing around with each other. Why would Kendall end up with Ennis's wife then? That sounds more like Kendall using Ennis to get Seven, he gets to knock down two birds with one stone. The only flaw in Kendall's plan was the lies the neighbors told.

Mae's next suspect was none other than Sylvia. It wasn't just the previous year before the murder, it was the behavior of the grieving widow that had Mae paying attention to her sister-in-law. Everything about the night circled around her, and the many half-truth's she'd given concerning the last evening of her husband's life.

She claimed they were happier than ever, yet she'd called the police on him that evening, somehow knowing there would be a fight. Now, if she was so concerned about his safety, you'd figure she would have willingly given the 911 dispatcher the necessary information.

"There's some doped up boys and there's going to be a fight."

No, she didn't have an address. No, she didn't give her name or where she was located. As a matter of fact, she refused to give them any information that could have helped or even saved her husband. Not that it would have mattered, because the police never showed up.

Around mid-night, she asked for a ride to go call her brother. She didn't go to her brothers, nor did she go home until her husband left over two hours later. She came in the door as soon as they left, irate at Cameron, and was already blaming her when Seven was either hurt or put in jail, or both.

Since the murder, she had a new, old boyfriend, Nathaniel Walker, whom she claimed was only a friend. She never admitted to being intimate with him, but she couldn't hide the fact they were seeing each other. No one said one word to her about it. As far as Seven's family was concerned, it was nothing new. Eventually though, Mae would begin to wonder if Nathaniel

Walker himself was involved. He had known Sylvia as long, if not longer, than Seven. Walker believed Bella was his daughter. Walker had also went to school with Seven, so they were not strangers to each other, and actually had a lot in common it would seem. Walker was also within walking distance of Seven's home.

Regardless, it was still difficult for Mae to believe that Sylvia would have ever wanted Seven dead. It wasn't hard at all to believe she had tried to have him beat up and successfully set up, oh and locked up. Was that her intentions that night, only things got out of hand? Did Seven wave a red flag at the bull, when he said, not to let Kendall Martin in his house?

Now if Mae could figure out why the neighbors were lying, she would have all her answers. David Smith had only known Seven for four months. In those four months, Seven had only visited David a few times. Some statements indicate that Seven and Sylvia had visited the yard full of people earlier in the evening. Sylvia had never verified that, so Mae couldn't be sure.

The game system had been stolen from David Smith's trailer. Was Seven going to tell David who had stolen it? Who knows? Mae felt the mere fact of the video system was a mute-point. No one killed anyone that night over a video game. It's a weak excuse.

Why would David Smith, his wife, daughter, and yard full of witnesses lie? Mae wished they could comprehend the peace that the truth could provide, yet they refuse. Why? Either they have something or someone to protect, or they are afraid. It would be easy for them to tell the truth, and put the killer away, so the fear factor doesn't work that way. Fear of being discovered? The parts that were contributed to the "ass kicking"? A bunch of young adults and teens, drinking all night in celebration of a birthday. No one would imagine the fellow they were kicking would actually die. It was all supposed to be part of a fun party night. When no one wanted to tell the truth, Mae's imagination began running away with her.

What was the deal with running to grab a shovel? Mae dared to say that would not be one of her top concerns after finding a beaten man, clinging to life, laying in her front yard. Mae knew they didn't find Seven. They watched him being beaten to death, and didn't call the police until it was too late. Then David worries more about his dogs walking around in blood than the fact a human's life had been taken away from a family who loved him very much. The same boy laying there beaten, had never done one thing, to one person in that entire yard.

David had the gun that night also. Why in the world, would he hold onto Ennis's gun for him? Finding the truth to the question about this deadly weapon being swapped around would give Mae many interesting answers. The murder happened in David's front yard, why?

Chapter Eighty Six

Seven was marked for death that night by Kendall and Ennis. He had worked all week out of town to support his family. When he got home that night, he had a clue that something was up. He was extremely intuitive and street smart, and had lived with Sylvia long enough to know when she was up to no good.

He didn't come home angry with Ennis Dorsey, Kendall Martin, David Smith or even his wife. His main concern was his wife being upset because he'd worked an extra day unexpectedly. Having to work through his birthday had been a bummer, but he worried more about Sylvia's happiness than his own.

As the course of the evening progressed, Sylvia began to complain about his love for her, and lack of attention. She also began telling her husband that Kendall Martin had been in his house, and had put the moves on her. At some point, Seven even went to the police department and made a report about someone assaulting him. One thing for certain, if Seven had been drunk and disorderly like so many claimed, he wouldn't have ever walked into Lanyard Police Department.

In the course of his last year alive, Seven had gone to the police department, three times for help. The first two times he went out of desperation, he ended up vilified, falsely accused and jailed. Now, this last trip for help, within hours, his life ended with his murder.

Mae knew Seven, and she knew his tactics. It was obvious he had picked up on something, and was attempting to fool those intending on causing him bodily harm. If they had jumped him, assuming him to be drunk, he would fully surprise them when he soberly whipped their ass.

Seven's target was obvious, Kendall Martin. He told several people that he had caught Sylvia and Kendall messing around with each other. In some ways, Mae believed it, but had a hard time believing Kendall's presence in the trailer would not have been noticed by Cameron and George. Of course, it was strange how they all came out to welcome Seven when he first got home.

His employer had claimed it had been one of the sweetest welcome homes he'd ever seen. Oddly, it was the first time to ever witness such.

When Mae asked Cameron about it, Cameron had some interesting facts.

"Sylvia insisted that we all go outside and welcome him home. She wanted everyone out the front door. As a matter of fact, she required we all go outside."

"Was Kendall in the trailer?" Mae asked.

"I don't know. Sylvia was back in her room."

There is a back door right beside Sylvia and Seven's bedroom door. Was Kendall inside the trailer? Was that why Seven got such a warm response out in the front yard, so that Kendall could get out the back?

Maybe Kendall was being used by Sylvia, and she had another guy waiting in the wings named Nathaniel.

One of the last things Seven had said to his wife was not to have anything to do with Kendall Martin. Out of all the men in the world, she would choose that one man to mess around with and then tell her husband when he got home?

Seven wanted Kendall away from his wife and kids. And killing Seven would be no easy task; it took them several hours to muster up the courage. They had come at him from behind, quickly and with extreme force.

Seven was no fan of the Lanyard Police Department, and in no way, shape or form, would he ever go in the building drunken and disorderly. His making that report, proved to Mae, her brother was fully cognizant.

At the hospital, the ICU nurse had informed Mary that Seven had only a small amount of alcohol in his system, and absolutely no drugs. When they had their day in court, the truth would make itself known.

The weeks and months after the first court hearing, brought many changes. Before the hearing, Seven's family wouldn't go near the DA office. Now, Mae and Mary walked the halls nearly every week. Mae couldn't give up the rights to her brother, to an office that refused to believe Seven had been set up. With the evidence the DA had, and the limited witnesses they would speak to, it was easier for them to believe that Seven had been up to no good that night. He was drunk and disorderly. No one cared about the fact he had been set up, the only witnesses that mattered were the ones present during the actual murder.

In the state of Alabama, there is no premeditation; it doesn't matter if they hold twenty meeting before the murder, concerning the murder.

It angered Mae that the Smith yard-full of witnesses, were being allowed to lie. If they didn't want to get involved, and refused to admit they watched Seven being beat to death, they had every right to refuse to talk. Even if there were more witnesses to the fact they were in their yard. The fact they refused to tell the truth had Mae convinced they were guilty of something, if not for contributing to Seven's murder.

Simply put, all that mattered was the seconds of the murder, nothing before or after. The DA had to prove those seconds, and nothing else. Why would they want to help Seven's family? How could they? Mae felt she had no choice but to somehow put it out there. She couldn't just hand over possession of her brother's memory to an office of strangers. After all, she had spent years praying for the blessing of siblings. Not only that, she'd watched over and protected him as best as she could. Sure her society had a developed judicial structure and ornate way of dealing with crime, but Mae elected herself as the one to make sure the record was played right. No matter whose toes she stepped on, or however many feelings she might hurt. Nothing could erase what she'd experienced, or what memories she had to live with. The world couldn't see the many layers Mae had, or the many personalities and characters that she had developed, in order to survive so many tragedies.

Seven knew Mae, and he loved her, no matter what Sylvia claimed after the fact. Her opinion will never count, or matter, as far as the love between two siblings. Once Seven was murdered, he didn't magically stop being loved by his sister. Marriage lasts until death do you part. There is no parting for blood relations. Seven remained Mae's brother, and she couldn't go out and so easily replace him like Sylvia did.

The grieving widow hadn't just told Mary and Mae she was moving to Athens, Ga. She was telling the church that had tried to help her after the murder. Many people were under the impression that Sylvia wanted to get away. Who wouldn't ? The homicide had made dozens of people in the county feeling uncomfortable enough to physically move. No one blamed Sylvia one bit, least of all Seven's family. Mary continued to help Sylvia pay her necessary bills, and many were willingly helping with the kids.

So why would Sylvia feel the need to lie?

Day's after she moved, Bella had been trying to call her Aunt Mae, and had left many messages.

"We've moved far, far, away to a place called Tusca...Tusca..." Her small voice tried to say the big word she'd heard spoken. "Loosa…Tuscaloosa."

Sylvia had lied about where she was moving. Instead of moving to her oldest brothers in Georgia, she snuck out of town with her lover Nathaniel Walker, who lived in the opposite direction, in West Alabama.

Why would she lie? What reason could she have? Seven's family hadn't turned on her in any way. Even after finding out Sylvia was living with Walker, the family kept the bridge of communication open with her. No one called her fussing, complaining or asking questions.

Mae was mad at Cameron, who had moved with Sylvia. When Mae confronted Cameron on the phone, her daughter explained she didn't know Sylvia had ever said they were moving to Athens. She was under the impression Sylvia had told them Tuscaloosa. Cameron said she didn't know about the lie Sylvia told, until she heard Nathan fussing at Sylvia for lying to Seven's family.

Cameron wouldn't stay long with Sylvia anyway. Two weeks later, Cameron was moving back home. She was full of information concerning what danger Sylvia was putting the children in. It sounded similar to the same behavior she'd had the year before Seven's murder. Fears and concerns grew for the children. Unfortunately to help them, you'd have to confront Sylvia, and she was dangerous when you tried to take something from her. She still had the system seemingly wrapped around her finger. Even though she had carved Seven's name into the court room wood, and they knew she'd done it, nothing would ever be said about it.

Time continued to move forward, no matter how bad it hurt. Mae worked tirelessly on the book, which was harder to write than she'd ever imagined. With so much pain inside her soul, the murder had whipped up a firestorm within her. She had a lot to say, and a lot to try to comprehend.

Ricky Levine died, one hundred and forty one day's after burying his only son.

For Mae, it was like a gigantic book, finally closing, once and for all.

Nothing stopped Mae from her determined obsession of finding the truth, and setting the record straight on Seven's ruined reputation. She put her energies into the next study on the time line of events. She placed index cards on her walls, with each hour, and what occurred within it. Though the decoration of cards all over the bedroom walls got Rex's attention, he never questioned his wife's obsessions.

Since she'd lost her brother, Rex didn't know how to go about fixing what had been broken. The murder had shattered his wife's sanity it seemed, and she was angry at him again for the mistake with Sylvia. This time though, his wife was angry for what had been done to her baby brother in the affair. Rex knew there would never be anyway for him to make it up to Seven. He reasoned that with time, his wife would calm down, and they could move past the mistake.

Chapter Eighty Seven

Before Seven got home that Saturday, Kendall and Ennis were seen walking around the trailer parks all day with Ennis holding his axe handle. Seven had been out of town since Wednesday morning, working. He was due home on his birthday, Friday, but ended up having to work an extra day out of town.

His wife never knew he wouldn't be coming home, and she didn't know where he was. Though he'd tried to get someone to go over and inform her, they never did. He couldn't reach her by phone; her pre-paid line was out of minutes.

Sylvia had baked a special strawberry cake, and when he never showed up, they all ate it.

At 5:00 pm, Saturday evening, Seven arrived home. His employer said that Seven was sick with worry over being a day late. He had to work through his own birthday, but his concern was over Sylvia's happiness. Seven was surprised when everyone came out the front door to welcome him home.

The three excited children were screaming, "Happy Birthday Daddy!" They were all wrapping their arms around him, thrilled to finally have him home.

His employer said any man would want to come home to a welcome like that . A co-worker of Seven's given him some bottle rockets for his birthday. Seven took the kids into the back yard, and they set the fireworks off. Seven absolutely loved fireworks, and enjoyed his children's entertainment. They all went inside and ate cake and ice-cream. It wasn't as special as the first strawberry cake, but Sylvia did manage to bake a second one.

Around 6:00 pm, they started giving the kids bath's to put them to bed early. Seven had asked Cameron and George to baby-sit so that he could take Sylvia out to their favorite restaurant, San Juan's Mexican. According to Sylvia, Seven was supposed to be kicking his niece and her husband out of the trailer. Instead, they were asked to watch the kids.

When Cameron was informed of her uncles intended actions, she couldn't believe it. She claimed Seven never indicated he didn't want them there. The only reason they had been asked to move in, was because two weeks before, Sylvia had spent a week in jail, and Seven had to work to get the money needed to bail her out. So Cameron and George moved in to watch the children. They had only lived in Seven's trailer for two weeks, the first one, Sylvia wasn't there. She was incarcerated.

It wasn't that Seven wished for them to move out, it was Sylvia who couldn't stand them watching her while Seven was out of town working. That had always been her problem with Seven's family, they were just too nosey in Sylvia's opinion.

They ate at the restaurant at 7:00 pm. It would be his last meal of nacho's and cheese, with a pitcher of margarita. If anything that night made him intoxicated, it would have been at this meal. The two remained gone for the next two hours. Now at some point in the night, Sylvia and Seven went by to see a guy named J.B. All that has ever been said about Seven and Sylvia riding around is that they were looking for something. What that something is, will just have to be speculated, because only Sylvia knows.

Cameron said that they got home around 9:00 pm. It was stated during the preliminary hearing that Seven and Sylvia visited the yard of people at David Smith's house around 9:30 pm. It was at this time that Kendall and

Ennis were also in David Smith's yard, and the time Ennis was supposed to have asked David Smith to hold his gun.

From 9:00 pm, until midnight, it's rather sketchy what was going on with Seven and Sylvia. They left and came back, as Cameron explained, many times. They were drinking weird beer. Cameron witnessed Seven pouring his beer out the back door, while George saw him pouring some down the kitchen sink. (Why?)

The only thing that George had to say about the hours between 9:00 pm, and midnight was that at 10:30 pm, Kendall and Ennis knocked on the front door. Seven and Sylvia were gone. Kendall asked George where Sylvia was, and was told she was out with her husband. Kendall wanted George to let them come inside and wait, but George told them Seven didn't want anyone in his house while he was gone.

Before midnight, the conversation turned to purchasing beer for Sunday. No alcohol could be sold in the county on Sunday, so Seven and Sylvia decided to go get some. George wanted to ride along with them, and Seven told him that he could. This upset Sylvia, who wanted to spend time alone with her husband. She began fussing at Seven.

"You don't love me anymore, you don't want to spend time with me!" Sylvia cried to her husband, who couldn't figure out what the big deal was to let George ride along.

"Up until then, Seven had been in an extremely good mood." Cameron explained. She had taken a shower, and in the time she was in the bathroom, things had turned around in the trailer. Both husband and wife were fussing. Seven went out the back door, followed by George. Sylvia went out the front door and walked off.

George would explain that Seven stated to him then. "If Sylvia starts hitting me, take me down, I don't want to even push her back."

Seven knew his wife well, and he knew when she was up to something. Her antics had been deployed on his entire family, and it hadn't been that long ago. He had sat behind bars already, accused of beating Sylvia to near death. The only thing he'd done to her on the October 2007 evening was push her off.

Sylvia came back inside, wanting to know where Seven was. He stepped back inside, and they continued to argue. Again, they went out the back and front doors, only this time, George followed Sylvia. Cameron said after a few minutes, Seven returned through the back door, asking where his wife was. She told him she'd walked off, and Seven marched toward the back door again. Angry, he pushed the door too hard and it swung back on him, making him madder. He hit a picture hanging by the back door. The picture was a family portrait. Seven's patience in his marriage, was running thin and dry.

His wife walked back in the front door, announcing she needed to make a phone call to her brother, and asked Cameron to drive her to the convenience store.

"I'm going to ask James to come pick me up, I'm leaving."

Cameron took her and watched as Sylvia made a phone call. After Cameron made a purchase inside, she asked Sylvia if she was coming home. Sylvia said no, she was waiting for her brother. When Cameron got back, Ennis and Kendall were inside the trailer.

"Ennis had his axe handle with him, and he wanted George and me too watch a card trick he had learned. Kendall was talking to Seven in the kitchen. Ennis was adamant about us watching his card trick."

Now it's at this moment that Mae wondered what is was that Kendall had to talk to Seven about? Ennis was obviously trying to keep George and Cameron's attention, so what was the important topic? Seven had never, in his entire life, ever, been associated with Kendall. They had never been friends, or even enemies. Sylvia was their only connection. Seven wouldn't have ever forgotten about Erik being so violently attacked by Kendall. Did Kendall tell him he was sorry for what he had done ten years before? Was that why these two showed up after midnight? Or did the two boys, one armed with a gun and the other an axe handle, just simply show up for a "birthday party"?

As for Sylvia calling her brother, well, James states he never received any phone calls from his sister that night. So who did she call? The bigger question would be what does it matter? Because it didn't happen within the seconds of the murder, it doesn't count.

Still it would be nice to know when Seven got the impression his wife and Kendall were, as he put it, "F*#!ing around with each other," and who he got that inkling of adultery from? Sylvia had claimed George told Seven. Cameron had claimed Sylvia did. Mae had even wondered if Kendall is the one who informed Seven.

From 1:00 am until 2:00 am, Ennis and Kendall were inside Seven's trailer. The entire time, Sylvia is absent. Cameron and George were present, and both claim Seven got mad at Kendall for talking about Sylvia.

At some point, Kendall started saying he needed to go buy some cigarettes. At first Seven asked Cameron and George to go, but Kendall didn't want to give them any money. He said all he had was a twenty. (He had claimed to Rex and Mae that while they were in the store, and the clerk was dialing 911 because of the fight Ennis was involved in out in the parking lot, that he handed the clerk a five dollar bill, and told him, to 'keep the change, he had to go'.) Cameron figured Kendall just didn't want them to keep his money, because he owed George for that gold necklace. So Seven asked Cameron if he could use her car. He promised to come straight back.

Cameron wouldn't tell her uncle "no". She gave Seven the keys, and the three drove off.

As soon as they left, Sylvia walked back in the front door. She immediately started questioning where her husband was. When she found out, she flipped out on Cameron.

"You stupid bitch! You know he is drinking! When he gets hurt or in trouble, it will be all your fault Cameron!"

Hmmm, her two favorite tricks she loved to play on her husband, the hurt or in trouble tricks. She'd provided him both, time and time again. Where did she hang out during the time she was absent? Wasn't it convenient for her to show back up, right after Seven left?

Chapter Eighty Eight

It's 2:00 am, and instead of stopping to buy Kendall cigarette's, Seven drives over to Taylor Boyd's house. Seven has never met this guy before in his life. Why did they go there? The bigger question would be why was Seven under the impression he needed to get away from his own home? He made many phone calls from Taylor's home. The first call to his brother Erik and then another to his friend Ava.

"He told me that he had caught Kendall and Sylvia. He asked me to come pick him and Kendall up, but I told him I would come get him, but not Kendall." Ava had revealed.

The third number he dialed was Brenda Tiller's.

"He called five times and left a message at 2:26 am, that he needed help. I answered on the fifth call and he said Sylvia was messing with Kendall. He said he had already made a police report, and he needed help. To come get him. I told him I wouldn't ride Kendall anywhere."

They stayed at Taylor's home for thirty minutes. During that time, Seven purchased a set of Taylor's hand carved mini bats. Seven was buying them for his nephew James Robert. As Seven reached into his front pocket to pull out a twenty from the ball of cash, there's no doubt it was a transaction being watched by Kendall. He knew exactly where Seven's cash was kept, as he observed him putting the money back into his front pocket.

Taylor claimed Seven was drunk acting, while Ennis was really loud and had to be told to be quiet. Ennis was also eager to go back to "that trailer" and get his gun.

The three left Taylor's house and drove straight over to Mary's house where Erik was living. Erik noticed the clock saying 2:37 am. Seven stood on the front porch, with his hands in his pockets, smiling. Seven hugged him and wished him happy birthday. Seven told his brother he loved him. Though many had accused that Seven was drunk, Erik denied that.

"Seven was stone sober and serious. I know my brother drunk, and he wasn't drunk or disorderly."

Seven asked Erik to come with him, and back him up. Erik didn't want to ride around with Kendall or Ennis, who was passed out in the back seat. Ennis was muttering something and Kendall told him to shut up. Seven kidded with Erik about decimating Kendall for him. The three left and drove up to the convenience store.

Kendall went inside and purchased cigarette, leaving Seven and Ennis in the car. Another car pulled up, and Ennis made a comment to the occupant. They started arguing, and Ennis got out of the car, and began fighting. This is when the clerk was dialing 911, and Kendall left the five dollars. Seven had gotten out of the car, to pull Ennis off the other guy. Kendall came out announcing the police had been called, and they all got into their cars and drove away. (Later, police would view the video surveillance.)

At 3:00 am, Seven begins to move into the last hour of his life. After they left the store in a rush, it was fifteen minutes before they were heard or spotted again in Ennis's yard. They could have driven straight there, the store wasn't but a minute or two away. It was after 3:00 that Sylvia started up about wanting to go check on Seven. She wanted to go to Ennis's to see if they were over there. George offered to go with her, but Sylvia insisted Cameron walk with her. At 3:15, they walked up into Ennis's yard where Kendall and Ennis were standing outside the driver's door, arguing with Seven.

"Ennis and Seven were in a heated argument." Cameron claimed. "They were yelling and cussing back and forth. Once we walked up though, they stopped. Seven immediately fussed at Sylvia.

"What? You don't trust me?"

He then looked at Cameron and questioned. "What are y'all doing here?"

"We're here to get my car." Cameron said. With that, Seven opened the driver's door and motioned for her to get inside.

"As I got into the car, Seven followed Sylvia around to the other side. They were fussing, and she slapped at him, and got into the car. As we quickly pulled away, Sylvia made a 911 call to inform the police there were some doped up boys who were fixing to fight."

She refused, however, to give them any pertinent information for them to actually help Seven. The police never showed up.

Ennis's wife Sissy was awakened during this time by the sounds of a female screaming in her yard. Alarmed, she went out to see what was happening, and Ennis told her to get her ass back in the house.

Seven tried to leave the yard, but Kendall admitted in the preliminary hearing that he said something to Seven that made him mad enough to physically pick Kendall up and toss him back down on his head.

(Sometime during the night, Kendall acquired the gun. He claimed in court that he went back at 11:30 pm to retrieve it from David Smith. He showed up at Seven's trailer not long after that. It's also another good reason that Seven would want them out and away from his house and children, with Kendall packing a loaded weapon. Yet Ennis was fussing at Taylor's house that he wanted to go back to that trailer and get his gun. He must not have realized Kendall had already gone and got the gun, but later, by the second fight with Kendall, he wants Kendall to shoot him.)

After Seven tossed Kendall onto his head. Seven showed up in his own trailer, asking George to come and keep it fair. George claimed that Seven went out to the front yard, and was looking for his oak stick. Mae felt this action on Seven's part made him look bad. After all, he could have shut the door and called the police. Oh, but he had already gone to the police that night for help. They'd also been called by his wife within the hour.

There were two males coming to his house. They both were planning on attacking Seven. One of the two had a loaded gun, while the other is carrying an axe handle that ultimately claims a life. So when Mae revisited those last minutes of her brother's life, she realized Seven was the one defending his life. Why would he wait for the two killers to get to his house? He wanted to keep them away from his family. It's known that Seven had a shot gun. That fact doesn't make him look any better, but he did. It wasn't something he toted around the neighborhood, passing it around for people to hold for him. He'd had it for many, many, years, and kept it well hidden. Seven knew exactly where that gun was, and he could have easily gotten it, instead of spending the time looking for an old burnt oak stick. Seven's intentions were to teach Kendall a lesson, like not saying vulgar things about his wife.

Everyone involved wanted to paint a picture of a drunk and disorderly Seven Levine. It fits so easily with the monster image. All that Seven wanted that night was for them to leave his family alone. Within the week of his attack, Seven had proclaimed to his family that Kendall Martin was dangerous. He requested that Kendall not be allowed around his family or home. Is it all that odd to believe that's exactly why he was around. His wife was playing her same old tricks. He was, after all, Sylvia's lifelong friend, who had spent hours, trying to provoke Seven to attack.

Seven grabbed his favorite stick, and took off back down the road toward Ennis's. They met up on the dirt road, where Seven attacked Kendall for a second time. He came at Kendall with his stick, breaking it across Kendall's arm that reflexively lifted. Seven swung at Kendall, knocking him off his feet. As Seven reached down to pick Kendall up, he was kicked in the groin, causing him to roll over. This gave Kendall the upper hand, and he was on top of Seven. As he claimed, he had his hands around his throat.

Ennis, meantime, took the opportunity to swing his axe handle at Seven, but George grabbed it. At this time, Ennis demanded Kendall. "Just shoot him, f*#! it, just use the gun."

George stated that Kendall didn't want to use the gun, instead Kendall said he wanted. "To f*#! up this mother f*#!er!"

When George followed Seven out the front door, Sylvia looked over at Cameron and told her. "Seven is more than likely fixing to whip George's ass." This frightened Cameron, and she quickly took off outside. Why did Sylvia say such a thing to Cameron? Why didn't she use the opportunity to call the police, when it was obvious they were fighting?

"Once I got outside, and started walking down the road, I could hear hitting sounds. I started screaming 'what the f is going on?'. George yelled at me to 'Stay Back! There is a gun!' I could see Kendall on top of Seven. I asked Ennis before Sylvia slapped him, why they were fighting?"

"It's just a man thing, when two men been away, they just fighting out the frustration." Ennis told her. (Odd that there is no mention of a video game at this point.)

Sylvia had followed Cameron and she ended up kicking Kendall in the head in order to get him off of Seven. She then attacked Ennis by slapping him repeatedly.

While Sylvia was arguing with Ennis, Seven kept asking Kendall. "Why'd you say that?"

After Ennis had walked over to the neighbor's yard, Seven and Kendall were supposedly hugging each other and making up. While they had fought, Kendall's necklace had been ripped off. They were both looking for it, as Sylvia walked up angry. (It would be interesting to note, Ennis would be going to a yard which was void of people, empty, dark and vacant. According to the neighbors who claimed to be in bed.)

"I told him that all the fighting was scaring me, and that I just wanted to go inside and go to bed. He laughed at me and said they were only playing around. (A real slap in the face if they all were trying to fire him up.) I told him it didn't look like playing to me." Sylvia stated she was sitting on the tongue of the trailer trying to talk some sense into her husband.

Meanwhile, Kendall went inside and sat on Seven's couch, and played one of Seven's favorite video games. George and Cameron were inside also.

George claimed that he heard Seven yell really loud. "I'm going to kill that mother f*#!er!"

Cameron, who was with George, stated later, she never heard Seven yell anything.

Sylvia explained that all of the sudden Seven was yelling. "I'm gonna get my sawed off and kill that mother f*#!er!" She said she was afraid, and didn't want Kendall's guts all over her living room, so she rushed inside, and forced Kendall outside, practically tossing him out the door.

"Sylvia walked inside, and held her hand out to Kendall, who then placed his hand in hers. 'I've known you my entire life, but now you've got to go!', was what Sylvia said to Kendall, as she pulled him up and pushed him out the front door." George and Cameron both stated this strange exchange they witnessed.

At this point, Sylvia looked at her husband, standing on the steps at the front door. She asked him if he was coming in. She then told him if you're in you're in, if you're out, you're out.

Seven debated it in his mind for a second or two. He's just been fired up enough to kill Kendall. What made him go from calling it play, to the rage of murder? Why didn't he come inside? Did he believe his wife was messing around with Kendall? If so, where did he get such an idea?

It's been stated that Kendall called Seven. "Come on Seven, let's go." Seven then turned his back on Sylvia and walked away. She slammed the door, and locked it. She walked to the kitchen, pulled a chair across the room, place it in front of the door, and blocked the entrance, so Seven couldn't get back in.

"I went to the bedroom, sat on the bed and smoked a cigarette. After I finished, I went to the bathroom. The house was dark, and I noticed right away, blue lights flashing through the window. Running through the house, I screamed at George to go outside to check on Seven, to make sure he was ok." This was Sylvia's version, which she neglected to mention the blocked front door.

Chapter Eight Ninety

Time was running down for Seven, and he didn't realize that when he turned his back on Sylvia it would be for the last time. Was the reason he didn't go inside and go to bed because he just wanted to be drunken and disorderly? Most of those who really knew Seven, figured he had had enough for the evening. His last walk was more than likely a trip to the convenience store, where he planned on calling someone to pick him up. Seven hadn't been in the habit of roaming the streets in years. Sure he had wanted to celebrate his birthday, but don't most? Seven was tired, he had to have been, having worked all week. He didn't abandon or leave his family that night, he was leaving because Sylvia was trying her best to entice him to fight Kendall Martin. It hadn't been the first time such a stunt had been pulled on him, and he'd more than likely had decided to leave for the night.

He could have also still wanted Kendall Martin away from his house and home. Sylvia had just said something to fire Seven back up. Or Kendall could very well have intended to finish what he started.

Three people had spent the last hours of Seven's life determined to set him off. Ennis must have had some personal problem with Seven. He wanted to shoot him or beat him to death. Kendall was bad mouthing Sylvia, or saying something one man shouldn't say about another man's wife. Sylvia was nursing this and adding fuel to the fire. Whatever she said to him outside that trailer to make him mad enough to want to kill Kendall, must have confirmed Seven's worst fears.

It's near 4:00 am. The only eye witness accounts of the next moments came from the two boys who had been trying to kill Seven all night. Kendall and Ennis. Kendall claimed Ennis came from behind, and just started beating Seven in the head. While Ennis claimed Seven hit him with the axe handle first, he took it from him, and whipped his ass.

Mae had her own view of what she believed happened to Seven. She makes her analysis based on what her brother looked like afterwards and all the different stories she's heard.

Seven's intentions for that evening was to get a ride away from Sylvia. He'd learned from experience, when he should just give up and leave. It was obvious she was up to something, and familiarity had taught him the further he got from her, the safer he'd be. He'd also had enough fighting, and was more than likely walking slumped over with his hands in his pockets. Kendall wasn't finished with Seven. He'd spent too much time mouthing off about what he was going to do to the mother f*#!er.

Mae's first question was why in the neighbor's yard? For whatever reason, he walked up into the yard, still full of people. The Smith's had a birthday party going into the early morning hours, and by this hour, many were intoxicated. Seven loved birthdays, and since his was on the same weekend, maybe he was going to finish celebrating. More than likely, he was exhausted from working a full time job, and wanted to get away from fighting with his wife. He was either called into the yard or led by Kendall or Ennis.

Ennis was intoxicated, but the entire evening had led up to this moment. He had to be drunk in order to accomplish the grisly task he'd bragged about doing. Kendall didn't need any alcohol to fuel his disturbing violent nature, and he was the one who had set the motions into action. The yard full of spectators had been told all night by these two boys that they were going to get Seven Levine. He didn't belong in the midst of them.

It happened really fast, because the first 911 call came in at 4:08 am. The deed was done by that time, more or less. Seven was all but dead. The yard full of people had to have some time to scatter.

Mae figured Seven didn't arrive in that yard until a few minutes before or after 4:00 am. The beating Seven took wasn't a quick slaughter. It lasted a good five minutes, because time fly's when you're at a party. They were having a blast. As Ennis came from behind, the yard full of people had to have seen it coming. Poor Seven was hit four times from behind with such force his skull was smashed into his brain. His temporal bone was fractured, which means someone was hitting at his head like a baseball.

That wasn't enough though, even though those injuries alone were terminal. As Seven was on his hands and knees, with a large puddle of blood accumulating, Kendall kicked Seven in the face, his shoe making contact with Seven's right eye socket. It shattered his face bone, and flipped Seven over onto his back. Even though he was mortally wounded, Seven continued to struggle, and in order to keep him on the ground, David Smith put his boot on Seven's chest, to hold him down. Once David did that, all his grandchildren, and their little drunken friends, took the chance to "get their kicks in too." Ennis continued to bludgeon Seven with his axe handle, as Kendall dug into Seven's front pocket, and stole his hard earned cash.

Some kicks were also being aimed at his massacred head, impacting his face.

Once they had all but destroyed Seven, they panicked and were forced to call 911, or have to find a way to hide the still barely breathing body. He lay right at their front door. Blood splattered all over everything. David Smith's first thought, was to run to get a shovel.

Chapter Ninety

Number one - of the top ten questions of Mae's was why in the neighbor's yard? They claim to have been inside, sound asleep. The claimed a disturbance was what woke them. They heard yelling and three loud pops. Statements from other neighbors in the trailer park, and even Kendall Martin's police statement, opposes their claims, and put's many individuals out in the front yard, all the way up to the attack. A birthday party had been held there that night.

In the months and years after the event, little bits of information trickled down. Teenage girls claimed to have gotten their "kicks" in. Other neighbors claimed it had been a planned robbery that most people knew Seven had worked, and would have had money on him.

Seven's sister Terri Lynn was visiting a friend, who had a bunch of people over. Terri Lynn said that she was sitting on the couch beside her husband when this guy started talking about the Levine murder. Terri Lynn said it was obvious the guy didn't realize she was Seven's sister.

"That boy was mobbed! There were at least thirty folks in the yard and seven or eight of them jumped him. They all beat him. No one would do anything because everyone knew they had a gun."

Terri Lynn had started shaking and crying uncontrollably as the guy bragged about what he witnessed. When the guy was told who Terri Lynn was, and why she was so upset about it, he abruptly left.

Number two - Why are the Smith's lying about being witnesses to a violent homicide? There are only two reason they could have for evading the truth. They have something to hide or someone to protect. Regardless, only if the tables were turned would they begin to comprehend what pain they are causing Seven's family by lying. They have to live with that lie, every day, for the rest of their lives.

Number three - Where were Seven's defense wounds? It's so easy for the DA, police and community to believe Seven Levine was a monster. If he was out roaming the streets, drunk and looking for fights, where was the physical evidence to prove it? He never had a chance to even defend himself, or his body would have exhibited such wounds.

Number four - Why did Seven go to the police department that night and file a police report? His asking for help didn't stop there. He asked three more people, calling them and visiting one. All were asked, none would because of the people he was with. No one wanted to be around Kendall Martin.

Seven wanted some to assume he was drunk. Yet those who knew him just couldn't see it. Seven appeared sober to his brother Erik within the hour of the murder. George and Cameron claimed, he wasn't drunk, and even witnessed him pouring alcohol out. In order for Seven to ever go to the Lanyard Police Department, it had to be something serious. The fact that he stepped foot into that police department makes it nearly impossible to believe he was drunken, disorderly and out of control. He was asking for help, but wasn't given any.

The list continues with question number five - Why is Ennis beating Seven to death? Motive could be as simple as anger or robbery. Ennis wants everyone, including himself, to believe he only hit Seven out of the self-defense.

Sometimes people lie so much they actually start believing themselves. He also claimed they were fighting over a video game. Bludgeoning another human, over an electronic gadget?

Ennis had been sitting behind bars since the day he attacked and killed Seven. In between the time from the murder to the trial, he would continue to get in trouble in jail. He was distributing prison contraband. He also physically, and unprovoked, slashed a younger inmates face. He would never apologize for any of his action's, because he would always believe what he did was justifiable. Ennis believed Seven was a snitch, and he had been bragging for weeks that he was going to get Seven Levine.

Once Kendall was asked by Sylvia to entice Seven, Kendall had no reason to fight Seven, but he knew Ennis did, having been hanging out with each other for weeks.

Kendall had a score to settle with Ennis, who had an affair with Kendall's girlfriend. He simply used Ennis. They were supposed to back each other with a justification of "self-defense". That Seven had drunkenly and disorderly, attacked for nothing more than a video game. Only when it came time for Kendall to back Ennis, he backed out. Instead of helping Ennis, Kendall took his wife and kids.

Number six - is a good question. Why didn't they simple shoot him with the gun they had? As grisly as it sounds, Kendall claimed he didn't just want to shoot him, he wanted to mess him up. After nearly beating his head off his shoulders, Mae believed he accomplished that.

Number seven - Why wasn't the crime scene ever secured? Well, it's been answered with the excuse that the police were short-handed that night, and they were originally called to answer an assault.

Number eight - Why is the crime scene being covered over, and why didn't any of the police stop him? Mae noted the total disregard for human life, while worrying about dogs getting into the blood.

Number nine - What did Kendall Martin and Sylvia Levine say to Seven within the minutes of his murder? Both said something that completely enraged Seven enough to physically attack Kendall. Sure Seven was a tough guy, but he didn't go around picking people up and tossing them on their head for nothing. As a matter of fact, only a few topics could enrage him to that level. Seven's top priorities were his wife, kids, family and home. So which of those topics did Kendall go after? Sylvia wanted her husband to attack Kendall, because she wanted him arrested for drunken and disorderly behavior, which she was so easily able to do. His probation was fixing to be up, and how would she ever control him then? No she couldn't afford for Seven to be free and clear, while she herself had so much trouble to deal with.

Number ten - Seven made a police report on someone for first degree assault. Who did he make that report on? The police wouldn't let Seven's family have that public information. Mary even tried to get the attorney Barker Reynolds to help, but he believed Seven was exactly what Sylvia had made him out to be. Most people couldn't see the tender hearted boy he really was on the inside. He grew up in a rough world with Ricky Levine exposing him to drugs, and robbing him of his own family's love. Seven went for help that night, but I imagine he ultimately knew the police wouldn't provide him with anything but a hard time.

After the murder, Mae couldn't help but feel bitter resentment towards those of the local police who had given Seven such a hard times because of Sylvia's brilliant acting skills.

Seven's family couldn't go to the police for counsel or advice. The lead investigator would refer to them as 'you people who likes to kick up trouble'.

Once Ennis confessed, the police were happy with that.

Investigator's should follow an objective, thorough, and thoughtful approach.

Or like Investigator Woody Muck liked to say, "They should follow proper procedure."

Chapter Ninety One

Ennis would get another opportunity after the preliminary hearing to make a plea, to which he pled not guilty. A grand jury examined the case, and it was true billed, pushing it forward for a trial. On the day of grand jury, Mary and Mae sat out in the courthouse hallway. They couldn't go into the room and listen to the evidence, but they couldn't be away either. Sylvia was called to testify and had returned to town for the event.

It would be an uncomfortable day for her, because Mary was too angry and hurt to confront Sylvia. When Sylvia decided to lie about where she was moving, it rubbed Mary the wrong way. There was no reason in the world for Sylvia to feel the need to lie. Since Seven was gone, Mary had helped Sylvia any and every way she could. With Sylvia disappearing with Seven children, it added to the agony of already losing Seven. It also made Sylvia look guilty.

Sylvia didn't like being ignored by Mary at all. She had a lot to deal with besides hurting Seven's family. Her own family wouldn't really support her either. Then when her sister Beverly married Charles Wheeler, all hell broke loose. Charles had been one of Sylvia's many old boyfriends. Once a man belonged to Sylvia, she never really let them go. Sylvia threatened to kill both

Charles and her sister. Beverly worried about it, telling Mae one day when they bumped into each other at a store, she feared for her life.

Cameron had made the mistake of befriending another one of Sylvia's ex's, Peter Roder, who was supposed to be Liam's real father. Though Sylvia was receiving a check from the state for Liam, being Seven's son, she continued to threaten Pete with child support court. Pete had actually moved his new family into Seven and Sylvia's trailer, and he was paying Sylvia rent. Once Sylvia found out that Cameron was hanging around Pete, she made many hateful and harassing phone calls to Seven's niece.

"Hey, you know what, f*#! Pete. F*#! whoever the f*#! you want to GD F*#! But I'm gonna tell you what, and I'm gonna tell you right now, you have GD done cross that f*#!ing line! Pete will be my old man! You will be my f*#!ing niece, and you know what Cameron, F*#! You! You f*#!ed a whole lot of GD people, hmmm, I'm not worried about it now. I'm just saying, f*#! you, cause you have GD crossed that f*#!ing line. And don't think I won't be there, every GD minute to be at you. You understand? Alright? Well, understand. Hell I loved you, or I did anyway. You rubbed everybody, GD everybody else off, but you never f*#!ing rubbed me off, and you have now. So f*#!ing ride this GD hard ass road out on your GD own. Giving up your kids, adopting them out, and f*#!ing who you want to. Getting whatever disease you want to. Ride it out. Don't holler at me. Pete is there with his f*#!ing dic!"

Cameron was friends with Pete's new girlfriend, and that's who she was hanging around with. Yet Sylvia, whose husband had been murdered six months before, couldn't stand Cameron being near Pete. Just like she couldn't stand the fact her sister married another ex-boyfriend. Never mind she also was rooming up with another boyfriend herself. Sylvia left Cameron two messages.

"Hey, you are of no longer of any importance to me. I care one f*#! less about you. I mean hook up on the internet you GD whore and find whoever you can find that will meet you in a week and f*#! you for that GD week. You piece of shit. But as far as my baby's daddy, and there is Pete GD Roder, and it ain't shit like that. But he is going to go on child support next f*#!ing week! And he can GD thank you and it ain't because I…whatever, cause, whatever. He could have picked anybody in the GD world. Still GD f*#! with Seven's GD family. You need to understand that Cameron and if you had any GD respect for him, you'd be on that same GD brain length, up, brain wave length. You'd be on the same GD one. Other than that, you ain't nothing but a GD piece of shit, like them mother f*#!ers who GD killed him. You ain't no GD better. Ride that F*#!ing attitude out. Be a piece of shit, just like they were, cause that's all you are obviously.

These messages were left the night before grand jury, so Mae was somewhat ill with Sylvia also. Mary and Mae's last intentions were to hurt Sylvia or anyone else's feelings that day. Their life still involved having to deal with her, and nothing about it seemed fair for anyone.

Sylvia had moved on with her life, and wanted to continue where she had left off. All the while she demanded the attention of being the poor grieving widow. Actions speak louder than words.

The day in court intrigued Mary to note Kendall Martin and Investigator Woody Muck appeared to be really good friends. Mary observed the two hugging each other a few times.

"Well if he's an informant, then I guess we know who he belongs to." Mary whispered to Mae.

After the grand jury indicted Ennis, Sylvia began spreading it around that Seven's family was being mean to her. That Mary had obtained all the money for Seven's murder. No money has even been obtained by Mary, no money what so ever, not even the funeral cost.

Seven's sister Angel paid a large sum on the funeral expenses, while Mary paid the rest on payments. It was obvious that Sylvia believed Mary was profiting from Seven's murder, while she was left to struggle all alone with his three kids. No one told Sylvia to move or stay. Any and everything she chose to do was without Seven's family's involvement. They had already experienced plenty of Sylvia's exploits, and lost their loved one, even before his murder, to her obsessive control of him.

The trial had months to come though, and each month had its own new book to write. Nothing changed, that's the point. Sylvia continued behaving the same way she always had. Nathaniel Walker was now the point of attack. She'd one night called her family for help, saying Walker had slashed all her tires and crashed in the front windshield of her vehicle to prevent her from coming back to Chambly County.

The family didn't know what to think of Nathaniel Walker, the man who was sleeping in the murdered man's bed, two months after the funeral. Within four month's he secretly moved Seven's kids across the state, hiding them from their family.

Because Cameron was still staying at Peter Roder's house, Sylvia wanted them evicted. Pete then had some information to share with Mae once Sylvia turned on him. He wasn't doing anything with Cameron, and announced his girlfriend was pregnant with his baby. Sylvia, didn't even know Pete had a girlfriend, much less one living in her trailer.

"She tried to kill me too." Peter spoke to Mae at her driver's side window. She'd come by to give Cameron a ride, and he'd come outside to speak to her.

His statement had Mae's immediate attention. "Really..." She replied, trying to appear like his accusation didn't matter, though she was close to opening the door and tackling him to the ground for his info.

"Yeah, she sure did. It was a lot like what happened to Seven." He stood with is hands on his hips, sweat running down his face from the intense early summer heat. "I don't really know if Liam is my son."

Mae didn't know what to say. "Really?" She knew Seven had gone through the same with that subject too.

"Yeah, I want custody of Liam, but I'm afraid my past criminal history would prevent me from ever winning."

Again, Mae knew Seven had gone through the same worries.

"How did she almost kill you? Why don't you know if Liam is you son? FIGHT HER FOR CUSTODY!" Mae's mind was screaming, but instead she didn't say a word or ask one question.

Beginning to feel uncomfortable, Peter excused himself and started walking away.

"Well Peter, you need to know if Liam is yours first, before you can fight for custody. I'd encourage you to do that if you are worried or concerned for Liam in any way." Mae's response had to be neutral, because Sylvia had a way of keeping her ex's in line. One minute they were angry and against her, the next they were laying out red carpet for her to walk on.

She drove off thinking about how similar Peter's situation was with Seven's. How many other men had she tried to kill? What gave her the invisible power to control so many people and get away with so much?

Mary entertained the thought of fighting Sylvia for custody, but with the long history of being Sylvia's victim, she was afraid. Trying to take anything away from Sylvia could prove to be dangerous.

Chapter Ninety Two

It wasn't easy for Seven's family members to be out shopping and walk into people like Kendall Martin or David Smith. It happened all the time. The pain it brought up made Mae elect to ride twenty miles away to another town's store in order to prevent such run-ins,

Kendall continued to break the law too. His name would appear in the paper every so often in the police reports.

Sylvia continued to show up in town for occasional court cases she had to appear in for past due fines and brand new charges. She'd gotten in trouble where she'd moved also. As the trial date got closer, she called to inform Mae she might have to miss the trial, because she could be in jail.

Mae called her back the next day, to find out if she'd gotten arrested, and Nathaniel answered the phone. Mae asked him if Sylvia was in jail.

"Oh no, I went down and paid her fine myself. Oh no, she ain't going to jail while she's on my watch. Now whatever trouble she has in yawls county ain't got nothing to do with me, but while I'm responsible for her, I'm not letting her sit in jail on MY watch."

His words made the hair stand up on Mae's neck and troubled her for weeks.

Seven had to leave Sylvia in jail for an entire week. The week before his last week alive. During his last week, he'd spent the majority of it out of town working. Did Sylvia get angry because it took Seven so long to get her out of jail? He had to work the whole week just to pay on her fines in order to get her released. He still had rent, water, utilities and food to buy, but every penny went to get his wife out of jail. Was that what had set her off? He didn't get her out of jail fast enough, so she wanted him in? Was she trying to teach him a lesson? She'd been known to do that.

Did it trouble Nathaniel? If he had been seeing Sylvia, and then she's locked up, it would have bugged him also. The last week of Seven's life, while he is out of town, his niece and her husband continued to live with Sylvia. Not giving them much time together either. It's just a theory, but the boy was over eager to take on Seven's family.

As the days turned into weeks, into months, other murders occurred in the county. Never before had Mae taken such things to heart. She cried for those families, realizing they now shared in her new permanent pain. It was like belonging to a morbid club. One which you could never escape from once your membership pin arrived.

Ennis Dorsey's mother being married into the Smithfield family would give her and Mae a chance meeting.

The Smithfield family was a large once, with many siblings making many uncles, aunts and cousins. It would be at one of the family members funeral's that Angie Smithfield would find the nerve to approach Rex and Mae.

"I have Ennis's power of attorney, and I need his tax papers sent to my address."

Neither Rex nor Mae replied, rather they walked away. It just wasn't the appropriate time to talk about taxes. The deceased cousin of Rex had also worked as a crew member for his business.

Angie Smithfield wouldn't give up though; she was determined to obtain her sons tax returns, though she had absolutely no rights to them. She began stalking Rex, and even went to the Tax Office, and tried to get the preparer to give her Ennis's tax forms. He called Mae and told her. So a few days after the funeral, Mae called Angie to see if she seriously had a power of attorney.

If so, Mae would mail the papers to her, if not, they would be delivered to the jail. The entire time Mae picked the phone up and dialed the number, she felt like she was doing something wrong.

Luke answered and handed the phone to Angie. Mae asked her if she had a power of attorney, and it upset Angie, because she didn't They both hung up the phone. Within a minute, Mae's phone rang and it was Luke, calling her back.

"We sure do need those taxes."

"I have to give them to Ennis, and if he wants to give them to you then he can." Mae was holding her breath.

"I didn't personally know Seven, but I'm sorry." Luke handed the phone to his wife, who was highly agitated.

"God will make the truth come out!" She was nearly screaming at Mae who was close to hanging up. "Kendall Martin is involved! He had something to do with it but he isn't on the witness list, only Sylvia and David."

Mae didn't know where Angie was getting her information concerning the witness list, except maybe through Ennis's defense attorney, Lenard Paul.

"The day after Seven's funeral, Sylvia and car load came by our house in a mini-van. They had shotguns. We had to call the police!" Angie was still highly emotional. "Do you know that Sissy moved the murder weapon? To hide it! The Friday night before, Ennis was at our house with his family, cooking out. They were invited to come over Saturday, but Ennis said they needed some family time. Sissy said that Kendall came over with some beer, and got Ennis to drinking. Then he started insisting they go to Seven's birthday. The gun Ennis had belonged to my brother, and Ennis had it in his pocket and forgot he had it. He asked David to hold it, while he was gone."

Mae couldn't hang up the phone. She was listening and writing as fast as she could. No one knew Ennis's side of the story completely, and Mae hoped within the dramatic woman's ranting, something new would come through all the gibberish.

"Ennis said he couldn't believe what happened. Seven was his friend. I believe Sylvia and Kendall used Ennis to get Seven, because a fight that would look like self-defense is what happened. They have pictures of bruises on Ennis's leg. Ennis said that everything Seven heard about the stolen game system and a stereo was a lie. They'd said Ennis stole those things, but he didn't.

Though nothing she was saying made a whole lot of sense, it didn't matter. Mae needed every bit of information she could get. Angie's tone turned angry.

"Lenard Paul believes Kendall had more to do with it. Sissy moved Ennis's kids into Kendall's trailer the day it happened!"

It was true, and had been a confusing action to everybody involved.

"Ennis's attorney wants Kendall and Sylvia on the stand. One day Eugene and I rode up to the store. (Eugene being Ennis's younger brother.) While I went inside, Eugene waited in the car. When I came out, Sylvia was inside a blue car, parked next to mine. The kids were in their car seats, and two guys were in the car with her. They backed their car behind mine, blocking mine in, then their back door opened, and the guy getting out was holding an axe handle. I heard them say, 'Ain't that Ennis's little brother?'. I told Eugene to call the police, and they heard me. They then pulled off. I got inside my car and pulled out to leave. That's when I saw them in my rearview mirror following us. I rode around until I lost them."

Mae knew how being a victim of Sylvia's felt. "We don't believe Ennis killed Seven all alone either." Mae wanted to say more, but felt she'd already said too much. She was feeling sick for even speaking to Angie at all. She feared that she could compromise her brother's murder trial by doing or saying too much.

After hanging up with Angie, Mae continued to feel light headed. They were not supposed to discuss anything about Seven's case with the public. It was a difficult demand on the victim's family.

It's only natural for a homicide victims family to want everyone on the planet to know what happened to their loved one.

Yet if they ran their mouth, they could possibly set Ennis free. Having that loved one in your mind constantly, it's difficult to find anything to say that isn't about what you've lost.

Chapter Ninety Three

Mae called the DA regularly to check on the status of things and ask new questions. She wondered if how she was handling the murder, was normal. Didn't everyone suffering such crimes, make weekly calls to the DA? If Mae couldn't get them to the phone, she'd drive over to the county seat, and walk in to see who she could find to talk to. She felt like she had to be driving them crazy, but she couldn't just sit back and do nothing. Sure Ennis's trial was in their hands, but Seven had belonged to her first.

She'd prayed hard for the blessing of sibling's, and she'd always counted them as gifts from God.

Mae felt that if she was going to find her answers, she'd have to work directly with the prosecutor. Getting a prosecutors attention is both easy and hard. If you commit a felony, you're bound to meet one. On the other hand, if you need answers, catching one is like finding a four leaf clover. You need lots of good luck. They are effectively busy people.

They do call special meetings with the family and sit down and answer all the questions they are able to. You get to hear what they are planning, even if you don't like it. With Seven's case, there were so many people claiming Seven was drunk and disorderly. Add that to what Sylvia had him made out to be, it was easy to assume that he had some blame in his own murder. He should have been in bed, not our roaming the streets, drinking and fighting.

Ennis wouldn't plead guilty, and the court ordered for him to be evaluated by a psychiatrist. It didn't seem fair that Ennis had so many opportunities to defend his life, though he gave Seven none.

Plea bargaining is a common practice for the prosecution to offer to reduce the seriousness of the charge if a defendant will enter a plea of guilty to a particular crime. It offers something to all those involved.

Prosecutors are able to dispose of cases more quickly, avoid long, drawn-out trials, eliminating the risk of losing cases, and build up better "election -worthy" conviction records. The accused, by pleading guilty to lesser offenses, avoid the danger of being sentenced for more serious charges.

Defense attorneys avoid incurring the expense of going to trial with a losing case or appearing to provide no service to their clients. By being able to handle more clients, they make more money.

Judges are able to dispose of cases on their dockets more easily.

Crime and punishment seldom work out the way the victims intend and wish for. Going through it can seem as painful at times as the actual crime.

The one year mark of Seven's birthday and murder was an emotional roller coaster ride. It was depressing how his birthday would eternally mark his murder.

Mae wanted to release some of the pain, and planned on having a balloon release at the site of the murder. Family and friends of Seven met, sang, prayed, and cried. They took the last walk that Seven made to the yard he was attacked in. They released some of the pain of his loss with each balloon. Missing from the event were Seven's three children, whom the family hardly ever got to see anymore.

As the trial got closer, it became apparent; that the only way to get Ennis was to let the court believe Seven was up to no good.

The DA wanted to paint a picture of Sylvia being the perfect wife. They didn't want it brought up that the married couple had been fighting, not just that night, but the entire previous year. Kendall would be their star witness, and the family should be grateful to him for even coming forward, considering all the witnesses who were lying.

Mae continued working on Seven's book, with the determination of a hound dog on a rabbit. Being confronted with so much pain, she needed something to keep her spirit and soul alive. She didn't care what people thought they knew about Seven. Her focus was on setting the record straight. The hard part for Mae, throughout her journey; she feared the pain her words would cause.

She didn't want to hurt Sylvia or anyone else. In doing so, she would be hurting herself. In telling Seven's truth, she wished to set his proper memory free. Mae obsessed he deserved it.

The trial date was set, and Mae was beside herself with dreaded excitement, until the day before.. It was an early Sunday morning. As the sun rose, a sheriff's car pulled into the Smithfield yard. Rex put on his boots and went out to see what the law needed. Mae felt it was a subpoena for Rex, since he had been the one to find the murder weapon.

What Mae didn't count on was being subpoenaed herself. Becoming a witness hadn't been in her plans at all. She'd waited patiently for over a year to sit with her family in the courtroom, and witness the murderer's trial. Being a witness would prevent that from happening, inhibiting her from the courtroom instead.

As Rex handed the paper to his wife, Mae completely lost it. Not knowing what to do, Rex left Mae alone with her emotions. It was for the best. She ended up lying on the living room floor in a fetal position. Her mother was on the phone with her, and thought she'd have to hospitalize her daughter. For a while, Mae was inconsolable.

"It's just not fair!" She cried to her mother. "I want to be in the court room, I want to be with my family!"

Chapter Ninety Four

Mae felt like she was being punished.

It's not uncommon for the defense to call in family as witnesses, to prevent the jury from watching them.

Whatever reasons there was though, were not good enough for Mae. In the end, she turned it around, and felt proud to be called a witness for her brother. If they wanted her to talk, then that would be their big mistake. She wasn't a grand speaker, but she certainly had spectacular opinions.

Sylvia was a called witness also, and she wasn't happy about it in the least. She did however, being the wife of the victim, get to sit at the Prosecutors table.

Again, for Mae, it wasn't fair. Sylvia might have been his wife for over a year, but Mae had been his sister every second of his life.

As the day started, Mae would be put into a little room to herself. Rex was in there with her, but he wouldn't have to stay as long, being called second to testify. The first day was hard, and Mae tried to pass the time in her room with Rex, by taking her usual notes.

Day One: The defense won't let me in. They are trying to claim Seven was still on meth. After lunch, back in my room, and it's about to drive me insane. The jury is being selected. (Rex is driving me crazy.) Even Sylvia gets to sit in on jury selection. Why can't I? Why am I being kept from my own brother's murder trial? (Had to stop and find tissues...tears.) Momma said Ennis is all dressed up. His momma stands all by herself in the hallway. David Smith and Candy sit outside. The DA's Investigator asked if we knew where Sissy Pasten lived, Rex explained where her parents resided. The evidence, pictures, clothes, axe handle, etc. is in the court room. Sylvia said they had pictures of Ennis passed out with dried blood all over his face. I am a weapon for the defense against Sylvia, I just know it.

I hate this, it's not fair. I want to be in there. Nothing is fair. Maxine Kemp said Sylvia was going to have to do something about the boy she brought with her, he was slumping over in the court room and it didn't look right.

A news camera is present, and Sylvia was asked to speak...

Mom explained what was being said in the court. That they were fighting and drinking earlier, and the fight was over a video game. Said that Kendall hit Ennis with the axe handle, dropped it and Ennis pick it up and hit Seven. That Seven and Sylvia were fighting and Ennis said he shouldn't have gotten involved. That Ennis only hit Seven once, but the prosecution disputed, putting the jury out of the room... that a doctor would be there Thursday to testify how many times Seven was struck. The defense claimed the police didn't do their job.

My opinion, the DA's didn't ask any questions of the people who could testify FOR Seven. It had nothing to do with an electronic game. It WAS premeditated. In the pre-hearing, Ennis claimed Seven hit him. Now he says Kendall did it. (Kendall didn't back him at pre-hearing, he stated, Seven DIDN'T hit Ennis.) This upset Ennis.

The TV news that evening reported the day's events in the court room.

Chambly County, AL. (WTVP) Monday in a Chambly County courtroom, a jury heard opening arguments in the murder trial of Ennis Dorsey. Investigators claim Dorsey bludgeoned a man after arguing with him over a video game system.

The deadly fight happened in the early morning hours of June 22, 2008.

Investigators say Dorsey picked up an axe handle and swung at his friend and the victim in this case Seven Levine, and cracked his skull.

Levine died several days later at the hospital. In opening statements we learned the defendant, the victim and a third friend, had been doing some heavy drinking and several fights broke out between the three friends that night.

The defense maintains the victim hit Dorsey first with the axe handle, so Dorsey took it away and swung back in self-defense.

Testimony is set to begin Tuesday morning.

Why can't the DA call people who will testify Seven wasn't drunk? They claim that the hospital didn't do a toxicology report on Seven, and there is no way to prove or disprove he was drunk or sober. How could a hospital neglect to take such an important test before surgery?

Seven wasn't drunk or high. He had gone to his parole officer the day before he left for out of town work...Why don't they call his boss, who had been with Seven the entire week, up until the last twelve hours of Seven's life. He could easily testify to Seven's character, ethics, sobriety and devotion to his wife and kids.

What could they possibly have to question me about? Does it depend on what Sylvia say's on the stand? I am going to get through this? I will only answer yes or no. God help me, do what's right, to say what's right. Help me to act the right way, and react the right way.

Before Mae left that first day of the trial, she had a chance to speak to Sissy, who seemed willing to share more than she ever had before.

"Ennis came in that early morning acting funny. He stated he thought he'd killed someone, and that he had to get out of there. I asked him what was going on, who did he kill? He said Seven, and then he went into the bathroom, and then passed out. I couldn't believe he had killed Seven, and I just went to bed. Then Kendall came over, and he told me it was true."

The second day in that little room was worse than the first and it really started to get to Mae.

Day Two: It's a rainy day with Tropical Storm Ida going over the South East coast. I'm back in my room, with Rex. Woody Muck and Kendall Martin are walking about the halls. DA Lewis Gold said Kendall claimed they were playing drinking games. That Ennis and Seven had trouble at the convenience store, and then they hid out. Then they had an argument in Ennis's yard. Da Gold explained he would explain to the jury how close the trailers were together. Gold instructed Sylvia to not sit there and shake her head back and forth. He told me that he knows I want to be in that room and he would work on it. It would depend on what comes out in testimony; they might not even call me.

I've seen Woody walking around, haven't had time for any stare downs. I'm stuck in this room, ready for something, but have this to look forward to all day. This room is situated in the newest section of the historical courthouse. My room has bright florescent lights, which hum constantly, like little bee's. It's very square, with a small glass insert in the entrance door, just big enough to look out into a portion of the hallway. Looking out of it, I feel like a zoo animal, as the passers glance at me.

Another locked door leads to an adjoining office. A circle grey top table sits in the center, surrounded by seven cushioned chairs. A large ceiling to floor window gives me a nice view of the old 1895 building across the street. A sort of historical renovation preserves the old antiquity of the town…

During the second day, Mae's calm demeanor began to unravel. Once her husband was called, he was free to leave, which Mae encouraged him to do. He had a business to run, and his presence would only unravel Mae more than help. Having brought a bag full of things to do, she couldn't think about anything but what was happening right down the hall. Before she knew it, she was crying, unable to stop. She couldn't stay in that room any longer. Just as she felt the need to get sick, the door opened. Court had taken recess, and the DA wanted to meet with the family. As they all took their seats around the table, Mae took the opportunity to express her feelings as calmly as she could.

"I'm not staying here. I mean, I'm going crazy. Seven was butchered and I had to watch him die! Now I have to sit in this room! It's not fair; I want to be with my Momma. I want to see Ennis punished! I want to hear what is said. I have to be in there. Please! I can't take sitting in this room anymore. It's killing me not knowing what is going on. I'm just not staying. I'm going home, where I can at least be comfortable while I'm going crazy. The defense can kiss my ass, if they want me, call me at home. This little room makes me feel like I've done something wrong. I've done nothing wrong."

Mae had started to cry, unable to stop herself. Her finger was tapping in pace to her demands on the table before her. In her mind, she was trying to quiet down her devil, Liz herself. SHE wanted out of that room!

The entire room of people was silent.

The DA looked down at his paper work while the DA's victims assistant, Maxine, shook her head, motioning how sorry she was to Mae, with tears in her eyes. No one could tell Mae any different. It wasn't fair, and they all knew it.

It wasn't until the trial, that the family would know exactly which DA would be fighting for Seven's case. To start with, the family had gotten to know, DA Dan Dobbs, who was sitting on the case. But the District Attorney who would become the most intimate with the case was DA Lewis Gold.

Lewis Gold had been involved with the previous year's history before the murder. During the court cases concerning Mary's run-ins with Sylvia, Mary had refused DA Holly Bass. When Mary's case was heard again, DA Gold stood in for DA Bass when it came time for Mary's case. So he was slightly familiar with Seven's family, and highly intrigued.

The young red headed DA was a fierce opponent in the court room. He was friendly, serious and liked to wear boots with his suits. Having taken a personal interest in Seven's case, Gold was determined to bring the family some kind of justice. It just wasn't as easy as it seems it should be. As he listened to Mae, he tried to calm her by telling her that he would talk to the defense attorney. Whatever he had to talk about was put off until after lunch.

Mary, Mae, Thulah and Sylvia along with some of their friends, all went and ate Chinese food. The family tried to get along with Sylvia, because they were supposed to be on the same side. Mary gave Sylvia some cash, while Mae paid for her lunch. They had a front to put up for the jury; that Sylvia was a welcome member of the family, a wonderful wife and mother, an amazing daughter-in-law, a magnificent sister-in-law.

Every hour felt like a year, while the year it took to get to the trial felt like forever. Over the course of time since the homicide, everything had seemed to move fast forwards , faster and faster, while feeling stuck in that senseless instance in time.

The same news reporter was present in the courthouse for the second day of trial. Sylvia had already given an interview. Oddly, the local paper didn't print one single word concerning the trial. Seven wasn't, after all, a prominent citizen, and what happened to him certainly seemed unimportant. Regardless, he was born and raised in the local paper's community, and Mae considered it rude on their part. It didn't surprise Seven's family, they felt it was typical of the paper to pick and choose what they wanted to print.

Walking back inside the familiar and historical courthouse, Mae hoped that DA Gold had talked some sense into Defense Attorney Lenard Paul. It wasn't right for the family to be forced out of the trial. Mae had been there every single step of the way, first in line. She was the only member of the family who wasn't allowed in.

Without hesitation, Lewis Gold was ready when the family got through the metal detector. He ushered them all into the same little room.

Mae hoped he had some good news, as his behavior had a hint of urgency to it. As they all sat down, he immediately started talking.

"The judge has filled out the Personal Prison Sentence Guidelines

Worksheet's. They represent Ennis's maximum sentences, which are the total scores at the bottom of the page."

As he spoke, he pushed two blue pieces of paper out on the table. Mary pulled the papers toward her, and began looking them over. As most conversations with the DA left them puzzled, this one would be no different.

Mae attempted to take in every morsel he spoke.

"One page represents murder, while the other is manslaughter. No matter what the jury decides, these are the sentencing commission's guidelines, and the judge has to go by them."

Everyone at the table looked back at him like he was speaking a foreign tongue.

"Well, the judge doesn't have to follow these guidelines, but if he doesn't, he is then required to write a report why he didn't follow them."

Because nobody spoke up, he quickly continued to explain the paper. The only one absent from the room was the victim's assistant, Maxine, who didn't know Lewis was meeting with the family with such important papers.

For the family, it was like the first day of school. As the students, they knew nothing about the surroundings or what they would be learning. They were trying hard to keep up with what was being explained.

"Well, the scores total higher on manslaughter, than on the murder worksheet."

Now he most certainly wasn't making any sense. How could there be a higher score on manslaughter than murder? Reading their puzzled faces, he tried to explain the dilemma of the state's judicial situation, while pointing out the facts.

"See, they ask questions, which coincide with a numbered score. At the end of the sheet, you total up, and that score determines your recommended sentence length. Now on Ennis's murder sheet..." Gold pointed to the blue paper as he spoke. "He had no prior felony convictions, no prior incarcerations, so his score is low on the sheet. On his manslaughter sheet, the score is on the higher scale, meaning if he is found guilty by the jury for manslaughter, then he will spend more time in prison on manslaughter than if he is found guilty of murder."

Mary looked over at Mae; they couldn't believe what they were hearing.

It would be Sylvia who spoke up first.

"What's that mean?"

Gold looked around the table of idiots. They'd admit it, they didn't have a clue of what they were being told. The little bit that was making sense sounded wrong.

He attempted to explain an intensely complicate situation going on in the States Legislature, which involved the states overcrowded and underfunded prisons. A State Sentencing Commission had been created to study, and ultimately fix, the problem. The blue pieces of paper were results of their actions. Every state in the USA was having similar problems finding money to pay for the rising inmate numbers.

All Seven's family wanted was for the murderer to be punished for the pain he caused. They wanted their chance to speak before the court, to Ennis, and personally inform him of the pain his actions had caused.

"It means, if he is found guilty of murder, he will more than likely spend less time in jail, than if they find him guilty of manslaughter."

Now it was hitting home. Could they afford to let the jury decide he was guilty of murder, to only spend less time in jail for it? They wanted him behind bars for the rest of his life, for the damage he did to Seven's head, and their lives. It wasn't self-defense! The only one defending himself all night long was Seven. Did Ennis go to the police for help? No! Seven did though.

"That doesn't make any sense!" Mae was shaking her head back and forth. They would have to allow Ennis to get away with murder in order to give him the maximum sentence.

"I know." Lewis Gold was fast to agree. He despised having to be the one the explain to bereaved family members how they would never receive the justice they deserved. The system no longer provides it. Every crime would be scored on a neat and tidy five question sheet of paper. No matter how cruel, brutal or heinous the crime, they were all put to the score on the blue pieces of paper.

"Let me express that Ennis will receive the maximum of manslaughter, which is 17 years. Granted he would be able to be put on probation in three years, but when he gets out, he can't get into one second of trouble, or he would be put back in to finish the maximum sentence. I can promise you, I'm going to be watching him, and be there if he messes up." Gold was trying his best to make the most out of the unfortunate situation.

The family agreed they wanted the maximum, but they didn't realize what was fixing to happen.

Lewis Gold got up, leaving the family to wonder why they had just agreed to let Ennis claim manslaughter. They all left the little room, leaving Mae to herself. She'd just started to freak out, when Gold opened the door and motioned for her to follow him.

"Go into the courtroom, sit down, and don't say anything." He whispered to her quickly.

Mae instantly slipped into the swinging courtroom doors, and took a fast seat. She attempted to be as invisible as possible. Soon, Gold walked in and motioned for her to sit next to him at the prosecution's table. This wasn't something she expected at all, to be up front, in the center of the action.

"I've got to ask Lenard if it's okay to have you present." He patted Mae's hand, then called out to Lenard, requesting she be allowed to remain in the courtroom.

The defense attorney looked at Mae, and nodded his head up and down.

"Finally!" Mae could feel her soul calming slightly.

Lewis leaned over toward her to whisper, while Investigator Woody Muck, who was also sitting at the table, watched with curiosity.

"Tell me… " He was smiling. "How did Rex found that murder weapon?"

Mae looked back at him. "I told him to go find it, and he did."

Gold continued to smile widely. "That was a brilliant move."

Mae didn't consider it brilliant, more like necessary. She hadn't believed the police really cared half as much as she knew she did. If her husband hadn't found it, she'd have been looking herself.

He leaned in close again. "I just want you to know, you're right."

Mae wasn't exactly sure what she was right about. She had many theories.

"About what?"

"There is more to it than it seems." He chortled at her, and nodded his head slightly.

She couldn't figure out why, but she felt she could trust Lewis Gold. However hard it was to trust anybody anymore. Mae desperately hoped someone would see through the ridiculous lies being told.

The court was called into order, and immediately things started happening.

First the jury was dismissed.

Next, Ennis's attorney announced a plea deal had been made, and Ennis would be admitting his guilt.

Mary, Mae and Sylvia were told to go stand in front of the court as Ennis was being brought before the judge. In the next few moments, they would receive their justice. Yet it was so fleetingly fast, and so minutely small, they all but missed what they got. They did, however, get to hear Ennis confess to what he did to Seven, as the judge asked him some questions.

Judge Steve Parker was presiding over the case. He had been an attorney before becoming a judge, and had at one time represented Ricky Levine in his divorce. Now he sat over the murder trial, of Ricky's only son.

"Are you pleading guilty before the court because you are guilty?" Judge Parker began to question Ennis directly.

"Yes sir."

Lenard whispered to his client to speak up.

"Yes your honor!"

"Are you aware of the maximum sentence for the crime to which you are entering a guilty plea?"

"Yes sir."

"Were you coerced into pleading guilty or offered anything in return for it?"

Seven's family stood with the prosecutors behind Ennis. Mae considered the prospect of attacking him while he stood there in his nice blue suit. The sound of his voice felt like sharp nails being poked into her ears.

"No sir."

"Are you satisfied with the representation afforded you by your attorney?"

"Yes sir."

"Give the court a description of what you did." Judge Parker pushed his glasses up the top of his nose, and looked down hard at the human confessing a serious crime.

"I took an axe handle, away from Seven Levine, after he hit me. I hit him in the head, many times, and I killed him."

"NO SHIT!" Mae wanted to scream. "We already know that! Tell us the real reason why! AND YOU'RE A DAMN LIE, SEVEN NEVER HIT YOU WITH ANYTHING!" While Mae was dealing with the irate darkness inside her, she wasn't alone in her torment.

Mary and Sylvia both stood with horrified looks on their faces.

"What have I done? STOP! NO! HE KILLED MY SON!" Mary had her own voice screaming inside her head. "I change my mind! I want the jury to decide his fate! Can't I change my mind? NOOO! What have I done? I've let my son's killer go free! "

They had allowed Ennis to get away with murder. Even with a felony conviction, they all felt unbearable guilt that they had just let Seven's deserved justice go far too easily. Like they didn't care to fight anymore.

"Your Honor, the State will require Ennis Dorsey's full cooperation in the ongoing case of Seven Levine's murder." Lewis Gold got it in that the case remained open and was actively being investigated.

Mae was a tiny bit relieved and wanted to tell her mother the good news. That Lewis Gold believed she was right, that there was more to it than it seemed.

Before she could, Gold again leaned over and whispered. "Don't tell anyone what I said. That's between you and me."

His words caused her more distress. Secrets wouldn't reveal the truth. She wanted the truth about everything known. How could the truth be told if it was kept hidden?

There would never be closure. With murder, there never is.

Mae felt it had been ingrained into her bones and DNA. It was now a part of who she was. That was just the way it was.

The Victims Assistant was stunned. She'd not been in the room when Lewis explained the sentencing standards. She would have advised the family to let the jury hear the rest of the case. Or at least have told them to really think about it. The decision had been made before they even realized they'd made it. Mae took a seat on the wooden bench next to her. The assistant sat with her arms tightly folded.

"When was this decision made?" Maxine whispered to Mae.

"Right before court resumed."

"Where was I?"

"I don't know." Mae smiled at the question. She had wondered where their assistant had been too. It was obvious to Mae; the fast decision upset her too.

The news reporter was packing up. Maxine nudged Mae. "This is your chance."

Mae knew something needed to be said, but her words came through her hands to paper with pen. Speaking required days of writing what she wanted to say. Mae looked at Maxine and was comforted by her presence.

"I don't know what I'd have to say about what's just happened." Mae frowned and looked down at her hands, ashamed that she wasn't as brave as she had hoped she could have been.

"Well, I'm not saying you have to say anything. I just wanted you to know." Maxine looked sick. "I just can't imagine what Mary is going through, knowing Ennis will walk free in a few years." She sat looking at Mary who appeared to need an ambulance, all the color having left her body.

Having one last chance to let the public know what had become of their loved one, Sylvia was encouraged by Mae to speak one more time to the reporter.

Sylvia wanted Mae to stand with her, and though Mae didn't want to, she agreed.

Listening to Sylvia explain how she wasn't happy at all with how the case ended, the reporter turned the camera to Mae.

"Who are you?"

"I am Seven Levine's sister."

"What do you think about the results?"

Mae couldn't believe it had come to this, a camera in her face. "Well, it's not fair. We will never get to see Seven again or hear his laugh. His children get to grow up without their father. We will miss him forever."

Chapter Ninety Five

We all have our own personal stories that most certainly deserve to be acknowledged. On the flip side, we all have shameful secrets we'd prefer not to ever surface or be revisited, much less be shared. Events or actions we would never wish to be analyzed and judged.

My lifetime of scars, will not create anything more than experience. I will not be ashamed of seeking help, nor will I be abashed for denying I needed assistance for just as long. It's all lessons learned either way.

On the surface, I will be courteous, polite and friendly, while beneath the skin, I am definitely no longer tame.

Being drawn into unknown journeys makes life and helps the soul not only develop but to gain True Knowledge. That is our Ultimate Goal. Learning occurs differently for different people. I followed my heart on this journey. I have found my calm through creating something to show for feeling so much rage and pain.

From the start I felt because this happened to me, it's happened to one and all. We've all been robbed of our innocence. Every day, someone or something tries to kill or destroy us. If one person is raped, we're all raped. If we hurt others, we're hurting ourselves. If we judge, we're being judged by the same measure. If we murder, we're killing ourselves. What you put out, returns right back to you.

I've shared to find my own truth. I hope through this story, my inner life is set back into motion and my compassion and empathy level grows to even higher levels. I won't feel that God has cursed me with certain people being placed in my life to cause me harm. Instead I'll have faith I've been placed in their lives, to bring light to the darkest part of their lives.

After Words

Chambly County, AL. (WTVP) A Lanyard man pleads to a lesser charge just hours after his murder trial gets underway. The jury didn't have a chance to consider the evidence before Ennis Dorsey entered his guilty plea.

Sylvia Levine is the victim's widow. She has three young children with the victim, Seven Levine. She said the justice system let her down.

"It's not fair." She said.

Tuesday in court Levine watched Dorsey end his murder trial suddenly by striking a deal with the district attorney's office. He pleaded guilty to manslaughter, and received a 17 year split sentence, which means he'll serve five years. After his guilty plea, Dorsey told the judge he hit Levine with an axe handle on June 22 of last year. The blows cracked his skull. Levine died 15 days later at the hospital. In opening statements, we learned the two had been arguing over a video game.. Now a son, husband and father is dead and his family feels they got cheated by the system.

"Seven is gone forever. His children don't have a father. His family can't enjoy him and watch him grow older. It's not fair…" said his sister.

The judge gave Dorsey credit for time already served leading up to the trial. So that means Dorsey will serve four years of that five year sentence.

The night after the trial was over, Sylvia called Mae. It would be their last true conversation. Sylvia was feeling like most of Seven's family, as if justice was a joke. She was also angry with the family.

Angel had tried to come to terms with Seven's murder by creating a web site in his memory. It had been online since his memorial. Sylvia had discovered it, and some comments she didn't like on it, made by Cameron.

"I don't appreciate Cameron making comments about me on the internet. Bella is the one who keeps seeing them. It was Cameron's fault that Seven went out anyway, he was sick of them being there. Seven walked away and never tried to come back in. The entire family had turned their backs on Seven, but not me. We were happier than ever!"

Mae listened with her eyes closed, wondering how happy Seven had to be to fall asleep every night crying.

Sylvia continued with her voice growing louder and louder. "Ever since Melina came over upset because you people took her baby away, and Seven came into the house crying, he told me he was so sorry for putting his family before her, it was a mistake, and he hated you. All of you."

"If I had thirty seconds to talk to Seven, I'd have set him straight over my daughter Melina. No one took anything from her, she gave her baby up." Tears started seeping from Mae's eyes. Sylvia's stabs were not hurting; it was the memories of how quickly Sylvia went from innocent victim, to destructive aggressor.

"Yeah well you never called him."

"I'm sorry, I neglected that, but I was busy dealing with Melina's actions myself at the time."

Mae hoped Sylvia would stop, before she lost her diminishing cool.

"NONE of you ever call Bella!" Sylvia was on a roll.

"Oh yes I have, it's just usually you never answer."

"Well I do have more important bills to pay then my pre-paid phone."

It grew silent on both ends.

"I swear on Seven's grave, I'm calling an attorney tomorrow to sue Angel, Mary and Cameron for their remarks. Since I can't go to his grave, I want him dug up and moved. I shouldn't have put him there anyway."

"Look Sylvia..." Mae attempted to calm the girl down. "I miss Seven, we all do." She wanted Sylvia to think rationally. "We all just have issues left unresolved."

"Oh I know the only reason you were nice to me at the hospital was to get in the room with him."

"Now you wait a minute, I take offense to that, even though it's true. I sincerely felt for you too. And you need to stop referring me to my entire family. I'm Marion Mae Smithfield, not my family. I can't control how they think or feel, but Sylvia I've always been straight forward with you. Yes, I'd put a line between Seven and me, but that was because of the dirt road escapades you had with my husband. As a wife, I was trying to deal with it."

"You know, Bella hates Angel now." Sylvia wasn't listening to Mae. "I know y'all think I'm living on Seven's benefits. That's why I had to get away from there. I was moving back, had even started making preparations, but now I just don't know." She was beginning to calm back down, since she wasn't going to be able to fire Mae off. "My attorney is Nathaniel's attorney in Opella. I'll have a civil case against Ennis in April."

"Well Sylvia, I think that's a good idea, you know, having your own attorney."

Again it grew quiet, and Mae wondered if she was finished. Sylvia was talking to one of the kids, and then came back on laughing.

"After the trial, Woody Muck tried to arrest me. I just laughed at him and told him to F off. I saw the axe handle and Ennis's shirt and shoes. They didn't have that much blood on them."

Mae hoped she was winding down.

"You know, Cameron was a sorry mother. She ain't nothing but a sorry drunk whore."

Nope, Mae thought, she's not done.

"All Seven wanted his family to do was accept me. He was so hurt that y'all wouldn't. I mean a little spit and broken windows shouldn't have caused y'all to push Seven away like that. You just wanted him to leave me."

"That's bullshit Sylvia, I've never tried to stop Seven from ever being with you, except for one time; that's when he put the gun in his mouth to kill himself."

Sylvia went berserk and started screaming into the receiver. "I have never put a gun in his mouth! I've never had a gun in my hands on the Baker property, except for one time. That was when Mary evicted me, and I had a gun in the yard, shooting it. But I never put a gun in..."

"I said SEVEN put the gun in his mouth over you!" Mae was correcting Sylvia but it was difficult for Sylvia to hear anything she was ranting and raving so loud.

"Seven never did that because of me!"

"Yes he did Sylvia, he told me."

"When did he tell you that? Not that day!"

"Yes, on that day, and we talked about it the entire trip to Muscle Shoals for the wedding. He was upset because you said Bella belonged to Nathaniel Walker. Seven was so tore up, he wanted to die, and I told him YOU weren't worth killing himself over. I told him then, he should just put you in his past."

"That's not why he tried to kill himself." Sylvia wouldn't let any truth into her life. "Your momma tried to get our kids. We saw her name on the DHR paper, and her signature. It pissed Seven off so bad, that's why he came up with the thousand dollars to move the trailer off the Baker property. And I'm tired of hearing how my trailer was Seven's trailer. It's just mine, NOT SEVEN's. My thousand dollar tax return paid for that trailer, and Mary paid five thousand on it. It was never Seven's trailer. I'm so tired of your family making me depressed. I ain't going to kill myself, like y'all wish I would. My kids have already had one parent walk out on them; I'm not going to do that to my kids.

Mae was relieved when the receiver went dead.

After the trial, Seven's family wouldn't see Bella, Liam or Cassandra for another year. At the two year anniversary, Sylvia moved back to Chambly. She was included with Seven's family on the day put aside to remember Seven. After dark, fireworks were lit and the family reminisced. It was as difficult for the family to be around Sylvia, as it is for her to be around them. The three children needed all of them though. The relationship between the parties, would stay on neutral grounds, for the children. Ultimately, somehow, someway, they would all have to learn to live with each other.

Once Sylvia moved back into Chambly, without Nathaniel Walker, the family was kept clueless concerning the couple's relationship. Bella explained to her Aunt Mae that Nathan had broken up with her momma with a text message. The next week, before Sylvia could get back to retrieve the kids and her possessions, Walker had already cleaned the entire house. Everything the children had, clothes, furniture, and toys, had been taken.

It upset Mae, to see Bella hurt. She had things her daddy had given to her that Walker had done away with. It was uncomfortable for Mae to hear, but there wasn't much she could do about it. If she had the chance, she'd tell him what a jerk he'd been. Taking things out on Sylvia was one thing, but to victimize three children, who had already had their father's life robbed from them, was taking it too far.

Things started making sense, once Mae found Nathaniel Walker's picture and information listed on a State's Registered Sexual Offenders page. Nathaniel had committed first degree sexual abuse against an eight year old female, back in 2004. He had served two years for the crime against a little girl.

So after, right after, Sylvia's husband is murdered, she puts a sexual predator in her bed. Then the two, run away with Seven's three kids, and hide them. Nathaniel Walker spent two years, with three minor children in his possession, Bella being the same age as his victim.

Now if anything could bring out Mae's Liz, it's a good old fashioned child molester. This sicko, had some nerves of steel. He was making himself look guilty just by being in Seven's bed after the murder. Yet, that wasn't enough, he was willing to go back to prison, just to move his brand new family into his home. Effectively taking Seven's place, and would finally be able to be known as Bella's "DADDY".

Some stories, just never end.